The Phelidae
The Hunted

SHELIA WEISS

Shelia Weiss

First Paperback Edition: September 2011

Weiss, Shelia, 1976-
The Hunted by Shelia Weiss –1st ed.

Summary: Thia and her brothers are forced to flee into the
unknown world with only the instinct to survive. But adaptation
into a world both biologically and socially alien proves difficult
until their desperate wandering leads them to a small remote town.
But the people of this strangely welcoming community hold
secrets of their own, and it is not long before Thia, Dae, and Shai
are entangled in a conflict between their mysterious hosts and their
unnatural predators. Through bonds forged in battle and blood, the
three Phelidae nomads are able to salvage a long lost hope that
they'd found home and the means to finally confront their
huntsman, never to run again.
ISBN: 978-0-615-49874-4

§
This book is dedicated to my dearly loved ones, both with me presently, and those waiting patiently in Heaven for the rest of us.

To my husband, Jason, thank you for your patience, love and support.
To my Meadow and Summer, I love you with everything that I am. Don't ever be afraid to intelligently chase your dreams.
§

CONTENTS

PREFACE

There'll be no fables or tall tales found about this kind. They carry on, hidden well below the story telling radar, invisible, just as they are trained from the beginning. In a timeless world of their own they keep to the deep woody mountains -- or used to. Opposite all of their supernatural cousins, they are the hunted. Only the old families and their secret keeping descendents know of their existence, not out of loyalty, but to obtain the ultimate prize.

Hunted

Leafs and branches graze their faces and thorns snag and rip their clothes as they flee through the woods. Two large, athletically built boys and a slender girl, appearing to be in their early to mid twenties, run fast dodging trees with great precision and speed. Thin sharp arrows wiz by in a high buzz, one getting as close as to tickle the fine hair on her ear, just barely missing. This didn't distract her though, her mind is somewhere else. Instead her attention is consumed by the dark and gut hollowing depression sinking in. Their lives have to again, start over.

When will this end? When and where will be the last time? The blonde girl asked herself finding it difficult to fight the tears back. She doesn't want to leave her brothers, but knows they must split up to lose the ones after them. Regardless she is tired of it. Each time becomes more tempting to break the rules to achieve freedom. Every time they get comfortable and start to call a place home, they are somehow found and have to run again. She knows they will meet up later, just like all the times before, but the months apart are always so long and lonely.

Thia started to break off but came back again. She wasn't ready yet to part ways.

"Thia, what's up?" Shai, the slightly smaller, tan and sandy haired one, was confused why she came back.

"Maybe we don't have to split up this time? I bet we can lose them together." She pleaded, desperate not to go.

Instantly both of her brothers understood why she was still traveling with them. The plan has always been that she is the one that heads off first.

Dae, the much larger dark hair and complexion brother, gently explained. "We've tried that before. It's too easy to track us together."

"Yeah, but..." she had nowhere to go from there.

After thinking for a moment Shai too attempted to offer comfort, "We won't wait as long. Will that make it better? And we have the Call now in case we need to use it."

The depression that consumed Thia suddenly gave way to embarrassment the moment she realized she had been found out, left to feel like nothing more than a needy burden now. Her brothers were on to why she hadn't left yet.

She was trying to compose herself when a large and shiny tranquilizer dart scratched her arm causing only a small barely noticeable rash that disappeared as fast as it came. This shocked her; she didn't realize she had slowed down at all during their discussion, much less enough to allow the Pallas, the ones after them, to get that close to her and her brothers.

Shai tried again to comfort her,"Come on T, it'll be okay. This time it will be different, I know it."

She couldn't decide if he was just saying it to make her feel better or not but there wasn't time to work it out. She gave them a teary eyed smile, "Until I see you again." and cut off to the right, away from them.

She was out of sight faster than they expected. But that has always been her way. Once she is able to get over the hard part, the rest was downhill or more like a straight drop. She gets that driven to move on to the next place faster to begin building happiness for them again.

Tears rolled down her cheeks as she ran however her emotions didn't slow her down this time. She already misses her brothers. Though they've been through all of this before, it still doesn't make this part any easier. They never get to say proper goodbyes. It's always just running. The group that followed her once she left her brothers quickly fell behind.

The fresh air blew through her hair and dried her last tears. She didn't get winded from the run, as a matter of fact none of them do. Instead ironically she felt free despite the chase. She blew past a herd of deer that began running with her, startled by her fast approach -- or, it could've been from the loud chopper over head.

The Pallas spent money this time. But rather than being intimidated by the step up in their pursuit and capture effort, curiosity set in. *What exactly do they plan to do with that thing? It's not like they can land it in here, it's nothing but trees!* Her question was quickly answered once the shower of dart like needles rained down around her. Now she was a little nervous. *I see. Guess I better get serious now.*

She ran much faster, zigging and zagging then cutting off in different directions. Still it was able to keep up with her every move and speed adjustment. *Crap, this isn't working.* Then she remembered something she learned when she was younger. Using her momentum she leapt off of the ground towards the very top of a tall sturdy looking tree.

This helped her come to a complete stop, then she rode the tree as it sprung back in the opposite direction. It worked. The helicopter tailing her had no chance of stopping like that. So by the time they circled back around she was gone. Thia leapt from tree to tree then hit the ground full out running in a staggered pattern until she was sure she was far enough away that they couldn't find her.

She stopped and quickly scaled to the top of another tall pine, a little itchy but bearable, and poked her head out to take a look around and listen for anyone or anything that might still be coming. Sure nothing was around, she swung from limb to limb like a gymnast down to the ground and continued on her way. She knew what general direction to head in by watching where the sun was positioned in the sky. For now she knew she wanted to head west.

Thia stopped at one of the towns she crossed briefly to grab something to eat and drink. As she walked through the small store she noticed that eyes kept following her as she passed by. She wondered what they were looking at but just shrugged it off as her being a stranger to the area. She remembered hearing people in small towns like to stare at strangers. So she picked up some sweet and salty snacks, sandwiches and water and went to the counter. She took her bag off of her back to pay for her items and found there was a large dart sticking out of it.

She was just as surprised as they were. *So this is what they were dropping. I better save it. Dae will definitely want this!* She pulled it out of her bag and brought it up to her ear to listen but didn't hear anything. However she did pickup on a foul odor coming from it. Then she noticed there was a thick yellow substance coming out of the tip of the dart.

"Gross", she commented under her breath. So she grabbed one of the local news papers at the counter and wrapped it up then packed it away in her bag to save for her brother. Dae loves investigating things and this was something she didn't recognize. *They must be trying something new. Oh he'll really like this!* She was actually a little excited that she had it now. She loves watching how happy he gets when there was something new to play with.

When she snapped out of her vision of Dae smiling like a little kid on Christmas morning she realized she wasn't alone during her inspection of the object. The guy at the counter was staring at her with a raised brow, probably for listening to a dart like a sea shell. Slightly embarrassed, she smiled sheepishly, quickly put down more than enough cash and ran out not waiting for change.

Avoiding any added attention she continued her jog into the woods continuing west. At the next town she stopped at a small gas station bathroom to freshen up a bit. Turning the key hanging from an awkward and heavy "lasses" carved board she begrudgingly walked into the disgustingly filthy, smelly and infested with buzzing flies facility. She made it quick holding her breath, all the while wondering, *Sick, why bother with a key?*

Doubting it was possible to get clean in such a nasty place she searched for the local library and went in to use a computer…but first, to clean up…again.

She sat at the computer the stereotypical librarian assigned her and let her instincts drive her search. *Shai is right, something has to change this time.* First she typed in "largest forest in united states".

Results popped up what would be the initial ideal spot, the Tongass in Alaska. The forest is virtually never ending so anyone could easily stay lost in there. However, though beautiful, it sounded like it is dark, cold and wet there a good portion of the time. Cats like the dark but don't care to be cold or especially wet. Just the opposite actually, napping in the sun is a favorite pass time. That's what they used to do a lot of back home.

They were young and only half through training when the final invasion took place. Never getting to finish their lessons and mature as adult cats properly, left them too wild and undone to be very effective. Most can never imagine being told of the superior abilities they possess yet warned never to use them for fear of exposure, capture and slavery or ultimately death. With training comes control, and this is the component in which they require extensive teachings and much practice.

Shai, Dae and Thia are of the Phelidae people. In the simplest of elucidations, the Phelidae are both human and cat.

Shai is the fastest so he usually lures pursuant foes in his direction during the chase. Once sure the other two have reached a safe distance, he stops toying with those chasing him, kicks it into high gear, and disappears into the unobtainable distance.

It seems like a noble thing to do, but then again Shai is also the one typically causing many of the chases. Everything about him draws attention despite his best efforts. Gorgeous, charming and a big trouble maker would be a fair appraisal, one he's proud to own. Regardless of all warnings throughout his life he just can't seem to restrain himself, for his own good, or those close to him.

Dae is the oldest, by a couple of minutes, wisest and most even tempered. Nothing really gets him upset, even when he has to constantly repeat himself to Shai who has little to no attention span or when he is the only one that can talk a worked up Thia down from some over thought conclusion. He's a gentle giant. Regardless of the fact that he is half very large predatory animal, he'd rather not take life, even when defending his own. He's always sure and looks for a more favorable option. It's in their nature. However this is not so when the fine line is crossed and he or his siblings are at risk. In these rare instances, thought nor planning belong or exist, only pure instinct.

Finally there is Thia. She's the uncharacteristically quiet and unwilling lead of the pack. Thia's real name is Athena. Her parents chose this because they knew she was special, dynamic even. From day one they were sure she had acquired the heart of an angel, and displayed the prowess of a goddess.

Not being one much for pride and things vain, instead she chooses to go by Thia only. Being a female makes her more complicated by nature however she remains absolutely unique. This is, as it's been explained to her, why she finds she doesn't really get along or fit in with most other girls. She does not talk a lot, much less on the topic of boys or enjoy keeping company with a mob of loud and more times than not catty women. She favors being with her brothers. What they are up to is always more fun and interesting.

They refer to themselves and are called siblings however they are not direct blood relatives. They don't look alike, not even close. When an explanation is needed upon introductions, to strangers they simply explain they are adopted to dissolve confused expressions. Dae is tall, very large and muscle bound with green eyes, dark hair and skin. Shai is above average height, has a more athletic build with light brown eyes, sandy colored hair and tan skin. Thia is slim and fair skinned with pearl grey eyes and champagne blond hair.

Thia scrolled through the hundreds of search engine results filled with miles of emerald trees, thunderous flowing water falls over massive cliffs and peaceful mirrored lakes until she stopped on one in Akron Ohio that thrust her back in time to when she first met Dae and Shai.

Her parents spent much of their time on head of tribe meetings and business so she sought entertainment outdoors, fed up and antsy feeling cooped up inside. It turned out to be somewhat of a sleepy afternoon roaming around alone deep in the forest following along the base of the plummeting ledges.

She wandered the woods practicing her jumps, scaling the rocks, climbing trees and smashing stumps from those fallen. When she got tired of that she meandered closer to the larger cliffs. She picked out a few golf ball sized stones and began throwing them up in the air bouncing them off of the side of one wall and catching them.

This was entertaining until the last one bound off in the wrong direction behind some pines and then she heard, "Ow!" Shocked that anyone was there she ran over to find Shai rubbing his head of perfect wavy hair and Dae, a fairly large and darker skinned boy sitting on a large rock by him with a great grin on his face.

Her stomach dropped when she saw them. Very embarrassed by what she did, intentionally or not, she tried to apologize, "I'm so sorry. I didn't know there was anyone else out here."

Still rubbing his head where it stung, "Maybe you could pick rounder rocks next time?"

"Right. Well again, I apologize." She looked down as tears began to well in her eyes. *Just the usual jerks from class,* she thought. Disappointed but not surprised she turned to go.

"Hey, don't go. Lighten up, I was only teasing!" Shai caught up and jokingly tapped her arm.

She half smiled quickly blinking away the tears she didn't want them to see and turned back.

"So what are you doing out here?" he asked.

She shrugged her shoulders, "Bored", then she smiled and rolled her eyes.

Shai looked confused, "Bored? Didn't think your kind got bored. You can pretty much have anything you want. I bet I could find countless ways to get into trouble with those kinds of options!"

"*My* kind?" she laughed. "nice."

"What?" Shai asked.

"I've never been sure what social category I fall in, but I certainly didn't think I was a *kind*." She raised an eyebrow at him.

They all laughed feeling a little more comfortable with each other easing the tension.

Thia nervously asked, "Mind if I hang out?"

"Not at all", Dae spoke up with a big brotherly smile.

His unexpected response surprised her. To Thia the large tough looking boy had just morphed before her very eyes. She'd always judged him to be a quiet yet massive bully based on poise alone, but once he spoke, he took on a cuddly teddy bear persona. *Now that I think of it, I don't think I've ever seen him fight. Could this gentle giant actually bring himself to hurt anyone with a smile like that?* It lit up his whole face, especially his eyes. *He better never smile during a battle,* her strategic section of mind inserted. *The opponent would never take him seriously, all though, that could actually work to his advantage.*

She is always thinking -- over thinking most of the time.

Forcing her thoughts back, "So what do you guys do?"

"Oh, we haven't seen Aurelia yet." Shai answered matter of fact.

Aurelia is a very unique member of their tribe as she has a talent to draw out dormant powers, if a Phelidae was marked to have them once they became of age. This is the single but very important and rare gift passed down through the females in her lineage. All with the special mark go to her when the time is right. Abilities don't fully develop until the human physical teen years, which arrived faster than normal humans. Once matured, a birthmark of sort forms on left inner bicep. All hoped for such a mark but few received it.

She laughed, "No, not that. I mean to pass time, you know, for fun".

Shai sarcastically replied, "Oh! Let's see -- sometimes we like to throw rocks at the cliff and see who we can hit on the other side!"

Her eyes squinted at him, "Funny! So you are the comedian then. Got it."

Directed at Dae, "And what do *you* do, other than laugh at funny man over here? So far you seem to be a man of few words?"

Shai cut in, "Not if you get him going on some of his geek stuff! Then you can't get him to shut up!"

"Thanks" Dae replied in a voice and demeanor too grown for his age. "You can usually find me somewhere around this punk."

"Punk?! Dude, I'll show you punk!" then Shai tackled Dae. They tumbled around throwing and kicking each other crashing into trees and rocks. Thia had to jump out of the way a couple times, until finally they were tired and called it a truce.

Thia just shakes her head, "Yep, I can tell already you guys are *special*."

Shai asked still a little winded, "Alright miss originality, what do you do to pass the time?!"

Across from them she hopped up taking a seat on a large bolder, "Hmmm…read books, listen to music, get kicked out of the house for my own good, come out here, find rocks, throw rocks. I see your point. Maybe we should come up with something."

Shai a little more serious now, "Hey we've been meaning to ask you something."

"Uh, oh" she said. *I knew it was too good to be true.*

"No, it's nothing bad." Shai reassured.

She was a little relieved.

Hesitating, he looked over at Dae before he started, "We were wondering why you fake messing up in training?"

Squirming inside now she too hesitated looking down picking apart a twig she found. Finally she shrugged her shoulder, "I don't know".

"They're just jealous you know, when they say that stuff. Dae and I think it's pretty wicked how you pick up on everything so fast, especially the first time we were got our chain whips. Remember how you thought you snuck off to practice but when you turned around everyone ended up watching you, *including* the teacher?"

Thia embarrassed by the now funny memory, "Yeah, I remember." Unsure she asked, "You really think that's all it is?"

"Yeah!" like it was obvious to all but her. "Actually the Sais look pretty cool too but the chain whip is best."

Thia smiles, "Thanks"

He continues, "Dae over here's been crying about wanting to meet you so we could ask you to help us with that one."

"Crying? Really Shai?" Dae questioned in sarcastic disbelief.

Thia laughed, "Yeah, you don't seem like the crying type Dae".

"Thanks Thia. He has part of it right at least. We have the Bo and Kamas down pretty good, but I do want to learn how to master the chain whip like you've done."

Shai couldn't resist inventing a whole new meaning for Dae's comment, "I bet you would!"

Dae and Thia both roll their eyes at the same time, pickup a piece of debris near and throw it at him. They all paused for a second noticing how strange it seemed to happen exactly the same. Then they just shook it off as coincidence and laughed.

"So how did you two come to know each other?" Thia inquired.

Growing up as the leader's cub, Thia was kept at home her first few years for protection. At least that was the excuse her parents used. However some in the village felt there might have been more to it than that as rumors of strange occurrences at their house after she was born quietly circulated.

"Our mom's hang out." Shai explained.

Dae and Shai met when they were cubs. Some of the mothers get together once a week for some social time and let all the cubs play together. Shai would stumble around to the different cubs but he didn't stay interested in any for long. Then he got to Dae. He playfully nosed at Dae but got no response. Dae, a very large, about twice as big as the other cubs in fact, pure velvety black panther just lay perfectly still soaking in the sun. His size was not a shock however as he definitely took after his father.

Dae ignoring Shai only made matters worse. Shai was average in size and nowhere close to Dae's mass but this didn't stop him. The shiny black and deep orange spotted leopard cub, having a serious troublemaking streak, kept at Dae nudging and pawing and chewing on his ear until he got a response.

Dae simply lifted his sleepy head just enough to see what was pestering him then without much effort his powerful hind leg kicked Shai sending him tumbling into some of the other cubs. Naturally Shai found this to be fun and returned many times for more.

From then on they were always found together in good times and bad. Sometime later, after they'd grown a bit, Shai wandered off and got in to some trouble with a full grown Brown bear. Shai was down and hurt pretty bad with the bear above him about to make its final strike until Dae appeared in front of him, ears down, growling and bearing his sharp teeth. Though they were not as old as the bear, Dae was just as big and powerful looking. The bear backed off a little startled by his sudden and threatening appearance, assessed the situation then gave up and left.

They shared some stories from earlier years but before they realized how much time had passed, a loud roar sounded from home signaling all to return for the night.

"Wow, I didn't think it was that late." Dae noticed after examining the sky.

They slowly headed back still getting to know each other more, then decided to split up close to home before they were spotted together.

"Just in case you know?" she said. They nodded. "We wouldn't want people to start talking, me being a *kind* and all." she said with a smirk. They smiled back and headed off toward their homes as she took the opposite direction to hers.

After that night Thia rushed out to see them as often as possible. Though her parents knew, given away by her sudden eagerness to go out, to do anything now, they were happy she finally made some friends in the village. It also helped that the boys weren't bad kids at all. Actually, Shai was a bit more – adventurous – than they liked but still a good kid at heart, in fact better than most.

The others she was strongly urged to join and befriend were no fun and certainly not bashful about showing their mutual disinterest in her. At first these were the only ones she was openly permitted to intermingle with. The rule was never explained outright but she understood. Some in the ranks thought they were better than others and so carried themselves with condescending snob like tendencies. According to them she was expected to conduct herself in a manner befitting her position.

However all of this pretentiousness faded into under-breath passing grumbles from the older ones as the trio grew older and closer no longer paying homage to ancient opinions. Times were changing and there were far more dangerous things threatening their way of life now to take social circles and status too seriously. Besides, being a "chosen one", which turns out all three were, trumped all nonsense.

A few of the Phelidae, the "chosen ones", possess a special ability beyond the common skills of their people. Thia tried her gift once, but vowed never to again. The angry scar down the middle of Dae's face served as a constant and torturous reminder. Though he forgave her the very moment it happened, she didn't, and probably never will.

Hanging out on the mountain side one cloudy afternoon they decided they wanted to sneak in some practice outside of class, an act not permitted of course. Shai, the most opposite sound of his name, being the eager and rebellious one chose to go first. His gift was controlling fire and earth. He'd endlessly watched his mother and father do it but now it was his turn.

"I've seen it thousands of times. It looks easy enough!" he said. And so he began. He concentrated hard on a carefully chosen rock he spotted. His eyes turned from a hazel to a very pale golden brown. Sitting off to the side Thia and Dae sniffed at the air filling with the smell of something getting very hot. They looked around expecting to find something burning. Shai concentrated even harder, perhaps a bit too hard as the small bolder he was staring at suddenly exploded into a cloud of dust.

Disappointed and covered in dirt, Shai admitted, "Awe man! I was trying to pick it up!"

"Maybe you shouldn't hold your breath next time." teased Dae. "I thought you were going to pop a blood vessel in your eye."

Thia burst into laughter. She tried to hold it in but Dae was absolutely right. That is exactly what his straining face looked like. But she was even more amused at how many shades of red he hit as the intensity in his expression escalated. She wondered if he was going to need to change his pants if he kept up like that.

This went on for a couple of hours. He did get a little better as time went on, breaking the boulders into bigger and bigger pieces, until at last he was completely spent of all energy. He had nothing left to even try his fire skill. Well, that and there was no fire around to be controlled. He can only control it, he can't create it yet. Dae was able to help out with that though.

The gifts revealed to Dae were air, from his mother and water from his father. Dae, always being the most calm and focused aided in an accelerated ability to learn, looked up to the sky as his eyes casually faded from his regular dark brown to a soft and foamy sea green as the iris washed from center out.

Thia always got lost in the color of his eyes, the feeling of peace and freedom the sea seemed to offer in all she read. They only ever get to see the various greens, browns and grays of the forest which can be undoubtedly breathtaking for a new set of eyes.

She closed her eyes and lifted her face to the sky as a gentle, cool mist fell relieving them from the steamy humid day. This began to clean off some of the rock dust covering them from Shai's trials. Slowly the small dots of water connected together and ran off sweeping away the dirt with them. Then the drops got bigger and cooler feeling refreshing has they hit. Shai shook his thick wet head full of wavy sandy blonde hair.

Then the clouds parted, a breeze blew and the big bright and warm sun shone down on them in the small clearing on the mountain side. *Now is a good a time as any for a quick nap*, Thia thought to herself. They all jumped up and laid down on a few of the huge flat topped rocks, smiled peacefully and fell asleep enjoying the gentle wind and warm sun.

Despite her best efforts Thia couldn't always keep her gift at bay. Occasionally if she had a strong enough dream or got too deep in her thoughts, funny things happened around her. These moments spread quickly becoming the topic of whispers among the villagers. But growing up with Thia the past few years, her seemingly now brothers couldn't care less and wouldn't contribute into spreading gossip even when questioned on witnessing such things. This was just another reason why her parents very much appreciate the boys being the good friends they are to her.

One afternoon they were all home relaxing and reading books in Thia's living room. Her parents were out so it was just them at the house. Dae was sprawled out on the couch, his great arms crossed on his broad chest, head back on a massive pillow he sunk into and eyes closed.

Shai sat back relaxed on the adjacent love seat flipping through and reading one of his favorite car magazines. Thia was curled up in the big comfy chair staring deep into a new book her mom brought home for her.

It was so quiet you could hear the rain plopping on the leaves and ground outside through the open screened windows. The whole week was mostly overcast cool and wet so everyone was indoors or running from one place to the other for cover. Occasionally the sun shone off and on as a breeze gently flowed through the house. Thia's mother never missed a chance to have the house open. "The fresh air always seems to awaken the soul." she'd always say.

Each remained deep into their pass times as a faint rattling noise started. They just figured it was probably a small tremor. They happen all the time but most go unnoticed by normal people since they can't feel the light ones. The Phelidae on the other hand were sensitive enough to detect them. Then it got stronger.

Dae opened his groggy eyes and looked around. Now that he was paying attention, it didn't really feel like an earth quake. It was slightly different. This you could actually feel in the air, like everything was vibrating. It even tickled a little. Dae sat up, and as he lifted from the couch, he could hear static in his clothes peeling away from the cloth on the pillow.

Then it hit him. "Thia", he called to her with a slightly amused look on his face.

There was no response.

"Thia!" he called a little louder this time.

"Huh?" she said as she snapped out of the trance she was in lost in her book.

The vibrating instantly stopped. Dae's face lit up. It confirmed what he thought might be the source of the anomalies.

"How's your book?" he asked half smiling now.

Wide eyed, "Oh, it's great! This chapter I'm in now is so intense!"

"I know", he said with a raised brow.

"Oh, have you read this one?" she looked at him slightly puzzled.

"No, I could just tell." this time holding in a chuckle.

"Ooookaaay", she was totally confused now.

Shai's attention to his magazine was broken sensing the odd tone in Dae's voice.

Dae began half hoping they would put it together before he reached the conclusion, "Remember that one week in class when the windows kept shattering while we were dissecting the frogs?"

"Yeah, that was weird", Shai answered.

"…and sad. Those poor little frogs. I can't believe they made us do that." Thia chimed in.

"And that time we *borrowed* that car you liked and then all four tires blew out for no reason?"

"Yeah, man Thia you were pissed!" Shai recalled.

"And the time Shai and I were messing around and that huge tree broke and fell almost crushing Thia?"

"Geez I almost forgot about that. Thia if you hadn't of woken up from that nightmare…"

"What is it Dae?!" Thia desperately rang out.

Dae looked at Shai and asked, "What was common all those times?"

They sat in silence as Shai thought for a minute.

Then he thought he might have it, "Thia was worked up about something?"

"Yes!" Dae smiled with pride.

As expected, Shai roared in laughter finding this new and tasty teasing material to be very entertaining. Dae was still smiling big being very pleased with his discovery. It took Thia a little longer not getting the connection, and then finally sunk in.

Her reaction -- a meek little chuckle and an apologetic, "Oops" came out.

After that day she paid more attention to how engulfed she got into her books. Dreaming however was going to be much more difficult. Her brothers knew this and could tell when she was upset and chose to sleep over on those nights. They typically occurred after a rough day of excessive teasing from her piers while her brothers were off in the other groups. They explained to her parents what was going on and that they would need to try to wake her before the disturbances became very noticeable.

In the broad scope of things, these were actually considered the fun times, then of course came the not so fun times. As they got older it intensified. If Thia got really upset or angry and wasn't carful, the damage was much more severe. One day she turned to yell at Shai during a silly little sibling-like fight that had gone too far and completely blew out the picture window in her house behind him.

She wasn't the only one that suffered from unintentional power surge side effects though. Dae, out of frustration, caused a hail storm one hot afternoon when neither of his siblings would listen to his theory proving the science teacher wrong on the topic that day in class. And Shai caused a rockslide when road rage set in after a rude driver cut him off as they were learning to drive in town. No one was hurt but there was quite a mess for the city to clean up.

Thia has never shared a particular feeling with anyone, not even her brothers, but she has always regretted, however unsure, *what* she is. Not from a martyr sense like most self-tortured half humans. Rather she is weary of being frustrated in possessing these supposed vast powers but forbidden to use them, or even get to practice to learn how to use them, though it is very much her birthright.

Growing up they heard only a few stories but countless times on the consequences of untamed rage, the result of misuse due to the absence of proper training.   Horror narratives of ancient assaults and battles prompted Thia to question, *But what did that have to do with today?* The nomad wizard, or so they assumed he was, sensing her distraction continued to warn her so many times it had become a reoccurring voice in her sleep. "We must remain cautious, the greater the power, the greater the use, the more detectable by both our kind and those that long to capture and use us."

This snapped her back to the now, to her search for a new home. Struggling to look beyond the moments of depression and dissatisfaction these memories brought, Thia still felt her world could be all right. Sure school and growing up was tough, but eventually everyone ends up being equal. She knew when the time was right all the tribes as a whole would one day come together when it really mattered.

Apparently now was not that time. Everything she once found bothersome at home no longer mattered. It was all gone now. But little does she know she is right, that her bloodline will not fail her. When the time is right, her star will shine bright.

The Phelidae

Before the final invasion that captured, killed and scattered all of the Phelidae tribes, they were a self-sufficient and peaceful people, though they didn't start off that way. Then again none are exactly sure how or from where they originated. All they have for history records were the stories provided from slave tribal descendents passed down through the lines.

As far as the stories go back, they mostly seem to begin in the Amazon. The Phelidae couldn't be sure if this was their origin but is all they've known. The tales are usually told around a massive bon fire, typically during festival times. The elders are the story keepers and pass them on from generation to generation. In addition, most parents also used them as adventurous bedtime stories, instilling pride in the values of their kind and old ways.

A few of the very old and broken stories were from long ago times in Egypt where cats have been known to be the preservers of life, keeping evil spirits in the underworld. However much of those stories were lost with some of the families trying to come over to America and so forgotten. Most surround the main and more recent legend of the old slave hunts in the rainforests.

From various countries the strong and healthy of the wild tribes, both young and old were stolen from their families. The raids took place at night with nets and tranquilizers. Once gathered, all were herded into a large plane. Upon reaching their final destination, they were then shoved out of the aircraft in mid air. Given old parachutes, that didn't always work, and no instructions, many landed wrong and suffered broken legs, ribs and arms from the fall. This proved to be even more dangerous when stranded on this remote island.

At first glance most would consider it just the opposite. With the mind awakening beauty found it must be a paradise. Waterfalls, varying in size, fashioning perfect rainbows through the sunlight and mist were spread throughout the land amongst the thick and fresh smelling foliage in every light and deep shade of moist green. Patches of never seen before flowers are sprinkled in every direction containing every vibrant color imaginable. Exotic birds fly through the air without a care donning a matching grace and beauty singing their inspiring songs.

However those actually left there with nothing more than the will to live, found it to be a completely different place, a horrible nightmare from which most would never awake. Whether it was the viscous baboons with their unheard of strength and the shortest of fuses tearing them apart like paper dolls, snakes with their quick and lethal strikes or the most innocent touch of a brightly colored but highly poisonous frog, it didn't take long for these healthy young men to meet an untimely end.

On the island there were hidden cameras and microphones in the trees. Now everything was set for the first ever sport of its kind. This event was for the wealthy to watch and place high stakes bets on which would be the first and last to fall. It was nothing more than a way to fulfill their evil cravings for forbidden morbid entertainment. They knew the corrupt governments would do nothing about the poaching of slaves from their land as it kept the tribes too weak for rebellion. In fact word got out that some volunteered certain areas that were being especially troublesome. It became all too easy to supply the prey.

In the early days of these games they tried releasing the slaves and just letting the wild take them out one by one, but the audience quickly grew bored and restless as they felt it took too long. The solution; human hunters were added. They hired the best of the best in the underground markets and paid them well to both participate and keep the secret. If one became too greedy, then they too became the hunted. This new format worked. The ones craving the live and gruesome entertainment drew more after the changes and it quickly made more money than the organizers ever anticipated.

Enjoying the benefits of their new success they put in more cameras to make the show bigger. But once the better cameras were in, they started to notice an anomaly on the island. The wild life seemed to be changing. Different creatures were showing up on some of the cameras that they hadn't seen before. From the brief sightings they decided the animals resembled extremely large wild cats, a lot larger in size than usual. It wasn't just one variety; it was a mix that seemed to intermingle, again something not typical of the species. As the appearances became more frequent they seemed to be moving closer and closer to the slave drop off point.

"Where are they all coming from?" the supervisor asked pointing at one screen in the control room that showed four of them close together.

"Maybe they were on the other side of the island?" another one guessed.

It was undecided if the new arrival of these animals was a good or bad thing. On one hand it could add a more exciting element to the hunts. But on the other, would a massacre end the hunts too fast. What of their expensive hunters? Should they warn them or should they have to prove their worth against both animal and human. All of this they wondered as they sat back and did nothing, waiting to see what happened next. However it didn't take long for them to promptly get their answer.

The chase began and almost instantly the hunter disappeared ending the show at once. The rich, who had waited a month since the last, aggressively expressed their deep disappointment and demanded another soon. So the hunt was postponed for a week and the prey wandered off to fend for themselves. On the rescheduled day they brought in three renowned hunters this time and a fresh group of slaves.

The hunt began and again and much to hosts embarrassment, one by one they also disappeared shortly after it started and before any kills. As they continued to search for the hunters a couple of cameras went down. The men monitoring each of the cameras notified their bosses that something strange was going on.

One young man was hesitant, "Sir, right before the first one went down – I think I saw a paw."

The supervisor had to confirm what he just heard, "a paw?"

Slightly embarrassed by the ridiculousness he carried on, "Yes sir. I think I made out very large claws before it swiped at it and the static took over the screen."

Getting annoyed, "So what exactly are you saying? Never mind, just point camera fifty three at the one that just went down."

This time they both witnessed, with the down camera almost in sight a human hand show on the screen and then that camera too went dead. They both jumped back when they saw it. The team started to get nervous.

The camera operator, attempting to understand what they just saw, what frightened him so, "Cats don't go that high in trees, especially animals that size. Those cameras are very close to the top. The trees wouldn't even hold them! And was that a human hand we just saw on the last one? How could the slaves have gotten up that far? We had to use helicopters to get those there."

"Is there anyone else on the island? I thought you did a sweep to make sure there weren't," the leader barked his accusation.

"I did, there weren't!" his underling quickly defended.

"Take the chopper out there and see what is going on. I want you personally to see to the matter." the leader demanded.

He did as he was told and had the pilot land in the area. He slowly got out and headed towards the edge of the small clearing. He stopped, and nervously looked back at the pilot.

"Stay put till I come back." he ordered over the headset with a poorly controlled shaky voice.

In a robot like tone the pilot replied, "Yes, sir."

He took faltering steps into the edge of the woods. He was sure to check in every couple of minutes, which the pilot thought was a bit excessive but said nothing. Then the man took a deep breath trying to calm himself and disappeared into the woods.

When the pilot returned to base without the man he claimed, "Sir, I think he said something like, 'What the...that's not possible!'" He then described a gurgling yell, then some rustling and that was the last they heard or saw of him.

Over the course of the next couple days one by one the cameras went down until there were none left. The entertainers were losing unfathomable amounts of money so they had to do something and fast to remove the strange animals before their audience lost interest. So they hired some highly trained and armed help to quickly find out what was going on and remedy the issue.

The big bad team of roughneck mercenaries arrived quickly and went straight in to assess the situation. After a couple of days and no word the entertainers almost gave up. But the team emerged from the woods unscathed, bags full and headed back to the hired headquarters.

They reported back with their findings which weren't much, but the little they did bring back was unnerving. Unzipping and overturning the huge duffle bag they dumped out some of the broken camera equipment and previous hunters clothing. The room was silent, all eyes fixed on the long table in the middle of the control room. Everything completely torn apart by what looked like an animal but couldn't be possible. The clothes which were made of a heavy canvas-like material looked like it had been put through a shredder. And the metal pieces left from the cameras had enormous groves in the thick plating but no signs of blood left from the sharp metal.

The leader of the group spoke up, "There's something else. I'm not sure why or how it's even possible but all of your slaves are still alive and healthy."

The supervisor thought for a moment, "Did you see anything unusual out there?"

"Sir?"

"Never mind", the leaders question was answer enough. He had not seen the large cats.

Extremely nervous, not only by the strange phenomenon but also by the lack of satisfaction for his customers, he paced back and forth until he came up with an idea.

"I assume your team is capable of killing - animals - large ones?" he was purposely cryptic.

The smaller but tough female of the group blurted out, "Ha, what like lions, tigers and bears?"

Another behind them whispered on cue, "oh my".

Their lead gave them a nasty glare before promptly returning to the question, "Sir, we can do anything you pay us to, no questions asked."

"Excellent", that was better than he wanted to hear.

So the hired guns went back in, this time hunting the large cats. The supervisor knew they had to be connected to the disappearances of the hunters and broken equipment. He wasn't sure how but the problems started when they came around and it was worth it to see if it would stop once the cats were gone.

The mercenaries were never heard from again.

Weeks later just before full night fall, in the high grassy area where the helicopter usually landed, the entertainers arrive trying one last time to find any sign of survivors. Indeed that is what they found and then some. All of the equipment they'd mounted throughout the jungle lay in a large burning scrap heap in the middle of the field. The captives danced a celebratory dance around it with their faces painted up like cats. The owners attempted to step out to take a look around but froze from what they saw next. All around the edge of the steadily darkening clearing all they could see were pairs of glowing eyes opening one by one. They got back up in the air as fast as they could and left, abandoning the project.

Somehow word got out to the right people and the slaves were found and returned to their homes. The stories of these guardian cats spread like wild fire throughout the lands and instilled hope in the people. At this new news the tribes were able to start fighting back reclaiming their lands. Attempts to relocate were futile as soon the hunts became more costly than they were worth so the wealthy eventually went away and so did the sport.

No matter how many times they hear it or who tells the story, everyone one in the village listens intently absorbing every detail. They are a simple people with few demands but possess big hearts and a great sense of pride. Hidden in various villages spread throughout the deep thick and vast woods they live never to be discovered by outsiders.

The Phelidae keep up with the times by use of altered generators and brief stays in a few of the towns on the far ends of the forest, selling their grown and hand made goods and buying things needed or wanted from the money earned. A few of the small stores in town provide a small spot to rent or trade on the floor to display what they sell. The items were mostly handmade jewelry, unique wood carvings, some fine crafted wooden furniture as well as clothes and food such as bread and corn. They also offered meat from over populated wild moose, boar and deer jerky. Back home the adults kept busy making things to sell as the young ones trained.

During the week it was the same routine. Everyone met in the field at dawn for calisthenics and physical training. Around noon they cleaned up and had lunch. After lunch for about three hours was nap time. And the rest of the day, into the night was lectures.

For training they all went to the same place at the start of the day. There was a large dirt field a little ways from their village. First was the warm-up. Everyone hated this part, mostly because they were still groggy waking up too early from their warm comfy beds and it was cold in the mornings. *Stupid, all of it with the jogging, jumping jacks and pushups.*, crossed most of the half-awake minds, if they were even thinking yet. The bland exercises were nothing more than tedium to them. However the actual training that followed was very fun and well worth the wait.

At the start of this part the young Phelidae were instructed to partially transform themselves from human to half human, half cat. This condition is referred to as the Coalesce state. This was required to train in the form preferred during a confrontation. They remain human visually but everything else is powered and influenced by their cat half. The advanced moves could not be done in human form alone. Once everyone was ready, the basics were reviewed first to establish a solid foundation.

They would work on some of the crucial skills such as running at top speed straight and through trees, jumping to peak height and striking objects with maximum force. There are two additional parts to running, sprinting and distance. A course existed, or more like a worn path, around the field where they practiced both. The other path wound a bit in between trees but this was by design as it forced them to practice being able to change direction quickly without losing speed.

Jumping was also taught in a couple different methods. One involved climbing two trees by springing from one to the other. Though it looked easy and very cool, it proved to be much harder than it seemed.

Thia, tending to do things slightly different, ended up resembling a gymnast who'd been practicing for years the way she bound from trunk to trunk then gracefully swung in circles around some of the branches, soaring to the other tree. Of course some of her peers called her a show-off, but the instructors ignored this amused by her creativity. They'd never seen another student turn a lesson into a performance like that.

Once at the top it was time for the next lesson, the second part. To get down from the top they were to free fall in various ways depending on height. Most of the trees in this area were only three to four stories up so this wasn't very high for them at all. Because of this they moved deeper into the woods to find the older, taller trees to learn how they handled the landing differently. Find a sturdy branch below to drop to and keep doing this until it was finally safe to fall to the ground.

The other method of jumping is based on distance rather than height and had to be done over the wide mouthed river further north. It had to be broad enough to present a challenge. The tricky part was learning to pickup enough speed in a short amount of space then planting and springing up at the last second. It didn't take the students too many tries to get it right as most hated getting wet, especially considering how icy cold the water was coming down from the mountain top.

And finally they worked on the art of blows and blocking. For this lesson, they practiced Martial Arts as their primary hand to hand combat style as it proved to be the most effective and efficient form of defense. Favorite moves from each style were chosen and some even altered and embellished a bit.

Some of the advanced techniques involved weapons. Thia's favorite was the fast and cool metal chain whip. It was one of the more precision instruments they taught, plucking the flame from a candle, dotting and piercing small targets from a distance and slicing when spun fast enough at a charging enemy...usually a melon or gourd of some sort.

None of the other students took much time to get good at it. In fact they quickly grew to hate it after earning many bruises. Thia too took her share of hits from it but that didn't stop her. It had her attention and interest now and she was up for the challenge. She rarely failed at things she set her mind to and this was one of those things. Unfortunately, thanks to her diligence, every time this lesson came around the teachers had Thia demonstrate it.

Though she enjoyed the challenge of the chain, she'd rather not have to show everyone up because of it. Still she obeyed as it is her place to set an example. When called on, she reluctantly walked by the others to get to the center. She was usually located in the very back and correctly anticipated the taunting whispers as she passed, "Showoff!", "Brownnoser.", "Know it all." This was the time before she met Dae and Shai and the classmates were much meaner.

Thia has always been one of the quickest at learning what she has an interest in. She found some of the lessons so fascinating she just couldn't help it. Still, on occasion, she would fake messing up so the others would be a little more accepting, or at least just leave her alone.

As a treat on days after much successful training, a ball was brought out. An advanced version of combination volleyball and soccer was the game they mostly enjoyed. The matches occurred at night by torch light surrounding the playing area. Seeing at night is not much different than seeing in the day time for them.

The volleys went on and on getting more difficult and fancy as the night went on. Much like soccer hands, heads and feet are permitted. The ball can be saved by someone going out of bounds. Many smaller trees didn't make it after a few of these plays, as the players made full use of their surroundings, jumping to all heights, twisting, turning and flipping to get at the ball.

Most looked forward to their time off on the weekends, however this was not the case for Thia. Thia knew the group she was supposed to be around due to her social status didn't care for her, nor did she them. She just sat on the side and watched them look down their noses at others and talk way too much about absolutely nothing.

To them she was too much of a Tomboy and strangely quiet. A quiet girl was one that couldn't be trusted. How should they know what she was thinking if she didn't blabber on about her every thought nonstop? No other female behaved like that, with the slight exception of her mother. The difference was, her mother carried herself differently, with a wealth of confidence and consequently respected and loved by all who met her.

Most of the Phelidae have never come to know anyone outside their land. Thia's family's tribe was the largest in the area so the other tribes typically traveled to them. They had many things the others did not and so drew frequent visitors to trade with and train.

Thinking back on the training in their village with their own kind for instructors, was nothing like the nomad's from what they could remember. The boring Phelidae instructors lacked the tricks and clever stories like Nomad used. Theirs was an old way based on nothing more than trial and error over the years. Everyone stood in a large sloppy circle, watched, attempted and learned from their painful mistakes. This included training with their new powers once revealed to them.

However after the accident with her brother, Thia was no longer allowed to try anything beyond the physical defenses when around the others. Before this decision it was months before she was even permitted to return to training with the other students. Needless to say they were not happy she was back. Some of the other parents kept their children away for weeks due to her return.

All of her life she consciously made an effort to keep the odd little relationships around her tolerable, but all that was ruined now. The changes in everyone around her -- the fear and hatred she saw in their eyes devastated Thia, but these were the smallest of upheavals that occurred.

The incident also brought forth many dangerous whispers about replacing the leader, banishing the girl, sending the boys away, on and on it went and only got worse. All of the treasonous discussions spread to the other tribes in the area eventually causing a historical meeting, the Council of Elders, to be called from all the Phelidae families in the area.

A meeting like this was unheard of and an unsettling thing among the people. One like this hadn't happened as far back as anyone could remember but unfortunately it was unavoidable now. Because word spread so fast to the other surrounding tribes and beyond, visitors from them started flooding to Thia's village, known as the Apex territory. The elders needed to first and foremost put an immediate end to the disastrous talk and restore confidence and respect to Amon, Thia's father. After all he was the first ever unanimous choice for the chair, and there are no mistakes made when one is selected.

The wise ones succeeded and the village settled. Now the focus turned to Thia, the root of such powerful rumors.

The oldest woman raised her hand and the room listened, "We must understand how it came to be and finally what to do with it."

Another tribal head spoke up, "No one anticipated the gift she gained based off of what she should have inherited from her parents."

The meetings went on in her home. Alienated by her peers she escaped to the woods.

Dae and Shai paid no attention to the constant buzz all around them and were definitely not afraid of her. Dae especially held no grudge against her. He knew she couldn't help what happened and loved her still, just as Shai loved her and she them, though they'd never come out and say it. Their bond was strong from birth, very strong some had noticed and brought up as they walked by.

"I have always said there would be something unusual with those five. First the strange things were happening at their house after she was born, all that shaking and noise and things getting broken all the time. Then once they brought her out of hiding, I caught the odd way the three reacted to each other. You know, when they would cry, if either of the others came near the crying would stop?! But *no*, no one wanted to believe me. I'm telling you, the other two would be mixed up in this too if they lived here. Like I said *all along*, it wasn't right, them all being born on the same night the great star Ara fell." an old lady carried on to two others in a loud whisper. The others just, Um-hmmm'd back to her with their squinty suspicious and wrinkly eyes.

"The five of them?" Shai questioned, since the three of them were eavesdropping the moment they heard *they* were the subject of the conversation.

"Yes", confirmed Dae. "The three of us and the twins."

"Who? Not Caleb and Kasha." Thia asked half not wanting to hear the answer.

Dae simply nodded.

The twins were born in the second largest tribe. Actually the other group used to be a part of the Apex tribe but chose to split off and return to stricter, older ways.

"oh" Thia and Shai were solemnly disappointed.

Caleb and Kasha, these are a famous pair of subtle menace. Trouble mysteriously occurred when they were around but were always sly enough to avoid direct blame. That usually fell on the others nearby which usually ended up being one or all of the other three.

The twins liked to harass Thia and her brothers. That is, Caleb thoroughly enjoyed it where as Kasha more or less tagged along with Caleb and joined in with nothing better to do. If it were left up to her, she'd have nothing to do with any of them too busy also looking down her nose at them; all are beneath her and her brother. But, she did as Caleb bid since they were typically inseparable.

Caleb is generally known for being headstrong and extremely over confident. Kasha, is very smart and equally unpleasant. Of course this greatly depended on who was doing the describing. Their aunt that resides in Thia's village, not having children of her own, couldn't be more proud of them and whole heartedly believes they are special and were absolutely perfect from birth.

The night all of them were born was the talk of the tribes for quite some time. Nothing like this had ever happened before. The mothers weren't even due at the same time. Thia was very early and the other four were late.

All believed it had to have meant something. *Is it a sign? Is it a blessing or a curse? Would they become all powerful? Would they turn out to be the next great leaders? Since our enemies are getting stronger is it nature's way of evening things out so our kind carries on?* Many speculations and hopes surrounded them throughout their early lives.

Phelidae are actually born as humans then at about a five months old phase into cubs. Because of this they learned to walk, hunt and basically survive much faster. Every moment of every day they were watched. Word went back and forth between the tribes on their progress. When one would do something a little advanced, excitement spread through the people. But after the first seven years of constant watching and waiting for something extraordinary to happen because of some cosmic alignment that must link them, all finally gave up convinced it was nothing more than a mere bizarre coincidence.

Due to all the attention in their early years, Thia and her brothers favored keeping to themselves as they got older. Thia never really meshed with the other girls especially. She is just more for adventure. She still likes the occasional pretty thing but mostly her interests are in exploring, figuring ways around things or occasionally making things, none of which require company.

There are times she has gotten a little too curious, which has no doubt gotten her into trouble. It may have been the result of her also being overly observant, which could explain why she is so quiet. When there is something she wants she can be somewhat defiant but when the time calls for it she is most importantly exceptionally loyal. Thia does error on the side of caution. She keeps a safe distance from those she is either unsure of, or has already found out the hard way cannot be trusted.

Boys on the other hand find her fearless, especially when compared to girls around her, which she detests, to be compared. She knows it just invites even more cattiness evolving into the very thing she loathes: drama. Thia has always thought women have the potential to have such a close connection if they could only get over the production and the competition. But it didn't seem that in this lifetime, anyone would be willing to give it a try. Whatever they chose to call what they were currently engaged in, she wants no part of it.

There may have been one last thing she had in common with them though. She loves cute, cuddly animals, cats especially. She doubted it was because she was part one or not as they weren't really that alike though they seemed so visually.

Boys being boys would mess with the domestic ones claiming they are inferior to them so it didn't matter. Still she's always felt pity for them and made them stop. She grew up with domestic cats for as long as she could remember. It might have started when she would sneak into town and steal them from undeserving pet owners that neglected them like some sort of low scale vigilante. So there might have been one or two more that followed her home. No one complained though since they kept the mice and other rodents out of the supplies.

One cat in particular holds a special place in her heart she will never forget named Tosh. He was a big black cat with bright green eyes. He reminded her much of Dae. He was carefree, kind and minded his own business for the most part. In his last days she watched as her little friend of half her live was fading away. It felt like a piece of her very soul was tearing. The pain was deep and dark. He was very independent but was always near when she was sick or sad. Now that he was sick, he stayed away like he tried to spare her the heart ache. She tried everything to help him bounce back but it turned in to simply making his last days as comfortable as possible. And then he was gone. After that she lost the last likeness with her would-be girlfriends.

Domestic cats weren't the only thing bad boys and judgmental girls tormented. On occasion during a trip to town some dropped inappropriate comments in passing to the other kinds. The Phelidae are the superior race but it's no excuse for rude behavior, same goes for ignorance and hidden fear of the unknown. Thia on the other hand had a strong fascination and respect towards those from different cultures.

Thia and her brothers detest the pretentious nature of some, majority of the time the repeat offenders were Caleb and Kasha when they were in town visiting and coming along for the town trip. Thia and her brothers so longed to put the two in their place though knew fighting was not permitted. Told time and time again, "Such behavior is not the Phelidae way." though she did not fully understand why as it seemed to be the honorable thing to do, not to mention enjoyable. However her loyalty to the tribe, her parents and their wise friend the nomad overruled all of her immature wishes.

Her parents noticed the constant bickering among the five but said and did nothing. For the most part she was a very good child. They always saw eye to eye when it came to how they would raise her and saw her bothers follow her down her path. They chose to enforce the basic rules but allow her to become who she was meant to be even if some of the others, mostly the old ones, thought it careless. Still no one dared say anything to them about it. They were too high up and well respected to be criticized by any of them. So like all of the other kids it was routine as usual, with an occasional judgmental glance and critical whisper on the side as she grew up.

Many times Thia found a quiet get away to escape the common areas and to avoid attention and ultimately possible trouble. On one of their many adventurous treks Thia and her brothers found a set of deep caves. After doing much exploring in them they found a small water hole.

"Who's up for a swim? T?" Shai asked taking off his shirt.

"No way, it's probably freezing!" Thia argued.

Shai stopped wondering if she might be right, "Find out. Stick your foot in."

She laughed, "I don't think so. You do it!"

So of course Dae did it, "It' actually warm. That doesn't make any sense. The cave itself is very cool so the water should be too, if not colder since it is most likely coming from the top of the mountain."

Before he was finished with is observation he heard a big splash and was drenched in the warm water.

"Wow! This is great! And it's so clear." Thia shouted.

Shai splashed Dae, "Come on in, the water's fine!"

They swam and played until the cave started getting very dark.

Dae looked around, "Suns going down, what time is it?"

"Hey, what's that?" Thia said looking down into the crystal clear water.

A light coming from somewhere was bouncing off of the silvery rocks below. She disappeared diving under the water to find the source.

"Thia wait!" could not be heard from Shai. "She's so impatient sometimes." Both Dae and Shai went down after her.

Thia swam following the path of the unknown light. Not being much of a swimmer she started to get nervous if she would have enough air and thought about heading back. But something about the light felt warm and peaceful calming her and kept her going.

Only a few feet in the underwater cave began inclining to another surface. First Thia's head popped up, then Shai and finally the slowest, Dae.

"Would you look at that?" Shai spoke for all of them.

The sun was indeed setting, filling the cave with fiery red and orange, shimmering in all directions off of the large chunks of crystals sticking out of the walls. The water on this side felt like a hot tub in comparison to what they left behind as the three slowly walked up the incline to the much larger but shallower cave opening.

"The sun must beat in here most of the day. The ground and water are so warm, almost hot." Shai said as he bent down to feel it with his hands then rolled over onto his back with his hands behind his head and let out a sigh.

"And look at the steam as the cool air comes in." Dae pointed out.

"This is heaven." both brothers turned to Thia to find a dreamy look on her face as she returned to the water and floated on her back.

The room was so relaxing that they all ended up stretched out on the warm ground and fell asleep. It was the best any of them had felt in a while. But once the sun had been down for a while and the day's heat ran out, the room quickly grew much cooler waking them up.

The sight they opened their eyes to was just as breathtaking as when the sun set. An artificial sparkling night sky, the moon light poured in through a hole in the top of the cave and reflected everywhere from the scattered silver rocks and crystals.

"This is amazing." Thia breathed.

"Wow it got cold pretty fast." Shai jumped in the still warm water.

Then Dae reluctantly added, "I hate to say it but we better head back before someone comes looking."

Shai quickly shot him down not wanting to leave, "Nah, as soon as they figure out all three of us are gone they will know we are okay. We take care of each other just fine. Hey T, remember that time you jumped in when those hyenas were tearing Dae and me up? I swear I'd never seen anything like that before. I didn't know you had it in you!"

Thia remembered a little annoyed, "Well what'd you want me to do? They had you guys seriously outnumbered and you looked pretty bad."

Shai chuckled, "Oh, I'm not complaining. That was a big pack and they looked pretty hungry. But I have to admit, you even scared me a little. You took out more than Dae and I did together!"

Thia started feeling bad about it, "I tried to warn them."

Shai smirked, "I don't think they speak tiger roar, T."

"They don't need to. The message is universal."

"Yeah, *don't mess with Miss Thia*.", Shai said with a head slide.

She shook her head, "Shut up dork."

"Awe!" he mocked.

She gave him a blank stare, "seriously"

Shai defiantly persisted, "Ha! I remember you drew them away to the other side of that hill and Dae and I freaked out and tried to get up thinking you took on too much – that was until the dogs started yelping and flying out!"

Thia didn't like remembering how hurt her brothers were so she got up and headed over to the water, "It's still a little warm. You're right Dae we better head back before they worry. That and it's a school night."

And so disappointed they headed home.

Thia became a frequent visitor to the caves. Even after her brothers lost interest she continued to go relax and even started practicing her dance there. It was the safest place to go now where she wouldn't be discovered or spied on. Only her brothers knew where to find her if they needed to. And she would know by the sound of the water that they were coming. The other opening was too far up to jump and too steep to climb.

When Thia came back from one of her practices she found nothing but tension at home. Something happened while she was gone.

Dae spoke softly standing next to Thia in the living room listening in on the meeting called, "Where've you been? A small group of humans in dark camouflage clothes and ski masks attacked."

This was very strange and had never happened before. The group proceeded, seeming to think they could conquer and take what they wished. Caleb and his sister were visiting during this. The moment they heard that a fight broke out they quickly left for home claiming it wasn't their fight.

All ended well, for the Phelidae with only minor injuries as the persistent intruders grossly underestimated their potential victims.

Thia's mother asked her father that night, "How did the humans find us? They've never found us before."

She was not one to be easily rattled but seeing she was very unsettled by the whole thing he offered the best explanation he could, "Perhaps our trips to town need to become less frequent. They may be drawing too much attention."

It worked, for now.

Later word got back to Thia and her brothers that a story about the twins running rather than helping had gotten out. Told more as a joke instead of focusing on the seriousness of the event, the incident was titled, Hollow Heroes Separate. It went on to describe in detail how the twins demonstrated their boastful speed as they turned and ran home in fear leaving behind their helpless aunt.

Caleb, outraged and embarrassed, spread his counter attack stating he would prove the vicious rumors wrong at the upcoming games. This didn't stop the stifled laughs everywhere he went and drove him insane with fury. So he feverishly planned his revenge. He would seek out Thia and her brothers, as he wrongfully assumed they were at the bottom of it, challenge them and prove his worth.

As time went on attacks became more frequent. Some started to speculate that someone bigger was behind them using them to uncover what was there and why the previous groups had not come back. But little did they know, none would ever be permitted to return and reveal their findings.

The daily lessons began to transform. History was the repetitive topic of late even though it had previously been covered. The young grew nervous by the signs of change. The lessons turned insistent on memorizing where they came from and the ways and traditions of their tribe. The teachings went all the way back to the origins of the Phelidae powers. Before they had a chance to ask what was going on, they realized, this is what was discussed when preparing for the ceremony.

The Ceremony

The time had come for the great ceremony. This event only takes place twice in most lifetimes thought this one seemed earlier than usual. In between them the famous stories of past ceremonies are told. Everyone in the village was spending the whole week before getting ready for the festival. Even school was on hold until after it. The other tribes were coming too. It was time to unveil the new young ones powers for those that carry the mark.

The Phelidae age quickly until teen years then slows and their powers mature, if they have them. The ones that will have develop a mark on the inner part of their left bicep. It first resembles a dark blotch about the size of a half dollar taking on no form. The ceremony is when its shape is evoked by Aurelia, one of the tribe's special members and its true meaning revealed. Traditionally those with marks are deemed defenders of the tribe and trained as such along with their regular training.

The women were in the kitchens feverishly cooking. The mouth watering smells carried throughout the village as giant steaming pots were found on every stove and flour and dough covered every counter top. Through the window sounds of hammering and sawing could be heard as the men were out constructing massive tents and repairing or building new tables and chairs. The boys helped working on the stage and gathering large logs for the giant bon fire as the girls were practicing their dances and putting the final touches on their costumes.

As members from the other tribes arrived they were welcomed into the homes of the different families. The relatives stayed with their extended and the others were invited into stay with the remaining.

The festival for the ceremony went on for three days. The first day consisted of receiving the guests and getting them settled in. The second day is when the fun began with the games and feasting. The men had competitions in throwing, running and jumping distance. Thia sat on the side to watch her brothers while the women caught up with each other and made more food or clothing and trinkets to be sold or taken back home.

Caleb as promised attended and didn't lose a beat in his strut. It seemed revealing his mark took second seat to making sure the trip was spent rebuilding his reputation. He showed off in front of all as Kasha sat unwavering, sneering in Thia's direction. Though Dae and Shai were also participating in the competitions, they kept mindful of where Caleb's attention was. They were all too familiar with his temper and assumed something was coming as payback for the stories they didn't initiate. But this is not what bothered them. They both noticed how he seemed to be looking at Thia recently.

As night fell on the third day, the festivities stopped and the whole village gathered together around the mountain of wood piled up like a teepee for the campfire. No one brought anything to ignite the wood. They didn't need it as there were two Fire Reapers, their official title, among them.

And the grand show began. As the drums pounded two small logs moved in rhythm on their own floating up in the air then scraping together to the beats. The wood got red and hot from the friction. Then a rainbow of sparks in yellow, orange, green and blue began to jump and dance all around, cascading down upon the wood pile that pointed to the sky. Then the heap burst into an explosion of fire and the crowd jumped back, then laughed and applauded.

Next the Wind Wishers sent a sudden current of air pulling the smoke up and out morphing it into a picture of a giant cat eye.

"Our eyes are not that of our simpler cousins. Instead they slide into sharp slits cutting through courage and striking fear in the very hearts of our enemies. Combined with our increased size, speed and strength, they are no match and thus we are able to restore peace and order again." the old woman shouted then turned back to the show of magnificent moving pictures above the fire.

A different story teller spoke about each of the great and fierce cats and their famous ancient battles.

As soon as the last story was told the Water Wakers took over. A fine glittering spray of water came from all directions out of the woods gathering in the center swirling above the fire. Then it split and solidified into waves of suspended water and spun on either side of the stage as it transformed into two enormous pillars then instantly froze crystal clear in a beautiful pattern of majestic tigers, leopards, lions, panthers and other great cats climbing to the top.

"Once the slaughters died down the Phelidae returned to the shadows until needed again."

The Earth Shifters sent giant slabs of polished marble with deep pits in the middle filled with more wood, floating to the top of the pillars. Then flames from the bon fire reached out and tapped the tops of the pillars like clawed fingers instantly igniting the brush and kindling on top.

The fire died down to a normal blaze as attention shifted to the emerging boys of the tribes performing around the fire. They rotated around the circle in tribal costumes juggling swords, spitting fire lighting the baton and poi spinning. One group toyed with a mix of pink purple and yellow flames forming the figure eight as the second group manipulated green and blue in multilayered circles all while the fire-spitters shot red and purple in between.

Following them came the girls.

The traditional female Phelidae dance is a version of Belly Dance though not in the popular movie fashion, nor the style done by the gypsies. Their way is tribal. No veils, beads or sequence are used on the costumes and the colors are not pastel or bright. Instead the fabrics were dark brilliant heavy and earthy. Deep blood reds, rich purples, royal and navy blues, browns and blacks are the basis of hues. The skirts varied a little but were mostly large flowing circle skirts of thick fabric.

One by one the dances went on. A couple started as solos then out came the pairs and groups. They move in sequence, some balanced swords and candles on their heads, hands and hips and others twirled canes embellished with ribbon and silk fringe. Everyone and everything moved in perfect unison to the music.

After all of the rest came the final dance, Thia's. Being the daughter of the tribal head, she was always reserved for last and much was expected of her performance. She would not disappoint but as anticipated by her brothers, she had her own style, a style she loved so much she didn't care what any of the other girls thought. She knew she stuck out anyway, so why stop now. Her mother wanted to see her dance but Thia wouldn't let her. She did however get to see her costume as Thia needed some help with it. Though it was not a fully traditional costume, her mother secretly favored what Thia came up with. She softly smiled with pride as she glanced over at her daughter, exposing it before them now.

The old man stood to make his announcement, "And finally Athena, only daughter of our beloved leader Amon and his gracious wife Lianna."

Thia stepped out into the fire lit half circle. Everything stopped and all eyes turned to her. The drummers began her song. Her heart sped up and her throat became dry. Then she forcefully brought her focus back to the music trying to forget anyone else was there. This was her favorite song as it made her relax and feel free.

She stood still at first in her pose with her head and eyes to the ground. With fluid control she ever so slowly lifted her eyes, hair slightly pulled back away from her face revealing her mesmerizing crystal blue cat slits. Next, her bold Tiger stripes began fading in, crawling up from the base of her back to her neck and finally out from all around her hairline. The crowd murmured in amazement, all but Caleb and Kasha of course but they were definitely paying attention.

"Please, what is she trying to do?" Kasha whispered to Caleb, feeling a little insecure.

"Don't worry about it. Tricks are nice but we have yet to see if she can perform." Caleb half attempted to rationalize to his sister.

She hadn't even begun yet and everyone was already impressed. *Not a bad way to start.* She thought. *Good thing I got bored that week.* She learned to pull out her stripes and eyes without fully changing one afternoon just to see if it could be done. Once it happened she continued to practice in the mirror until she could control it at will.

She wore the same hues; however her skirt had much less material and separated into panels. Hair pins made of bones and beads, feathers and exotic flowers decorated her head. A string of metal beads draped across her forehead and long thin leather strips with shells and coins on the ends cascaded down around her face swinging gracefully with every movement as she began her dance.

As she floated around the circle, her body swayed and twisted like a snake in a trance. Her arms perfectly accented every move, lined with netted arm socks, old beaten metal arm cuffs and big stone rings on her long narrow fingers. Her stomach rolled like waves in the sea, top to bottom then in reverse. Her hips dropped and lifted effortlessly tossing the tassels, beads and jingling metals dangling like a curtain. Around her shimmying torso thin vines of ivy had been perfectly painted on. Her leg slid out from behind the front black panel and through the torn shear strips of purple and blue revealing her anklets of shells, stone and glass beads and old coins that were strung down to her middle toe mocking a sandal.

She got lost in her dance and the music. All eyes never broke from her for a moment. It was a dance they'd truly never seen prior to this. Before any wanted it to end, including Thia, the song was over. She gracefully ended her last movement, bowed her head slightly, politely saying, *Thank you dearly for your time*, turned and walked back to where she started slowly dragging her feet just like a large cat with heavy paws, her hips guiding them along.

The moment she was out of the circle and out of sight she flew home to change. She didn't even want to wait to learn their reaction. She threw back on her festival clothes. They weren't as comfy as her normal clothes but way better than her costume. Then she headed back to the festivities to find her brothers.

Along the way she found her mother who was already searching for her.

Her mother gave her a loving hug, "Thia -- that was absolutely beautiful. You should hear what everyone has been saying. I think your father was proud too. He seemed to be sitting up a little taller than usual while fighting off a grin."

"Only you would know mom." Her father didn't really share his feelings.

Her mom just smiled. "Dear, why did you leave so fast?"

She tugged at her clothes, "Mom I'd much rather be in these clothes than my costume. If I'm expected to stay here all night I'm going to be comfortable."

Her mother smiled knowing how she is, "Very well. I think Dae and Shai were looking for you over by the stage a moment ago."

"Thanks mom!" as she gave her a kiss on the cheek and hurried in that direction.

Getting there took longer than she'd hoped as she was unable to avoid all of the stops every couple of feet to receive the many compliments on her performance.

"Hey T, that wasn't bad! I liked your trick with your stripes. You been holding out on us?" Shai found her in the crowd.

"Thanks! No, I only just got it to work. I was going to show you." she smiled.

Dae found them and joined as Shai went on to explain one reaction in particular, "Oh, you should've seen how pissed Kasha got! It looked like Caleb was trying to talk her down."

Thia just rolled her eyes, "I don't really care. I can't wait till they go back home."

Dae got a little serious, "Speaking of Caleb, watch yourself around him Thia. Shai and I have been noticing he's been acting a little…funny this trip."

Shai adding some detail, "Yeah, and the way he's been looking at you is kinda creeping us out. We don't know if he's got something planed because of the story or what."

Then the conch shell horn sounded.

Thia's face lit up as her heart jumped, "Oh my gosh, it's time! Are you excited? I am but nervous too."

They talked amongst themselves on what was about to happen as they headed to their designated spots in line.

The horn sounded once again and the old man stood up, "Each carries their own unique tribal mark which represents what power they possess. However none have been able to invoke the true mark but Aurelia and her ancestors."

She never explained how it was given to her, as they are forbidden to do so, but when she came back with the gift, everyone recognized it. Some say the invoking gift chooses the perfect Phelidae for it, when the time is right and the next one is chosen they are sent for. Some remember when Aurelia was young she was summoned; she left and was gone for weeks, then came back changed. She returned white-eyed and blind, in the traditional sense; however she must have taken on a new type of sight. She was forbidden to explain this as well but anyone could tell she was able to somehow see as she got around without trouble.

Upon the elevated stage sat, a large chair resembling a throne, constructed in dark, thick heavy wood, sanded down so fine it felt like silk to touch. Polished colored glass, beads and metals embellished the arms and legs of the chair. Thick deep plum cushions covered the back and seat. Candles scattered everywhere providing a soft glow.

Most all the students were already lined up by the stage to be read. They were positioned according to Aurelia's order, spoken to her by her gift. *Still at the end. I can't get a break*, Thia thought, again placed last in line of about ten. She couldn't help keep checking on her brothers. First she spotted Shai was third and Dae was fifth then *stupid Caleb and Kasha* were shortly after them. *Bet they love being placed behind them. At least their time here is coming to a swift end.*

The time came and Aurelia began her slow and deliberate approach from one of the nicer homes, along a candle lit path, through the quiet and attentive crowd to the throne, placed her large staff against it and sat down with her hands folded on her lap. She was wearing another type of tribal ceremonial gown and head dress but hers looked very old and worn. A mix of shells, beads and feathers decorated them. Most must have been imported or traded for since none of it was from their woods or even found at the town stores. The beads looked hand made out of crystal and gemstones and the feathers were exotic colors, not found in the area. Even the shells had to have come from a beach far away.

She wasted no time starting, one by one calling each up drawing out their true mark and moving on. After the reading was done, she would shout out the result and the crowd clapped and cheered. The first couple went quickly and then it was Shai's turn. Thia instantly felt butterflies in her stomach for him. Then she noticed some of the crowd whispering, she thought she made out that they remembered he was *one of the five.*

Aurelia placed her hand on the indeterminate blotch on his arm and closed her eyes. The crowd was still watching the light pour from beneath her hand and then fade away. Thia couldn't help but to notice the most serious look on Shai's face that she'd ever seen. But her observation was quickly diverted as Aurelia lifted her hand, only enough so she could see what she'd drawn for him. Her eyes widened with surprise, unlike the other two that went before him. She paused for a moment sorting through a flood of thoughts.

What happened? What is she waiting for? Is it not clear? What did his turn to? Poor Shai. Thia suffered for her brother.

Aurelia stood up still with a firm grasp on his arm, as the audience stared at them in suspense. "His revealed powers -- are earth **and** fire." She peeled away her hand and jerked his arm displaying his result to the crowd. Everyone including him starred dumbfounded at the spot on his arm. Indeed there were not one but two symbols there. Once it set in, the whispers began.

"Did she just say *powers*?", "I knew those kids would be different!", "I wonder what the others have now.", "They should go next, skip the others.", "What does it mean?", and on they shouted.

"Read the other four now!" one man rang out above the buzz of loud whispers as the rest speculated amongst themselves, then turned to agree with him. The tribal heads grew concerned as the group got louder demanding the other four be read out of turn.

Aurelia released Shai, grabbed her staff next to her chair and slammed it down with a loud thunderous boom causing everyone to jump in alarm.

She was not happy and would not tolerate such insulting and disrespectful behavior, "The children *will* be read *in* the predestined order! Stay and be silent or leave, the choice is yours. Now if you *please*, there will be *no more* interruptions!"

Everyone straightened up and remained quiet as the ceremony moved on. All applauded and greeted with aggressive handshakes and hugs as Shai finally made it off the stage. A few more went and were met with a lesser degree of enthusiasm. Then it was Dae's turn. Again Thia was both nervous and excited for her other brother. In the fire light she noticed his clothes didn't exactly match. *Sweet Dae, he sees the best of all of us at night but his colorblindness does him in sometimes*, she humorously thought to herself adoring him. But again her thoughts were interrupted. The crowd began speculating in a low hum, paying him special attention as she suspected they would after Shai's news.

This time there was a roar of applause when his gifts of air and water were revealed. The same greetings and congratulations followed. Shai gave him a solid punch to the arm. *He's so rough with him, not that Dae notices*, Thia just shook her head. Normal people would've been holding their arm in pain from the blow he dealt.

A couple more went with their single gifts revealed and then it was time for the twins. The anticipation was making for a very tense ceremony every time one of the five stood by Aurelia, but it was moving a little faster now that they knew what to expect. Caleb had wind and fire and Kasha had earth and water.

At long last the belief that the births were not mere coincidence came true.

"I told you all but you wouldn't believe me." The same old squinty eyed lady proclaimed to those around her. They just rolled their eyes expecting as much from her as she's known to say many things.

The rest went after the twins but before Thia, truly robbed of their own special experience as everyone seemed to only be interested in the five. Though their parents tried to pay special attention to them, deep down all were wondering which two Thia would end up with.

Some tried to guess, "I bet it will be wind and water. You saw how she moved during her dance.", "Oh you are crazy. Earth will be one for sure. Weren't you paying attention? She controls her stripes!", "No, her father is Earth and she's nothing like him. She will be wind like her mother."

As the second to last walked off Thia felt all eyes fall on her. Extremely nervous, more than when she was up to perform, she glanced over at her parents. They were beaming with love, pride and superiorly controlled anticipation. She snuck a smile to them and they returned it...even her father, once sure no one else was looking.

Aurelia called to Thia in her low stern voice, "Athena, please join me."

She made her way to Aurelia hearing nothing, like everyone was holding their breath. Thia's hands were ice cold and she began to tremble. Opposite her parent's kind and loving gaze, Aurelia's face was cold and somber. Her task was an old, serious and respected one. She requested Thia's hand just as she had the others. Thia offered it. Aurelia firmly took her by the wrist, pulled and turned her inner arm towards her. Aurelia laid her warm left hand over the mark on Thia's arm.

At first Thia felt a strange tingling sensation, then it got warm. *Funny, no one's ever mentioned you could feel anything before,* she thought. Then, it began to burn and the light came. *This is getting a little uncomfortable. I wonder if everyone's was like this. It must have been. Quit being a baby and suck it up, it'll be over quick.* Only it wasn't. It kept getting hotter and hotter and the light brighter and brighter. *It can't keep getting worse can it? No way did they feel this and not show it.* It was so hot it started feel like sharp red hot nails sticking her.

Finally she felt she couldn't take it anymore and whispered in desperation, "stop".

Aurelia's grip got tighter and the wind picked up speed.

Thia started to panic. Louder this time, she pulled to free herself, "Stop"

Aurelia's eyes shut tighter as her claws came out digging into Thia's arm drawing some blood holding her in place. The ground began to shake.

"Stop it!" came out as half scream, half cry. And faster than anyone thought possible her brothers were at her side growling. The bonfire exploded to three times its size.

Thia felt a sudden wave of white hot warmth wash over her. But this hot didn't hurt. This hot made her feel strong and fierce. The fear was gone and replaced by anger. The light under Aurelia's hand went from white to blue.

All of the delicate twinkle lights hanging down the back of the stage burst like little firecrackers.

Everyone watched nervously as Shai and Dae tried to pull the two apart, but their skin singed their hands and a force threw them back. Thia crouched down panting and bearing her teeth as her stripes came out getting ready to strike. Neither Aurelia nor Thia noticed the boys. Bright light still pouring from under her hand, Aurelia's eyes opened reacting to Thia's stance and light poured from them too. Thia's eyes changed to swirling silver and light blue around her cat slits as she began to growl.

The pain jumped in intensity bringing Thia to her knees and her head fell back angrily screaming from it. Then her anger grew turning the scream back in to a vicious roar. A curious smile appeared on Aurelia's face until she finally grabbed Thia's forehead with her right hand. A blinding and crackling clap of lightening knocked everyone to the ground. Everything was dark and silent again.

Aurelia slowly stumbled back into her chair exhausted, eyes and nose bleeding. Thia lay collapsed on the floor before her. Shallow gasps were heard all around as the crowd sat up collecting themselves. The candles relit themselves returning light to the stage.

Aurelia sat gathering her strength and sorting out what to say as Shai and Dae came back to Thia, testing her skin before lifting her head to see if she was okay. She regained consciousness wondering, *what just happened?* But before she could voice her question, Aurelia stood up with assistance, wiping the blood from her nose the same time Dae cleaned Thia's.

"oh, thanks" she whispered to him, still sitting on the floor.

Very concerned, "Sure. You okay?"

Still feeling a little out of it, "yeah, I think so"

Donning a brand new silver streak in her hair glistening from the moon light Aurelia rang out, "I have only heard of this in stories. In all my years have never seen it, until now." grabbing Thia's arm again with a tight grasp pulling her to her feet. *Ow, she's pretty strong for an old lady.* Thia looked over at her parents again afraid to see what anyone else's expression might be. She found they, like the rest of the crowd were wide eyed awaiting Aurelia's next words. And then they came.

"This one has a single gift".

Low whispers began. "What does it mean?", "The other four had two.", "How can this be?"

Aurelia put her hand to the crowd and they were quiet again. Her grip on Thia was starting to hurt, but not like before, but was definitely cutting off her circulation as she was now losing feeling in her fingers.

"Her gift is energy, energy in its purest form." Everyone looked around at each other confused and back at Thia. She had no idea what it all meant and wasn't all that interested anymore in finding out. All she could focus on was locating the nearest escape route home once she was set free from this old woman's death grip. She looked back at her parents. They were the only ones that seemed unsure but pleased. This at least made Thia feel a little better. *It must not be too bad. Mom and dad don't seem to mind.*

Aurelia finally turned to her as the others talked among themselves.

"What you have been given is rare and powerful child. Learn it well and use it wisely young one." At this she finally let go of her, walked off the stage and was escorted home to rest. Thia followed off with her bothers on each side and quickly made her way to her parents. They met her with big hugs as all three of them were congratulated by everyone in town. Knowing Thia was uncomfortable in the spot light, her mother kept her close by her side between them.

She was finally able to join the party and find Dae and Shai once the last of the members had spoken to them and the well wishing visitors died down. Her throat and mouth were dry and her cheeks sore from trying to keep smiling as she thanked everyone like she knew her parents wanted her to. She looked around but couldn't find her brothers. The crowd was too thick and she was no longer on the stage up higher than all of them.

She desperately wanted to head over to where the beverages were being served but there were too many old people there talking to each other. She was so thirsty but didn't want to get stuck answering all of their boring and or intrusive questions. "When are you getting married? Why don't you come to our village and meet my son? You should settle down with a good boy, this would make your parents proud." *Well, they would probably be right about that one.* But there was plenty of time for that later. The thought of getting married and having babies didn't even cross her mind. And on and on they would prod, especially now that she has this rare and wondrous gift she knows absolutely nothing about. She was too tired to tolerate any of it and decided it just wasn't worth it.

As she turned to begin searching again through the crowd, Dae shows up in front of her with drink in outstretched hand.

"You are a lifesaver!" she gratefully accepted and started drinking as fast as she could. It was perfectly refreshing and exactly what she needed. The cool sweet wet soothed her scratchy dry throat and quenched her thirst.

"You looked like you could use it." He glanced over to where the old ones stood, "We got extras early so we wouldn't have to hear them prattle on too." he said insightfully.

"They're just so nosy!" she looked around. "Where's Shai?"

Dae nodded his head behind her and to the right as he finished swallowing, "He's over there talking to some girls"

"Figures. Showing off is he?" his behavior didn't surprise Thia at all.

Shai was more like the others than Dae and Thia were. Being good looking with a magnetic personality tends to help. Drawing attention happened naturally for him. But he didn't have much patience for the common things so he typically didn't last long with them, as evident with his timely return.

"God! I keep forgetting how awful it is talking to them. Or maybe I am subconsciously hoping they've found something new to talk about since the last time we've spoken. But no, they just yammer on about the same boring stuff in that high pitch giggly voice!" He stuck his ear in Dae's face, "Check, I think my ears were starting to bleed."

Thia mocked him, "Awe, you poor perfectly social thing." Then glanced over at them, Oh, great, so you draw their attention over here?! Now I guarantee they are probably wondering why you hang out with the likes of us. No offense Dae, I meant me."

"None taken." he said with a simple smile.

"Yeah they mentioned something like that." Shai admitted.

Both Dae and Thia turned to Shai. "...so what'd you say?" Thia was curious what anyone in his position would say. What drew him to the misfits when he fit in so well, so naturally? Not only did he fit in but he could own them all if he wanted to. They already hung on his every word as if they were swooning over a famous celebrity they'd finally gotten to meet. Thia was sure Dae wondered the same thing.

Shai came clean not being the subtle type, "They asked why I hung out with you guys so much since you're so weird."

"Not surprising." Thia was a little bitter now.

"So I told them how sometimes you guys do like freaky experiments and stuff..."

Thia freaked, "You didn't!"

"Ha ha, I'm just kidding. I said you guys were not weird but actually pretty fun and you weren't really friends but more like a brother and sister to me. The looks on their faces was priceless. But after they got over the shock, they went back to talking about which of them was cutest and their new clothes or something. I couldn't take anymore so I left."

Thia's heart jumped and suddenly she found herself on cloud nine. *He told them I'm like a sister.* She beamed. She knew she felt that way about them but wasn't sure exactly how they felt. For all she knew they might just be tolerating her or showing mercy out of pity.

Shai playfully swiped at Thia's face, "You can wipe that big goofy smile off of your face Thia. Don't go all girlie on me now."

Dae just laughed. Thia embarrassed, tried to swipe back and kick at Shai but missed of course. Guys were always good at dodging solicited attacks.

"But really, you guys are great. And of course you already know I'm great so it just makes sense for us to hang out." They all laughed as the real Shai reemerged from his sentimental time out.

She brought her mood back down to about cloud six but she had to fight to keep it there. Thanks to a – weird but successful big night and Shai's comment, she was off the charts happy.

From then on they were a permanent fixture in her life. She had them come over to her house so often her parents came to know them as almost children of their own. She completely trusted them and they her. They practiced, explored and relaxed together. They learned from each other which helped each of them round out their personalities and abilities as they became young adults. Dae spoke more, Shai spoke a little less and Thia got out more -- with them.

The day after the ceremony Thia woke up refreshed for a new day. She found her parents with some of the elders and Aurelia in the living room.

All were focused on Thia's mother as she spoke, "It was just a dream, no? It is common for pregnant women to have unusual dreams."

Aurelia shook her head, "With recent events, I must disagree. What she has now is very powerful. It took much to expose. Had I not ended it the moment it was fully realized -- Lianna, we must know everything, every little detail. Now, when the old spirit woman spoke to you, what did she say again? Please try to remember her exact words. We must to try to understand and record what might have caused this."

Thia's mother closed her eyes remembering the dream, "She laid her hand on my stomach and said, *To be a star, she must shine her own light, follow her own path, and worry not about the darkness, for that is when stars shine brightest.*"

One of the elders spotted Thia was there and cleared his throat. They stopped talking and turned to her.

Her mother broke from the serious discussion and gently pulled her in the kitchen, "Good morning honey. Are you hungry?"

"No, I'm okay mom. What's going on?" curious about what she just heard.

"Oh just boring superstitious talk." She said dismissively.

She watched her mother make more coffee, "Have they figured out what that was that happened last night? Or better yet why all the weird stuff happens to us?"

Lianna did not believe in lying to her daughter, "We are working on it. The problem is that it's been so long since the last time anything like this has happened, not much is known about it. But we are trying. Why don't you run out for a bit and come back for lunch? We'll talk then, okay?"

"Yeah, okay." Thia was concerned but respected her mother wishes.

Her brothers were a little too rowdy last night so they were restricted to their homes until further notice. Shai of course couldn't resist a challenge, especially from Caleb. When cheating was suspected after it wasn't going well for Caleb, a fight broke out and that's when Dae got dragged into it. So Thia found herself off wandering alone after getting kicked out of her own home so the grownups could converse regarding her new oddities.

She strolled along her usual path but it was somehow very different. She didn't notice anything obvious that might have changed but something was unusual. Everything felt energized and busy, but nothing was moving. The wind blew through a bit but that was not what she was feeling. Something – she couldn't quite put her finger on it was very different now or rather she felt everything now. She was looking all around taking in how different the trees, leaves and even sky looked.

An orange and black butterfly gracefully floated by then came back to her. It bobbed all around her then headed off again. She smiled at how playful it seemed and decided to follow it. Then she noticed he had a strange trace of color trailing behind it like the lines in the sky left by an airplane. It flew faster and farther so she sped up to keep up wondering where it was going. When it seemed to reach its destination it stopped and started to climb, higher and higher. She noticed a couple more where that one was going and then there were many more and they all had the same weird and wonderful tail. *Wow, they're so beautiful and free. There's so many, I wonder if there is a nest or something up there.*

Busy staring up walking around taking in the new sensations she suddenly stopped and turned to see what she felt behind her. She was about to back right in to a tree but something stopped her. She slowly placed her hand on the tree and without actually touching it she found she could feel it, every bump and grove in the bark. It too looked like it had a faint glow to it. Then she looked all around. *That's it!* It occurred to her that everything was glowing now. It's not an obvious glow, just brighter, more vivid -- alive.

At the most inopportune time she was interrupted by a voice all too familiar, one that had not gone away yet like she'd hoped.

"Thia! There you are!" Caleb called out to her jogging in her direction.

"And there I go." She said as she turned to leave.

Acting innocent, "Hey, come on I just want to talk."

Not falling for it, "Caleb, you never just want to talk. You start trouble, it's what you do. And I don't want any part of it right now."

"I just wanted to say Hi." Still carrying on with his fake innocence.

Annoyed she quickly responded, "Okay then, Hi! Now I'll be going and you'll not be following."

He followed anyway, "Awe, don't be like that. Let's start over. There is no reason we can't be friends."

She sighed, "Caleb, I'm not looking for anymore friends. I'm good with what I have. Thanks anyway."

Caleb getting a little condescending now "Oh stop. That is no way for the daughter of the chief to behave."

She tore around angry at him, "How dare you try and tell me how I should behave!" She tried to calm down, "Alright I'll bite. How about you just tell me what will make this end faster?"

Completely ignoring her last remark, Caleb quickly changes the subject, "So, Energy huh? I knew you were special."

Thia recalling one of the many unpleasant conversations in the past, "Ah, so that's what you meant when you called me a, oh how did it go again? *Lonely freak loser*, right?"

"Oh, I was just playing with you." He explained as he got closer to her.

She backed up in response, "What are you up to?"

"I'm just trying to be nice." His face changed a little, less fake friendly and more creepy.

Thia shivered as a very uncomfortable chill ran up her spine, "Why, you feeling okay?" Then she just couldn't help herself. It was button pushing time, time to end his little game, "Did you bump your head when Dae knocked you to the ground at football yesterday?"

Bingo! Caleb blew up, "He didn't...he caught me off guard!"

Thia wryly smiled, "There he is, the real Caleb we all know and love! Are we done now?"

That creepy look resurfaced as he looked Thia up and down. Fighting off the goose bumps on her neck she paused for a second and looked around. "Say, where's your sister? I thought you guys were connected at the hip."

It worked; his face changed again, more plain and absent now, "You know, honestly, I don't think she likes you."

She chuckled, "Yeah, I think I've picked up on that by now."

Now his blank stare through her was getting under her skin. Something was not right.

"She'd be really upset with me if she knew I was here with you."

Thia raised an eye brow, "Well we wouldn't want that. By all means, GO."

Thia finally wore Caleb down, and his face softened a little as he shook his head. Then it rushed out, "Thia, I wanted to compliment you on your performance!"

Thia was taken back, mostly by his shouting at her but also by the surprising revelation. Whoever was in front of her was no longer the typical Caleb. His comment seemed a little off, almost genuine. All of his swagger and condescension was gone. What stood before her now seemed to be a raw and vulnerable insecure man.

"Okay, thank you." She wasn't quite sure what to say to him now. She was actually a little nervous seeing this new side of Caleb. It was unexpected and kind of unsettling. *Does maturity come with our powers?* She couldn't help but wonder.

"And I'm sorry about being a jerk all the time."

Thia just stood there in disbelief, *Okay, now I think I need to pinch myself. I must be still sleeping. Or he might be sick. I was just kidding but maybe he did get cracked in the head?*

But before she could figure out how to respond he said something that changed everything, making complete sense of the whole situation, "What'd you say we hook up? You and I...we could be unstoppable with our powers and talents together."

She just shook her head in disappointment, "I see, now. I get it."

"Get what?" lost on what she was referring to.

"You're unbelievable. Is power and popularity all you are ever after?"

He grew frustrated, "If you won't of your own free will then I could always make you."

"Ha! Now you're threatening me? You are unreal!"

"I could ask your father for you." He jabbed in desperation.

Now she was angry with astonishment, "My parents would *never* do that to me!"

Then the look came back, the one that's scaring her a little more each time it returns. He got real close, too close, "...or I could just *take* you!"

She backed away from him but he just approached faster backing her into a tree leaving them face to face with his hands now wrapped around her waist.

She panicked, "Get off!" and shoved him to the ground.

She realized she was in trouble now as he was stronger and faster than her. He got up and back handed her across the face sending her to the ground. Her eyes watered from the strike as her heart sped up. As she licked her lip to clean it, he yanked her up and into him by her arm, digging his other hand into her side to the point a rib cracked and bruised. She still tried to push off of him with her hand in his face. He found another smaller tree, dragged her to it and wrapped her arms back around it holding them by the wrist with his large crushing hand. He went to kiss her but she turned her head, until he grabbed her face, lip still bleeding a little and forced it back to his.

She squirmed, growled and gritted her growing teeth as her eyes started to turn and her stripes faded in.

Seeing her transformation, especially her stripes developing reminded him, "Oh, I forgot to mention, your little markings trick is quite a turn on."

He aggressively kissed her smashing his lips into hers, pressing himself into her and began pulling at the neckline of her shirt. Then in a panic he stopped and suddenly pulled away looking for something in the woods. Then Thia looked sensing it too. Something was coming; it was something big and fast. Caleb's eyes widened and stomach dropped as Dae and Shai suddenly appeared in the distance heading straight for them swift and furious. Shortly after their growling could be heard as they got closer. Caleb jumped away from Thia before they got there. He was a little stronger than Shai and faster than Dae but knew he couldn't take them both at the same time.

First Shai then Dae stopped on a dime at Thia's side still growling with sharp teeth and eyes turned at Caleb as leaves small twigs and dust caught up and floated past them carried by the current of air their speed generated.

"You okay Thia?" Dae asked breathing hard and angrier than she'd ever seen him.

"Yeah." Thia replied a bit shaken, but relieved.

As Thia reached up to wipe the rest of the blood from her lip, Shai caught sight of the black and purple bruises on her wrists. Knowing they already had plenty of time to fade, he snapped and lunged at Caleb ripping up the ground where he stood the instant he changed into the immense leopard version of himself.

Caleb didn't anticipate his attack and fell back under Shai's force. Caleb managed to change into his cheetah form as they grappled around smashing into trees, growling ferociously, biting, tearing out clumps of fur and swiping thick heavy claws in a vicious cat fight until Caleb finally broke away and ran off bloodied and beaten. His slight advantage in strength didn't help him this time. Shai was enraged knowing Caleb's intentions for his sister.

Shai came back in human form with barely any scratches. Dae threw him his clothing scraps as he questioned Thia on what happened.

"Nothing, thanks to you guys. He just came out of nowhere acting funny, and apparently doesn't take rejection well I guess and attacked." She was embarrassed by the details and chose to leave them out. That and she didn't want to cause Shai to go after him again.

Dae took his shirt off and threw it to Shai to cover up with since the scraps were not working out, "You can keep that."

"thanks" Shai was out of breath, livid and flush.

Thia was amazed how fast they got there for she had wandered pretty far, "How did you guys get here so fast? I thought you were stuck at home?"

Shai tried to catch his breath during the answer, "Not sure. We both had a feeling something wasn't right with you and ended up sneaking out and heading to your house to check on you. I picked up your scent but it was a little old, then I caught Caleb's and knew what..." Shai let out a growl. "...*mood* he was in so we hurried."

Dae continued on, seeing the anger festering in Shai, "When Shai smelled your blood on the wind he lost it. I could barely keep up."

She felt bad, "Thanks you guys. You'll probably get in trouble now. I should've listened to you, I shouldn't have gone out so far. I'm sorry."

Shai snapped out of his trance from her ridiculous apology, "*You're* sorry?! Thia you just got attacked and almost raped!"

The word made Thia's stomach drop as a wave a nausea hit.

Shai didn't notice and kept at her, "You need to become a little more selfish Thia and stop worrying about others so much. The moment you saw him you should've ran home! Didn't we tell you we didn't like the way he was looking at you?"

Thia started off defensive, "Yes, but how was I to know he would...never mind, I don't want to talk about it anymore. You guys better get back. Maybe they didn't notice you are gone yet."

Shai was still determined, "Besides you think we are going to get into trouble once we tell everyone what happened?"

"Oh! Please don't tell!" Thia begged.

Shai's eyes started to change as the discussion quickly escalated to yelling, "What do you mean, *don't tell*? He needs to pay, T! He can't do that to you and get away without punishment. Someone needs to teach him a lesson."

She knew Shai was right but was desperate to avoid the embarrassment and tried to get out of what he was proposing, "Shai, I'm thinking the beat down you just served might have been enough to teach anyone. I'm fine. Anyway he's going to have to come up with something clever to explain away all the marks you left on him. And if we are lucky maybe he will just leave sooner now."

Dae wanted to stop the fighting without being too obvious so it would work, "T, why are you out so far?"

Thrown off by the new direction in questioning, "Uh, I don't know. I got kicked out of the house because they are having some meeting so I just started walking. Oh and then I saw this beautiful butterfly and... hey, do you guys feel any different today?"

Shai was calming down a bit distracted by curiosity now as he listened, "Yeah, a little bit. You too?"

Heading back to Thia's house for lunch they tried describing the new consciousness they seem to be experiencing. However the boys' descriptions were centered around what they could do now rather than the overall changes Thia was talking about.

When they entered the house, they found the meeting was not yet over. In fact the group had gotten larger. Thia's mother escorted them off to the kitchen, found Shai some pants and provided a most satisfying meal, one of her many known talents.

While they were all around the table eating, Thia wanted to bring up something she noticed, "You know, I find it funny how no one seemed surprised you had no pants on Shai, including my mom."

They all started laughing and went back to eating and attempting to listen in on the conversation in the other room. Another, more wanderer than teacher or elder, who went by the name Nomad was sharing his theory on how four of the five of them received two gifts instead of one like the rest, the fifth exception being Thia.

"Well I am not sure where the star fits in but I believe the reason the parents and their class mates, unlike the four, have only one power each is because somehow nature logically dictates the mating of like powers every so many generations to bring back concentration of the power. Once the density of a power drops to a certain level of dilution, attractions change, as if like powers are attracted to each other with a special bond. This bond I believe is something like a unity of a soul mate and instinctual survival. I have also found often times it crosses prides, also strengthening alliances. The Phelidae are not meant to be a separated people. "Nature has a way of preserving things, even with supernaturals."

"So that explains the parents but what about the four children?"

"Ah, yes. I was getting to that. I believe sometimes the potency can get too strong. The parents have such strength in their powers that both passed on to the children instead of one dominating the other, in turn beginning the dilution process again. It has happened before but it was a very long time ago as the process takes centuries. Aurelia I do not mean to discount your theory as I do think the fallen star has some part in it however I have yet to find a sensible explanation. I agree the alignment, and the births are all too coincidental."

The discussion was somewhat interesting but not enough to keep the attention of Thia focused, "Hey you guys better head back home now. I bet they haven't even noticed you are gone yet."

Shai huffed, "I'm sure they've figured it out by now. I'd rather get in trouble later."

"Let's go see, I'll go with you. Let's try at least! I can help. I can distract them at the front door while you slide in the back, yes?"

Shai shook his head and took another bite, "Nope, let it go."

Thia knew when to stop with them, "Wanna head out to the caves then?"

"Yeah, I haven't been there in a while. I could use a good dip." Shai said looking a little happier.

And there they spent the rest of the afternoon, swimming, and laying in the sun until it went down and they returned home. The boys did get into more trouble and were confined to their homes until school started up again.

Caleb and his sister left very early the next morning. That was the last time they saw them.

The Accident

Thia started having nightmares due to Caleb's attack causing new, more potent anomalies in the village. Thia faintly heard her mother calling, "Athena, wake up. Athena!"

She finally opened her eyes and sat up breathing fast and hard.

"Dear it's okay. It was just a bad dream." her mother explained while brushing the hair from her face. "Come, let's get you some tea."

As they made their way to the kitchen there was a knock at the door. Thia's father answered and it was their friend Nomad.

Nomad was clearly concerned, "Is everyone alright?"

"Yes, why what's going on?" her father asked him as they all sat at the table.

"The barn is destroyed."

"What?! What happened?"

"No one knows. There are no signs of tampering or weapons yet."

Nomad turned to Thia with a gentle but suspecting look, "Did something happen?"

"No, like what?" she played dumb to avoid the embarrassment.

Another knock at the door, then it swung open, it was both of her brothers.

Shai headed straight over to Thia, "T, you okay?"

Then Dae continued, "Half the town is up wondering what brought the barn down. They all think something hit it but haven't found anything in the mess yet. Shai and I could tell it was you, but don't worry, we didn't say anything on our way over."

Then Shai cut in, "It wasn't...*he* didn't...attack you again did he?" Shai began to boil.

Thia rolled her eyes and huffed as she turned red and started rubbing her temples to stop the oncoming headache, "no, just a bad dream about it".

Thia's father was thoroughly confused and started with Thia, "Someone attacked you?" She just shrugged. Then he turned to Shai and Dae, "What do you mean you knew it was her? You mean she brought the barn down? How could that be?"

Nomad spoke up now sure of what he suspected, "I'm afraid Dae must be right. As you know they have a special connection we still can't explain. And, I believe, now that her power has been revealed, it is more concentrated than before. Before, when she was younger, the anomalies that happened here at the house, was just a hint of what was to come."

After the festivities were over and all the visitors left, it was business as usual. Monday rolled around and they all reported to the field for calisthenics. The mood definitely changed since the last time they'd been there. Practicing the basics was cut short to make time for learning their new skills. Now lessons were getting interesting. They were very excited and knew the time would come but they had no idea it would be this soon. It usually wasn't from what they'd heard.

Typically a solid couple of weeks went by before it was even mentioned again as everyone worked to put everything back as it was, but not this time. Dae wasn't sure why but he felt a little uneasy by the unexpected rush to get to it. Thia was concerned only because she knew Dae was, but Shai couldn't have been happier.

One of the single powered girls, Miranda went first. As revealed to her, wind was her gift. The instructor, most commonly referred to as Madden, put a rickety chair in the middle of the field and had her stand a couple feet in front of it as he stood off to the side spouting instructions. Everyone else sat in a large circle around them watching. After about 15 minutes, and two tantrums later, the chair jumped about an inch off of the ground accompanied by some dust. Then she leapt off of the ground dancing and clapping. She was so happy it finally worked. Then Madden sent her off to a far corner of the field to keep practicing with the old broken chair.

Next to try her fire skill was Naomi. Madden put scraps of wood down in a pile in the field. He then told her to stand in front of him and she did. "Now I want you to look at the wood I placed over there. Study it and the area it is in. Now focus on it. Remove everything else from your mind. Now imagine it catching fire. Focus...focus...focuuus...", and then she jumped with surprise when one of the broken boards exploded into flame. She too jumped around and giggled in excitement. Then Madden told her to try another one. And again she did it.

Three times she was successful until, the unintentional fourth time.

The instructor inserted a lecture between individual student assessments when suddenly Shai's shirt caught fire. Shocked, Shai ripped it off and threw it to the ground. Naomi instantly turned red.

"Apparently Naomi was just now very focused on something else instead of listening to the lesson." Madden teased and the whole group laughed. "Class you must be very careful when using your gifts for they will take much concentration and focus to control".

Devin was watering rocks, trees and anything else he could find within the first few minutes of his lesson.

Then it was Dae's turn, first of the double powered few. Dae listen intently to what the instructor said. This was how he was anyway but now that he had something of his own, he really wanted to master it. Madden had him imagine it snowing and it did, then rain and it did, then the sun out and it was. Dae was very good, a natural he said. Then Madden really tested him requesting an ice sculpture in the middle of the field and it was the grandest sculpture anyone had ever seen. Wind and water could do many things when separate but even more when used together.

Next went Shai. His gifts matched him like Dae's did. *Perhaps that was part of it, how it works*, Thia thought. *You are given what you are or rather what fits you.* But when it came to her it explained nothing.

The instructor took a deep breath bracing himself for Shai's turn. He knew how much of a test he was already on the basic stuff. Now he would see how he was with his own special abilities. He started off trying to play it safe and told Shai to build a dirt hill.

"Seriously?" Shai challenged in disbelief.

Madden didn't budge, just looked at him. So Shai bent down to the ground and started scooping dirt into a hill with his hands.

"No boy, with your mind, your gift!" Madden corrected him, after figuring out what he was up to.

"Oh! Ha ha!" Shai laughed in relief. So he looked at the pile he started and took a step back. He focused on it, and focused, and focused until finally there was a gigantic explosion of dust. Everyone was coughing and trying to wave the dirt away from their faces and clothes.

"I think you may have concentrated a little too hard. Instead remember how the dirt felt in your fingers. Imagine the dirt is soft and light. Then concentrate again but this time imagine you are scooping the dirt with your fingers again, soft and light." Shai tried again imagining like he was told and a neat little pile formed.

Next was Shai's fire. Madden, very hesitant this time, lit a match and told Shai to take the flame over to the fire pit and light it. So Shai began concentrating very hard, again too hard as the teacher patted out his singed eyebrows from the massive burst the small flame detonated into.

Shai always starts off extreme before he figures out how to turn it down. The brave teacher tried again. This time was more successful though his eyebrows were already gone and that awful burnt hair smell still lingered. Dae tried to whisk it away with a nice moist breeze but the smell would have to be washed away. Satisfied for now, Madden sent Shai off to another, further section, to keep practicing.

And finally came Thia's turn. Madden stood and studying her, though he wasn't really looking *at* her. His gazed seemed to pass through her as he mulled over his approach. As she waited, she become aware of what she thought she had escaped; everyone was staring now when they were supposed to be distracted with practicing. Even Dae and Shai stopped to see what would happen.

They all wanted to see what the big fuss was about at the ceremony. Thia wished for a somewhat private lesson as the others seem to get, but should've known better. She really didn't care for all of the attention. And it only got worse as a few more onlookers, standing a little inside the woods arrived hoping to go unnoticed. Those from the village too were curious. Now she *really* wanted to leave. She was thinking about how she could squirm her way out of this one and maybe catch up with him later. She could claim she wasn't feeling well and would go home. But they would never buy it. Maybe she could fake an injury? No, too late for that. *I better just get it over with,* she concluded after attempting to come up with a few more poor pathetic options.

The teacher took a long deep sigh still saying nothing. Thia half smirked back uncomfortably ready for whatever. He turned his back to her and paced taking in their surroundings. He showed no sign of acknowledging the larger audience. Instead he seemed a little annoyed, she hoped it was from a lack of ideas. Antsy now, she half searched too, though not sure what she was looking for. Just then Madden came up with something.

"Ah!" he said quickly. "Okay Thia here's what I want you to do."

Thia was startled by his sudden revelation but grateful it finally came. At this very moment in time, she decided that there was no one else around, just like when she danced. *Some music would be helpful,* she wished but there was nothing. It's only she and the teacher now. So she took in every last word and tuned everything else out that she knew would distract her. It was the only way to get past the attention of the masses that were steadily growing in number.

"Do you see that tree over there?" He was referring to a single lone tree in the forest. *That sounds kind of oxymoronic,* she thought. *Focus,* she forced her mind back to the task at hand. All the trees were still bare from the winter as spring approached. The one small tree though, seemed to hang onto its leaves even through the heavy wet snow falls. It was a captivating sight actually. It had a pale glow of hope in the grey of sea of sleep.

"Yes" she answered back.

"I want you to focus on that tree and I want you to imagine wrapping your hands around the small trunk. Then I want you to shake the remaining stubborn leaves off of it".

Remove the hope? Don't be ridiculous they're just dead leaves, focus!

"Okay" she said out loud.

At first she was fighting being put off by this. *Sure, bring my attention to how pretty it is and now I am to destroy it.* She shook her head slightly to get back the objective.

"Should I get closer? It's kind of far away over there on the other side of the field." she stopped and asked.

"No, I don't think that is necessary if you can see it clearly."

"right", so she began. Again, she pushed everyone and everything out of her mind. Then she closed in on the tree, the size of it, the fragile nature of it, the light colored leaves of hope. It was a baby. *Still, I must focus and embrace my lesson. I'm just shaking off the leaves, that's all.* So she did exactly as she was told.

Just then the tree rushed in on her. It was a little startling at first but then she assumed it must have been like this for the rest so she went on. All other things went blurry but the tree. Then a dark haze around her vision highlighted the tree now. She pictured wrapping her hands around the base of the small tree and squeezing. Then she pictured herself shaking the tree. The muscles in her arm contracted as she shook back and forth. Just gently at first….

"Thia STOP!!!" boomed in her head and she snapped out of it.

"AH!!!" she yelled holding her head.

"Huh?" she was still dazed from trying to focus so hard. Then she blinked a few times trying to get her mind and sight right. When she was sure and clear again she looked around to find just about everyone around her was on the ground writhing in pain.

"What happened?!" she yelled panicked. "Did someone attack again?!"

"Yeah! YOU!" a voice screamed angrily, but still blurry she didn't see who.

"What? What do you mean?" Thia was sick with confusion and worry.

A crying and unforgiving voice drew Thia a vivid picture, "While you were trying yours, everyone started having difficulty breathing, like they were being squeezed. When Madden figured out what was happening he asked you to stop but you wouldn't listen. When he started to approach you to tap you, the squeezing got worse as he got closer and some of their ribs, including his, started cracking so he stopped. Some of those watching came from the woods to help but as soon as they got close then they too couldn't breathe." Thia blinked hoping to clear her eyes, looked over and was able to make out figures of some of the parents on the ground recovering next to their children.

Tears welled in her eyes and she began to uncontrollably shake.

"Shai saw the teacher couldn't get to you so he tried to run at you thinking he was fast enough, but was thrown like he hit a wall once he got too close. Then Dae made sure he was okay. He thought he was big enough, that he might have a chance to tolerate it. So he kept coming at you even through the cracking ribs.

Thia covered her mouth. She looked like she was going to be sick.

The girl relentlessly went on, "Then his nose started to bleed."

A whimper escaped from Thia.

"He even let out a little yell when he got real close, and then..." the girl cried in horror of the replay, "...his face just split open!"

Thia struggle for breath herself as the tears poured down her face in a river. She scanned the crowd and spotted Dae.

"nooooo" she sobbed quietly and fell to her knees as they gave out.

Blood was everywhere. Her heart dropped to the ground. Shai was next to him, his burnt shirt bunched up on Dae's face. His parents came from the clearing and ran to him. By this time many of the parents were there collecting their injured ones.

"What did you do?!" one of the mothers wailed in her direction.

Thia curled up crying. Her face buried in her arms.

Her parents came running out of the woods and stopped. Her mother was frantic looking around and her father stood in awe. Stunned they tried to appraise the damage. No one had died from what he could tell. They were mostly moderately injured. Finally they saw her on the other side. Her mother heart broke when she saw what state she was in and rushed to her side. As they walked her through, many still on the ground being helped, she passed out overwhelmed by what she saw. When she woke she was home, in her bed.

Thia entered a deep and dark depression after that day. She didn't go to school, or the woods where her recovered friends were waiting for her, regardless if the whole village called them insane. At first she didn't leave the house and wouldn't even let her family in her room claiming she might harm them.

When they came she refused to see her brothers. She didn't eat or drink and slept a lot, mostly during the day. Her brothers were getting restless and more insistent in seeing her, spending every night over. So one day before they knew she was up, she snuck out and ran off to the caves to avoid the chance of hurting all who cared for her. For months suffocating mental pictures continued to haunt her flashing fresh images in her head of that day, of Dae's face...covered in blood...because of her.

Summertime came but didn't feel like it. The rain fell much more than it should've, sometimes not letting up for days at a time. Dae felt Thia's depression as did Shai. He recovered faster than most thought he would. They both desperately wanted to see her. They felt the emptiness and guilt devour her over and over. Being a complete outcast he accepted her fate long before anyone needed to say anything.

Her brothers also became outcasts themselves. Not intentionally, their people weren't afraid of *them*. It didn't matter though. Their home had changed; the people were no longer who they used to be. Shai and Dae had no desire to know any of them anymore. If Thia was to be banished then so they would go too.

The boy's parents tried to talk them out of being mixed up with Thia but this only outraged them. Both families backed off instantly realizing she was very important to them as generally the boys were not easily angered. For the first real time they recognized there was something there, something deep rooted and strong. Not knowing why they now understood that whatever it was, was supposed to be there and was bigger than all of them, so Dae and Shai's parents let them be.

Much time had passed and they could take it no more so her brothers set off to find her. Before long they figured out where she chose to hide out and intruded. She woke up from her nap to their splashing. She knew who was there and wanted to run but there was nowhere to go even if she had any energy.

Shai gasped at the sight of her. Her bones stuck out, her eyes sunken in and she couldn't move though he knew she wanted to. Very weak and frail it was evident she hadn't eaten in days.

For a split moment she was half grateful for the company but fear quickly dominated causing her to lash out at them, "Why are you here?" Her voice was broken and distressed as the rest came out in a loud whisper. "Get out!"

She tried to sit up but had to lean back against the wall of the cave and slid down it exhausted.

"T, what are you doing? Are you trying to kill yourself? You know you can't avoid us forever, and we aren't going anywhere without you. Enough is enough." Shai told her more serious than he'd ever been.

Dae turned to Shai, "I'll be back. I'm going to get her something to eat."

She heard him and shook her head, "Don't bother. It won't stay down. Apparently if you don't eat long enough, when you finally catch something and try to your body rejects it. It's my time and I'm fine with it." She ended in heavy breathing from trying to talk and laid her head back on the wall.

"We'll fix it Thia." And Dae dove back in the water.

She hid her face in her hands again. She knew Dae was gone but she still couldn't bear the thought of looking at him. The vision of his scar and the repeats of that day had only begun to fade. Seeing him again so soon just brought it all back again as if it happened yesterday.

Shai sat next to her and she jumped not used to company. She looked even worse up close with her split dry lips and chattering teeth as she shivered. Shai took off his wet sweatshirt, rung it out and wrapped it around her. Then he began softly, "Thia, it wasn't your fault. We know that. Dae, knows that".

She said nothing. She didn't move. He wasn't sure what else to say so he held her. It seemed to relax her as she started dozing off again.

Waves grew in the still pool so Shai rubbed her back to wake her. Dae came out of the water shirtless, panting and carrying a large heavy plastic tub. He sat it down next to them and opened it up. He pulled out a covered bowl of hot soup, tea, crackers and some warm clothes. The weather had turned much cooler in the time she'd been gone now that summer was ending.

Over the next few hours they worked on getting her fed and changed. It was rough at first but they were patient and took it slow. As the tea and soup went and stayed down, color returned to her face. This made her brothers hopeful and happy. Still Thia would not look up at either of them.

"Thia please come home. Your mother begged me to bring her here, but I refused knowing how both of you would react. Do have any idea how hard it is to refuse your mother anything?" Dae pleaded with her.

She caught his attempt at making her smile but hearing his voice broke her heart all over again and she started to cry.

"Thank you but please go." she whispered through sobbing and streaming tears.

Dae knelt down and placed his hand on her shoulder in an attempt to comfort her. But with the last bit of energy she had she sat up and crawled away from him and collapsed on the other side of the cave.

"Don't *touch* me! Have you learned *nothing*?!" as she unintentionally looked over at Dae in disbelief.

All breath was robbed from her and she turned completely white then passed out cold. What she saw was too much. Across what was once a beautiful, smooth and handsome face was now a dark, long, thick scar ripping from one cheek up over his nose through his forehead to his hairline. A nasty scar that would be there forever, a scar she put there, on someone she loved as her own flesh and blood. If she could do this to someone so important, what was she capable of doing to anyone else? This was the question that burned within her like an eternal flame.

When she came to, she found she was thankfully still in the cave but her brothers were also still there softly discussing something. They heard her move so they walked over and sat in front of her. Dae was now wearing a scrap of material around his forehead.

Dae tried to address her uncomfortable stare at it, "Shai thought it was a good idea…for you not to see it, so we could talk."

She turned her head as tears rolled down looking out the mouth of the cave to the sky, wishing there was a way to fly out of there.

They made sure she ate again before the session began. There was no way to avoid it, she knew from the determined and stubborn look in their eyes. And she was right, the debate lasted for hours. The boys refused to stop or leave without her.

It got colder as the night went on so they build a small fire that warmed the cave and everyone around it. For the first time in months Thia was content and comfortable with food in her stomach and wrapped in layers of oversized warm cloths. But most of all she was happy her brothers were there with her, even if they refused to shut up and leave.

They were going to convince her she was not alone and that it was nothing more than an accident and everyone was fine now.

"Thia, if anything it's the tribe's fault for not being prepared. They should've done more research before just winging it." Dae pleaded with her starting to sound a little more like Shai.

They were all beyond exhausted by this point and Shai started showing signs of getting loopy.

Shai looked over at Dae, "His time for initiation was up anyway. I got cracked in the head when we all first met by that small bolder you were tossing around, and this was Dae's turn. I actually think it's kind of sexy.", as he gave Dae a wink.

There was a brief moment of silence until Dae burst into laughter, then so did Shai.

Dae shook his head, "That rock gets bigger every time you tell that story."

Finally, Thia bordering deliria and dried out from a day of crying, let out a tiny weak laugh.

"There it is." Dae said with a warm smile.

"Why?" was all Thia could get out at first, slowly shaking her head back and forth, eyes closed.

Then she took another breath, "Why can't you two be normal and just exile me like the rest? I could've easily just wandered off, never to be seen or heard from again and no one would care. Even my parents would have a chance at getting back some semblance of normalcy."

Shai shrugged uncomfortably, "Just can't." He wasn't one for super mushy stuff so this was as close as he could get to it.

"You are one of us and always will be." Dae filled in for Shai. "We don't much care for what anyone else thinks."

Tears filled her eyes looking at both of them.

In a quivering voice, "Can we go to sleep now?"

All three laughed and Shai covered her with a blanket.

Dae woke up early the next morning and brought back some warm breakfast. They all ate and packed up. With a little more nudging and shooting down of her excuses they got her to agree to go back home. They took the back route so no one would see them. Her parents were more than thankful to her brothers.

Thia still refused to go out in public for months. She knew what waited for her. Regardless slowly word leaked out that she had returned. As she anticipated the town buzz grew as worried members voiced their concerns. And so Nomad returned and chose to step in.

Nomad

After the accident a stranger took mercy on Thia. He was an older man dressed in long traveling robes, with long grey hair, beard and wise and friendly wrinkles at the sides of his eyes. Thia's parents knew him well but she'd never spoken with him or seen much of him before recently. Once the nomad obtained permission from her parents, he promised the village that he would ensure everyone's safety by taking her far from the village to teach her. The older members trusted and believed Nomad's goal was to help her discover the true use of what she'd been given and edify control. All had faith in his word and abilities, and so the lessons began.

Starting the very next day every morning they set off, bothers in tow. The boys refused to leave her side. She was nervous and they knew it without her saying a word. They tried to follow unnoticed at first but the nomad was much more observant and smarter than he let on. So, without much of a fight, he gave in and allowed them to come along. Nomad found their bond to be intriguing so he chose to use this as an opportunity to study them in addition to honing their skills. He knew their destiny, though not yet discovered, would without a doubt be significant.

All three watched him cautiously as they followed him through the woods to their training destination. He was not trusted yet among them. He was hiding something. He was overly simple on the outside and how he carried himself. The helpless old wanderer image cracked when with the wave of his hand he parted the brush the boys were hiding behind. They didn't put too much thought into it though as they'd seen earth benders do that before. Thia noticed something too. Unlike the rest of the villagers, but much like her brothers, he was not afraid of her, or even nervous for that matter.

He instructed them to sit down on the fallen tree and proceeded to lecture. More common than not, lectures are considered boring, but they had not been talked at by him. Hours flew by feeling like minutes.

"He is absolutely magical." Thia called it. "His stories swallow you whole. How does he do it, his face, his expressions and his words? They draw out any emotion they please with the greatest of ease, even from the emotionless."

One particular tale, of his fair wife, left an impression in all of them.

"She is a sweet and loving woman of few words. Ah, few words, a quality sought after by most men, rarely realized." Nomad began closing his eyes and smiling.

"Shut it." Thia cut off Shai before his predictable comment made it out.

Immediately at the very mention of his wife, a veil of pure peace washed over his face causing every single muscle in his audience to relax. He went on to explain, though she was a tolerant woman, he dared not cross her for she would become just as potent with anger.

He described in finite detail their first fight ever; her face contorted from a soft and beautiful flower, into a being he never imagined possible. Her sweet smile twisted down into a dark, frog like wrinkled frown. Her eyes normally bright and sparkling crunched down into a half squint, dousing any luminance from them. With her nose flared and her gaze piercing she let out a screech harpies themselves would cringe.

Immersed with him in his vivid memory, the three of them went from complete relaxation to utter horror.

"Good Lord! Why would you remain with such a beast?!" Shai asked with frightened wide eyes.

"I travel a lot." He said with a wink and a smirk that instantly won all three over as they broke out in laughter.

Once story time was over, it was time for what Thia dreaded the most. He invited them to try their gifts. Shai, ever excited to play was always the first to go. Next passively Dae accepted. And finally Thia, who initially refused every time. Finally after many talks and convincing from all, she agreed but under one strict condition. She demanded they be miles away where she couldn't harm them when she attempted her lessons. Begrudgingly, all for their own reasons, they agreed to her compromise.

During one of the first few lessons, they came back at the agreed upon amount of time to find her first few tries didn't go well. She chose to practice on her prey while hunting alone. She concentrated just as the nomad explained. Very disappointed in herself she described what happened.

"I was trying to stun him. I was a few feet away and focused on him while he ate a patch of grass next to the tree." She focused. She stared. She concentrated some more. Suddenly she noticed something strange. "It was like my vision was blurred for a moment. Then it looked like it was vibrating?" Next she heard a series of small muddled BOOM's. She blinked a couple of times, looked around and then realized what happened. The buck and a few trees by him blew apart into thousands of pieces.

Shai, leaning against a tree, fell off it roaring with laughter. Then something dangling on the branch above him caught his eye. "Hey, deer jerky!" he announced pulling it down.

Despite Thia's tense mood from the experience, Shai had everyone laughing.

Each lesson Nomad tweaked his instructions to them and their results improved, not tremendously, but it was enough to keep Thia trying. Some time went by and though she still needed a lot of work, she did get good at the smaller scale stuff, in particular, shocking, like the zap from dragging feet on carpet. Nomad appreciated the relationship between Shai and Thia however it seemed one sided.

Shai teases her every chance he gets, but until now she had no way to really get back at him. That all changed once she perfected her new trick. And she made sure he never saw it coming. She didn't have to physically touch him as Nomad showed her how to make it travel through things. That made it twice as fun for both Thia and Dae.

Nomad tried to teach them to always be aware of their surroundings but they didn't get much time to practice since that part didn't change much. Nomad taught them many things aside from their special gifts. Though not all of the Phelidae had special gifts they did share some common talents. Since it was in them to protect life, all had supporting skills to do this. Nomad's favorite of these was the stealing of wounds. Nomad revealed he, being half Phelidae and half nomad wizard, is able to demonstrate much of what the Phelidae can do.

During one of their hunting trips Shai earned a set of gashes on his upper arm, along with some other bumps and bruises, when playing a little too rough with a full grown brown bear. Nomad took this opportunity to show them how to steal the wounds. He had Dae go first, as he too knew he was always the most focused and therefore successful. He took Dae's hand and placed it on one of the large cuts then instructed him to close his eyes.

"Closing your eyes blocks out visual distractions and increases your other senses. Now focus on the wound. Feel the moisture and warmth of it.

"gross", Thia's stomach turned a little from the description.

"Yeah baby...ouch." Shai teased and winced from the stinging.

Nomad was not annoyed by their comments as he knew this would not distract Dae in the slightest.

"Now imagine it peeling off of the skin like dried glue on a finger. Pull it into the palm of your hand. Imagine it slowly moving up your arm to the same place. Now…open your eyes and look under your hand."

The gash was gone. Then Dae cringed for a second and then looked at the throbbing, burning spot on his massive upper arm under his loose sleeve.

"Huh.", was all he let out, as if he found it more interesting than painful.

Shai and Thia were amazed, "nice!"

"Thanks man.", Shai said slightly relieved some of the pain was gone.

Nomad offered for him to take it back as his turn came up.

"Nah man, I'm good!"

Next Thia was up. Though she was nervous she tried to do the exact same as Dae. She unintentionally covered two of the three partially healed, but still very deep remaining cuts. All watched in anticipation as she closed her eyes and concentrated. It only took seconds to perform when they first started. She opened her eyes and furrowed her brows in pain. Then she smiled removing her hand to confirm she successfully stole his wound.

Nomad realizing Thia ended up with two rather than just one, placed his hand on one of hers and closed his eyes to take it. Thia, famous for her stubbornness, believing she could take it and caring about all those that surrounded her put his effort to an abrupt end. She went to pull away but he had a good grip on her arm, reminding her of Aurelia's. So she too closed her eyes and imagined locking the cut where it was.

Nomad tried again but nothing. When he opened his eyes, confused to what just happened he found Thia's cat eyes staring back at him with deep intent.

For the first time in a very long time Nomad was taken back in real surprise.

"Thia! What...no student has ever done that before." A moment passed as he stepped away and paced deep in thought, "Much less on their first lesson." He scratched his head both confused and excited, "Oh, this is a fine thing. Tell me, why did you stop me?"

"I heal faster than you." At once she replied but looking more tired than before.

"I see" he said with squinted studying eyes.

He had to know more, "How did you know what to do?"

She thought. "I don't know. I didn't really think about it, it just happened."

Then she wavered a bit in her footing, closed her eyes and attempted to stabilize herself.

Nomad supported her by the arm and escorted her to the base of a tree to rest, "Are you feeling alright?"

"I'm really tired."

"Yes", he said as he looked at all of them. "The skill can drain you at first, but with practice you will become faster and stronger at it so it will not tire you."

What she said was true, the gashes were a third the size they were minutes ago, still it didn't make the pain any less. She assumed since he was only half Phelidae that he would heal much slower than they would. That and the females tended to mend even faster than the males.

There was more she didn't share though, something she would never share. Her brothers would certainly tease her to no end for it but she had a pretty good idea why this skill came so naturally to her. *Is it possible they haven't noticed?* She was always one for the feel of things.

She loves to close her eyes and slowly run the tips of her fingers across whatever she was studying; the coarse and ridged bark on a tree, fine liquid sand in its dry state and grainy in it's wet state, cold solid rocks, smooth feathers that zip closed at the splits, smooth still water interrupted by a gentle dip of the finger then the heavy drops that collect and fall from it, and so on. Discovering the intricate details of piece was fascinating. But now it was like she could feel each unique energy signature like a finger print.

The next part of the lesson was better use of their delicate sense of smell. Beyond the everyday odors they all experience these three were being trained to pay closer attention to find something more.

"Each person has their own distinctive scent. I'm not referring to the over powering perfume of a bath gel, deodorant or cologne but the personal and unique smell that comes from the concentrated places, such as hair by the root or in the nape of the neck."

Thia already had everyone beat on this one as she could tell who it was when people she knew approached faster than anyone. Unfortunately more times than not memories came along with some familiar smells, like when Caleb's aunt would walk by. She didn't smell exactly like him or his sister but the common family trace was there. However, the holidays, especially Christmas, made the tag-a-long worth it.

But little did Thia know someone did notice, Nomad of course. But it's what he does. Somehow he seems to sense all. Nomad knew absolute observation was crucial in order to unlock complete control and to uncover the unknowns of her gift. And so he remained ever so watchful of her. She was too young and surrounded by too many young adult worries and distractions to be able to take in what his vast life experiences help him weed out.

Each of them still wore their first lesson in stealing wounds but they knew there would be no scars since they healed so fast. Only the really bad ones left marks. This they were reminded of every time they looked at Dae.

Thia thought of this. That afternoon when everyone was napping Thia snuck over next to Dae. Doubtful, but worth a shot, she gently placed her hand over Dae's scar. Before she had a chance to really focus on it he grabbed her wrist.

He spoke gently to her, "Don't. It is the mark of my gifted sister. I earned it and am proud to wear it. She is marvelously unique and incredibly powerful. I am honored she doesn't mind me tagging along." He ended in a sweet smile, kissed her hand and rolled over back to sleep.

She just watched him thinking about what he said. She wanted to pet his hair but didn't want to wake him again, so she sighed and went back to her spot to rest. *Perhaps he will return the favor one day,* she thought just before she faded to sleep.

Next week's lesson was hand to hand combat. Shai signaled disappointed until Nomad explained this was not exactly the type they had already been taught. Nomad expressed how crucial it is for them to learn the exact way the bounty hunters fight first, and then later add enhancements. There was some redundancy since Martial arts was popular among humans too. But Shai didn't mind being a big fan because he thinks it looks really cool, so there was less fooling around from him during these sessions.

Since their powers are to be hidden until absolutely needed, the physical method was absolutely vital. The lessons lasted longer than he planned. They practices for weeks. The three were so in tuned to the flow of it that they didn't want to stop. They insisted that Nomad keep teaching past the basics, past the advanced, they wanted to be the best there was at it. In his expected fashion, he was very pleased by their enthusiasm as well as engulfed in curiosity and therefore granted their repeated requests.

The lessons carried on from weeks to months. They'd become so disciplined in focus, one might think they were in a trance. Nomad was impressed by the fluidity and precision they continued to perfect. He saw evidence that it boosted the power for both the defense and a strike moves and as an added bonus a trace of each gift accented their moves.

Dae struck an old dying tree and at the same time a mighty wind knocked into it as the last bit of water it contained, sprayed from it. Shai flipped through the air practicing his kicks and round houses when Nomad spotted small bits of wood floating up and twirl with him accenting his moves. When Thia was off meditating, everything around her, the chirping crickets, the calling birds and even the leaves became peaceful. These signs were both good and bad. They were good because they were becoming one with their powers. But they would next need to learn to conceal them.

After the extensive combat training ended Nomad set out to see how the lessons affected the use of their gifts. And as he hoped, their powers too appeared intensified and more defined. He's trained many of their kind before them but never witnessed this type of outcome. More than ever he had to find out what was so special about them. This was the burning mission in his mind, his unsolved puzzle. He was sure it must have something to do with Thia. But there had to be something special about the boys too or she wouldn't be so closely connected to them. The mystery liked to drive him mad. Another piece had been uncovered but still left with the feeling he was nowhere near to the full picture.

Nomad announced the next tutorial, "Another just as important part of survival is the art of fleeing."

Shai clearly disagreed, "How can you possibly consider running like a coward, an *art*?!"

Nomad addressed his misconception, "When done properly and skillfully it is possible to disappear without a trace, like a magician." With his cleverly placed spin Shai was more agreeable. Nomad urged, when it was time to flee they were to keep a small pack that contained anything they might need to move on. They also learned some of the skillful ways to lose their trackers. And if they were to get separated Nomad shared the story of The Bond.

"James Bond?" Shai uselessly blurted out thinking he was funny.

Nomad ignored him, like they typically have to, "Have you three heard of the Bond?"

Dae spoke up before Shai could say anything else inapt, "I think I heard my grandmother mention a little bit about it. Isn't something about trading blood and being able to contact the one you traded with?"

Nomad agreed with a nod, "Very good Dae, that's exactly it."

Thia looked a little grossed out, "Now when you say *trade* with someone, what exactly do you mean?"

"Consume or better, drink", Nomad was not a man who bothered with beating around the bush nor had much sensitivity for weak stomachs.

Thia swallowed hard, "That's what I thought you meant."

Dae wanted to know more, "So is the story true? Does it really work? Can we try it?"

"Dae! Did you catch the part about drinking blood?" Shai was squeamish about it too.

"Yes, but it's a small price to pay for its benefits." Dae shot back at Shai.

"That is true Dae but I am afraid it may be too risky to try. Though I am still researching, the stories never describe how much or who exactly can ingest it safely. Long ago a greedy human attempted to consume too large a quantity and died...painfully. The blood was not compatible. His temperature cooked his human brain and his heart raced until eventually every organ in his body ruptured. There are these kinds of details I have yet to find out. Though like you Dae I am most curious. However the risk is not worth the potential price for now."

Once Nomad finished his tale on the Blood Bond, Thia asked something that had been lingering in her mind for some time now, "Nomad, how did you come to know us, our people I mean? You aren't like us, are you, but you can still do what we can?" Both Dae and even short attention-spanned Shai, straightened up, alert to hear his response.

Nomad took a moment to consider how to answer her surprise probing yet overdue question. They'd trusted in him thus far without doubt, as is their way. Still he felt they earned an answer.

After a purposeful breath he began, "Yes, where to start. Thia, you are correct I am not like you exactly. Those that raised me believe I am half Phelidae. My mother," he paused. "She was human and my father they suspect is Phelidae. You could say my mother was a bit of an explorer. She got into trouble a lot, or so I'm told, for running off with no warning for long periods of time. But she always came back with some kind of treasure or bit of news that effectively distracted her guardians from punishing her.

The last time she returned married and carrying me, but her husband, my father, was not with her. She wouldn't say who or what he was when asked, afraid that I might be found. They tried to get her to tell, to help her through the strange transitions hoping to better understand them, but even on the days of her poorest health she refused. She did share that their marriage was forbidden and that she was sure the baby would not be permitted to live and that is why she fled."

Thia couldn't help herself and interrupted, "You keep saying *was* like she is gone?"

Nomad continued on, "They are not sure if she is or not as she never returned after that. They suspect it was to keep my existence unknown, to protect me."

"Are you mad at her for that?" Thia asked looking upset herself.

"No, I believe she felt she was doing the best thing for me. I would like to know if she is alive and who my father is. I am sure my father is still around as you know, the Phelidae age slowly, though it is too hard to tell if my mother is still alive considering how old I am now. Still there is a small bit of hope."

"Hope, how?" Thia insisted.

"Geez Thia", Shai was getting antsy.

"Shut up." she hushed at him.

"The extraordinary things that she was experiencing were signs of the Phelidae line becoming part of her. Her heart beat was far faster than that of a normal human, still her body sustained it. They suspect her body was able to carry on due to the way the blood was introduced. Though there was a lot of it, it was gradually mixed with her own. Also some of the physical abilities became hers. She'd broken numerous things adjusting to her new found strength. I do not believe that after I was born, any of her new gifts faded away with my absence for the Phelidae blood is a lasting endowment."

Shai excited by this new news and tired of all the nurture talk interrupted, "Nice! So what kind of cat are you?"

Nomad chuckled, "Shai, I've always admired your enthusiasm. However I am sad to say I cannot change. Only full Phelidae can change into the beast that best embodies their soul. Dae you are a very large black panther because you are passive, physically powerful but passionate. Shai you are a brilliantly colored leopard as you are charismatic and swift. And our dear Thia, you are a snow white tiger because you are powerful but shy and know not yet of your grand purpose."

"How did you come to know our parents?" Dae asked this time.

"I found your people…"

"Our people", Thia corrected.

Nomad was moved by her amendment, "…or rather *our* people when I was much older. You've probably noticed I have a bit of the wandering trait from my mother as I find it difficult to stay in one place too long. As a result one day I left the castle in search for my parents. Years later I was walking along not very far from your village and spotted a baby cub all alone napping in a spot of sunlight in the woods. It was you Shai."

"Ha!" he was proud Nomad found him on one of his adventures, even if he didn't remember it.

That is until Thia chimed in, "That's a big surprise, Shai meandering off never where he's supposed to be."

Nomad paid their bickering no attention used to it by now, "First I looked around for any other cats. It is unwise for one to go near a cub if the mother is near for you will certainly meet a gruesome death. Once I was sure there were none around I picked you up and went in search for your parents. At first I was afraid they were killed and that is why you were alone. That is typically the reason for abandoned animals as in the normal species the cubs do not stray far from their den. However I rapidly found, you too have quite a wandering streak in you, for later that day I stopped to rest and turned away from you for only a moment. When I turned back you were already at least twenty feet away. At that moment I knew you were trouble. "

"Ha ha! He had you pegged at only days old." Thia laughed.

"I wandered for days unable to find your home or parents. Then I had an idea. Shai seemed to struggle when I headed in certain directions then was calm when I apparently found the correct course. Still the direction seemed to change so I decided to put him down to see what he would do. First he just sat down and looked up at me with those big eyes. And just when I thought my idea to be wrong, he picked up something in the air as he sniffed around and ran off tracking it. Though I have added speed from my father, it was difficult to keep up. He moved even faster when a rabbit or some other type of prey caught his attention. As a matter of fact, his appetite grew daily as fast as he did physically.

We encountered a couple larger animals too big for him to fight off but I was able to handle them. And they made hardy meals as well as rugs once properly cleaned and treated. Finally at the end of our trip we came upon a lioness. Shai was sleeping over my shoulder, I was barely able to carry him at this point. It didn't take long for me to learn the general direction he insisted upon which I assumed was home. She stopped dead in her tracks when she saw us, as did I. Her eyes moved up to him then back to me as tears began filling them. She was undoubtedly tired and hungry but it quickly turned to anger.

Sure that she was his mother, I spoke. *He is not dead, merely sleeping. We had a full meal today and I didn't want to lose time finding his home. Your son certainly enjoys his naps.* And right then, before my very eyes your mother stood up on her hind legs, I have to admit it made me nervous, and walked behind a thick tree then came out from behind it human. After that moment the draw to find my own family had never been stronger. Her beauty was breathtaking."

"Okay, stop right there! I don't need to know how hot my mom was...is, whatever." Now Shai was getting grossed out.

"Shai, that's not what he means and you know it." Thia scolded his ignorance.

Shai held his hands over his ears, "I don't care, I don't want to know."

Again Nomad paid them no mind, "She showed me the way to your village. Your people, OUR people…" he corrected before Thia jumped at it. "…allowed me to live and study there for years. In return, to show my gratitude, I taught them lessons I learned from my home and did what I could to help whenever possible.

Your tribe took me in when others probably would not have. I came to love and become a part of your families and people as my own, in part realizing I may never find mine. Consequentially my aggressive search to find my blood relatives lost momentum. This is how I came to know all of you. "

He turned to talk to Shai, "I also promised your mother I would keep an eye on you when I could as that would prove not to be your last time wandering off seeking adventure. However once you met Dae, my looking-after services were no longer required. Dae has gotten you out of many a conflict since you seem to particularly enjoy challenging opponents greater than your current abilities."

"So did anyone know of or offer to help you find your parents?" Thia asked hoping her family would've done the right thing.

"I did ask and they did not know of my mother or father. They promised to speak with the other tribes but were sure if it took place in one of the older ones, they were sure to behave as if the humiliating event never occurred.

The Invasion

Life and its everyday routine were slowly getting back to normal. The historic council meetings had come and gone and the people were more at ease even though things were not fully figured out yet. But most importantly trust was restored in their leader and his family not only from the council's word but also due to his willingness and demonstration in getting his daughter proper training in the safest way possible. All agreed the lessons seemed to be going well as they witnessed fewer and fewer upsets.

Now that Thia was older she found how she wanted to spend her time was changing. Going out to venture around became less appealing. Instead she enjoyed spending more time at home with her mother, helping and learning from her. Her mother noticed her new behavior and couldn't have been happier. Until now she felt disconnected from her only daughter but wouldn't force her to do something she didn't want to. She knew if it was going to happen, it would in its own time. And so their relationship grew.

Thia learned how to make things to sell and spent more time in the kitchen with her mother trying out the different recipes and asking her mother about her childhood.

Baffled by the amount of fun things she never knew about her own mother, "Ha! Turns out you are the one I got my adventure streak from! So how did you and dad get together if you are so opposite?"

"Well you could say we were somewhat forced. Well not quite like that. We were certainly forced to meet as the council and our parents thought we were a match. I'd never met him before so I was very nervous and had no idea what to expect. I think the worst part was when they sat us down at the little round table for dinner and left us there. They didn't go far so they could watch to see how it was going. It was very quiet at first until I could take it no more."

Thia was on the edge of her seat, "So what'd you say?"

Her mother giggled, something Thia had never seen before, "I said, *so what do you think of all of this?*" she loved the suspense on Thia's face but wouldn't make her wait for long, "And he said...*It's weird.* That's when the tension got the best of me and I broke out laughing causing him to too. We couldn't help it. The occasion had been so built up that it created a completely apprehensive situation. It was nice that he was good looking but even better that he had a sense of humor. And that was that."

Thia thought for a second on what her mother just told her, "Dad laughs?" Thia's half tease got them going on a giggling fit.

For the first time, Thia's mom was not just a prim and proper mother and wife to the tribe head, but almost a girlfriend she could trust. They laughed and shared things, Thia even talked a little bit about what happened with Caleb. She witnessed an exciting dark side peek out from her mother.

"I'll admit, I have to take Shai's side on the matter. Just because you can overpower someone doesn't mean you should. And there is always a price to pay, be it immediately or much later, it will come back." she stared off remembering something.

Thia was a little unnerved by her mother's expression, "Wow mom, you're kinda freaking me out a little."

She blinked out of it, "Sorry dear. I had a friend that wasn't as lucky as you in friends. There are choices in my past that I am not proud of, but what I did to him I am embarrassed to say I will never regret."

Thia slid to the edge of her chair, "What'd you do?"

Lianna's head dropped, "Something I shouldn't have. He is fine but *will* think twice before behaving that way again."

She sat stiff waiting for her daughter's reaction, hoping she wouldn't ask her to go into detail.

Thia in turn knew the way her mother answered meant she didn't want to go further with it so she doused the incredible urge to insist on the answer and replied only with, "nice!"

Thia just looked at her mother and shook her head, "Geez mom there's so much cool stuff I don't know about you."

"All you have to do is ask." She smiled.

And that she did, "Tell me everything!" She even got to see her father smile when he was in the kitchen during one of the stories involving a snowball fight.

Thia especially loved being home around holidays, in fact she rarely left the house anymore. Her mother's true passion shone during the holidays. Christmas being her favorite, the house was covered in red, green, silver and gold and the fire place crackled as an apple cinnamon scent fill the air and old Christmas music played in the background.

Back in the kitchen actually helping her mom now that she knew many of the recipes, they baked a sea of cookies in all flavors, shapes and sizes. Most were for the annual party held in the newly rebuild barn Dae and Shai helped with. The rest were set aside to deliver to all the village homes on Christmas Eve.

Her brothers didn't mind the change in Thia. They too lost interest in their old woodland adventures. Whether it be that they'd done everything and gone everywhere already or if it could just be part of growing up, it didn't really matter as the three were still inseparable.

The boys always found at the house helped with the "sampling" all they made and washing it all down with warm apple cider. Bellies full, they migrated to the living room with Thia's father napping and a game on TV. The warmth of the fireplace made it all too easy to fall asleep.

Thia peeked out to check on them and the scene was nostalgically breathtaking, *This is perfection. It can't get any better than this.*

Actually it does once you have your own family, she suddenly heard in her head, like someone was speaking behind her. She looked around the room for her mother, certain she left her in the kitchen. *Did I say that out loud?*

No, you didn't. I'm a telepath Thia. No one knows beyond my mother, and your father, but he has sworn not speak of it. Thia turned to look at her sure she was just going crazy. Her mother turned to Thia from the pot and gave her a reassuring wink, *It is true. You can't tell anyone though. Not even your...brothers. At least not yet. Maybe the time will come later.* Thia agreed by nodding though she was very stunned. She stared at her mother a little longer then again shook her head and smirked in disbelief.

Am I one too?, Thia questioned in her mind.

No it doesn't seem so and for this I am glad. It is very hard to conceal such a thing and it is not accepted among our kind. Though our tribe is not as strict, my mother insisted we tell no one so we were sure to be accepted. She didn't want to take a chance.

We don't read other minds unless we have to. We respect privacy. I only listened in as you looked so happy and I so wanted to know what finally made you that way. That and I wanted to share this with you for so long. The time felt right, so I did. You never know when this kind of knowledge may be needed, or how some might take it.

Why wouldn't you be accepted if Aurelia is? She's different than the rest of us.

I imagine because her special gift is crucial to our kind and less invasive.

Mom, I'm so sorry.

For what dear? her mother asked returning her attention to cooking.

For taking so long to get to know you.

Thia sat down at the kitchen table and began picking at her nails. She was still digesting all that was just revealed to her. But after a while she decided to drop it, too afraid to expose all that her mother had worked so hard to hide.

"What are you so deep in thought about?" her mother sweetly asked seeing she was consumed by something.

Thia first looked up at her with a smile and raised eye brow thinking, *Shouldn't you know?* Her mother winked back and there was still silence in her head.

"Mom, what am I to do with my life?"

"What do you mean Honey?" she replied in the warmest of voices patiently stirring the contents of the large steaming pot of dinner. She had to accommodate for the larger portions now that the boys were there all the time. But she didn't mind at all.

"I mean, what do I do when it's time to leave home? I don't really have a trade." Thia had been thinking about this as she knew she was getting close to the appropriate age.

"Oh, I wouldn't worry too much about it. Whatever it is you will do will come to you when it's time. In the mean time you can stay here as long as you like. I'd be happy if you never left."

Thia smiled, got up and gave her mother a giant hug.

Since the children were rarely permitted to leave the village and the adults didn't really leave much either beyond their in-town trading, there was the need for the villagers to take on different roles. Thia was unsure where she would fit in. There were leaders to make the decisions, farmers to provide the food and the militant ones for security, both external and internal.

Hmmm, I could do security I think.

Fights among their own kind, typically about territory or jealousy, were rare but could get pretty extreme if not settled quickly. However, things got real interesting when a would-be natural predator stumbled upon the village and didn't know what it was really getting into. Most times the animal could smell that something was off about their potential dinner and would leave, but if it was hungry or stubborn enough it took its chances.

Unless the beast got too aggressive the tribe would try to rough it up just enough to send a message that it is out matched and needs to move on. And most of the time it worked. But on occasion for the unwise ones, the villagers tried to make it quick and the most of what was left.

But change was coming. An increasing amount of animals flooded the area stealing food. The people knew this was a telltale sign that something big was taking over where they used to live, driving them further into the woods…closer to the Phelidae.

Unsure of what threat was on its way, the best of the gifted and trained were immediately called upon and sworn to protect the decision makers and elders from any impending intruders. The location was chosen because it was remote and secluded. It was too deep in for humans to tread and had all they needed to be self-sustaining with the area being half mountain, and the other half was woods and flatland. But all that was seemed to be at risk now.

All Phelidae could easily ward off normal hunters, but what they didn't know, what was coming for them this time, was a new breed of hunters. These had a single mission. They were seeking out the Phelidae, these great animals with power. They somehow knew of their existence and location now. The hunters not only knew of the Phelidae people but knew a lot about them, too much.

"Contact our sister tribe. Send for help…" Thia's father ordered speaking before a group of men, but a young member from that very tribe came running into the village beat up and bloody. Before he could get the words out, the invasion that followed him began.

Nomad, Thia and her brothers were off on one of their lessons. Nomad took them farther in the woods than they had been before to the Lake with the Giant Tree. It was the most beautiful place they'd ever seen. Appropriately named there was indeed a giant tree with a large and deep lake at the base. Exotic looking fanning ferns and massive elephant ears covered the trunk, roots and massive rocks all at the edge of the water. Lilly pads the size of a coffee table floated under the shade of the tree.

Nomad wandered off in search of some berries or mushrooms to eat as Thia and her brothers sat on the edge of the lake relaxing for a bit after a rigorous first session. Dae provided soothing waves in the lake that crashed against the great rocks. Thia and Dae were already lying back enjoying the peace and quiet…that is until Shai cannon-balled a huge rock into the water, thoroughly drenching them.

Thia gasped. "I'm going to *kill* you!"

She jumped up to run after him but Shai popped up a root tripping Thia. She fell and the moment her hand hit the ground she zapped him good sending him to the ground as well.

"Payback sucks doesn't it?!" Thia gloated with a somewhat evil smirk.

A very wet Dae and dry Nomad watched and laughed.

Shai got up and dusted himself off, "It sucks now that you're better at your power. But you still only have *one*, so there!"

They all laughed again until the moods of both Shai and Thia instantly dropped to a panic. Both felt something wrong, something terrible was going on back home. They read it from their hands still planted on the ground. Dae summoned a wind from home and sniffed the air for what news it brought him. It took Nomad a couple seconds longer but he too picked up on it.

Shai confused by what he smelled, "Why does it smell so strong like Coyote urine, metal and humans? Did a pack roll in human garbage?"

Thia kept her hand to the ground, "Something's not right. There's a lot of activity and negative energy coming from home."

Nomad would've been impressed by how advanced his students had become in what he considered to be a relatively short amount of time, but he was more concerned with the news they reported.

"We must to go back *now*. That smell is someone attempting to cover their scent." Nomad declared and they left without another word.

Shai shouted as they ran, "That first attack a while back wasn't just a bunch of lucky hillbillies, they were scouts!" Fear shot through all of them and the three took off even faster.

"Remember, stay focused and together!" Nomad reminded knowing he would arrive later.

They approached home running full steam into smoke bombs and utter chaos. Humans in military clothing were shooting darts, spraying something in their people's faces, tearing through their homes and hauling them away. In passing a few lay dead.

The trio did not slow down. They chose a target and handled them. Progress was made as they helped some get away while dodged the tranquilizers that flew by. They tackled, slashed and threw the enemies bodies where ever they could. With Thia and Shai at his side, Dae sent a wall of wind through to clear the smoke exposing those hidden in it, then another knocking the remaining down. Shai tried to raise walls of rock all around them but found it was too advanced yet for him. So he redirected by shooting large stones at them as Thia sent jolts at anyone aiming anything their way.

They were able to take down the few left but it was too late. The Phelidae never knew what hit them. Many of their members were either dead or missing now.

When it looked clear, Thia ran off to find her parents. She spotted her mother off in the distance helping anyone left get away safely. She handed off a little boy to one of the other adults and shooed them off, as she turned back she was hit. Nomad, Thia and the boys arrived just as it happened.

Nomad, "That bullet just hit the biggest, most genuine heart to ever exist."

"no", Thia ran and caught her mother in mid air as she fell to the ground.

Thia forgot about all around her, there was nothing else, only she and her mother. She pulled her mother close and looked in her big beautiful eyes, the brightest sweetest most innocent eyes, now filled with tears as the light began to fade.

"Why" her mother whispered. "What did *we* do?"

Thia whimpered, "nothing mother" as she stroked her soft strawberry blonde hair. "We didn't do anything" a huge tear plummeted down her cheek.

Her mother put on a gentle smile as if there was no pain. She softly brushed away her daughter's tears and kissed her hand.

"You have always been my life Thia. I love you more than you will ever know". Thia heard a long struggling breath in…then another out…and then she was gone.

"mom? mom? No…no, you can't. It's not time…it's not your time…" she held her tighter.

Some said Thia's scream was what abruptly ended the still lingering invasion. It started off sorrowful towards the sky, then came down and contorted to unadulterated fury. Anything in her path was instantly destroyed. It resembled like the after affect of a bomb. Trees blew apart and all of the homes and structures pulverized. There was no mercy, no care, no life in her, only wrath.

This unknown intruder pillaged one of the very few things in life that mattered to her. Any soldiers within her immediate range burst into dust. Those out of her sight were struck dead. Some further away managed to escape either blind or deaf with many shattered bones.

Nomad was able to shield the boys in time from the bulk of it.

She cried until she had nothing left. She lay motionless holding her mother, staring at the ground with swollen eyes and shallow breath for a day. When her body violently shivered, wise and gentle Nomad covered her with a blanket and then let her be. Those that stayed behind knew better than to disturb her during this time.

Her brothers outright refused to leave with their parents and the few survivors left. They chose to stay and deal with any that may return. They sat by Thia's side, not touching her or talking to her -- just sitting. When it could be put off no longer Nomad buried her mother in the traditional and most honored and respectful way, then took the three and vanished with them.

Thia had nothing left to resist with. They didn't speak for weeks, all in mourning. Dae carried Thia where ever they went as she slept the whole time as if in hibernation. Their home was completely abandoned, what was left of it.

Throughout their journey evidence of her sorrow lasted for miles, as even the animals wept for her. Eyes sad and faces wet, days of howling and even the biggest of animals just sat in a daze paying no attention to anything that passed by. The closest town they visited off of the woods reportedly went through a period of unexplained deep depression.

Months of lonely wandering went by. They'd setup camp and some mornings Nomad had already gotten up and wandered off. His things were still there so they he wouldn't be gone long and they should stay put and look after Thia. He always returned after a day or two.

Shortly after Thia started eating and talking again Nomad announced it was time to part ways, "I have to go away for a while and you three will have to be on your own."

"What? Why?" Shai anxiously asked.

Nomad's tone was somewhat distant. He didn't want to but knew he must, "There are some dire matters I must handle immediately. We have traveled far to a safe place. You must remember all I've taught you, especially concealing what you are so you blend in. It is a very small town and you now own a place on this far end of it. Your family earned a large amount of money but never had use for it, so now it is yours. You will need it."

Nomad pulled out a small brown bag from his large sack, "In this bag you will find all you need to get started. Remember the lessons, especially on control, keep low and stick together. Your training will have to be completed at a later time. But for now it is too dangerous."

Nomad spoke as he packed up, "There is a traitor among our kind, some suspect from one of the closer tribes. This is the only way any of this could've happened. Someone was sharing information, educating the enemy. They too have money and could offer extremely tempting rewards for such information."

Furrowed brows and concerned faces all around were trying to figure out who it could be and what was happening to them, "I can go no further with you. Keep heading in that direction and you will find the place. You will hear from me again, I promise this." At that he quickly left.

Thia and her brothers just watched as Nomads image shrunk down to nothing. They were alone and on their own now.

The Pallas

Years later, memories of their talks with Nomad left Thia often thinking what a pain it must have been in the times without cell phones and the internet with the various networking sites. *How did they find anything or get anything done? They must have felt trapped without knowing what is going on all around them. I lived that life too but I have no idea what I did with my time anymore.*

Out of necessity, the three of them followed their lessons and had their various pre-planned screen names and sites they would later connect by once they felt it was safe. The reconnecting part they were very good at by now with all of the practice they've been forced into.

Though they were technically being "hunted", the early chases turned out to be almost fun, at least after the first few raids. The newbie's, as Shai labeled them, had no idea what they were doing which worked out well because neither did the three of them yet, so both committed simple mistakes. The first groups of hunters began attacking at the wrong time of day, approaching from the wrong direction.

These *basics* are covered at the training facility, however somehow they always seemed to miss one seemingly small detail or just flat out forgot. Probably too caught up in why they were there, dreaming that this time *they* would be the one that had the successful mission and gained all of the glory and wealth. These distractions and mistakes prove costly.

During one of their first attempts they thought it was a good idea to break in during the late evening hours. The plan relied on the chance that all would be fast asleep so they could catch them off guard. All set to go with every piece of the latest high-tech expensive gear available they made their move.

Among the many items they carried the night vision goggles, special dark camouflage and fine tuned listening devices were thought to be the most useful. The most important part they failed take into consideration was their targets. These people are part cat. Had they done their homework they would've realized that cats are nocturnal and actually roam at night. As a matter of fact they are most active at night. So, when they made their grand destructive entrance into the house, of course they were shocked to find no one was home. Instead they made so much noise trying to surprise the empty house that they knew at this point it had most likely announced their presents to the targets and chose to leave.

When they finally got that right they forgot another well known attribute of a cat. They have an acute sense of smell. So approaching downwind wasted another very expensive attempt.

When the weather is nice, Thia loves to open up the house, just like her mother did. The fresh summer air filled with the natural smells of pine trees and the sweetly scented flowers freshly planted flowed through the house, invoking the most relaxing mood as the sheer curtains swayed from the breeze blowing in.

As fate would have it, it was this type of day when the Pallas approached. It only took seconds before all three picked up the scent. To them it was more like an assault on the senses comprised of a repulsive mix of sweat, war paint, gun oil, bar soap and electronics. It wasn't difficult to figure out what was coming after putting all of these together.

Through fumbling trial and error the Pallas eliminated repeating the same easy mistakes, and so came the next level of difficult challenges. The Pallas are simply not fast enough. They had plenty of expensive toys but didn't know how to really use them to their advantage. They could locate the three but found the equipment useless after that. If they didn't catch them before they had a chance to get a little distance between them, the mission was an automatic failure. The woods were too much of a complication. The only item small and fast enough to help in keeping up with Thia and her brothers on foot was a bike. But even that didn't help them. The woods are too thick in parts and the ground was too uneven. All of the riders were thrown from their bikes as they flipped over the large thick roots.

Sometimes out of frustration some men would open fire during a chase, knowing full well a dead catch was no good, or worse even a punishable offence, but done still in desperate hopes of at least slowing one down for capture. Despite their efforts, just about all of the bullets ended up in trees, ricocheting off of rocks, roots and buried deep in the ground. A few were just bad shots, but sometimes there were misses that seemed to be caused by strange anomalies. From time to time there would be a sudden mysterious increase of weapons failing, backfiring or duds. And occasionally there was a peculiar change in the elements. A strong wind blew on a non windy day from the wrong direction, an odd landslide swept their feet out from under them, or rogue hail storm pelted the troupe. Never witnessing such events before, some of the superstitious members of the group were beginning to think the woods might be haunted.

But the experienced ones of the militant group just laughed at them knowing it was no less than a sign they were heading in the right direction. The three were known to have special abilities, a side affect not uncommon to the supernatural, but this was not shared with all. The less they knew the better, for the mission to carry on. After all, the majority were not there to think, but to do.

The specific gifts these three had were still unknown to their hunters but they had an idea what the basic options were. A sample of just about every other gift from various other species had already been collected and observed then sold to those who paid the highest amount. All of these types of beings were useful but for some reason none yet believed to be as powerful as these three combined.

Money opened many more doors for the Pallas than were available to the Phelidae. They knew more about some of the legends and set out to find the truth by any means possible. Ultimate power was the end goal.

The poachers quickly learned how inefficient sending the new ones out too early was for them and delayed the recruits, taking care to train them longer. They could not afford to keep losing men on the same three again and again without coming any closer to bringing even just one of them in.

The expense rapidly climbed its way to the owner's attention. The cost in weapons and surveillance alone was staggering but the training of brand new recruits grew to twice that. In addition to that finding the right type of person with a human hunter mentality was already difficult and rare. Only the coldest of hearts would do. There was no room for a conscience in this job. No questions asked, no answers given.

Obtain slaves with special abilities to command as anyone that owned them saw fit. The Pallas sold the idea well, the entertainment, the power, the weapon they could serve as. The Pallas knew the money their clients would pay to employ those who ruled such a thing. They already had some of them captive and were using them in some of these ways.

But these three, are special. Owner of few words, descendent Hiram Pallas, secretly withheld another purpose for them. His secured diary holds an excerpt best describing it, *"Oh, I will have you, for you alone possess the might to bring gods and monsters alike to their knees. And power belongs only to those with the will to wield it."* Still he knew the rest were too feeble to understand and kept with the entertainment farce. Some out there have anything and everything they could possibly want, yet stay bored restless and unhappy.

History shows us that greed is proven to be one of the greatest motivators. Love however is another powerful motivator. Some might even argue Love to be stronger than Greed. The remaining Phelidae hope so knowing it is this that drives Thia and her brothers.

Later the trackers became more experienced, as did the Phelidae. This is when *fun* begins. Shai hated the chases because he hates artificially running. So naturally he was very pleased when running didn't work and they instead had to turn and fight. Though his siblings outwardly showed disapproval, secretly, Thia enjoyed fighting back too.

Then again it really wasn't much of secret. Her brothers could tell her heart was into it, regardless if she chose to admit it or not. Dae, on the other hand, couldn't care less either way as long as he didn't have to outright kill someone, which unfortunately was sometimes necessary.

The attacks were therapeutic in a way. Shai concealed nothing when satisfying his need for an outlet. To him these times are a long awaited chance to play a little hardcore without much worry about control. But Thia used it as a release from being so pent up and restricted. She trusted herself enough to know it would never be a total loss of control, but she was grateful for any moment she could get to set someone straight.

So often the hunters attempted to force upon their victims arrogance, so rarely deserved. It was this pet peeve of ignorance that drove her to actually enjoy a fight. Putting someone in their rightful place has its own selfish rewards. Though the three couldn't completely let loose with everything they had, as it is their way to only match force to be fair, they subtly made it known they had no problem holding their own. It was enough to bring down the enemies numbers and send the remaining retreating back to base, for now.

The hunters thus referred too are a group called the Pallas. The Pallas could also fairly be considered as poachers, bounty hunters, hired guns or any other form of unlawful highly trained self-interested humans for lease. The wealthy and either power hungry or just bored of the world finance them. No one knows for sure where exactly they reside. It is said they relocate as often as the ones they hunt.

When an organization receives the magnitude of funds this one does, it is not difficult to obtain the latest in weapons and tracking technology. They can even afford to come up with their own. However, regardless the abundance of resources, this target is as smart, if not smarter, than the hunter, has special powers they don't have or understand yet and must be captured alive.

But all of this effort is just to attain them. The hard part doesn't start until after. Once captured the subjects then had to first be broken and then trained like wild animals. Thia and her brothers have already had much training but this was not the same as what the Pallas had in mind.

Captives are abused and robbed of their free will then conditioned for whichever program the Pallas deemed fit for them, be it for testing, rent or sale. They were sorted by skill level. The less impressive are reserved for experimental testing and or demeaning circus like entertainment, where as the ones with real talent are sought after for more military type services. Those that fall in the middle somewhere could go either way but were mostly used as expendable opponents during live training.

All of this information has been supplied via stories told by a couple that managed to escape. A Phelidae and the other referred as a *cursed one*, explained they believe the main base is somewhere underground in a large desert in the western United States. They couldn't tell where exactly. As they were escaping they didn't think to check the license plate to learn their location. They admit the only thing on their minds was getting away unnoticed as fast as possible.

That night when the two were clear of the base, they snuck into the back of a pickup truck speeding down the dusty deserted road. With no one else around they were able to catch up on foot and stay close behind, matching speed as they slid under the flapping tarp covered bed of the truck. The male Phelidae had to carry the other as she couldn't run fast enough.

Once in, they were careful not to move around too much so the driver wouldn't hear them back there. This worked out well and got them far from the facility. Still to be cautious they took turns resting, and keeping on watch just in case.

One stop during the trip was unexpected as it should've been a hundred miles till the next crossroad. The Phelidae peeked out to find a check point in the middle of nowhere, and on the side of the road sat an unlabeled black helicopter. The couple knew the Pallas must have realized they were gone and were already searching for them.

The Pallas have enough money to afford convincing fake credentials to fool the small time local police into thinking they are true military. As they inched closer to the inspectors the two knew they had to come up with something. So they both quietly slipped out the back and up under another larger truck behind them hauling a bed full of loose hay.

Luckily the driver, distracted by the scene, happened to be following very close and there was no one behind him, so burrowing under the mountain of hay went unnoticed.

The hay was moist and heavy and created a burning sensation in the Phelidae, Thomas's super sensitive nose. It wasn't long before he strongly desired the relief of fresh air to clear away the toxically sweet and thick aroma they were now buried alive in. Nausea took over knowing he couldn't have his precious air for as long as it would take. Next the moisture sinking into their clothes caused itching as Thomas felt a stinging sneeze coming on but held his breath trying to hold it off for as long as possible.

Fortunately the girl, Sarah, was a mind reader. She told him how close they were so he would know when to let it out and not. When their new truck reached the checkpoint she told Thomas, when and where to move as she knew where they were planning to dig and poke in the heap.

The checkpoint men finally gave up after they too had enough of the smell and the itch and let them pass. Unable to withstand the environment any longer the stowaways decided they were far enough out and snuck out during one of the driver's meal stops. Returning home was not an option so they set off with nothing to their names to make a new one.

Though the actual location would've been very beneficial, Thomas and Sarah were still able to expose the contents and functions of the base. All news and details traveled via word of mouth so no documentation could be found. The Phelidae could not afford to let on that they knew such things. If this happed it could result in the Pallas moving in turn causing all they'd learned, any advantage they may hold now, completely worthless.

The facility was nothing but concrete, observation windows, guards and cameras. When subjects are captured they are kept drugged at first unable to do much. Vision and sounds were all blurred and muffled at best. A few days later the new ones are herded in to a room with some others and given the reason they were there and what was expected of them.

Those that flat out refused at first were severely punished with variations of water and sound torture until they gave in and did as they were told. Fire was considered but the healing time took too long. They were also warned worse would happen if caught trying to get away.

The two that escaped, Thomas and Sarah, stayed together during one of these orientations. As they'd hoped they were placed in a cell together since like creatures were kept separated at all times to avoid any hope of teaming up. They comforted each other despite the strict rule of no talking, as she read what he was saying in his mind and she verbally answered. They agreed to find a way out so they lay low obeying orders and watch for any possible weaknesses in security.

Weeks went on as they studied the routines of their captor. The constant time spent together gave them a chance to learn much more about each other, causing them to grow closer developing an even stronger connection. Sarah told stories she hadn't shared of her family before and the challenges of hiding what they were. Thomas spoke of his tribe and their ways, including why a relationship like theirs had been attempted before but tragically quickly ended as the union was strictly forbidden.

At meal time all were sent to a locked down cafeteria looking room and were fed oatmeal looking slop and water. It was enough to keep them alive but weak. It was best if they stayed a little tired but not hungry. The half animals, which are about three quarters of their slave population, get violent when they are hungry. They were also always kept with the one they roomed with. This was to avoid on sets of panic and acts of desperation and motivation to escape.

Finally Thomas and Sarah decided they had studied enough, came up with a solid plan and were ready to give it a try. Figuring the air vents had to lead out to fresh air, this was going to be their way out. On best behavior at all times the guards subconsciously trusted them and therefore paid them less attention. So nightfall came on the very evening they chose, the night of the lazy guard's patrol.

They went to bed like good little inmates, passing the eleven pm check in. Once the guard moved on to the next they stuffed their beds making no sound at all and headed for the vents. They climbed in and followed against the flow of air. As they traveled through the tunnels there were heavy jail-like lead bars installed throughout the air tunnels. Typically this would be enough to stop anyone however it didn't end up mattering much as Thomas was good at manipulating metals from his Earth bending gift. This was the reason why getting into the air ducts went so smoothly and why he was also able to put the cover back like nothing happened.

The ones that ran the facility never did figure out where they went or how they got out. Cameras were installed in the rooms after that. They didn't even know what their abilities were yet, much less the extent of them. Getting to that was scheduled for the following week. They changed that too to earlier in the plan going forward. This group learned via trial and error.

"Thomas suspects his story has been discounted as a rumor, probably planted somewhere down the line by the Pallas themselves to save face and discredit him." but Dae got the story straight from the couple and was sharing it with Thia and Shai. "I ran into Thomas, that's the other Phelidae's name, at the grocery store today."

Dae continued on, "It was strange. It felt a little like Déjà vu. Like I knew something but I didn't know what exactly. Something felt familiar when nothing there should."

"That makes a lot of sense!" Shai rude and sarcastically interrupted out of frustration. Thia just shot him a look

Dae kept going, "My stomach was growling and I was getting very hungry looking at the thick fresh steaks they just brought out when it, the feeling distracted me. Once it was too strong to brush off, I looked around for...whatever it might be. Then I saw Thomas. He's older than us, about in his early forties, tall and thin with dark hair and a goatee. Something felt like I l already knew him but I know we've never met. Then I noticed he too was looking around for something, or someone. The second he saw me I could tell he found the same thing I did."

"Awe, true love!", Shai couldn't help it.

"Shut up Shai! Go on Dae.", neither could Thia.

"Automatically he walked over but we both felt...off and not sure what to do next. I knew he was one of us but I have no idea how. So I scratched my head showing off my mark and just told him the first thing that came to mind, *We're having a cookout at our house tonight. I know it is short notice but would you care to join us?* Then just like I hoped, he too held his arm out to shake, and also had a single mark, and he just said, *Yes, thank you.* So we exchanged contact information and met up shortly after in the parking lot to talk. Oh, sorry Thia for the short notice but I brought the steaks home. I couldn't help it. We haven't seen our own kind in so long. It felt like what you say all the time, *meant to be?*"

Thia just smiled back at him, "It's okay Dae. I have time to prepare."

Shai was almost bursting at the seams with real excitement now at the chance of talking with more of their own, "Really, I can't believe it! What time is he coming?"

"I told him around 8pm?", Dae answered sheepishly, not looking natural on his massive size at all, from still feeling bad for putting Thia on the spot.

"Ooh, it's almost seven, I better get started. Hey, I don't want to miss anything. Come in the kitchen with me so I can hear everything." Off she ran to get started and they followed.

Suddenly very interested Shai asked, "Dae, you think that is how we can tell when we are around our own kind?"

"Maybe? I can tell you I've never sensed anything so strong. But it was odd, the woman that was with him didn't have the same affect. She must not be Phelidae at all. He is still bringing her though."

"Plus two! I'm on it.", Thia grabbed more food from the fridge.

Dae went on about his experience and telling the story until what seemed like only minutes later the door bell rang.

"It's them!", Shai said excited.

"Geez, eight already? Dae, you should get it since they would recognize you. We don't want them to be uncomfortable right away." ,Thia suggested, always trying to be considerate.

Dae answered the door with Shai behind him, "Hello, please come in."

He welcomed them in and showed them to the breakfast bar to sit and meet Thia.

"Thia this is Thomas and Sarah.", Dae politely introduced.

"Hi, it's very nice to meet you both.", Thia could instantly feel what Dae was talking about. The Déjà vu was only with Thomas, not Sarah just as he said. She glanced over to Shai to see if he felt it too but was slightly shocked then embarrassed when she caught the way Shai was staring in amazement at them. It was all too evident he was experiencing the connection as well.

Only Thomas spoke as the Sarah stayed close to him wrapped around his arm, "It is nice to meet you too."

"So, Dae told us what happened at the store and that you seem to have like...tattoos?", Shai is not good at subtle. He is more of an up front and all out conversationalist.

Thomas laughed from the poorly disguised exploration, breaking up the tension, "Yes, it is true."

Shai, pleased to find a like earth bender, "Wow, Dae you were right! Hey why can't we tell your friend is one too?"

Thomas chuckled, "You are much better at direct questions friend. I am glad you ask. You don't sense her because she isn't *one*. She is something else."

"Thomas!" she whispered cautiously squeezing his arm extremely worried.

Thomas patted her hand reassuring her, "It's alright Sarah."

She tried to whisper but by now knew it was a little pointless, "You don't even know them."

He nodded, "True, but they are my kind. We can tell."

She was still unconvinced and uptight, "What from some tattoo? Theirs isn't even like yours."

"No, it's more than that. It's difficult to explain how exactly."

Dae acknowledged what he was referring to, "Yes we are getting that too. Do you know what it is?"

"The people from my tribe said we should be able to sense our own kind. I assume this is what they meant. Back to your direct question Shai, she is what is called a *gifted or cursed one* depending on what tribe you come from. She is not Phelidae but human with special...*talents* shall we say."

"Interesting. We've never met anyone like that." Dae commented now intrigued.

Sarah asked softly, "Thomas how do you know they aren't the traitors?"

He shook his head, "I do not believe they are."

He turned to Dae, "I've heard of you three. Two with the double marks and...", he looked over at Thia and stopped.

The room was silent. Thia exchanged looks with her brothers and when they nodded she slid her cardigan down her shoulder to confirm her mark.

"…the girl with the lightning bolt." he barely got the words out as he stared in awe.

His gaze made Thia uncomfortable, "Would you like something to drink?" she blurted out as she threw her sweater back on. "Food should be ready shortly. Um, Sarah, how do you like your meat? I think we prefer ours the same, yes Thomas.", Thia didn't look at him when she asked.

Sarah shook him out of his daydream state when he didn't answer right away, "You would be correct Athena. It has been too long since I have hunted as I assume it has been for you as well."

She swayed a little, sick from the rush of fading memories of her mother calling her by that name, "yes…and you can just call me Thia."

Her brothers felt the affect and had to stabilize themselves as well. Her affects on them were getting stronger.

Looking to shake off the unsettling motion sickness, Shai chose to change subjects, "Where is the rest of your tribe?"

Thia, put off by the timing of his invasive question felt Shai was being just plain nosey now.

"I am not sure. I have not seen them for quite some time.", both Thomas and Sarah looked very sad at the truth of this statement.

"I'm sorry." Thia apologized for her brother.

"It's alright. We…left before the invasion on our tribe. You see my people did not approve of our union and therefore gave me an ultimatum and finally banished me."

I wonder if they are from the same clan that Nomad's parents are from. I better not ask now but I hope I get to soon, Thia instantly thought to herself, half hopeful and excited for Nomad.

Dae, ever investigating things was still curious, "You said your people talked about what we are experiencing. Did they say anything more in how it works?"

"Only a little. Since we were already around our own kind all of the time, there was no way to tell how the connection would feel. But now being away for so long, it is quite strong. They said at first, since we are not masters at it, we will only feel it when the other Phelidae is very close, such as in the same room like we were. But once you know the feeling and get better at recognizing it, it is possible for some to sense miles away. This however would take much practice and fine tuning to pick up on it."

"Fascinating" Dae's mind was going full steam ahead now.

"Judging by your age, you were young when they came for you?"

"Yes." Shai said sadly.

"They were well informed, you were lucky to get away..." then Thomas stopped dead in his tracks remembering something. "Oh...you three actually ended the raids." Then he remembered more as the story refreshed in his mind. "I...I do apologize..."

Sarah very confused by Thomas's backtracking pulled at the arm she was still attached to, "What, what is it?"

Genuinely regretful to his new friends, Thomas ignored Sarah, "I do not mean to drudge up such a horrible experience for you Athena...uh, Thia. I am very sorry for your loss."

Thia quickly dismissed the whole thing, "It's fine." She stayed focused on dinner.

Dae jumped in, "We are quite eager to learn all we can from any that will teach us."

Thomas relieved by the new subject, "I will gladly share all I can."

"Dinners ready!" Thia said in an almost too cheery tone.

They sat down at the table and ate, told stories of their adventures up until now, and discussed differenced in the tribes. Thia decided it was now or never to ask.

"Your tribe sounds more traditional than ours. Did you ever meet a wonderer that goes by the name Nomad?" Dae and Shai knew why she asked.

Thomas thought for a moment, "I am afraid that does not sound familiar to me."

Thia wasn't quite ready to give up, "Did you ever have...I guess you could call it, a scandal occur in your tribe?"

"Ha! You mean other than us?!" getting that Thomas knew them, the girl Sarah was much more comfortable.

"Yes." Thia confirmed.

Thomas still declined, "Not during my time there. Even if something before then happened I am sure no one would've spoken of it."

"I see.", Thia was clearly disappointed thinking she just may have caught lightning in a bottle.

Thomas was curious by her sudden and somewhat specific interest, "May I ask why?"

Thia seeing no harm in it, "We have a friend that is searching for his parents. Their marriage too was forbidden as she was human as well."

Thomas immediately understood, "Ah, and they had a child. Yes, if they were from my tribe, they were wise to abandon him."

Thia didn't care for the coldness of his comment. "I guess, but it would still be nice to find them for him."

They finished up their visit and headed to the door, "It was truly a pleasure meeting you. I hope this is not the last of our encounters. It has been too long since I've had such freedom to reminisce and discuss the things of our people."

Dae reassured, "Definitely not, you have our information and we have yours. We will surely make use of it."

"Please stop by any time you like." Thia politely insisted.

And they did. Dae mostly spoke with Thomas via email, multiple secret screen names, sites sometimes using codes, and visited with them on occasion to be safe but never spoke over the phone as they worked together to learn and share information.

No longer completely alone, some hope had been restored to Thia and her brothers. If Thomas is out there then so are others, now it's just a matter of finding them. Hiding and relocating had been wearing on them for some time now. But you have to do what you must to survive. Being a little more informed was helpful but it was nowhere near enough to get them where they wanted to be yet. Still they were grateful for a start in understanding what they are up against. Until now all knowledge has been acquired the hard way and rarely shared.

The Pallas hit like a force they'd never known before, attacking the various tribes capturing all they could and spreading out the rest thin enough to prevent any chance at reuniting and fighting back. They continue to do the same now any time even a hint of the Phelidae turned up.

Regardless, meeting with Thomas and Sarah revived the deep down and over time greatly diminished desire to find their people and be great again after being afraid for so long, but they had yet come up with a safe plan to begin the search. They had no way to know where to start or who to even look for. Knowing what the others would feel like helped. But for the present time it was clear they had to stay focused on staying hidden. Recently, even this was proving to become more difficult as time went on.

The evening after their dinner with Thomas, a strangely quiet evening, Dae stared sadly into his food and said, "History's repeating itself, only this time we are the hunted."

Something Different

She'd left the library and continued her trek shortly after finding something...special. Backpack of essentials strapped to her back, Thia slowed to a jog the moment she picked up a sound the wind carried of a truck passing on an old town dirt road about a mile ahead of her. Approaching the edge of the woods she had her story down pat. *I hitchhiked the whole way from NY. Thought I would try modeling or acting but it fell through. So I took up a waitressing job until I got some extra cash and am now heading back home. Where is home? Geez, I'm such a bad liar. How about they don't need to know!* She just needed to find a car she could afford that would get her the rest of the way.

She crossed the street about half a mile down the road from a small old settlement. This way no one would see exactly where she came from. Out of the five buildings there, one fortunately happened to be a used car lot. The place was dingy, old and run down. The signs, drastically faded from years of sun exposure, were barely visible with all the dust that had settled on them. The owner, salesman, mechanic slash receptionist, was a large and dirty man. His face hadn't been shaved for at least a week, and he smelled as if his last bath was just as far away. Of course it had to be one of the worst hot and humid days.

Transportation being the first thing she wanted to get out of the way, she put aside how repulsed she was by the sweaty, smelly man, found and bought a car at the old lot. She paid cash and only filled out the basic paperwork with one of her predetermined aliases, for what most would consider a beater car.

She wasn't sure what model or make it was as those emblems had rusted off long ago and the paper work didn't mention it, but all-in-all it didn't really matter to her. She knew if it wasn't fast, Shai would fix that once they met up again. It closely resembled one of the cars he's owned in the past. Even she could tell it needed some serious body work and didn't sound all that healthy, but it ran and that was all she needed for now. She actually preferred it that way. It brought her comfort looking forward to seeing Shai again. This of his hobbies definitely came in handy obviously by getting a better than new car, but mostly by keeping him out of trouble...at least until the test drive of said car.

Over the years of running they gained the wisdom of how to stay untraceable but didn't feel they needed to completely deny themselves some of the finer things in life. All of them enjoy speed, it's in their blood, an indulgence they often took part in abusing but also helped a time or two in escape in the past. Or at least it was their rational.

The money Nomad set them off with was spread out in accounts kept everywhere. They too were wealthy and educated despite their remote location growing up. One member from the tribe was sent out every so often for a couple years to keep up with the outside and what was going on. When they finished their assigned time out, they brought back both items and knowledge to educate the rest. Beyond the trinkets the women made, a few also wrote books sold under a pseudonym that were mostly fantasy based children books. Many of the books made a lot of money and the wealth was shared. Everyone contributed in their own way and therefore every one gained. The agent never asked too many questions. He appreciated the larger than normal percentage provided for the guarantee of privacy.

Each account purposely held a modest amount, and kept under the most common names to keep out of any spotlight that may be searching and tracing the locations of the withdrawals once flagged as a possible target. When they needed cash often times they would close one of the accounts taking the money in small bills typically no higher than a twenty dollar bill. If they had to settle in a small city, which is where they usually ended up, they would stand out handing over large bills that didn't match their usual "we're nobodies" persona. Besides, most people didn't have change. The preparation for these small inconveniences was well worth the security and peace of mind they got in return. It was also the least they could do for the potential trouble they were sure to unintentionally bring with them.

Thia did her research and shopping from the internet at libraries which are both public and anonymous. But what she found this time was a small old abandoned military training facility in a small town named Lionesta not far from Cleveland, and it was going for cheap too. She thought it would be different enough from what they had in the past and might even have some perks to help keep unwanted visitors out. She actually got a little enthused about the idea, pretty sure her brothers would like it too, once she finished applying her own special touches that were already piling up in her mind.

As she looked further into the area she found Cleveland, only a few hours away, seemed to be large enough to be interesting but small enough to still be somewhat nice, the people that is. Thia knew Shai would not be happy that they weren't going to be directly in the city this time but she made sure there were some city life options for him still. Dae only ever wants the ability to research, so he was all set anywhere they ended up as long as there was internet access.

She continued reading into the history she printed out, *Apparently this city used to be famous for its burning river in 1969 but now sells something called Burning River along with another powerful seasonal favorite named Christmas Ale. It also has some fun things going on that might prove entertaining and worth an occasional drive to the big city. It looks like a young ball player has been making quite a name for himself. Yes, my bothers will like this area.*

So Thia made up her mind and purchased everything online. Now she just needed to get there and pick up the keys for their new home and a small club to clean up and run. She already scheduled to have a truck deliver everything she ordered a week later. Once she arrived she stopped at local shop to pick up some basic food and toiletries until the rest showed up.

She also wanted to pick up some new clothes since hers were ruined, but couldn't quite find what she was looking for. She visited their quaint little clothing shops and experienced a rude awakening noticing the differences in options compared to big city stores. Giving up on this she moved on to the diner next door for a quick bite before heading to the new home.

Finishing up her meal quicker than she planned, to get away from all the stares and whispers, she left. Her car seemed to sound worse than before. *Hmmm, must be from hauling all this stuff in it now.* Trying to envision her destination, she expected the worse of the soon to be converted facility and was right.

Her car made it up the long pebble drive way to the stone cold, dark grey box with tiny windows and old graffiti. "No wonder there were no pictures. I have to give the writer credit, the description was quite creative."

Not blinking once she climbed of the car, stood and stared, "Where to start? The day's almost half over so I better see what the inside looks like."

The large heavy rusted metal door opened much easier than she expected. Flipping the light switch a few fluorescents flickered on in response revealing piles of dust, dirt and cobwebs. She refused to take another step forward without some sort of defense against it all. So she ran back to the car and unloaded most of it into what she would make the foyer.

Seeing that the electricity had been turned on in time, she brought in the stand lamps and fans she bought and set them up. The fans she put in the window to blow out any dust she kicked up during cleaning. Also expecting the heat not to work she bought a little portable stove to heat the main room she got clean enough to stay in and to cook on. A bit tired from her long day and forgetting to consider perception, a few of the stock boys stood shocked at how easily she was able to load the cast iron appliance in the trunk of the rust bucket she pulled up in.

In between fixing up the place, Thia ate out at all the restaurants for the first week getting a feel for the town and the people in it. As expected, news of her arrival spread quickly.

"Oh, you are the one that bought the old training place and rundown pub right?" a tall skinny young man about her age abruptly spat at her during a visit at the local hardware store. "What would someone like you want that old place for?"

It was still hard for her to adjust to how nosey they were in these places. She wasn't good at hiding this fact either. So she quickly had to recover from it.

They don't mean anything by it, they just don't have much to talk about in these parts, she constantly tried to repeat to herself.

This part she got good at, in fact it was almost too easy how fast she became a natural. The tried and true Damsel in Distress bit, worked every time. Men, especially the unsuspecting and well mannered ones, like this guy, couldn't help abiding by proving their chivalry. With the flash of a sweet little smile, a bat or two of her sweeping thick black eye lashes and a slight bite of her lower lip, the cold, rude image of her initial reaction instantly vanished from their minds. Then shed' ask for some help and which direction was North. After all being from a big city, the poor girl probably didn't know any better.

Switching between small and big cities seemed to be the best way to keep the enemy guessing. It was easy to get lost, blending in with the busy crowded areas both day and night. The last couple of times, which lasted about five years, they stayed with the larger cities. The first in the cement jungle and the second in a little more secluded but wealthy area. Trying a very small town this time will definitely take some adjusting. This reality became more apparent the more she explored.

Gone are the days of mass chain restaurants, chic bars and huge grocery stores with anything you could possibly want in them. Goodbye chai tea lattes and tofu. Here they just look at you funny. They would also have to get used to distance measurements in miles rather than minutes, directions explained via map and compass and the town rolling up the sidewalks dead after ten o'clock.

Though inconvenient it's not all that bad once you get use to it, Thia thought taking in a deep long breath of fresh clean air, something not found and greatly underrated in the big cities. *It's kind of nice to slow down. Shai will not agree at first but I think it will grow on him.* With the sleepy town came simplicity and a sense of cleansing, both of the body and mind. No more java induced over night marathons to meet impossible deadlines from past city jobs. Everything here moved much slower.

Thia knew Dae would probably even like the new place better but she anticipated a very unhappy Shai knowing he loves everything about the city. Somehow the everyday jerks and rudeness of it all brings him to life. Though not a jerk himself, he seems to thrive off of the challenge. He is so good at getting even the most threatening to stand down. Everything about him oozes confidence with an accent of unfamiliar wild.

Thia stopped by the local Sheriff's office claiming she was trying to find where to research any residential and or building codes. She explained that she wanted to be sure to follow the rules while renovating their new home and place of business. Seeing as how her brother was a frequent overnight visitor of the city jails, mostly from bar brawls or street racing, this was the actual motivation in why she decided to meet the people and get a peek at the accommodations he would undoubtedly be taking advantage of in the not so distant future.

They seem nice enough. It looks pretty clean too so he should be okay in there when the time comes. I doubt even this town will be able to slow him down. Thia reminisced on some of their adventures. In the city Shai actually became cronies with the cops since he spent so much time there. Unlike the vast majority of the temporary residents, they actually liked him because he was just a young and rowdy boy, not a true trouble maker like the typical scum brought in. The officers never admitted it to Shai, but they secretly hoped Thia would be the one to come and get him.

One night while waiting on his ride, Shai ended up helping out with an unruly group of new prisoners. It was an unusually large drug bust and the office wasn't staffed enough that holiday night to handle it. During the chaotic mix of cursing and yelling, one beast of a man broke free. Ripping off the arm of the old wooden chair his cuff was attached to, he grabbed the officer interviewing him as he attempted to fill out paperwork. He swung the officer around pulling a short thick and very sharp knife from his sock and placed it at his throat.

Shai, still very young at this time, felt his instincts violently kicked in. His face changed from a playful punk to that of a crazed animal. Only one smaller member of the bust saw the transformation in his face. It was so severe that it scared him so bad he soiled his pants as he sat shaking in the chair.

Shai sprung over the two large old grey metal desks in the way. The huge man with the knife froze stunned by the underestimated speed and agility. Shai, not permitting him time to come to his senses like he would in the silly fights we was usually engaged in, grabbed the hand with the knife and with enormous force twisted it around his back accidently causing a snapping sound at the wrist and elbow. Before the man could cry out in pain, Shai leveraged his weight and threw the guy pinning him to the wall. The room fell silent. No one could tell if it was the unlikely strength of Shai or the shear mass of the man that caused the crater and shower of dust in the drywall as he slid down it unconscious.

Dae arrived just in time to witness the crash and find Shai at the center of it.

Shai smiling awkwardly, seeing that all eyes were on him as everyone seemed to be awaiting an explanation, tossed out the first Dae inspired idea that came to mind, "Momentum?"

Thankfully his brother rescued him before anyone had a chance to put any real thought into it, grabbing him by the arm, signing the clipboard and dragging him out.

Even that night never slowed him down. Shai kept up with his usual antics well after coming so close to exposing himself he still managed to draw trouble. One thing did change, ever since the fore mentioned incident, Shai found he received more warnings and was arrested less and less regardless of the trouble he may have caused.

Understanding what was going on, all three took advantage when they needed to let loose every so often and got pulled over for some serious speeding/reckless driving. But as many good things do, sadly the benefits of this fortunate turn of events came to an end as the pace picked back up with a new face in the office. Routine returned and the police once again were habitually visited by Dae and Thia taking turns collecting their brother.

After the fact, Dae suspects the new rooky might have been planted there to confirm news they might be located there. He remembered catching the new 'Officer Brown', the Pallas were not very creative with names, peering at him longer than an ordinary person would. Once the officer realized Dae was watching back, Dae noted the new officer came off a bit anxious. Dae is very good at picking up on subtle body language but this one was all but shouting at him. The stiff unnatural walk, always peeking out the corner of his eye and watching reflections on the windows really gave him away.

One evening about a week later Shai was picked up for street racing, again. On their way home Dae noticed they were being followed. Brown thought he was back far enough not to be noticed, but cats have very good eyes, especially at night. Hunters should know this. Dae subtlety change course heading out side of city limits. The car followed. This guy was not very good. Still, they were raised and trained to be very cautious as things are not always what they seem. This obvious clod could just be a decoy. Shai called Thia at home to warn her. As they were on the phone, she scrambled to pack a few things preparing for the worst.

All senses were at their peak but sensed nothing yet. The brothers grew anxious and uncomfortable with Thia home by herself, not yet knowing the scope of this possible hunt.

It was too quite as Shai became annoyed, "If something is going to happen it should just happen already. I'm hungry and want to go home. Jail food is crap. What'd T make for dinner?"

"roast" Dae answered steadily watching the rear view.

"Oh, I love her roast. I can smell it in your clothes now. Just ditch this guy and let's eat!" Shai demanded shifting around in his seat.

Dae didn't react, "Call Thia back. She shouldn't stay at the house alone."

Once Shai heard all he needed from her describing that she thought the coast was clear, he ordered her to the club where they would meet her after they lost the tail.

She arrived first but knew stay mobile, to drive around until the boys got there. A large dark blue Buick slowly pulled up next to her at a stop light. She had a funny feeling about this car. Or maybe she was just being paranoid. She admitted to herself that the call from her brothers spooked her a little. Not to mention, she was in the middle of watching a scary movie, after all it was almost Halloween already.

The streets were empty as it was pretty late now. She wanted to look over into the car but couldn't, it would be too obvious. Her stomach growled attesting the popcorn unsubstantial knowing there was hardy meat awaiting them. The light turned green and she drove on at a normal speed. The blue car was matching her pace now sitting in her blind spot. She decided it was time for a left turn. She waited for the next main intersection and made the turn without any indication. She watched in her rear view mirror as the blue car kept going straight keeping a normal pace.

She let out a deep sigh of relief as she rolled her eyes at the ridiculousness of it all, *Stupid movie*, she thought. At the next intersection she turned left again to head back to the club. As she approached the club for the fourth time the very same blue car came out of nowhere cutting her off and forcing her to turn into the club parking lot next to the building. Half pissed and half scared she looked into the car to find Shai driving and a very annoyed Dae.

She got out of her car slamming the door behind her, "What the hell?!"

"We wanted to be discrete", Shai came back with a smirk.

No longer scared but furious, "You call *that* discrete? You ran me off the road. Moron."

Dae just rolled his eyes in agreement with her as they entered the dark club.

"So where did you get that beater?" Thia asked.

"Jacked it", Shai proudly answered with a big smile.

"Shai thought it would be better to arrive in a car that was not one of our own. So he suggested we...borrow without permission, someone else's so we wouldn't be recognized on our way back here", Dae explained.

"nice" was all she could get out staring in disbelief.

Dae turned the key and they followed him in.

Shai went for it, "Hey, did you bring the roast?"

"No idiot." Thia whispered back.

They all gently walked around the rooms, listening intently in every direction. They examined air vents, dark corners, under counters, in drawers and behind doors. No words were spoken until their search was conclusive. Police bugs let out a high pitch sound they could easily pickup on. Even the most high-tech listening and visual devices were unable to avoid this dead giveaway. Since this equipment was still somewhat mechanical there was no way around it. The unmistakable scent of hot wood and metal tends to stick around after being freshly installed too.

Thia's brothers were off in the kitchen and office. She came out of the women's bathroom and entered the men's. *Filthy Neanderthals. They're so smelly and disgusting,* ripped through her mind seeing and smelling the grime everywhere. She didn't even bother turning the light on for fear of what it might highlight. Opening the last stall door Shai jumps out at her scaring her so bad she fell back into the rust stained leaky sink.

"What's the matter with you!" she screamed at him until he grabbed and sniffed her.

She shoved his face away with her hand as he said in a dreamy tone, "Mmmm, roast."

"Don't be creepy dude." They both laughed remembering a movie they liked with that line in it.

Eventually satisfied there was nothing there, the three returned to the bar area.

Thia, hoping not, but worried they would have to move again, "So no signs of anything else yet, just this new paranoid cop so far?"

"No, nothing more so far.", Dae confirmed.

"Where'd he end up going? Wasn't he following you guys?"

"Apparently he lives out that way in a boring little cookie cutter house. We lost him when he turned off so we went back and found his car in a driveway."

Thia was hopeful, "So it's probably nothing then, right?"

But much to Thia's dismay Dae shook his head, "I'm not willing to call it yet. I think we should lay low for a few days so we can keep a close watch on Brown."

And so they did. For the next two weeks they took turns watching every move the cop made while staying out of site. Dae took first watch while Brown was still home in bed and then observed his morning routine.

Rather than peering in through the window and risk getting caught they hid as far away as possible, relying on binoculars and their hearing to keep track of what the officer did. Dae added that they should keep a log to compare as the week went on. Dae's & Thia's entries looked something like:

6:30am – woke up, worked out, showered & shaved, got dressed

7:00am – coffee/news paper

7:30am – watched news & packed sandwich lunch

8:00am – left for work

8:30am – arrived at work

9:00am to 5:00 pm – answered phone calls (consisting of pranks, complains of barking dogs and reported road kill), checked on prisoners, took food to prisoners, ate lunch at desk, more calls, more food did some time tracking and left for the day.

6:15pm – arrived home, changed & cooked frozen meal

6:30pm – watched the news & ate

8:00pm – watched part of a recorded game

10:00pm – went to bed

Shai's entries were a little different:

6:30am - woke up way too early, I guess you can call that a workout, showered with the worst smelling cheap bar soap, shaved, put on ugly uniform

7:00am - drank cheap week coffee and skipped good stuff in news paper

7:30am - watched boring news & packed nasty lunch

8:00am - left in noisy crap car

8:30am - finally got to work obeying speed laws to an excruciating degree

9:00am to 5:00 pm - blah, blah, blah, left for the day.

6:15pm - back home, changed & ate probably decade old mock food

6:30pm - watched boring news again

8:00pm - looser watched part of an old recorded game from a non team that was great like five years ago

10:00pm - finally went to bed and Thia saved me from crying from all the boringness suffering!

This carried on all week. The routine became very predictable.

"Too predictable," Dae was not convinced by the show. "Something about this is not right."

Shai whole heartedly agreed with him, "You got that right! I'd kill myself if I had to live like that! I almost wanted to, having to watch it. Why would anyone choose to?"

"There's something to be said for a simple life. I'd take that over what we're forced to do." Thia longed for the running to end.

They all felt it.

"Brown has to be a decoy of some sort, but why, for what purpose?", Dae thought out loud trying to figure it out.

"Maybe a scout sent to draw us out? Get us to act different?", Thia suggested.

"Maybe. We need more to know for sure."

They decided to snoop around town more looking for those that might not belong. Maybe there were more around than just him. This was not an easy task considering the various districts are made up of all kinds. Still, they had an idea of the type they were looking for. They would be much like the cop, a little too stiff and suspect including his perfect little schedule.

A few days went by and turned up nothing so they eased back into their normal lives while still keeping an eye out. Thia stopped by the little twenty four seven corner store near the club picking up a couple of things they ran out of. It was just a quick stop in between the every-other-week grocery store excursion. Men eat a lot, especially big ones.

Dae was finishing up at the club and said he would be right behind her. Suddenly she felt very uncomfortable. It was a funny feeling like she was being watched. She risked a sneaky glance up at the security mirror and saw two men in drab nondescript clothing, one in same isle behind her and the other an isle over, both looking back at her. She didn't recognize them and they were standing in the way of her path to the door. *They should know animals don't react well when cornered*, she thought feeling increasingly agitated.

She tried to stay cool, grabbed her last item and turned to pay at the counter. She was ready to defend if need be. When she got around to facing the man she found he was no longer staring at her but reading the back of snack in his hand. *He doesn't look like the type to be watching what he eats.* She slowly slid past him whispering "excuse me" and headed to the counter.

She paid in cash and left. Still no sign of Dae, she wasn't sure what to do so she decided head back to the club but took the quicker shortcut through the ally. Not because she was stupid and liked getting robbed but she knew it was the shortest way back and if they were who they could be, she would rather keep the audience minimal in case the situation got hairy.

The uncomfortable feeling returned, the two guys were now behind her and advancing fast. She picked up the pace, wondering what could be keeping Dae, and they did too. Before she reached the end one of them grabbed her arm. Then he immediately let go after hearing a heavy thud. She turned to see where the noise came from. Dae was there with one guy behind him on the ground and had the forearm of the other one. Cats can be very stealth like when they wanted to be. The men never heard him coming.

"Who are you and what do you want? I strongly suggest you answer quickly and truthfully for I am not a patient man." Of course he was lying, Dae wouldn't hurt a fly, but he could still be pretty scary when he wanted to be. It was a side of him so rarely seen.

"...I ..." the man looked at the other one out cold the ground.

Dae stared him directly in the eyes, another effective form of intimidating interrogation. Watching the man's physical reactions, Dae would be able to tell if the man was lying and if so would use other methods, but hoped wouldn't come to that.

"I just…it was his idea! He saw her coming out of the club and said she would have some money on her. We weren't going to hurt her, swear!"

A big sigh of relief came from Dae. Thia calmed down too. They were just petty thieves.

Once they were out of the ally Thia asked, "Where'd you come from?"

"I finished up so I stopped by the store looking for you. Then I followed your scent down the alley."

"Boy I'm glad!" she said.

"You could've handled them." he said with a reassuring smile. Though both of her brothers are very protective of her, they knew her strength and what she was capable of.

She surveyed the area cautiously as they walked, "Yeah, I know, but I couldn't tell if they were mere pocket pickers or Pallas. All of this watching has me paranoid now"

"True." He said now deep in thought. "Have you seen anything else that caught your eye?"

"No, nothing yet. That was the first time anything like it has happened."

They confirmed with Shai that he too still noticed nothing. After another week of strict caution they finally let their guard down and it was business as usual. Shai got taken in again, this time for buying stolen car parts. But when he got to the station he noticed officer Brown wasn't there anymore.

"Hey what happened to that one officer, Brown was it?" Shai faked like he'd forgotten the name.

"He just up and quit last week, no notice or anything. Said he had to move due to personal reasons." the officer explained.

Shai told them the news, in the kitchen for dinner.

"Very strange" Dae was again concerned, though it probably never really stopped.

Thia's heart sank, "Are we going to have to move now or what? I can't take much more of this back and forth stuff."

Dae disagreed, "No, too risky. They could end up following us and then we start all over with this again before we even got settled in. I think we need to stay put and just be ready. Maybe we should change some of our habits, starting with you Shai."

Shai a little shocked thinking he isn't predictable at all, "What do you want *me* to change?"

"The biggest thing is stop getting in trouble. We need to lay low for a while. Not to mention we are tired of bailing you out."

"No doubt." Thia seconded.

Shai had a hard time agreeing giving up his fun, "Easier said than done but I'll try."

"Thia you switch up what days you do the shopping. And we'll change our shifts at the club." They both nodded.

"Oh, and you guys are going to have to cover for me. I'm going to take off for a bit." Dae said with some hesitation.

"Where are you going?" Thia asked worried.

"And for how long?" Shai added also a bit concerned.

"I need to see if I can find out more. I'll be back as soon as I can." Shai and Thia looked at each other as Dae left the room to pack.

Thia looked to Shai. "I'm worried."

"I know, but he knows what he is doing."

She had faith too but didn't like it, "How will we know if he gets into trouble? Nomad told us to stay together."

Just then Shai thought of something and called for him, "Hey Dae!"

Dae came out from his room with a bag, "What's up?"

Shai began, "Remember when my old bat…"

"You mean your aunt?" Dae corrected him.

Shai continued on as if he didn't notice, "…when we were like nine and she was retelling one of her boring stories about the old times and she mentioned something about a Blood Bond, the same thing Nomad mentioned later? Do you remember how it worked? Wasn't it something about sharing blood or pinky swearing or something and then there was like this *mystic link* to each other forever after that. You remember?"

Dae held his tongue till Shai was done, "Yes, I do."

"Well, how'd it work?"

Dae explained it as he remembered, "Hmmm, I think they said you have to ingest it for it to work. But they didn't know how much. Then no matter where that person is, you can somehow connect to them. They also warned our kind has to be careful though because our blood can be fatal to others. Keep in mind how the story ended."

Thia threw caution to the wind, "Shai you're a genius! Let's do it!"

"Whoa, wait a minute. How did this even come up?" Dae asked.

"Thia was worried about you leaving and us having no way to know if you got in trouble and then it just popped in my head", Shai explained.

"We don't know if it will actually work or if it is nothing more than folklore." But Dae caved once he glanced over at Thia and her hopeful eyes, "But I guess we could give it a try."

"Well here's to only one way to find out." She ran out of the room and came back with a needle from her mini emergency sewing kit. "Okay, who's first?" and at that she pricked her finger.

They all took the needle and did the same then stood there.

Shai laughed at Dae, "Dude, I'm not licking your finger"

"Oh come on!" Thia chided. "Just do it, real quick!"

He starred almost cross eyed at Dae's finger for a second, "Nah, I can't."

"ggrrr!", and she left the room again. This time she came back with a small glass half filled with grape juice. "Here, prick your fingers again and dip them in here fast before they heal. Then we'll all take a drink. This juice is so strong we won't even taste it. Better?"

Shai thought about it, "Yeah I guess, but no back wash! Never mind, gimme that thing, I'm going first." They did as she said and stuck their fingers in the juice, stirred it up a bit and Shai took a drink. Dae and Thia watched him in anticipation.

"Anything?" Thia asked.

He waited expecting something, "Nope, nothing."

"I'm doing it anyway." and Thia took a drink then handed the glass to Dae. He too drank from the glass and finished it. They all were careful to take equal amounts stirring it before drinking.

They stood there expecting, some hoping, but there was nothing.

"Well that was gross and worthless." Shai declared and plopped down on the couch and turned the TV on.

"I didn't know you guys had heard the story before. So what else happened? "Thia asked.

"What do you mean what else happened?", Dae asked.

"You said *keep in mind how the story ended*. What happened? How'd it end?"

"Oh. It was a lot like Nomad's version except she said that the human that tried our blood, thought because we age slower that it must be something like the fountain of youth."

"Wow, I wonder how he found out about us."

"That part was never explained but I would guess the Pallas had something to do with it. They too have been around a long time."

"Yeah, I guess so." Thia was disappointed, "I really wish it worked. Maybe we didn't use enough? Should we try again?"

"No, I think we used plenty. Don't worry, I will contact you with regular updates once a week."

Thia's stomach sank, "Once a *week*? How long do you plan to be gone?"

"I am not sure Thia. I hope not that long. I just need you guys to hang tight and be extra careful until I get what I need. Alright?"

"No, not alright, Nomad said we are to stay together." Thia was going to fight it as much as she could, trying to convince him not to go, especially alone.

"I know T, but I am less noticeable alone and I can't take a chance in endangering Thomas and Sarah. That wouldn't be a very nice way to repay them for all their help."

She didn't like it one bit but knew he was right. She also knew she wouldn't be able to talk him out of it, so she let it go.

She wasn't sure why but she felt a new sense of peace take over. She was calm now, much calmer than she normally would be in this situation. Maybe she was learning to trust in her brothers after all they'd been through, knowing they were both tough and smart and could handle just about anything.

So that evening Dae ran off just after dark with just a small bag. He didn't bother taking his car. Cars can be bugged. She wanted to know where he was going but he wouldn't say. He explained it was safer for all and supplies deniability. You can't tell someone something you don't know.

A couple nights later Shai and Thia were sitting in front of the TV watching a horror movie when Thia turned to Shai, "I have a huge craving for pot roast."

Shai's eyes got wide, "Me too! It's like I can already smell and taste it. My mouth is actually watering. We just ate and I feel like I am going to explode, but now I'm hungry too."

Thia's eye went wide, "Me too! How can that be?" Then Thia's tone turned sad as she sat back in her pillow packed oversized chair, "I wish we could call Dae, he would know."

Shai missed him too but tried to comfort Thia, "I know, he'll be back soon." Then he thought of something, "Hey I have a date tomorrow night with that girl I met at the party the other day. She said her brother thinks you're cute. I'll set you up! At worst it'll at least take your mind off of things."

Thia laughed, "A blind date? I don't think so, but thanks anyway."

"No, not blind, you met him too. They were both at that party. I'm pretty sure I caught you checking him out."

"Oh, *that* guy?! Hmmm" she thought it over remember how good looking he was. "Yeah, what the heck. But not a double date."

Shai fully concurred, both somewhat sickened by the idea, "Agreed. I'll let her know."

The next night came fast for Thia especially, *God, I haven't been on a date in forever. I hope he's not weird.*

Shai was heading towards the door, "So when's he coming to get you?"

Thia was just sitting there, "He's not…"

Shai cut her off, angry, "Did he stand you up?!"

"No, no, we are just meeting at the restaurant. I have a few minutes to kill before I have to leave."

Very relieved, "Oh. Alright, I'm out. Good luck T!"

"Thanks, I'll need it.", she mumbled.

"Nah, you'll be fine."

"I hope so. The last one didn't go so well."

"Huh? Oh yeah! Ha ha, I forgot about that one. Yeah, guys don't like it when you show them up in sports. Good thing you are just going out to eat this time."

"Yeah, I guess so. See ya."

Taking one last look with adjustments in the mirror by the door, "What no good luck for me?"

"We both know you don't need it.", and she winked at him as he waved and left.

Thia took a deep breath, also made sure everything was in place, picked up her purse and keys and headed out.

The night began well, all parties but Shai a bit nervous. They ate and decided things were going so well they would extend the evening and catch a movie. Thia thought it would be safe knowing Shai was going to see one but they were in different parts of town so they would probably not run into each other.

Both movies began and the couples were content, that is until Shai's slightly tipsy and overzealous date decided she was more interested in getting to know him better rather than watching the movie as her hand slid down his thigh.

"Hey!" Thia slapped her date, on the arm, remembering at the last second not to hit too hard.

The guy looked surprised, "What? What'd I do?"

"You just grabbed my leg." Thia explained with accusing raised eyebrows.

"Huh? How could I? I've been holding this cup the whole time.", as he lifted up the cup.

Thia sat back both embarrassed and puzzled, "Oh, sorry. I swear I felt something." So she looked around but there was no one anywhere close enough to have done it.

He put the cup down in the holder, "It's okay. Hey, I have to run to the restroom. I'll be right back."

"Okay" she watched as he left. "Yeah, he's not coming back" she rolled her eyes and whispered to herself.

But five minutes later he did return, also bringing with him a heavy cloud of mouthwash and cologne. Thia held her breath right after it hit her for as long as she could then took a breath. *I can't take it.*

Shai and his date were kissing until he suddenly backed away with his hand over his mouth and nose, "What *is* that?!"

His date looked shocked and hurt, "What is what?"

"Oh, that smell. Did someone just spray really strong cologne in here?"

"What are you talking about? I don't smell anything."

Thia started sneezing after taking another dreaded breath.

Shai started turning green, "I think I'm gonna be sick." And he ran out of the theater. His date followed him.

Thia turned to her date, "I'm sorry but I need some fresh air. I think I may be allergic to your cologne. I'm so sorry. Thank you. I had a nice time."

Her date just sat dumbfounded as she left.

Thia went home, driving with the windows all the way open, hoping to get the smell out of her clothes and hair. When that didn't work she hopped in the shower to get it off then got cozy on the couch in her sweats to watch a movie. She took advantage of her brothers not being home and found a good romance flick. Thia then day dreamt of being on a date with the star of the movie instead of stinky man. It'd been a long time, if ever, since she'd been held and kissed right.

Shai and his date were in his car outside her house...kissing again, making up for running out. As he kissed her, she suddenly turned into a man before his eyes and he jumped back hitting his head on the rearview mirror, "What tha.."

"What now?" she yelled at him.

He blinked and the man was gone, "I...nothing." And he slowly pulled her close again. But before he got to her lips she became the movie star again. He sat back in his seat staring strangely at her, "I...I'm not feeling well. I have to go."

"Fine!" she yelled as she got out of the car. "Weirdo." And she slammed the door shut.

Shai pealed out messed up by the whole thing. When he got home he looked exhausted and confused.

Thia was still on the couch watching the movie, "You're home early."

"That's him!!!" he shouted and pointed at the TV.

Thia jumped, and held her chest where her heart just about jumped out of, "Him who, what are you screaming about?!"

"I was kissing him!" Thia's eyebrows dropped down like she couldn't have heard what he just said. "I mean, it wasn't him it was her, but she looked like him." Shai spat out trying to make sense of it.

Thia's brows went up, "Oh, wow, that's not right. You hooked up with a girl that looks like a man?"

"No. It's...hard to explain.", and he sat down in defeat rubbing his forehead from the on setting headache.

"You think that's bad? I had a ghost feel on my leg while we were watching a movie and I hit my date for it."

Shai was still half out of it, "A g...wait, what?" Then it all hit him like a ton of bricks, "Oh...no, no, no. You think that bond thing worked after all?"

Thia gasped, "Oh my gosh, I bet you are right! Dae must have been having pot roast for dinner that night...and you were the one getting...ick, never mind."

Shai squinted at Thia, "Were you kissing the TV or what...oh. But worst of all was that smell..."

Thia embarrassed, "Yeah, that was my date after came back from the bathroom. I couldn't hold my breath anymore so I told him I was allergic and had to go."

Shai's stomach turned from the memory of the scent, "Man, I'm glad you did, that was bad! Ha, someone was getting ready to make a move."

"Oh, the mouthwash? This bond thing is not all it's cracked up to be. I'm getting a little too much information. We need Nomad more than ever now. What are we going to do with it? You think Dae is feeling...", and they both jumped when the phone rang.

"Dae", they laughed in unison.

Shai answered putting Dae on speaker, "What's up brah?"

"You two need to not date until we figure this thing out. I'm getting way too much over here."

They all laughed and agreed.

Thia chimed in a little disappointed, "I think I am done with humans all together. We're just too different."

"And it's too risky." Dae added,

Dae came home shortly after that with little new information. It wasn't a wasted trip though since he had a chance to see his friend again and now had a new challenge to tackle with the discoveries of The Bond.

Days went on, Dae disappeared in his room on his PC doing research, Shai was out and about being at least a little less rowdy and Thia was planted in the living room sucked into reading a new Saga series that just came out. Before they knew it, it was Halloween. Thia, happy as can be had their home decked out in all things Halloween and setup the massive bowl of candy ready for any that came.

Her cell rang. She had a feeling and was right, the display said it was Dae, "Hey T, I'm heading to county to pick up Shai. We'll be home soon."

"Okay, I'll keep dinner warm. Be careful." she hung up and waited for them, flipping through the channels for a classic Halloween movie.

An hour passed and there was no sign of them yet, *something's wrong.* A blinding flash and a thunderous boom knocked her to the floor. She immediately sat up to find the house was fine. *Oh, no. County!* She jumped in her car and sped, weaving in and out of traffic, to where her brothers were supposed to be.

When she arrived it was surrounded by smoke, police cars and fire trucks. The front of the brick building had a gaping hole where men were dragging bodies out of.

"A couple are dead from the blast but most are just unconscious from the gas", her heart sank as she heard one officer say to another. "A prisoner we were releasing and his step brother are missing too. Not sure why someone would come for them though. The big one is usually quiet and the other one is just a reckless punk kid."

Thia felt a little better but began to panic realizing who had them. She tried to focus in on them and mentally tried calling them hoping the bond thing would kick in but she felt nothing from her brothers. She was breathing heavy trying to figure out what to do when she instinctively singled out an all too familiar scent. She stole a nearby motorcycle and followed the trail to its source. It wasn't long before she caught up with the unmarked truck and its precious cargo. She could smell the nondescript black metal box on wheels that had her brothers...but not for long if she could help it.

One of the guards dressed in all black spotted her in the side mirror, hung out the window and immediately began shooting at her. She was able to dodge most but was hit once not slowing her down at all. Instead the pain angered her as her body naturally worked to push the shallow item out. Then the truck sped up, pulling away from her. Thia took advantage of the dark empty road and leapt off the bike leaving it skidding and sparking behind her, and softly landed like only cats can do, on the roof of the truck.

She landed so perfectly no one heard a sound. The gunman witnessed the bike go down in his mirror and laughed with pride assuming he got her.

"See they're not so tough." He snorted arrogantly.

She hung over the edge to take a look in the back window. Her brothers were bound and motionless but breathing. Thia then saw two gunmen inside laughing and kicking her brothers while waving the tips of their guns at their heads. Rage immediately erupted in Thia. She dug her fingers into the thin metal like butter and pealed the roof off the truck, exposing about five men with guns in total. She flipped back and clung to the corner of the truck. Again so quietly they couldn't tell where they needed to start shooting.

A few seconds later of letting them sweat it out, she swung up and over the side like a trapeze artist and down into the middle of all of them. Stunned and frozen by her sudden appearance, she worked to take each one down with her bare hands. As she attacked one, two grabbed her so a third could stick her with a needle to drug her, but she broke free slamming all of them into the walls. Then another tried to spray her in the face to knock her out but she used the one behind her as a shield. And the final lone guard pulled his gun but much too slow as she broke his arm and threw him out of the truck through the open top.

Just when she thought she could take a breather to check on her brothers, two of the three in the cab stuck their guns through the little window and let loose. Two struck Thia in the back and leg until she growled, lunged at them and bent the hot tip of the one gun closed and ripped the other free breaking his wrist. She smashed the barrel and threw it out and into the woods on the side of the road.

The driver slammed on the brakes causing Thia to fly into the wall. One arm grabbed Thia by the neck then slid a thick metal cable around attempting to choke and restrain her. It was latched to the inside of the cab and was too short to slide or twist out of. She closed her eyes and screamed desperate to work free but unable to break the thick hook.

A raspy voice spoke in her ear, "My your are a feisty one! You'll fetch a handsome price and probably a promotion."

The sounds in the cab went from three laughing to two gasping and one yelling. Thia opened her eyes to find her brothers on either side of her and their arms reaching in through newly punched holes.

Thia smiled so happy they seemed okay she was ready to cry, "You're awake!"

Dae looked concerned, "Are you okay? Are the hits bad?"

She just shook her head, "No, I don't think so. Did they hurt you?"

"Please!" Shai laughed off the thought and threw the head of the man he held into the windshield cracking it.

Dae then did the same then unhooked the cable freeing Thia. Knowing he was all alone the remaining driver opened the door turned the wheel hard to the right and jumped out. All three looked at each with wide eyes and Shai spoke their thoughts, "That's not good."

Dae yelled, "Jump!"

Shai and Dae just made it out before the truck flipped over but Thia got stuck. One of the guards in back with them grabbed her leg pulling her down. She kicked free and fell hard against the side of the truck cracking a couple of her ribs. Thia's bothers caught up alongside and jumped in to get her.

The truck came to a stop and they all ran out and into the woods for cover before they were noticed.

Dae grabbed onto Thia's arm to support her, "Let's get you back home."

Thia pulled back a bit, "We can't, what if they are there?"

Dae looked at the spots she was still bleeding from, "We need to tend to your wounds."

Thia not crazy about taking the risk, especially on her account, "I don't think they are that bad."

"We will be careful." Dae assured knowing it was worse than she let on.

She gave up and they walked on, "So what did they drug you with? It must not have been very strong, you guys weren't out for long."

Dae had it all figured out, "No, it was stronger than what they've had before. I think *you* woke us up. We could feel your rage and pain. I felt my heart rate speed up as a reaction and I think it ran the drugs out of our systems much faster."

Thia sniffed, "Now that you mention it you are all sweaty and smell funny."

"Yeah, back to the rage thing? *Wow*, are you all like that? Cuz if that is anything like PMS..."

Thia abruptly stopped him, "NO, that's not what it's like!"

They arrived back at the house. With no signs the Pallas had been there, they patched up Thia, packed some things and left, together for a change.

Thia mentally returned to the small town jail. Seeing there were plenty of windows and doors for escape, unlike the solid brick box her brothers were trapped in before, Thia was pleased. *Yes, this quaint little jail will do just fine.*

Homecoming

Dae, Shai and Thia's unexplained natural bond from birth, only compounded once they triggered the blood union. Through trial and error they grow and adjust from the various experiences but never lose who they are inside. Shai, kept up his part in being the fun, outgoing and chaotic element. Dae remained the laid back, supportive, intelligent one. Thia's role seemed to be the glue, cement, or some other indestructible analogy for adhesive found. She brought and kept everything and everyone together, but when all alone, her mind sometimes drifted to her birth family.

She loves her brothers more than anything but still misses her parents terribly. She found her mind would wander back to her mother over all. She too was a quiet being but not in the awkward sense like Thia. She was respectfully quiet and very observant, sweet with the kindest of personalities so that everyone couldn't help but love her. Her beauty was moot after talking with her. Whoever was fortunate enough to have her attention felt special.

Thia's brothers could tell when she was feeling down. Things literally move slower when she is sad. Mechanical devices were the first to go before they figured out what was the cause. They went through a lot of car batteries as they found them drained of all power. Lights fade and even the water runs slower, which makes showering tricky.

On occasion Dae fell in tune with Thia and subconsciously became depressed too. Those times resulted in rain when the forecast called for sunny skies. She felt bad once they figured it out but her brothers were there for all she had been through and understood. They too became very fond of her mother from all the time spent there. They truly were family and it was a serious loss for them as well. She tried to control it but just in case they learned to keep a generator ready, they wouldn't expect the impossible from her. For the most part she was usually either content or in a very pleasant mood.

To keep from getting lonely or restless, Thia starts big projects and gets lost in them. The best is when it's time to make a new place home – just like the new base. She applies all her effort, refusing to think about the probability that this will not be their final home.

She started on the interior. When she was finished no one would ever have known it was an old smelly, dingy, grey converted military cement block in the middle of the woods. She thoroughly cleaned and then painted with bright and vivid colors in all rooms so any light that entered through the small windows filled them. She had thick padding and lush soft carpet installed in each of the bedrooms, halls, and living room, deep golden brown wooden floors for the dining room and large beautiful rustic tiles for the kitchen... at least that is what the rooms are now, who knows what they used to be.

She giggled with excitement when the delivery truck came right on time bringing the larger items. Appliances, beds, end tables and hope chests, lamps, curtains, coffee tables and accents were also dropped off. She generously tipped the drivers and sent them on their way. This is when the real fun starts. The nasty dirty work was done, now to put the rooms together.

A week later the inside was complete. She slowly walked around judging each room and ultimately smiled pleased with the finished product. "Phase one complete. Now for the outside!" she gleamed.

She walked outside, it was a little chilly but not cold enough for a coat. She went about fifteen feet from the front, turned around and assessed the situation. Just as described before, nothing more than a cold looking cement box surrounded by flat dirt.

"Hmmm, what to do with his?" Then ideas started jumping like crazy in her head. She hopped in her rickety jalopy and drove into town looking for a nursery and hardware store. The hardware store she found without a problem. She picked up some shovels, a pick, a ladder, lots of spackle, cement, sand and other stucco ingredients, paint, some wood and nails. The nursery was another story.

They didn't have such things in this part of town. The overly helpful gentleman explained she had to go to "in town" for that kind of fancy stuff. *Funny, I thought this was town.* So she headed back home, unloaded what she purchased and ran out again following the written directions on the brown paper towel to the place mentioned.

Thirty minutes later, "Well this certainly isn't close. I hope it's worth the trip." The car sputters a bit. "Better yet, I hope this hooptie makes it there and back."

She had her windows down just a little for some fresh air. The car smelled as old as it looked. She wasn't even sure they would go back up if she took them down any further. Then a new smell invaded.

I must be close, she thought trying not to breathe through her nose.

Dirt, mulch and fertilizer aromas rushed in from everywhere flooding the car. A moment later she spotted the place and pulled in. It was a decent sized nursery and she was happy as it looked like it had all she would need so she wouldn't have to run around all day. Excitement filled her again impatient to get started. She walked around pushing an overflowing cart piling on more and more as the ideas and plans blossomed from passing displays. She knew she wanted mostly perennials as she didn't want to keep starting over every year with the planting.

As this thought crossed her mind she stopped and felt the sadness hit her blindside. She had been working so hard to fight it off since they parted ways. As temporary as it may be she found peace in her constant projects. *Are we ever going to get to stay somewhere long enough to actually worry about such things?*, she blinked out of it and went back over her new ideas again pushing the bad feelings away. *This is going to be my best one yet,* she decided.

She finished up her shopping just in time for her stomach to growl at her and she felt a sudden wave of weakness pass through. Hours pass like minutes when she dug deep in her planning and shopping, so much so that sometimes she flat out forgot to eat all day. *Wow, I'm actually really hungry. I think I saw a little diner on the way here. I'll stop there on the way back home.*

Driving along she became distracted by the sky. The day started off grey and hazy. The sun peaked through from time to time but it didn't rain yet. She was glad for this as her car was as packed as it could be, or more than it should be actually. Thia doesn't like to make more than one trip anywhere if she can help it. Not to mention she wanted to get started on her outside project as soon as she got home. The nursery promised to drop off the dirt and rocks she ordered later that same day.

Very excited about what she had planned, but knowing she wouldn't be able to do it if she didn't get something in her system first, she found and stopped at the diner. It was a small and old but clean place. Not knowing if it was because of how hungry she was or the amount of butter being used, but the food cooking smelled extremely good and especially fattening. It had been a very long time since the last time she'd eaten anything that smelled this greasy. Her mouth began watering uncontrollably as she drew it all in.

She was greeted by the hostess then escorted back to a small patched up red faux leather booth at the far end and sat down. The waitress, a giggly young and simple girl came to the table. Thia ordered some coffee first to shoo away her yawning. There was still half the day to go and she was determined on getting a lot done if not all before it was over. No time for a nap.

The girl returned with a friendly smile and a heavy country accent, "Here ya go. And what can I get y'all to eat?"

Thia was unsure still looking through the worn plastic menu, "Umm, do you recommend anything?"

"um, the cheese burger's pretty good" she happily replied.

"That sounds really good actually.", again her stomach agreed and mouth began to water.

Geez, I didn't realize how hungry I am, she thought a little embarrassed by the girls surprise at the noise.

"I'll tell him to hurry with that."

As she sat there finishing her meal, the waitress came back and dropped off a piece of pumpkin pie and another cup of coffee.

Thia looking thoroughly puzzled asked, "Sorry, I don't remember ordering desert?"

"No ma'am, the man over there…" just then she turned and pointed directly at him, then waved, "…got it for you. He has us just call him Matt." Then she got down and whispered with a wink to Thia as if it were not an overly obvious move. "Well his real name is Matteus or something. I know it's really weird but he's pretty nice." then straightened up again.

"Oh…how nice." Thia was at a loss for words, mostly stuck on the whole whisper-n-wink fiasco. *Does she actually think he wouldn't notice that…especially after pointing right at him? Wow, this is awkward.* She thought. So she leaned to the side around the waitress and gave a friendly little wave and smile and mouthed the word *Thanks.*

I gotta get out of here.

She dove into the pie, which turned out to be quite good. She didn't want to be rude so she ate it, quickly. Then she got paranoid. *I need to be more careful! What if they did something to it? What if ...no they couldn't have found me already, I barely knew I was coming here. Oh, I can't wait to get started.*

"You're not from around here." an unexpected voice acknowledged.

She gasped not realizing he'd gotten up and approached her table. She was already in her head planning out what to do first. It never takes long for her to jump all in on her garden planning especially when all of her goodies and supplies were right there to stare at just outside the window, hanging out of various parts of her car.

He seemed to feel bad, "I am sorry. I didn't mean to startle you."

"It's okay I was…day dreaming. Thanks for the pie, it was really good." she failed an attempted friendly smile. She really wanted to skip pleasantries and escape as fast as possible.

"Sure, I've heard it's the best around", he stood, not moving and confident.

I don't think he is from here either. Good looking, proper in attire and speech...actually a little too proper there. Like an English professor trying to be cool but doesn't quite have the hang of it? What did that girl say his name was again? Crap. Forget it, this place is weird.

"Wait, you've *heard*? You mean you haven't actually tried it?" *How odd, why would someone send something they've never tried?*

"No, I'm unfortunately allergic to just about everything.", it was strange, every time he spoke it came off very pleasant, no matter the subject.

"Oh" She didn't know what else to say. *Sorry* didn't seem to fit.

"May I", as he gestured to sit down across from her.

"Oh! Sure, sorry for forgetting my manners. But I do need to go soon." she gestured to her car.

He saw what she meant, "Ah, I see. I will not keep you long then."

He began again, "So, you are not from around here? Am I right?"

She nodded as she instantly thought, *here we go.* She has had many conversations recently that started off like this.

"Yes, I am new to the area." She politely responded with a better attempt at a pleasant smile. She had been practicing, but the first time she was caught off guard.

"I had a feeling."

She pursed her lips and nodded.

"You are not going to ask me how?"

"Well, I guess I have to now." She quickly snapped back at him with a raised eyebrow. Then she instantly felt bad. City responses were much faster and dripping with sarcasm, nothing like here. She quickly corrected herself.

"Um, sorry. How did you know?" very embarrassed now.

"It's okay, there is an adjustment period. We city folk tend to stick out in places like this."

She half smiled agreeing with this comment, "Yeah, I suppose we would."

"I must apologize; I don't do this very often and am afraid I am out of practice. I haven't properly introduced myself. I'm Matt.", and he held out his hand with a gracious smile.

Thia shook his hand, "Matt? Not Matteus?"

He was a little surprised by her correction, "She told you then?"

"She did." She let out a stifled laugh, "You didn't notice?"

He laughed, "I did notice her pointing me out to you, yes."

Thia straight to the point, "So which do you prefer to go by?"

He cocked his head not used to the getting the option, then smirked, "I guess that depends on who is asking."

She shrugged her shoulders, "Okay, let's say I am. What would you like me to call you by?"

He studied her for a moment, "What is your name if I may ask?"

"Ha! A Dodger fan are we? Okay, I'll play. I'm Thia", she studied him back. There is definitely something attractive about him, beyond appearance.

He was completely thrown off by her comment, "A fan...Oh! Very good!", and this time a little chuckle escaped him. Thia sunk deeper into him helplessly drawn in by his warm smile. But she could help but laugh at his almost childlike ignorance.

A little uncomfortable, unsure how long she had been staring, she laughed, "Uh, thanks. Been away from sarcasm that long, huh?"

He, still very focused on her name, "So, just Thia or is it short for something?"

"It's Thia", she smiled coyly.

"It's a beautiful name." He hesitated, "Very well then. For you I am Matteus."

Thia blushed a little. His wording made her feel special but awkward at the same time so she did her best to squirm her way out of it. "For me huh, or rather my city folk *kind*?"

He smiled catching her sarcasm this time, "Yes, your...kind."

"Very nice to meet you Matteus." She said politely.

"It's all my pleasure Thia", then he gently took and kissed her hand.

Red rushed her face, not expecting the sudden depth of his charm.

"Starting a garden?" he suddenly changed direction.

Thia followed his lead working her out of the daze, "Yeah, we bought a new place not far from here. It needs some work, a lot of work. But the town we moved to doesn't have a nursery so they sent me here. Where are you from?"

"North of here." was all he divulged.

"Okay, that's pretty...broad!"

"Yes, I...travel a lot, so it is difficult to call anywhere home right now."

"Ah, nothing apprehensive about that." She said with a sarcastic smile. She couldn't help herself. She was getting a little impatient and untrusting now. People that talk like that are hiding something, then again he is good looking. *This is taking too long and he is a bit too vague. Can't get involved, there is much to do. I've spent enough time here now to pay off that pie.*

"Well, I'd better be going." escape now the goal. He isn't going to play fair then she was finished playing.

"How about lunch?" he quickly but confidently counter offered.

She sat stiff not sure what to say.

…awkward silence…

"I will not be offended if you choose not to. I just, I thought I could show you around, if you'd be interested." this time with a charming smile.

Still unsure of him and not willing to gamble, "I don't really go out much."

"Maybe you would if you had the right tour guide."

He made her struggle internally; *I have to admit I am tempted. I mean, it couldn't hurt to get to know the area a little better, right? No. I need to get back to the house so it's ready for when Dae and Shai come home. We'll explore once they are here.*

"I really can't. I have a lot of work to do over the next few days. Perhaps another time?" that last part slipped out faster than she could stop it.

He kindly accepted, pushing no further, "Absolutely. You know where to find me."

Thia was confused, "Uh, not really…you don't mean here?"

"Yes", he simply confirmed.

"You spend a lot of time here?"

"I come here often enough."

"Okay. Thanks, I might just take you up on that, later." the reoccurring lack of common information exchange bothered her again.

"I certainly hope so.", again with a magnetic smile.

"Okay, see ya." She gathered her things and left.

Thia arrived home faster than she thought she would but couldn't remember any of the drive. It was like the car was on autopilot. Her mind was consumed by him and their strange conversation.

With renewed energy, she unloaded all of her new treasures. She started on the outer front part of the building. She worked for hours mixing and applying the stucco to the whole thing. Once it was finished she let it dry and would paint it a pastel color later. Next came the part that she knew would make the most difference, decorative trees, shrubs, flowers and plants.

She dug, mixed and planted through the rest of the day. It steadily became colder the darker it got, but she never really noticed keeping busy trying to finish. She hadn't even realized it was the middle of the night by the time she decided she was at a good stopping point.

She yawned and again stepped back to take a look at all she had accomplished. The soreness settled in her muscles but still she smiled as the picture in her head was coming to life right in front of her. She then went in, took a hot shower and melted in her new and extremely comfortable bed in her beautiful new room. For the first time in weeks, she slept very well that night.

Maybe a little too well she thought waking up around noon. Feeling refreshed she prepared and devoured a big breakfast and dove back into her renovating again.

A very long awaited week later Dae came home. Thia being considerate and observant knew which rooms each would enjoy the most and how they would like them to be decorated, or rather equipped. This happened to be one of her favorite challenges. And it paid off. Dae was very happy with what Thia had done for him. That day he too especially appreciated the new bed. Traveling was long and exhausting.

Shai was the last to arrive. Both Thia and Dae smiled with joy once they heard him pulling in with a revved up truck this time, big red and build like new with all the extras enhancements and modifications of course. But that wasn't all, he brought something else.

This time he brought presents with him. In the bed of the truck were three perfectly shiny new crotch rockets. Thia and Dae heard each other's hearts jump at the sight. They knew which was for who, red for Shai, black for Dae and sparkly purple for Thia. He pulled up next to her car, took one look at it and a huge smile spread across his face. She smiled just as big back knowing the fun he was going to have, and the fine car she would end up with.

Hopefully I'll get to keep it for a while this time, she thought as her smile slightly faded.

They ran out and Thia attacked him with a big hug.

He hugged her back and laughed, "Where'd you find this piece of crap?"

She shrugged her shoulders, "Some old lot. It runs."

They stood in front of the house before they went in. *Our new home.*

Shai still looking around taking everything in, the house, woods, old car, "T, what made you pick this place with the little nowhere town and converted military base?"

Staring at all her work, then back at them, a little worried now that he didn't like it, "You said it would be different this time. So I'm helping it along."

He smiled remembering he did say that and shook his head, "I have to admit, you did good. I would've never guessed this was something else before."

"Thanks! So what's with the new toys?" Thia pointed back to the bikes spotting the new sparkle in Dae's eyes.

"This idiot was practically giving them away! It pays to know mechanics. There was hardly anything wrong with them so I got them cheep and fix them up. I'm sure you can figure out which one's yours."

They were all happy to be together again. Thia had them come in so she could conduct the tour then serve dinner so Shai could get settled in and finally rest on a full stomach.

Thia escorted them down the hall, "And this is your room Shai."

Shai's room was all about speed, covered in race cars and bikes. She painted the walls cherry red with black accents. She plastered the latest and hottest up and coming cars all over the walls, with the bikini models too, rolling her eyes the whole time.

"This is great T. I especially like the posters." Shai gave her a hug and took his bags in.

"Something told me you would."

Dae's room was a bit more relaxing. She made sure he had a giant work area and plenty of book shelves for his various collections.

Thia's room was soft and dream like. Twinkle lights on the ceiling, lilac walls and plush white carpet. Her mattress was the kind that molds around the body like a cloud.

The day was coming to an end. The cars and bikes were safely parked in the massive and well equipped garage. They had a good feel for where everything was, put all their things away and had a nice home cooked meal.

They all crashed in the living room to unwind surrounded by the fresh smell of leather from the brand new couches, mixed with burning candles and the faint left over smell of paint. Both brothers weren't able to fully relax though. They could feel something was off. Not new place off, but Thia wasn't sharing something, off.

She avoided their suspicious stares for as long as she could trying not to think about the very thing she couldn't stop thinking about. *No need to worry them*, she justified to herself. She wanted them to get comfortable and feel at home. But they were too distracted at this point. She could tell their attention was not going to be swayed.

"There was a minor incident, okay?!" she blurted out knowing they would ask at any moment.

"What happened?" Dae asked concerned.

"I was good", she took a stab at what he was probably asking about. "There was a guy, drunk, wandering around behind the dive bar next to the hardware store. I only noticed him because I just missed him as he staggered out the back."

"What were *you* doing there?" Dae followed up.

She answered, "My usual get-to-know-the-new-area rounds.", then continued to explain.

The vision of that night came to her. They were together again and back in tune so they somewhat saw it too.

Dressed in a simple jump suit she walked around the small dark plaza. The loud music and thick odor of stale cigarette smoke mixed with beer repulsed her, very close to the point of gagging, so she quickly headed around to the back. Before the fresh air was able to cleanse out the stench, she heard the back door slam open and a burly scruffy sweaty man backed out yelling obscenities to someone inside.

Thia jumped out of the way before he could see her and hid behind the door. She watched as the sloppy man slowly staggered over to his car and miss getting the key in the door five times before giving up and sitting on the ground. He then laid his head against the car and began to snore.

Thia was about ready to come out from behind the door and move on until she spotted a small pack of large wolves exiting the woods just behind the bar and head towards the defenseless sleeping drunk.

Awe, come on. I have to defend that? she thought quite disappointed.

She didn't move at first to see what the wolves had in mind. The wolves kept an eye on the noisy man, growling and quietly barking to each other as they got closer and closer.

That's odd it looks like they're talking to each other. Not to mention they make them big out here, Thia thought as she continued to observe, not yet ready to reveal herself to them. She wasn't looking for trouble but would act if needed.

The lead wolf stopped short as the second and third continued on. Then one of them crouched down and then so did the other. The lead just sat and watched.

This isn't good.

The moment the aggressive one of the two started barring his teeth Thia quickly confirmed there would be no possible witnesses, let out a warning growl, startling all of them and stepped out from the shadows. The drunken man was still snoring loudly. The wolves all straightened up and looked at each other.

Thia continued to walk towards the man to get in a better position to the animals still too near him. The wolves watched. She stopped at the man's car and climbed up on the hood and sat with her legs crossed. The wolves were clearly unsure on what to make of her. They again chattered back and forth and then the aggressive one slowly advanced.

Again, she made sure no one was looking, and there were no cameras to catch her. Then with not much room between them, she sprung high in the air off the car then came crashing down to the ground in front of the man with such force it up heaved a cloud of dust from the dirt parking lot. The aggressive wolf jumped at her as the others howled. She caught it by its chest holding it stunned in the air for a bit then whispered to it, "I don't want to hurt you but will if I have to.", and threw it into the dumpster against the wall padded full of garbage bags and rotten food.

Embarrassed, the wolf climbed out and headed in her direction again. The lead wolf gave a stern bark and he reluctantly stopped.

All the noise roused the drunk and the wolves ran off back into the woods, "Hey what's going on?"

He grabbed Thia's leg and she pulled away in absolute disgust, "There's nothing going on. You are drunk and stink. Go home."

Back with her brothers she finished up the story, "He couldn't even stand up. I was so aggravated by him and his smell that I didn't even want to wait to see if the wolves would return, so I broke his door open, threw him in, jammed it shut and left. See not so bad, just some wild animals and a drunk."

Dae gave up, "Yeah, I guess. I'm tired and going to bed. Good night guys."

Shai was tired too from traveling, "Yeah me too."

And they all slept sound the first night together in their new home.

Thia dreamt that night, remembering Nomad's lesson #1 – Always stick together. And that they did and she would continue to do no matter what. Where they went, she would go, even if it could mean their last goodbye. She would never leave their side just as they had done for her. In their most desperate times they had each other. If either of her brothers end up chasing the dark, she will be there too pulling the other. If they are on a cloud nine, she'll work to kept them there as long as she could sustain. She takes pride in the belief that it is the woman's place to be a pillar of never wavering support. Behind every strong man is a strong woman. She had two to cover.

Support, it's such a feeble word for such an imperative and thankless task. Yet she is all but too glad to realize it. He brothers had done the same for her in her darkest times.

Though she picked up the keys shortly after she arrived at their new home, she had no desire to visit the place that would soon be their cover for income. But now that the house was in order and her brothers were at long last home and settled in, it was time to go see what they were in for.

Thia had copies made of the keys and handed one to each of them. In turn, Shai too happily handed out keys. They all hopped on their beautiful new bikes and rode off. It was a quick ride, considering how they drive, Thia leading the way.

As they pulled in Shai began to laugh, "Just what I expected"

"What?" Thia asked surprised.

He shook his head as he crossed his arms, "A broken down old western saloon looking thing. All that's missing is the swinging doors."

"Oh come on, it's got potential, it'll be great!" trying to sell him on the vision.

They sat parked in front of their new eye sore, catching the eye of everyone that passed by.

"Motorcycles must not be common in these parts", Shai added with a smirk and a twang.

"It looks...sturdy" Dae said trying to be supportive.

"Really guys! All it needs is a little landscaping, some paint, a touch up here and there..."

Shai cut her off, "Have you even been inside yet?"

"...no, I was waiting for you guys. It can't be that bad." She said hopeful.

"We'll see." Shai turned to Dae, "Care to do the honors?"

"Sure."

Dae turned the key and opened the door. They were instantly hit with an overwhelming assault of stale beer, cigarette and urine.

Holding her breath, "I'll get the windows." as she stepped in to open up the place.

Shai was next to go in, "I'll get the back door. We are going to need to hose this place down with bleach. Hopefully that'll kill the smell. Or we could just burn it and start over. That might be quicker and easier."

Thia was able to get a few of the windows open and Dae worked on propping the front door open. Shai walked around the bar to see if any goodies were left, but it was all cleaned out, "Awe, no welcoming gifts?"

Then a rat flew out the open door.

"That's not what I meant."

"See, once we clean it up, it won't be half bad. We can reuse a lot of what is in here."

They agreed most everything just needed to be sanded down and refinished. The tables, chairs and bar were built well and sturdy. The style was plain enough that they could work with.

"We will need new lighting." Shai mentioned looking up at the old flickering florescent lights. Just then they surged. Both Shai and Dae knew what this typically meant.

"What'd you find Thia?" Shai asked for both of them.

Thia got excited the moment she saw it. "A stage guys! This is perfect! I knew I had a good feeling about this place."

So for the next two weeks they spent hours, day in and day out cleaning and repairing. Dae and Shai first got the new lighting in. Once they did that Thia was able to take over on the inside while the boys moved on to the outside. Dae was up on the roof patching. Then fixed some of the outer wall holes and finally worked on painting. Shai finished moving the furniture outside to be worked on then spotted the sign.

Shai stopped, "Hey guys, what are we calling it?"

"Hmm, Good question." Dae took a break and sat on the porch next to Shai.

Thia came out with a tray of some fresh lemonade and tuna sandwiches.

"Wow Thia, you're fitting right in." Shai said sarcastically.

"When in Rome?" Then she stuck her tongue out at him.

"Mmm", was all they heard from Dae once he got started on his sandwich.

"I didn't really give it much thought." She hesitated, "Well I did have one come to mind but it was stupid and would probably give us away."

Shai could tell she was a little embarrassed by it, so he couldn't help himself, "What was it?" Shai blurted with a huge smile on his face. He could barely sit still now.

"No way, I'm not telling. I already told you it was stupid."

"Oh, now I can't wait! Spill Thia!"

"Fine, just to get it over with – Paws"

Shai thought for a moment disappointed. "Awe, that's no fun. It's not half as bad as I thought it was going to be. Kind of girlie though. Give me something else. I really wanted to laugh at you."

Thia laughed, "Shut up jerk! That's all there is. So let's come up with something."

They all sat consuming their drinks and sandwiches thinking in silence.

Thia was staring off then casually suggested, "The Haven" Then she braced herself and looked at Shai out of the corner of her eye waiting for her persecution.

He hesitated, mulling it over, then finally spoke, "T, I like that one! Like it's an escape from their boring, boring lives."

They all laughed and nodded in agreement. They finished up their lunches and got back to work.

The Date

Finally, it was the last day of finishing touches. Thia ran out in Shai's truck, after much reassuring him that she would be very careful with his *baby*, to pick up some remaining items like food, kitchen supplies and stock for the bar. She'd been a bit clumsy that morning.

The stores in town didn't carry all they needed and she hates running all around so she went to the next town to get everything all at once. Thia was perusing the beverage isle, holding a bottle of wine when a voice out of nowhere startled her...again.

"Hello." It was Matteus.

She jumped and dropped the bottle which hit the hard lament floor and smashed into several large pieces.

Matteus felt terrible, "I must apologize, I did not mean to scare you, again."

"No, that's okay. I'm not sure why I am so jumpy. I think I'm a little off today." She admitted as she bent down to pick up the larger pieces. Nervous and eager to clean up the mess before much attention was drawn, not paying enough attention herself, she quickly reached for a large piece of the bottle. "Ow!" she pulled her hand up to find she'd cut her finger on a point of the glass.

In a split second Matteus gently cradled her hand, "Allow me" and he placed her finger in his mouth to clean the cut.

This took Thia's breath away for two reasons. His hands were cold like he'd been holding a jug of milk too long, but more so he is charming, so unexpectedly breathtakingly charming.

When she looked a little faint from his trance like effect, Matteus slid his arm around her waist to secure her. Even if she wanted to, she could say or do nothing. Her eyes were still fixed on his lips until they slowly wandered up to his eyes. She fell even deeper in his arm realizing how close their faces were now, sharing the same breath. Then a loud maintenance man at the end of the isle hurried to their side to begin cleaning the mess. The abrupt appearance and noise brought Thia back too and she stepped away, suddenly embarrassed.

Attempting to restore a light mood and her comfort, Matteus commented on Thia's selections, "Must be quite a party."

As soon as she caught her breath she looked down at the remaining bottles in her arm. She spoke slowly still in a daze, "Actually we, um…my brothers and I, are opening our club soon so we are trying to get everything ready. You should stop by."

"Interesting." Was all he offered in return.

Her brows furrowed, "Okay, I'll bite. What's *interesting*?"

Matteus laughed a suspicious laugh and finally answers, "I didn't really see you as the club owning type."

Her daze cleared by his comment she chose her response carefully, oozing with sarcasm, "Surprise!"

"I wonder what other surprises you have for me." His voice took on a suggestive tone.

First her face dropped, then she couldn't help but blush. Matteus just smiled. Thia noticed the pleasure he enjoyed at her expense and became irritated. She doesn't appreciate being manipulated. Matteus felt the sudden shift in the mood.

"I've overstepped. Again I must apologize, I do not mean to be rude." He was back to charming now.

Thia, not knowing what to say just turned and tried to return her focus to shopping.

"I must admit to you, I've never had to do so much apologizing to a single person before. Please allow me to make it up to you. Some friends of mine are having a small get together tomorrow night at a nice place not far from here. I would be honored if you would accompany me as my guest."

Every part of Thia froze, even her breath. *What...is he? What is his deal?*

Once she started breathing again, "I guess it's only fair that I admit something to you." She turned and looked him straight in the eyes. "I often find myself at a loss of words with you." Fell out of her thoughts and right through her mouth. Then her heart dropped once she realized what she'd just openly admitted.

He seemed to be in a hurry now before she had a chance to decline, "May I take that as a yes then? Shall I pick you up around eight?"

Eight? "Don't people around here normally eat at six or so? I meant the whole town shuts down around ten."

"I suppose the normal ones might." He glanced over to the man still cleaning then leaned in close to her ear and neck so only she could hear, "But something tells me we have more in common than I initially thought."

Intrigued by his comment and fighting the distraction of his proximity, "How so?"

"Club owners tend to be night people. I too am a night person." he replied very matter-of-factly.

"Ah" she had a lost look in her eyes. *Is this really happening?*

"So is it a date then?" he confirmed in his tone.

The word *date* brought back her attention.

"Ah, yeah, okay" she said in a daze. *What am I doing?! I can't go out with him. I don't even know him...* her mind ran off in a thousand directions.

He smiled, "Very well then, tomorrow night at eight. It was a pleasure seeing you again. I very much look forward to tomorrow."

Anxiously she blurted out, "What do I wear?"

He chuckled, "Don't worry about that. I'll take care of everything."

Just then, as if something had hit him, he placed his hand on his chest, took a deep breath looking a little confused and flush. He quickly composed himself, nodded to her and left.

Hey, why's he taking off so fast? Actually, he looked a little red, maybe he isn't feeling well? Wait, what does he mean he'll take care of everything? Geez, I have no phone number, no way to get out of this. Oh, what have I done? Shai and Dae are gonna freak.

She took a deep breath trying to calm herself then checked her cell for the time. *I better get back. Shai is so going to have fun with this.* So she finished up her shopping and headed back to the club.

While she was putting everything away she kept thinking to herself, *I'm not telling them. I'll make something up! Who am I kidding? They'll see right through it, I'm such a bad liar, especially to them. I have to stop thinking about it before they notice.* Shai was too busy working on finishing the last adjustments on the sound system to notice how nervously Thia was behaving. He was fighting with some static he was getting, not yet putting together that it might have been caused by Thia. She was able to calm down and force the impending situation out of her mind. The static faded away. Shai sat up proud believing he'd fixed it with his mad rewiring skills.

Dae brought in the refinished furniture he had been working on all day. He was on his way back out to grab another chair when he found a man at the door with a gift wrapped box in his hands.

"Hello, is a Miss Thia here?" the man said with a heavy French accent.

Dae studied the man, "Yes please come in."

"Thia" Dae called for her.

She stood up from putting glasses away behind the bar, "yeah?"

Who's that? She thought once she saw the man with the fancy deep purple package and a huge platinum bow on top.

"Bon jour madam, I have been sent from Monsieur Matteus Farra. He sends you this gift."

Oh no! She thought now panic stricken but also quite surprised, *Man, he's quick!*

"What's this sis?!" Shai suddenly appeared at her side with a very wide smile.

Great, here we go. Defeated she took the package and thanked the man. She attempted to tip him but he wouldn't accept.

"Oh madam I couldn't possibly. Thank you." He bowed his head slightly and swiftly departed.

Shai started in on her without delay, "Who's this Matteus? You've been holding out on us!"

"It's nothing really yet. He's this guy I met a little while after I got here. I stopped at this diner on the way back after shopping for the house and he bought me pie."

Shai was almost in her face with anticipation, "Ooooh! Do go on."

Thia wanted some space so she headed to the bar to set the box down and sit.

"I ran into him again today at the store and he asked me..." she hesitated knowing what was coming. "He asked me if I wanted to be his guest at a party tomorrow night."

"You're going on a *date*?! What have you done with our sister? Ha ha! I knew you had it in you, old girl." And he sat down right next to her.

"Gee thanks, and how about you quit talking to me like I'm an old horse. I'm sure you remember I have been on a date before....smelly guy?" she was not enjoying his taunting enthusiasm and decided to take a stab back at him.

Of course, patience not being one of Shai's virtues completely ignored it and pressed on, "Well open it!"

"No"

"If you don't, you know I will." He threatened as he reached for the box.

"You drive me insane, you know that?" And she proceeded to open the beautifully wrapped package. It was a large and deep box. She pulled the top off and pulled back the silver tissue paper.

"Wow" fell out of her mouth after her jaw dropped. Her brothers behind her were also speechless.

In it lay a perfectly folded simple yet exquisite shiny black dress matching purse and pair of high heel shoes. Shai snatched the shoes.

"Have you ever even put something like this on before?" as he turned them around in his hand.

"Shut up! Of course I have! What do you think I wear at the club! Are your hands clean?!"

She put the box down on a nearby bar stool and lifted the dress out of the box. It was the most beautiful thing she had ever seen. Not only did it look it, it felt super expensive. It was a short spaghetti strap cocktail dress with flowing vertical ruffles all around the top and the rest plain and gently form fitting.

"Go try it on!" Shai was even happier bathing in her torment than when he was when he thought he fixed the wiring.

Dryly she asked him point blank, "Why do you enjoy torturing me?"

He pushed her to the bathroom, "Oh, come on. You know you want to!"

"Fine", she folded as she took the box and its contents to the bathroom.

She sat the package on the counter in the bathroom and looked in the mirror. Only a dirty frumpy looking girl stood before her. *Oh my, is this what I looked like when he asked me out? Maybe he needs to have his eyes checked. I wouldn't ask me out.*

So she cleaned up a bit, threw her hair up best she could and got dressed. Once she had her shoes and the dress on she turned again to see how bad it was. But it wasn't what she'd expected at all. She felt beautiful. The dress was snug but comfortable. It fit her every curve and laid on her perfectly. It was like the dress was made just for her. She even liked how the top of the dress didn't point out that she wasn't very well endowed. Actually it somehow had the opposite effect. Feeling kind of good now it was time to go see what her bothers thought.

"So what do you think?" then she braced herself waiting for the worst of it.

Again she was surprised. When her brothers saw her they said nothing.

"Well? Be honest.", again she cringed.

Dae broke the silence with an endearing look. "You look great."

"Yeah?" she smiled. He helped her feel a little less self-conscious. Then she slowly turned to Shai waiting for his flood of mockery.

"Tell us about this guy. He certainly knows how he wants you to look for his little party. What are you, his little dress up doll? ", Shai's big brother instincts had completely overtaken him and he was now demanding information on this stranger.

"Where's he from? What's he do? How old is he? What's he look like? Where does he live? What does he drive? Where are you guys going?" Dae had joined in and they were hitting her non-stop digging for information.

With a sign of relief she was willing to do her best, "Stop, stop. I don't really know too much about him."

"Apparently he as money judging by that outfit and its arrival. Hey, how did he know what size you are?! How much time have you spent with him? Don't hold back on anything T. We need to know what he wants.", again they couldn't help themselves.

"I told you everything, I swear! I have no idea how he knew."

"I wonder if he does this a lot." Shai suspected out loud.

Thia threw her hands up, "Thanks Shai, way to ruin it for me."

Shai was in no mood, it was all business now, "Seriously, what do you know about him? We can't have some nut job kidnapping you."

"Ha ha! I highly doubt that is the case. Besides, I'm pretty sure I could hold my own against some random *nut job*."

"That's not the point. We don't doubt you could. Just give us something more to go off of." Dae pleaded.

She furrowed her brow, "Mmmm, let's see. He's super polite...but kind of sneaky."

Shai reacted to the last part, "Sneaky, I don't like that. What makes him sneaky?"

She knew then she shouldn't have mentioned it, but it was too late now, "I don't know. It's funny but I never hear him coming, or going for that matter. He's just there and then not sometimes."

Her brothers look at each other, concerned.

Shai started shaking his head, "I don't like it. You need to back out. There are plenty of nice hill folk out here for you to choose from. Sure they can't buy you nice dresses and shoes but what would you need them for anyway?"

"Oh, stop it." She hesitates, "Besides, I can't."

"Why not?"

"I don't have a way to reach him."

Again they looked at each other very uneasy about what she was wrapped up in.

And the last bit of information she didn't want to give, she gave, "Look, you guys can meet him tomorrow. He's picking me up at the house at eight."

Shai couldn't believe what he was hearing. "So he knows where you live but you can't even get a phone number from him?"

"No, we didn't actually exchange that type of information."

"So how's he know where we live?"

Dae got this one for Thia, "Shai, it's a small town. Everyone knows where we live and where the club is." Thia nodded.

Father Shai was not letting up, "Oh, right. Okay, why so late?"

For the first time in this interrogation she agreed with him, "Yeah, that's what I asked. I guess he and his friends are night people?"

Shai even shook his head like a disapproving father, "Thia you really know how to pick them."

She had no idea what he was talking about, "What's that supposed to mean? He's the first that's ever outright approached me."

"Not the first Thia." Shai said quicker than he wanted to.

Dae instantly knew what he was referring to, "Shai, Caleb doesn't count. She didn't ask for that."

Shai prepared and proving his point, "I don't mean who you pick but who you attract."

"That doesn't make it any better. Drop it." Dae warned Shai.

"Guys, just talk with him tomorrow. I gotta get out of this stuff before I get it dirty.", so she headed off to the bathroom.

"This isn't done yet Thia", Shai informed her.

"I know.", but she kept walking.

Before she changed back into her work clothes she took a long look in the beveled full length mirror she had Dae install in the renovated women's bathroom. She turned and posed and played with her hair trying to decide how to wear it. When she was done dreaming she neatly put everything back in the box including the pretty paper and bow then headed back out.

Gratefully her brothers were already back to work and nothing was mentioned about the date the rest of the time. Once they were sure everything was just as they wanted it, they finished up and headed home. Thia wondered why it wasn't brought up on the way home but certainly wasn't going to be the one to start anything. She decided they were probably too tired now to argue. Besides, there is all day tomorrow for that.

The next morning Thia slept in a little longer as she assumed her brothers did from the long day of work they'd just had. Deciding to get up she got dressed and walked down the hall toward the kitchen, thinking about what to make for breakfast, when she heard Shai shout to Dae.

"I can't find anything on him. You said the card spelled it F A R R A, right?"

The boys were already on the computer trying to find out anything they could on this Matteus Farra.

"You guys are something else." was all she could say.

"We're just looking out for you." Dae justified.

"I know. And I can't wait to return the favor when your times are up." She said her attitude more sadistic as she passed.

Now that the club was ready for business, they knew the next step was picking an opening date and getting the word out. So Thia made some flyers and the three of them scattered the promotional material everywhere they went. The local area was covered but they made sure they hit the surrounding areas too. Dae and Shai worked on the clubs web site.

They spent all day advertizing and were good at it, calling radio stations, newspapers, posted on the club site as well as general list and blog sites. Being unfamiliar with small town people, they weren't sure what kind of turn out they would have. Regardless they made sure it wouldn't be because people didn't know about it.

Finally Thia's long dreaded evening was fast approaching. So she slipped away to get ready for the big night. She showered, did her hair and makeup and put on her fancy new dress. She grew more and more nervous winding up like the clock she watched as the all important number eight sped up on her.

"Thia! Calm down, you're messing up the TV", Shai yelled from the living room.
"Sorry!" then she took a deep breath and tried to relax.

"Thaaanks!" he shouted confirming the it worked and the TV was fine again.

It hit eight o'clock and the doorbell rang. Thia's her heart instantly sped up. *Not eight already?!*

Matteus was right on time. Both of her brothers answered the door inviting him in.

I better get out there before they attack him with a million questions. She thought as she checked herself over one last time.

She walked into the living room to find all of them strangely sitting in silence, "Hi!"

Matteus, with much style and grace, instinctively and immediately stood up signifying a lady had entered the room, "Good evening. You look beautiful, better than I imagined."

She blushed, "Thank you very much for this." she shyly glanced down to her outfit. "They're amazing." Then she started to feel awkward with her bothers there.

"Would you like something to drink?" she offered assuming her brothers hadn't thought to ask.

Matteus politely declined, "No, thank you. Your bothers already graciously offered"

With half a smile she turned to her bothers both surprised and proud of them.

"Can I assume you've also introduced yourselves?"

"Yes" Shai said sneered back at her.

"Okay then. Shall we go?"

"Alright" Then Matteus turned to her bothers, "It was nice meeting you."

They simply nodded at him and watched.

Thia grabbed the matching purse and turned to her brothers, "Dinner is in the fridge". And they left.

Like a perfect gentleman he opened the door of his black shiny car for her. Suddenly self-conscience about being graceful, she slowly sat down. Luckily she caught it in time before falling into the highly expensive, low sitting car like she normally does. Thia glimpsed in the side mirror as they pulled away confirming her suspicion that Dae and Shai were watching them leave through the front window.

In the silence, she started imagining what they might have said or asked him before she came out, "I hope they didn't badger you too much. Sometimes they can't help themselves."

His eyes never left the road, "It's quite alright. If I had a sister, I would want to know everything about her visitor too."

"So what is the name of the place we are going?" Thia gets uncomfortable in a quiet car and remembered she was supposed to get better at getting information out of him per a promise to her brothers.

"It's called The Red Lounge." his eyes ever scanning their surroundings.

"Oh, I've seen that one. It's right on the edge of town, yes?"

"Yes that is the one."

"Um, not to be rude, but aren't we a little over dressed for there?"

Matteus awoke from his over attentiveness to the environment and laughed, "Oh, we won't be out in the common area. There is a private room. Ah, before it slips my mind." He reached into his jacket and pulled out a small box with a bow.

"Oh, no, no, I can't possibly accept..." but he cut her off.

"Please, I insist. It is just a small token."

"You do too much." Very uncomfortable now she slowly opened the box. It was a silver necklace with a large pink teardrop stone, with matching earrings and ring, all of which seemed to be producing their own light to sparkle like a star in the sky.

Thia's jaw dropped, "Small?"

"I wanted to thank you for coming with me tonight.", he said sweetly.

Still in shock, "And you didn't think the dress and shoes were enough?"

"It was the least I could to for imposing so last minute."

"Ha, the least you could do, yeah." she couldn't help but stare at them. Purple actually being her favorite color, the soft pink and accent diamonds were no less than breathtaking.

Thia, in a humble tone, "Thank you. Can you take them back after tonight? I can't possibly accept all of this. It's too much."

"I'm afraid not. They are yours now to do with as you wish." And that was the end of it.

She put the earrings and perfectly fitting ring on and gazed at it. Again she wondered how he knew what size to get her. She wanted to know much more about him. She had her own questions as well as some of the ones her brothers hit her with at the club but couldn't bring herself to ask just yet. She didn't want to come off intrusive considering he'd given too much already.

Before she knew it they were there. They pulled in to the parking lot, through the front then over to the side and parked next to a number of expensive cars already there. It was a small stand alone building that resembling a petite winery in the middle of nowhere.

He shut off the car, turned to her and motioned to the box still holding the necklace, "May I?"

She gave him the box and he helped her with the necklace. His close contact set her heart racing.

He sat straight in his seat, taking her image in, "You are simply stunning."

Overwhelmed and feeling like a manikin on display, she shyly smiled back and looked down. *All of these things, now this place and his friends yet we still know nothing about each other. This is not me, not me at all. He had to have seen this. Why did he ask me?*

He sat back concerned, "Is everything alright? You seem to be drowning in your thoughts."

"Sorry, I'm fine, just not so good at these kinds of things." Then for the first time she looked him straight in the eyes, "Please promise me you will let me know if I embarrass you in front of your friends." She half laughed, "It's sure to happen."

Her unexpected direct gaze and gentle smile affected him as his breathing deepened, "I do not think it is possible."

Attempting to shake the onset of nerves, she playfully corrected him, "Don't be so sure. You don't know me yet. You'll see."

"Very well then. Shall we?"

She nodded and reached for the door out of habit until he stopped her, "Please, allow me."

"Oh, right. Told ya.", so she quickly pulled back her hand and sat back in the seat.

He opened her door and offered his hand. She took it feeling like a princess in an old movie, and stepped out. He closed the door behind her then slid her hand under and around his arm. For the first time ever, with any man, being at his side and holding his arm was the most comfortable place in the world. *Mmm, this is nice.* At this thought she unintentionally pulled closer to him as she looked around learning the new place. She didn't see it but he was very pleased by the gesture as a slight smile appeared and he too held a little tighter.

He opened the lounge door for her and they walked in. He escorted her through the front room full of people sipping drinks and loud chatter. By this time the common patrons had been there a while and were feeling pretty good. The bar on the left had bottles of every shape and color imaginable. The tables full of people on their right one by one, turned and looked as he guided her through. Her grip tightened disliking the added attention.

"Why is everyone staring at us?" she asked in a low voice.

"Surely you know locals by now. They notice new and different people."

She turned her focus to straight ahead trying to ignore them, "Right, seems a bit rude."

He reassured her, "We're almost there."

They came to what looked like a large closet at the end of the room with coats hanging on either side and a floor length mirror.

We're going into the closet?, she thought.

As they got closer, the small wall with the mirror opened up and they continued through.

That was cool, she thought with a childlike joy, until she saw what awaited them on the other side.

"Matteus!" an older sophisticated man called out as he grabbed and aggressively shook his hand.

The room was full of them, High class society. She immediately preferred going back to the other side of the mirror.

The introductions began, "Giles, I would like you to meet Athena."

Her grip on Matteus tightened even more to the point her knuckles were almost white, but she forced a smile and presented her hand, "Nice to meet you".

She didn't like going by that name. The enemy knows that name. *Come to think of if it, how does Matteus know that name? Dae or Shai must have told him? Weird, that's not like them.*

Giles took her hand and kissed it. "The pleasure is all mine." Then his eyes moved down from her face, "My, what a beautiful necklace." But Thia was distracted. The man seemed strange to Thia. It was like he was moving in slow motion. His wide eyes barely blinked. His hand movements were slow and precise. Even when he spoke, every word was very deliberate.

"Um, thank you. It was a gift." She looked up at Matteus's face, hoping to find some comfort. He looked back at her with a warm grin that made her feel much more at ease. Her hand loosened, returning color to her knuckles.

Matteus brought her in further to meet more people. All appeared to be forcefully polite failing to hide their blatant prejudice. Their body language confirmed Thia didn't belong. Thia can read body language as good as Dae. A few of the women looked confused, then appalled as he proudly escorted her around the room keeping in constant physical contact with Thia on his arm.

After she met just about everyone it was time for dinner. Everyone sat around the long table decorated in fine linen, china and crystal. Matteus pulled out Thia's chair for her then sat beside her. Next the plates of food came out with a stream of mouth watering aromas following. Thia had to keep from staring as she was quite hungry by now.

Thia was surprised to find all of the meat on every plate coming out was extremely rare. When her plate was placed in front of her, it was a colorful salad with grilled strips of chicken on top.

Matteus leaned in to her, "I hope you don't mind but I ordered chicken for you. I hope you like it."

"Thank you. It looks wonderful." She looked around but no one was touching their food yet so neither did she. The rare steaks looked so good to her. It'd been so long since she and her brothers had gone hunting. *I need to get a grill for home. Mmm, rare seared steak,* the thought appeared as a dream to her.

Matteus leaned in again to her and whispered, "If my food is unpleasant for you to be near, please let me know."

She looked over to find one of the rarest.

She let out a little laugh. "No, it's fine".

Shocked by her reaction, "You mean you are not repulsed by how rare it is."

She looked in his eyes and tilted her head finding his shock cute, "No, not at all. My brothers and I don't believe in ruining a quality cut of meat either."

He continued to speak very low, "Yet again, you surprise me." For once she caught him at a loss. This pleased Thia and she wanted to enjoy it as long as possible for it too was rare.

Giles spoke up singling Matteus out, "Matteus, I can't remember the last time I've seen that look on your face."

Matteus quickly looked up at him shocked, then caught himself and relaxed his expression.

Giles behaved as if nothing happened, gave a half smile and spoke louder continuing on to the real reason for his announcement, "Thank you all for coming. Birthdays are truly a special occasion for celebration. As you all know we are here to celebrate our dear friend Matteus."

Everyone politely clapped and smiled then toasted in his direction.

Thia's jaw dropped as she turned to Matteus in disbelief.

Once all of the well wishing died down and eating begun, Thia leaned over to Matteus and whispered, "It's your birthday and you didn't tell me?! On top of that you bought me all of these things...for your party?"

Matteus said nothing and continued eating.

Dinner was over and everyone moved over to the bar socializing. Giles and another man, Thia couldn't remember his name, asked to have a word with Matteus. He looked to Thia for approval and she sheepishly nodded to say of course. They took him to the other side of the room to have their discussion. Thia found a small group of open bar stools next to her and sat down.

"May I get you anything?", the bar tender offered.

"Could I just have some water for now?"

"Of course." And he brought it to her. She politely thanked him unlike the rest that just ignored him.

She looked around, taking in the different choices in decoration when she heard a group of three ladies speaking in a low tone on the other side of the bar. Normal ears could not have heard it but Thia's are far from normal. She listened, careful not to look at them.

"Why did he bring her?" the brunette started.

"Yes, she's very awkward." the redhead added.

"Doesn't he have plenty of women of his own kind to choose from without needing one of the locals to toy with?" the blonde stated.

Thia rolled her eyes and tuned them out. She couldn't help but smirk a bit from her thoughts, *Snooty but still catty like all the rest. If only they knew*, she thought. *Forget them, if only he knew!* At this realization she glanced over at the men.

She became concerned as their conversation didn't appear to be a light one. Matteus wasn't very happy either considering it was his birthday. The other two men's backs were turned to her so only Matteus noticed her concern. He gave her a quick comforting smile that she returned and then turned away, embarrassed he noticed, to have some water. Before she knew it he was at her side.

As usual she jumped in surprise, "Oh, hi. Sorry I wasn't trying to be nosey but is everything okay? You didn't seem very happy over there."

"I received news that some," he hesitated, "family members are coming to visit soon." He looked away as he spoke of them.

Thia noticed but chose to respond differently, "Oh, that's nice."

"Not really." He admitted faster then he meant to. "They tend to cause more trouble than they should."

"Oh, *that* kind of family." She smiled understanding what he meant.

Perplexed by her reaction, "You are familiar with this?"

She shrugged her shoulders, "You could say that. Shai has been known to get a little unruly at times. It would seem he can't help himself."

His disappointment faded as he became pleasantly intrigued, "I see."

Despite the topic she was happy she now had him talking. Perhaps now might be the perfect opportunity to start asking questions without appearing nosey. *But what to ask? Where should I start?*

Then something random she noticed came to mind, "Why do all of your friends have such old names?"

He thought for a quick moment, "I am not sure. Maybe we attract our own kind?"

Thia laughed at the ridiculous comment, "Really? I am not your kind. You have to admit, I don't exactly fit in here."

Without missing a beat, "You too have an old name."

"Yeah, but…hmmm." She was stuck.

He proudly smiled at her knowing she had nothing to come back with.

She laughed, "Okay you got me."

He pulled her closer to him, "Do I?"

She looked up, deep into his eyes. He was close now, very close. She knows for certain now that she likes him, his smile, his touch, the way he talks and carries himself with a modest but powerful confidence. For the first time ever she is comfortable. She very much likes that he is closer now. And now that he was closer she found she also likes the way he smells. He didn't have overpowering cologne on like most that have money like to bathe in. As it was, he didn't have anything on.

More than anything she wanted to wrap her arms around him and lay her head on his chest. She wanted to kiss him on the cheek and softly wish him a happy birthday. But she did neither. All she managed to do was smile and look down at her hands which were fidgeting with her nails. She found a sliver of courage and was able to lean her bare shoulder into him. He smiled again pleased by her gesture and in return gently wrapped his arm around her slowly pulling her in a little tighter. She'd be happy if this moment never ended.

The night went on as the group became much more relaxed and having fun, laughing louder, hugging more and frivolous toasts popping up everywhere. Still Matteus stayed at Thia's side the whole time in constant affectionate contact. He didn't stop holding her as various people stopped by to talk with them and bestow birthday wishes.

Only one thing distracted Thia from fully enjoying the evening. She could just about feel the displeased looks from members of the party that unapproved. The distain was escalating, but she said nothing and tried not to pay attention as she was sure he hadn't noticed them yet.

"Another toast!" one of the men cried out. "To Matteus, for finally making it interesting."

Thia smiled with the others. Then when she was sure no one could hear, asked Matteus, "What does that mean?"

He finished his polite laugh, "Nothing really, he's just drunk."

Then one of the sneering girls spoke up, "In bringing such a savory..."

Before Thia could clearly hear what the girl had to say Matteus scooped her up, "Thia I didn't realize how late it was. I should get you back home. I wouldn't want to anger your brothers."

She was completely caught off guard and confused, "Wha...no, it's okay. It's just starting to get fun and it's your birthday."

"Leaving so soon?" the very same blonde girl from the group before appeared in front of them, faster than Thia thought possible, much like how Matteus does.

Matteus's grip around Thia tightened around her waist pulling her in close and slightly behind him. His embrace was exhilarating, but she could tell something was wrong. His odd behavior was making her a little nervous now even through her infatuation with him.

He attempted to go around her, "Simone, as a matter of fact we were just leaving."

The girl saw how tight Matteus's hold was on Thia. She slid in front of him and stroked his face. "Oh Matteus, don't be ridiculous. It is your pet. She can't possibly be your mate."

"Besides, we've spent no time with your…little friend." Simone looked Thia up and down.

Thia's eye brows went up in disbelief, *Little friend, It, pet? This girl is unreal.*

In a very low and controlled tone Matteus made an effort to get her to stop, "Simone, perhaps you've had too much to drink..."

She cut him off, "DO NOT try to embarrass me in front of the clan." she hissed at him and the room went silent.

Clan?, Thia wondered. *Now I am sure of it. She is not right in her head. She is taking this upper class thing to a whole new and unhealthy level.*

Matteus very unhappy now looked over to Giles for assistance but he was already on his way.

"Simone. Might I have a word with you?" Giles politely but sternly interrupted.

She sneered at Matteus.

"Of course." she said coolly turning to Giles.

"Come." Matteus grabbed Thia's arm, keeping her close, and swiftly headed for the door.

They were almost to the car when he noticed some patrons outside whispering and staring at them. Matteus then realized how fast he was walking and slowed down. Once they reached the car, he gently pulled her close, glanced back at the door then looked her in the eyes. She was silent only looking back at him. Though she was ready to fire off the growing list of questions building up in her mind at him, it was evident to her he desperately wanted to say something important, so she held her tongue.

She waited a couple of seconds but the suspense proved too much for her, "What? What is it?" she asked as her eyes searched his. Deep down she wanted him to know he could tell her anything.

Then he started finally finding where he was willing to start, "Thia, please accept my most sincere apology for the way tonight turned out. I would very much understand if you didn't want to see me again," he hesitated, "but I must be desperately honest with you and admit I pray this is not the case. Please know, even with the small amount of time I've had with you, you are very special to me. I cannot yet explain it, but it is the truth."

She stood shocked by how open and vulnerable he was suddenly being. Tonight somehow turned out to be a giant leap in the depth of what they were.

Not wanting to lose momentum on their progress and being quite honest herself, she wrapped her arms around him and gave him a big warm smile, "I can assure you that is not the case."

With a deep sighed of relief he hugged her. Then he kissed her head, looked back at the club entrance and opened the door for her.

He sat in the driver's seat and put the key in the ignition but did not turn on the car. He turned to her, "I hate to ask another thing from you but I find I cannot help myself at this point. I've been more open already than I've ever been with anyone. I don't want tonight to end, at least not like this. Would you mind terribly if I take you somewhere else?"

"I would like that very much." She found she cared about him more than she should so soon. Maybe it was simply curiosity, but she believed it was more that kept her interest in him, something she too was unable to explain it. All she was thinking now was how his birthday was ruined and she wanted to do what she could to make it better.

"So where are we off to now?"

"I don't believe much else is open so I thought our favorite meeting place might be nice and relaxing."

"Okay, sounds good."

Some silent time passed as they both replayed all they'd just been through.

Matteus was the first to break the silence, "May I ask you something?"

"Of course."

"When we were leaving, the people outside were staring at us. Do you know why?"

Hoping he too couldn't see right through her poor lying skills, "Oh? I hadn't noticed."

"I think they may have been surprised at how fast we appeared to be moving. I have a tendency to walk very quickly on occasion when I am in a hurry. I couldn't help but notice you had no problem keeping up."

"Hmmm, I guess I tend to walk fast myself." *Geez, note to self, I need to pay better attention to that.*

The silence resumed, as both thought more on the event.

They arrived at the diner, where they first met and went in. The waitress greeted them and took them to their seat.

"May we take that one?" Matteus requested one of the more private booths against the far wall.

"Sure" and she seated them.

Thia's phone beeped from at text message. She answered it back.

"Am I in trouble?" Matteus playfully asked.

She laughed, "No, they're just checking in."

The waitress took their initial orders for water and left.

"I hope you don't mind this seat. I thought we could use a little privacy."

"Not at all, it's perfect."

Neither were sure where to start so after some time Thia thought she would just go for it and just ask what kept popping up over and over in her mind. After the water came Thia spoke up, "So what did your friend Simone mean by *clan*?"

Matteus thought for a minute, slightly distracted, "Ah, we are an old fashioned family and use old words."

Then Matteus countered, "You are certain I wasn't walking too fast for you?"

"Yep", Thia ended that line of questioning more abruptly than he did hers.

Neither were getting anywhere with their questions, nor did they know where to go next. Thia was disappointed by how things were going. Regardless she very much wanted the holding from before, but there were no signs that was going to happen, especially with a table between them now.

Thia decided to try taking it back to the basics, "How do you know all of them? I know you call them family but I got the feeling they are not actual blood relatives?"

Matteus seemed grateful for the new line of questioning, "You are correct. Giles is like an uncle to me. He and my father are close friends."

"Where is your dad? He wasn't there was he?"

"No, he lives far from here and I believe is off traveling. He doesn't usually stay home long."

"Your mother goes too?"

"No, my mother passed away when I was born."

Thia felt terrible, "Oh, I'm sorry."

"She was a lovely woman from what my father has told me of her. And what of your parents?"

"Both gone. My mother …they both died a few years ago."

"I am very sorry for your loss."

"They too were great people."

"I believe you. Children can often be a reflection of their parents."

Thia blushed, "You are very kind. You give wonderful compliments and gifts. Tell me, is it always so one-sided? Do you ever receive or take?"

He adjusted himself, uncomfortable by her question, "In my younger years I took more than my share. Now it is my time to give."

Thia shook her head, "I don't believe it. You are not the type."

Matteus bowed his head, "You must simply trust my honesty then."

"I don't see how? How could you have taken so much as you say?" Thia pursued.

But Matteus would not give, "That is a conversation for another time."

"Right.", she was a little frustrated and it showed. Then again she wasn't trying hard to hide it. "So, what *will* you tell me about you then?"

Matteus did not like to see her upset, "I am sorry. I do not mean to be so closed off, especially with you. There are sensitive parts of my life I *will* share with you in time. Please believe me, I don't ever want to hide anything or lie to you. So I ask that you try and understand, if you ask something and I avoid it, it is because I am unable to answer it at the moment."

Thia shook her head, "I don't get it. You act like you are in the secret service or something. Help me understand how I am supposed to get to know you then."

"Spend time with me.", he answered quickly with a smirk.

His charm almost succeeded in diverting her but she wanted answers more than anything right now, "Aren't we spending time now?"

His curiosity blocked out what she said, "I must figure it out."

This only frustrated her, "Figure what out? And why are you dodging my question?"

He gazed in her eyes, "Why are you so magnetic and addicting?"

She refused to be swayed, "You really can't tell me anything, at all right now?"

He dropped his head, "…and persistent. Very well, I will try, for you."

She was suffocated with questions, "And why do you keep saying that?"

He straightened up and started off more stern, "Quite frankly because I don't answer to others, I am not accustomed to explaining myself."

"Excuse me! So why am I so special? I am no one, and didn't approach you. By all means if you don't care to explain anything to me then don't bother.", and she started to get up to leave.

Unbelievable, I knew it was too good to be true! she thought about to storm off.

He gently grabbed her wrist, "Please don't go. The last thing I mean to do is upset you."

She could tell he was upset so she took a deep breath and sat down but didn't look at him and said nothing.

He released her hand, "It appears I am in need of some further adjusting. I don't intend to come over rude. A better way to put it would be that we keep to ourselves and don't really have the need to interact much with others. As for your other questions, I cannot explain why you are different, just that you are. I find the experience both intriguing as well as frustrating. From the moment I saw you, I had to know you."

Thia said nothing but her angry expression softened.

"Now for the information you rightfully desire. Let me think, I grew up in Europe. As you've noticed, my family and their friends are very close and accustomed to behave a certain way, so when we moved here years ago, it took adjusting. Some of the older people, around when we first arrived, do not care for us because of this."

"Why did you say, *my family and their friends*?"

"You are a much focused listener. I've found this to be a rare trait in your gender. As mentioned before we don't mingle much. Because of this I do not get many opportunities to establish my own friends. You could say it is somewhat frowned upon, betrayal being the greatest of risks. Long ago my family line almost ended due to such treachery."

Thia yawned, "I'm sorry, that's terrible. Oh, and sorry for yawning too. Today began much earlier than I am used to." *Do I tell him that I can relate? No, it's too soon. Not safe yet.*

"You do seem tired. Would it be alright with you if we continued this another night, presuming you have not given up on me yet?", he reached out for her hand.

She placed it in his, "I would like to see you again."

Matteus dropped Thia off at home. Thia, knowing her brothers were still up gave Matteus a hug, wished him a happy birthday and went inside. Matteus drove away.

Then it hit her, *Crap, I still have no way to get a hold of him! I'm so bad at this.*

She awaited her game of twenty questions but her brothers were too tired so they all went to bed. The next day she did not escape so easily.

The Club

It was almost opening day so they wanted to send out and post a few more flyers as reminders. Thia took the ones left over and went to the popular places she could think of like the mall, various shopping centers, libraries and even telephone poles at traffic lights.

On her last stop at the nearest mall to home a group of boys shouted some rude and suggestive comments at her. She heard something but wasn't paying attention too focused on last minute preparations for their big day.

"Ha! She didn't even notice you!", the one boy poked at his friend.

"She *will* this time." And they followed her giving in to the made up challenge.

He tried again, this time much more aggressively, "Hey! I was talking to you!"

Thia heard him this time realizing she was the only one in the area. She glanced back at him, became annoyed and kept on her way. She didn't intend to acknowledge the ignorant boy, it was more of a reaction.

This aggravated him and made his friends taunting worse.

Now that her surroundings had her attention she heard another set of footsteps...*sounds like another...man*, approaching from the other side. *This will be fun.*

"Hello", he said before she had a chance to see who it was.

But once she heard his voice her guard dropped. She was very happy to find it was Matteus, and surprised she heard him this time.

"Hey" she said back with a little grin, absorbed in his charm. She turned and they hugged. His arms wrapped around her like a perfectly secure blanket. The boys following her continued until both Matteus and Thia broke from their embrace and turned to look at them at the very same time with the very same cold stare. They stopped dead in their tracks as it sent a chill down their spines how unnaturally synchronized they were. Snapping out of it they high tailed in opposite direction.

"I was hoping I would see you again." Matteus admitted bathing her in his appeal.

"Well, here I am." she said with a big childlike smile.

He checked her hands, "What are you doing here so late all alone? I see no bags. Didn't find what you wanted?"

She showed him a flyer, "No, not here to shop. We are just reminding everyone about the opening. We have no idea how many, if any will show. A few seem suspicious of us. So I thought I would spread the word out further hoping it might help. I was just heading back."

Consumed by what just happened more than her motivation for being there, Matteus wondered, "You know most women would be afraid or at least nervous by what just happened, yet you seem only annoyed?"

She struggled to come up with something convincing. This being something she is not good at, "I've taken some self defense classes. I'm confident I could hold my own if it came to that."

Unconvinced, he questions further, "They were large and three of them to your one. What if they used their size and numbers against you?"

Stubbornness being her only ally at this point, "Nope. Still could take 'em."

He couldn't help but be amused by her bullheadedness, "You never cease to amaze me, dear Thia." A little more serious now, "Still, you need to be more careful. Some may be stronger or more clever than they look."

She took a breath and held her right hand to her heart, "Oh my, you know, you are right."

He stood back, intrigued to see where her thick sarcasm was taking them.

"Thank you for the advice...*dad.*"

Then she broke with a smile, "What are *you* doing up here so late?"

"Ah, yes. I am on a hunt to find the perfect gift."

Thia shook her head, "Always giving. So, what's the occasion, maybe I can help?"

They started walking, "Well, you see there is this new club opening up soon, and I wanted to …"

She stopped, instantly on to where he was going with it, "Oh no you don't!"

She was already over her head in his generosity. She was not used to receiving gifts as it is, much less getting used to the feeling of being spoiled.

She grabbed his chin and pulled it close to her, "Just show up, and that will be gift enough."

Then a thought interrupted the perfect setup for a kiss, "Though we are the staff so I won't be able to spend much time with you. We did recruit that nice waitress from the diner."

"A familiar face, how nice. How did you manage to do that? She's been at that little diner from the start of her working career."

"You would be proud, I was very cunning. I mentioned how much she might make in tips. That and she said she could keep her day shift there so you won't have to miss her after all." Thia winked.

Then concern took over her expression, "Hey, promise me you won't buy anything? You ruin me too much as it is."

He held her hands, "I'm afraid I cannot do that Thia, for I cannot help myself.", and kissed them.

An elderly couple passing by appreciated their affection.

Thia's voice dropped to a whisper, "No, please promise me? We are not used to such things and though it is very nice it can at times be uncomfortable."

"Oh, I do apologize. The last thing I wish is to make you uncomfortable. Very well I promise."

She felt bad, "No, that's not what I mean. I have no idea what you like. I…just can't return the favor."

Matteus released her hands and held her face, "Thia there is no favor. If you only knew what your attention alone means to me, you might demand much more."

Taken back by the depth of his response, all she could say in response was, "No gifts then, yes?"

"Very well if you wish it", he kisses her forehead.

"I'm sorry but I do. Thank you.", she hugs him.

Suddenly aware and very uncomfortable by how deeply he affected her, she backs up and diverts the mood by playfully handing him a flyer, "Here you go, in case you forget."

"I doubt that is possible, *however* I'll be sure to spread the word."

"Thanks, we appreciate it."

He straightened up, "Considering I am no longer shopping for a gift, what are your plans for this evening?"

She thought for a moment, "I guess my plans just ended."

"So you are free now?"

She couldn't help but be honest with him. He seemed to pull it out of her, "Yeah, this was my last stop so I guess I am."

"Will you do me the honor of coming to my home so I may cook for you?"

Her insides jumped with excitement. *I don't even know where he lives much less have even been there. Wow. Today is turning out not so boring after all.*

Realizing she hadn't answered him yet she smiled and just said, "Uh…sure."

Matteus gave her a ride in his car to her bike in the other parking lot. It was very dark out now but she had no problem following him there.

She tried to pay attention so she could remember the way but it was difficult with her thoughts racing, *What am I doing again,* she thought. *On our first date he just dropped me off at the door and took off because he didn't want to move too fast. Now I'm going over his house so he can cook for me? I wonder how this night will end. I better let Dae know I'll be home late.*

They turn down a stamped stone driveway. The black iron gate opens automatically and they drive through. It's a long driveway leading to a large old beautiful house. Matteus pulls up to the front and Thia parks behind.

Matteus walked back to her, "I must admit, I was concerned but you ride well."

"That'll teach you about doubting me.", she smiled as she hooked her helmet on the bike.

He gestured to the house, "Welcome to my home." Then he escorted her in.

They stood in the foyer. Thia was frozen in awe at the small mansion.

He took her jacket and hung it up in the closet, "Would you care for a tour?"

"Okay", he took her hand and showed her around, last stop the kitchen.

As he cooks for her she stood against the island looking a little uncomfortable. Matteus, getting good at reading her, sets the spoon down and walks over to her. He wraps his hands around her waist, lifts her up as if she weights nothing and sits her on the counter top. She giggled feeling silly but it worked. He had a feeling after visiting their house a few times that it would help her be more comfortable.

After dinner he took her by the hand, "Come I want to show you something."

They walked out the back through the kitchen, "My very own private escape."

Lit only by the bright moon, they followed a path of beautiful stones through an arch covered in flowering vines with a wall of tall hedges on either side. Once through the arch it opened up into a secret garden of flowering trees and bushes in full bloom. In the middle was a crystal clear pond with a small waterfall that contained every color fish imaginable.

"Oh, it's beautiful!" Thia said in awe as she slowly spun around taking it all in, almost dancing like the falling pink and white petals in the sweet perfume of a very large cherry blossom tree.

Matteus affectionately watched her, and when he could take it no more stopped her pulling her into him.

He looked deep into her captive eyes, "Thia, I adore you." and kissed her.

Thia melts in his perfect arms as if they were a mold made just for her. He holds her close and she him. Her whole body and mind buzz with exquisite warmth, enjoying his lips, so soft and absolutely faultless. The moment could go on forever as far as she is concerned. Until now she'd never known such bliss. Then there was a faint but funny noise. It sounded much like...*purring*?

Realizing it was coming from her, Thia jumped back slightly pushing away and gasped in a panic, "Oh, sorry"

She thumps her chest and coughs, "I...I've been a little congested. Allergies I think."

He pulled her close again this time meeting her forehead with his, "No, Thia I am the one that must apologize. I know it is no excuse but when I am around you I am not myself."

Both stood still embarrassed for their own and very different reasons.

He continued, "I beg of you, please do not leave yet. I promise I will better control myself."

This is not what Thia desired but she could think of no way to admit this to him without it sounding bad. So she simply agreed, "I can stay a little while longer."

"Thank you. Come, I want you to see something else. I think we are just in time." And he again led her by the hand under the center most breathtaking cherry blossom tree. There he sat down and gently pulled her to sit on his lap and look out from under the tree. It was very dark now. Then one by one little lights twinkled on and off.

"Lightening bugs!" Thia felt like a kid again. The show was magical. There they sat holding each other. The night was perfect with the fragrant flowers softly filling the air, sounds of the soothing waterfall and chirping crickets, the sky clear and full of stars and…the doorbell.

"That's odd, I'm not expecting anyone." Thia attempted to sit up but he squeezed even tighter.

"You don't want to see who it is?"

He buried his nose in her hair, "No, just the opposite, I wish for them to leave so I can be here with you."

She smiled, pulled his arms tighter around her and laid her head back on his shoulder. He sighed full of joy that she wanted to be with him. They both closed their eyes, dreaming in the moment, all once known troubles - forgotten.

"Ah you *are* home you naughty man!" Both Thia and Matteus jumped at the unexpected greeting from Simone barging in through the back gate.

"I was in the area and saw your car out front so I thought I would stop by to make sure everything was okay.", she lied oozing with fake concern.

"How very considerate of you. I am well thank you." Matteus politely but dryly replied.

Thia feeling like it was time she should go, especially remembering their last encounter, again attempted to sit up but again Matteus gently pulls her back into his wonderfully welcoming embrace. Though feeling a little awkward still, she relaxed against him understanding despite the unexpected and seemingly unwelcome company, he was not yet ready for her go. They both had longed for a moment just like this. He was determined not to let her ruin their time *again*.

As Simone paced around the garden rambling on about her day, Matteus nuzzled Thia. With his nose buried again in her hair, he inhaled.

"Intoxicating." He whispered so only Thia could hear.

Thia turned to the side and sunk even deeper in his arms and pushed her cold nose into his neck. Normally Thia would be very considerate of those around her. She didn't want anyone to feel uncomfortable due to her actions. And she had noticed Matteus didn't seem himself. Typically very proper, tonight he was ignoring his surprise guest and supposed friend. Tonight both were so drunk with passion it half felt like they were still alone.

"I'm sorry, what was that?" Simone actually did hear him and seemed annoyed.

Thia was shocked, *how could she have possibly heard that? There's no way.*

"Oh, nothing", he sighed.

"Say I'm a bit parched, let's have a drink, shall we?" still dripping with unconvincing kindness but careful not to acknowledge Thia's existence.

"Of course." He was not happy but his manners hadn't completely abandoned him. Still he kept a firm and caring grip on Thia's hand as they all went inside to the social room.

Simone turned to Thia and asked while looking past her, "Dear, would you mind terribly if I take a moment alone to speak with Matteus?"

Thia fought not to crunch her eyebrows as she wondered what the heck she was looking at, "Of course not."

Matteus did not want her to leave, "Don't go anywhere. I need to talk to you about something."

"Okay"

He gave her hand a little squeeze, "Promise"

She tilted her head and snuck him a smile, "I promise."

"Ehem" Simone was growing impatient standing by the kitchen entrance.

"go" Thia urged him in a whisper trying to free her hand.

He reluctantly followed Simone to the kitchen. Thia didn't bother looking at Simone's expression, for she knew it would not be a pleasant one, but instead kept her eyes fixed on Matteus. Once inside they began and spoke low, but of course Thia could hear everything.

Simone insists upon him, "Matteus, I was hoping I wouldn't have to spell it out for you. Surely you realize by now that our clan has chosen *us* to join, they just haven't made it official yet. Naturally it would be us all along as we are the best of our kind. And quite frankly I find it embarrassing that you insist on carrying on with that...girl."

There was no response from Matteus as he stared at the floor in the direction where he longed to be, where Thia waited.

Angrily Simone snapped at him, "Matteus, are you even listening to me?!"

He broke out of his daze and spat straight to the point, "What exactly is it that you need Simone?"

Taken back by his aggressiveness she backed down but still stood her ground, "A little respect for your own kind would be a good start."

How strange. They really take their social status seriously, Thia thought as she listened in.

Matteus wanted her to leave more than anything and as soon as possible, "Can we discuss this another time? I would very much like to get back to my guest."

"Your *guest* Matteus is the very issue. You've been changing since you met her and everyone is noticing. It doesn't look good. You need to stop seeing her."

Matteus stood up straight, slid closer and stared straight in her eyes, "I will not be dictated to by *you*. You were not invited nor are you welcome. I would appreciate it if you would leave...*now.*"

Thia stiffened up nervous, not sure what to expect, *Uh-oh, she's not going to like that one.*

Simone hissed, "You will be sorry.", and then stormed out of the kitchen.

She didn't bother looking at Thia and slammed the door on her way out.

Matteus grabbed Thia, "Now that the interruption is gone."

Right after he said this, the sound of tires pealing out penetrated the house.

Thia cringed, "That's going to leave a mark."

Then her mood changed as she affectionately looked up at him, "Hey is everything okay? She didn't look very happy. I don't want to cause trouble for you."

"Not at all. In fact the *problem* just left."

Doing her best to ignore the fact that he takes her breath away she continued, "Because you know, it's usually not a good sign if the new person in someone's life ends up pissing off the ones that were already there."

Matteus walked her back to the dining room where he poured drinks and handed one to her, "I noticed you took much care in avoiding any commitment defining titles."

She took a sip leaning against the serving table and smirked, "I am not one to assume."

He moved over to the table next to her, "Thia, I would be honored if you would allow for us to take the next step into an official couple."

She became uneasy, "You certainly have a way with words yourself." Then she considered it, *I've never been an official anything before. What the heck,* "Sure, we could try that."

Then her phone buzzed, "Oh I forgot to tell them I would be late."

"Though I do not want you to go, it is rather late so I will release you against my will…for the evening. May I drive you home? It is quite dark now."

"No, it's okay, I don't have trouble in the dark. Thanks though. And thank you for a wonderful evening. It's been the best I've had yet.", it was a risk being so honest but tonight overcame many hurdles already.

"The pleasure has been all mine."

She got to the door when she remembered, "Oh, before I go, what was it you needed to ask me about?"

"Nothing, I just didn't want you to try and sneak off.", then he pulled her close and kissed her. "I'm finding it increasingly difficult but forgive me if I am ever too forward with you."

Still holding him, "You are fine."

"You'll let me know though, yes?"

"sure", and they said goodbye.

Opening day at the club arrives. The stories around town about who the new owner were and where they came from so far have been pretty harmless but enough to keep them unsure who would come. The towns' people murmured about the three new comers that mostly keep to themselves. Two large men that looked nothing alike, or more like opposites, and one fair skinned girl with platinum streaked hair and light grey eyes that looked even less related, yet called each other brother and sister.

However much to their surprise when it was time to open the doors, Dae found the parking lot was already full and there was a line running back around the building. All three of them had been so busy inside setting everything up; they had no idea of the crowd that was building just outside.

It was an odd combination of people. As they shuffled in, Dae recognized a few locals, some from the spots outside of town but many he'd never seen before and couldn't place what area they might have come from.

Dae's primary function was bouncer and help behind the bar as needed. Shai, the DJ and Thia behind the bar and serves tables when needed. The waitress from the diner was there, greeting those she knew. They posted for help in the kitchen and found one from the other side of town they liked and hired named Ben.

The night started off smoothly. The music was just the right mix and nonstop, the food and drink was top notch and the service, the service was all Thia. She treated everyone with the same amount of respect whether they dressed up or came wearing overalls and she taught the staff to do the same. They were making sure this was a true Haven. All felt important and welcome.

Shai started with angry heavy metal off and on. He thought it might help the early crowd let out their days pent up aggression. When he thought that worked its magic, next came some hip hop in the mix. After the rough day it was time to let loose and have fun. The crowd responded well. They just wanted to drink, dance and feel good. Finally at the end of the night was a special show. Shai put the other music on, the kind Thia loved to dance to. The audience had no idea what they were in for.

Thia at a very young age knew the dance and her infatuation with it. She performed it at the traditional ceremonies but as she got older it took on a new purpose. It became her escape. She needed something to devour her time and energy when her brothers are away or when she feels cooped up. Her passion for Belly Dancing grew.

At home one day, completely by accident, she stumbled upon a video of an adaptation to traditional style Belly Dancing called Tribal Fusion. This was the style that called to her. It was the direction she already headed in but had no idea of the places it could go. She dug in full force. Thia is nothing if not the very definition of determined to find every little morsel of what she is looking for. Her focus is clear and fixed on the thing until completely satisfied.

Glued to the screen she played it over and over. Her brothers came home and tried to get her out but she sent them away. Every movement spoke to her telling its own story, a tale that could not be ignored. She continued to search and watch any and all she found absorbing everything. Then she noticed something. As she viewed the videos again and again she found the shape of the women widely varied. Still all of them took this art and made it their own, forming it to their own style and will. And each choice was unique and beautiful.

This was what she's been waiting for. This is the answer. The art of Belly Dance was non-judgmental. It was something so very precious and rare in the female species. Something that felt natural, comfortable and right. Finally knowing this was her place and that it existed outside of the tribe, she immersed herself and mastered it.

So now it was Thia's time to perform. She was a little disappointed that she hadn't seen Matteus yet, but tried to stay focused on the routine she created for the song. Though she was nervous she still decided to take one last look out to see who her spectators were.

"He's here!", as she peeked out of the curtain.

She found Matteus in the audience and her nervousness abruptly escalated. "Oh, I shouldn't have looked. You know the last time I remember any serious attention from a guy was when we were growing up? I have no idea what to do with this."

Shai shook his head, "You are *not* talking about Caleb. Thia it doesn't count if it isn't mutual."

"I guess you're right", then the first of the few dark times came to her. A time right before the attempted rape, a time she never told her brothers about. It was the warning sign she never saw.

Hanging out in the cave relaxing, knowing her brothers wouldn't be able to make it again as they were grounded. They were often up to no good but it didn't usually involve breaking things. This time they broke something and it was expensive.

Still, hoping they might catch a break or even sneak out, she stayed at their spot a while longer. This also happened to be the same time Caleb and his twin sister were in town staying with their aunt so this probably had something to do with it too.

Thia was taking a dip then practicing her running up and flipping off of the rock wall when she heard someone coming out of the pool. She hoped down excited so sure it was her brothers, or at least one of them. There were only one set of steps as she dried off then threw on her sweat pants. *Which one got away?*, she wondered. But excitement turned to distress as the scent was neither one of theirs.

Caleb, annoyance immediately set in. *What does he want? And how did he find this?*

She watched moving closer to the wall, *maybe he doesn't know I'm here yet.* She waited, wishing she could jump out of the opening but they hadn't tried that yet as it's too steep. But it was too late, he caught her scent and was at her side in a split second. She stared holes in his hand, wrapped around her upper arm, then snapped up to his eyes in strict warning. He got the message, removed his hand and raised both in the air as he stepped back.

"Sorry, just wanted to get your attention. What are you up to?", with a fake innocence she thought. "I just want to talk, swear."

"Right, well I have to go so maybe some other time." She tried to step around him to the pool.

"Oh come on" he grabbed her arm again. "Please?" with a rotten, no good smile.

She shook off his grip and got some distance between them, "Talk about what? And how did you find this place?"

Caleb was seemingly oblivious to how much she outright despises him, "You want to do away with the pleasantries, okay."

"Nothing about you is pleasant." she secretly blamed him, knowing it was more likely her brothers were taking the fall for something he did.

Stubborn as ever he carried on, "Have you ever been to the city?"

"No", she was short with him hoping it would speed up the unwelcome meeting.

"I went a couple of years ago. I didn't want to come back. It was amazing! Makes these places look some poe-dunk hole."

"Fascinating" she sarcastically lied. It would've interested her, if it was anyone else talking about it.

"I was thinking of going back soon."

This got her attention, "Don't you have to be chosen?"

"Not if I don't plan on asking."

"Nice, well good luck with that.", and she turned to try and escape.

He finally made his point, "Wanna go with me?"

She stopped dead in her tracks. She turned to him in disbelief in what he just proposed, "Ha! You're kidding."

"I'm not." He got close, leaned in towards her, his hands quickly slipped around her waist.

She realized what he was trying to do and broke away, "Not on your life!"

"Why not?" Caleb was less friendly now, actually angry, not taking rejection well. He was a good looking guy, very in fact, but knew it which in turn ruined it.

"I'm out of here."

"Fine, I get it. Let's just chat then.", he didn't have his fun yet.

She packed up her things, "I have absolutely nothing to say to you."

He further prodded, "I heard a rumor."

Thia was getting seriously fed up, "That's great for you! If it's about me believe whatever you like. I couldn't care less."

"But it's not, about you." He went dark and evil, "It's about that big, frail baby you call a brother."

She ordered with a growl, squaring up to him glaring straight in his eyes like she was burrowing through them. "Now, *you* need to leave."

Now crazed with curiosity he invited the challenge, "Ha! There it is. Come on, show me what you got. I heard it almost squeezed the life out of everyone around you and even split that big guy's empty head! Show me!"

She saw the look in his eyes, gritted her teeth, "Leave me alone! You're such a freak!"

His head fell back in laughter, "Ha ha, I'M the freak?!"

"Enough!" and she launched out the cave opening not caring anymore what happened after that. She sailed over to a couple large trees, grabbed on bending the top riding it close enough to the ground to make the final jump. This time Caleb did not follow.

"Thia you're up!", Shai yelled over the music startling her out of the memory.

The lights dim and her music starts. She sulks onto the stage like a wild cat stalking its prey. The song began slow then quickly picked up. Bending back at a ninety-degree angle, moving her arms like a pair snakes, then sliding from side to side down to the floor and working her way back up, as before, kept all eyes fixed on her. Service came to a complete halt, with the staff too absolutely entranced by the vision, but no one noticed. It was a show none could ignore. Her fingers swirled and her wrists turned as her arms brought them past her eyes removing a mask never seen before.

Seeing her dance many times before, Shai and Dae took a moment to relax and enjoy the first moment of peace from their insanely busy and successful opening night. They had fun gauging the reactions they knew Thia would later ask about. It was all too clear the Haven's visitors had seen nothing like this before now, as conversations ceased and even blinking became rare.

Thia finished and Shai moved the music on to the next hit but the crowd was frozen. One by one, they blinked out of their trance and began applauding. Thia changed back into her server self and returned behind the bar. Most didn't recognize her when she passed by them. Then Matteus approached.

Very excited to see him, "Hey, you made it!"

He took her hand and kissed it, "That was absolutely incredible Thia."

A girl sitting next to him turned in surprise, "That was you up there?! Wow! Can you teach me?"

Thia laughed, "sure".

Matteus in an urgent tone, "Is there somewhere we can go to talk?"

Thia grew concerned by his tone, "Yeah, I can get away for a few minutes."

She took him back into the office and he gave her a big hug and held her tight. Then gently grabbed her face and softly kissed her lips. "Will I ever stop learning new and wonderful things about you? Speaking of which, I hadn't realized you favored tattoos."

At first she was puzzled then she looked down at her arm, "Oh this, yeah."

He ran his fingers over it, "How have I not noticed it until now? You must think me not very observant."

"Hmmm, I don't know. I don't have many sleeveless things. And the ones I do have I usually wear a sweater over. I'm such a freeze baby. Speaking of which you feel a little warm. Are you coming down with something?" she felt his forehead and face as he looked a little off.

"Does it mean something?" like he didn't hear her question.

Not sure what to tell him she got a little nervous, "Um, it's kind of an inside thing between me and my brothers." This was the best she could come up with on the spot.

"Ah, so they have them too?"

"Yep." *Time to divert*, she thought and wrapped her arms around him again. "I'm so glad you could make it!"

"I am too. It looks like you had a nice turn out."

"Yeah, thanks for your help. Oh and your friend was here earlier, Giles. And Simone was with him. Much to my surprise she didn't look very happy." she said sarcastically.

But Matteus didn't laugh. He didn't even smile. Instead he looked troubled by this news, "really".

"Is everything okay? You look upset or not yourself. Are you okay?"

He seemed somewhat non responsive at first, "Yes, it's just I was unaware they were planning on attending."

"Oh, I assumed they heard about it from you."

Shai flew in and gave Matteus a manly pat on the back as he headed to the shelf, "Matt, how's it going?"

"Good, thank you." He was staring off but managed to nod and smile cordially.

Shai grabbed a folder of music and ran out just as fast.

Her brothers got along with him now. He seemed to treat Thia well and she was happy with him. That and they did all the background checking they could and he came up clean. It also didn't hurt that Matteus brought everyone gifts every so often, nice gifts like expensive watches and gadgets.

"I'm sorry, I don't want to keep you from your duties. I should let you get back." Matteus was distracted and not even looking at Thia when he spoke.

She knew something bad was bothering him, "It's okay, I don't need to get back right away. Please tell me what's wrong?"

"I have to go. You are right, I haven't been feeling well for a little while now...I will try to explain later."

She gently grabbed his face, "You are making me nervous. What is wrong? Please let me help?"

"No, you can't. I...I have to go away for a little while."

Seeing he didn't want to talk long, she kept her questions short, "Oh. Do you know for how long?"

"I'm afraid I don't." she noticed he was looking flush and a little panicked.

Is he breaking up with me?

If this was the case she was not willing to prolong this type of thing, "Look I know I don't fit in with your group but, you know I could try harder. Is that what's really going on? Are you really leaving *me*? You can just tell me. I'll understand."

His refocused eyes met hers as he took her face in his hands. "No Thia, it is nothing like that." Unable to breathe he looked back down the hall to the club entrance to find Giles and Simone staring back at him.

She was desperate now, "Please tell me something, anything? You're scaring me."

"I can't right now. I have to go."

They were heading his way now so he pulled her further in the office where they couldn't see, held her close and kissed her hard. They entered the room eyes only on Matteus. Giles respectfully took him by the arm and they escorted him out.

She just stood there at a loss watching them leave. Matteus did not look back but held his head down.

After a few minutes Thia physically went back to work but her mind was running in another direction wanting to understand what just happened.

What is he sick with and why couldn't he tell me? Why won't he let me help? And why does he have to go away. What is going on? He's acting so strange, especially once his friends showed up, even the very mention of them. I know she doesn't care for me but that's not what is bothering him. There's something more, something big he's not telling me. The last time I saw him behave weird was on our first date when Simone said I should be his pet not his mate. She paused at the thought of mate. She felt butterflies in her stomach and smiled. *'Mate'. Focus Thia! He was not happy when he found out about his family coming too. But why? Is she not the only one that thinks I am no good for him? Do they all disapprove? Maybe it is better that he goes, I seem to be making his life harder for him. Then again he did seem physically not well. Maybe he really is sick? This is going to drive me crazy.*

For the rest of the night her thoughts consumed her wanting to know why he had to leave her so suddenly.

The next day was Saturday and the turnout even bigger. Some from the night before came back and brought more people with them. Positive word spread fast hopefully guaranteeing their chance of success in their new home town.

But throughout all of the excitement, Thia thought of Matteus.

It didn't take long to learn not to create trouble while being a guest at the club. An example was made of a couple of rowdy bikers passing through who decided to act up during one of Thia's performances. They thought they were big enough to do as they pleased; throwing glass bottles at the walls, obnoxious hoot and hollering and stumbling up on stage with her, but their actions met an eerie end.

Size is nothing when numbers are great. Dae the one having to typically deal with the rare but occasional issues, watched in awe as the disapproving crowd handled this situation themselves showing the irritants just how much they didn't appreciate the interruption.

Shai killed the music and everything fell absolutely silent. Thia stopped and backed off with a smirk and a nod motioning their attention to the audience. The two large, leather-bound men turned, expecting the crowd to laugh and join in, froze, wide eyed and jaws dropped.

Instead they found everyone in the entire place standing in front of the stage in a solid mass staring angrily at them. The two men cautiously left the stage and made their way through the room and out the door ultimately avoiding the need for intervention from the authorities.

As time went on the police in fact never had a problem with them. Thia always chummed up with her big warm and friendly smile when they stopped in "just for coffee". It was the kind of smile that gave even an older aged man a slight glimmer of hope when a younger woman paid them a little attention. However it was a bit more genuine than that. Strangely much like her mother, they had an unspoken respect and longing for her to trust them. As she got older this became her affect on most. Their respect ran so deep that even when she danced it was seen as a dance of beauty and grace, not seduction like the form's unfair reputation.

"Children of the Night" only scratched the surface. These three *are* the night life. Cat naps during the day paid dividends when the 11pm rush rolled around. First prep time before the doors opened, the show and cleanup after the doors finally closed, whenever that was. If there were guests left, the placed stayed open, which happened to be most nights. No one was in a hurry to leave.

A few suspicious theories from the paranoid floated around, "They pump extra oxygen in the vents so you don't get tired", and "They must put drugs in your drinks so you want to stay longer". None of which were true, of course, they simply didn't want to admit the real reason they didn't want to leave. There had to be something evil about it to draw so many.

But in fact, Haven did just as the owners had hoped. It drew a crowd of all kinds from near and far. It was a simple and nonjudgmental place, a place of escape. All come to feel like they were on the same level as everyone else for a change, blue collar, white collar, all alike. Sit back with their favorite drink, a little on the heavy side, watch the shows, and get to be someone else they couldn't be outside the Haven's doors.

Play Time

When they aren't at the club entertaining, or at home relaxing they could be found out and about the town sometimes, but normally most of their play time was spent deep in the woods at their favorite new clearing. Very deep in the forest where no cars, dirt bikes or even ATVs can make it and normal people would have to set up a few days of hiking just to get there on foot. The trees are too big and thick and the roots drastically molding the ground to range both high and deep. Only a helicopter could get someone there fast, if there were something to go there for but none seemed interested up until now.

No tall ledges like home but close. It'll do, Thia found it one night on the second of four parameter runs her first week there. This task was on a virtual checklist of action items performed after relocation. Nomad's lesson #2 – Know the Land, essential for quick escapes.

Unlike the last place they tried to call home, a mix of everything was here in this undiscovered treasure of land. A flat meadow in the middle, a small creek carelessly wandering through the trees on the south end, small piles of boulders on the one end next to a large pond, and thick walls of established sturdy trees all around. It reminded her of home, their real home. Very different indeed to the city parks they had gotten used to. Those sad little trees couldn't take even the smallest of blows from playing cats.

The day she found it she researched all the local and internet maps to confirm it was a complete and insignificant blind spot. Land surveyors must have just gone in only so far, assumed and recorded that the rest was a sea of nothing but trees.

Returning there often running through in her soul freeing Phelidae form, she observed the variety of plant life and animals keeping a mental note of each for hunting. She first passed by many squirrels and ground hogs then found deer, a bear and some wolves the deeper in she traveled. However, these were not like the pack from the night with the drunk man. Those wolves stuck with her as she hadn't seen any that big before. But it was no matter; she found their special place, their place of escape, their own haven.

Though they resembled normal humans, they were irrefutably half animal. And with animals, come animal needs. They ate normal food like normal people, but could not avoid the occasional and overwhelming craving for something fresh...*very* fresh.

A couple weeks went by and trees in different parts around the clearing, took on the appearance of scratching posts. While it was helpful in sharpening nails, these served another very useful purpose. Particularly in the winter months, deer came to visit these trees first to eat the bark that had already been roughed up and easy to pull off. This made hunting them all too easy, which was fine by Thia since the chases at some point ended up tearing through the water. They have thick coats in the winter but do not favor wet fur in the least.

Generally the plump ones were the target. They ran slower and these were the ones over eating which meant the others were getting less than they should. It also didn't hurt that they were very tender. Not once did it cross their mind that hunting was cruel or barbaric. The kills were always quick and in the end it's the same as eating a rare steak found at a favorite steak house.

After hunting the three cats return to the field. To any onlookers they were more than twice the size of standard big cats. Dae took the form of a massive but sleek and velvety black panther. Shai was a deep fiery orange and black spotted leopard and Thia was the barely noticeably smaller but breathtakingly stunning snow white and ebony striped tiger.

Even though they weren't biologically family it was still awkward seeing each other without clothes which was the unavoidable after affect of changing back to human form. So they made sure they kept something Thia came up with on them at all times. Long cargo-like shorts for the boys and for Thia a lighter linen dress. She wrapped the material around her ending up with a shorter version of a gown a goddess might wear, secured by two ropes, one around her ribcage and the other at her waist.

When traveling in cat form, the garments were bundled up and hung from the neck. This was not ideal though when hunting as it could get caught on a tree branch so instead they would hang them somewhere to come back to. When in human form, if they remembered, the package was carried on their belts, in their bags or over the shoulder just in case they hit any trouble and had to change destroying the clothes they were already wearing.

After a well earned meal comes time to unwind. On sunny days they laid around and either napped or talked about whatever came to mind. This time Thia brought up something new.

Lying on her back with her eyes closed she dropped the thought that had been building inside since they met Thomas, "You guys think we will ever find the others?"

"What do you mean *the others*?" Shai half knew what she meant but felt like being a little cold as he was annoyed by her untimely and complicated question. He didn't appreciate such deep conversations on a full stomach.

"I mean the rest of us." She snidely replied knowing it was obvious and he was just being lazy.

"Thia, what makes you think there *are* any more of us?" Shai quickly and grimly replied forgetting how sensitive Thia can be, especially on this topic.

Completely taken back by his carelessness, a large lump suddenly formed in her throat, "You don't mean that. Of course there are." She felt some of her courage return, "Shai, our kind are strong and you know it!" She took a moment to collect herself. It wasn't common but did happen. Something triggered a spark igniting what started as a pilot light but could rapidly fester ready to explode into a full out Armageddon if pushed to that.

However she shook her head in precision denial dousing the freshly lit flame, "We are just a little scattered now. We just need to figure out a way to find the rest, that's all. If we got back together again we could stop, no put a *permanent* end to the Pallas attacks."

Exhausted and uncomfortable from over eating, he grew irritated by her over exposed and dripping sense of hope and snapped at her, "That's a fine dream Thia but don't you think by now we would've found someone, *anyone* like us?", Shai was being uncharacteristically mean now.

But before Thia's heartbroken and defeated whimper could be heard, Dae spoke up, "No Shai, I think she's right..."

Shai interrupted completely tired of the topic, "Dae, no need to come to her rescue! She needs a solid dose of reality sometimes. It's not healthy to dream all the time, especially about something like this."

Dae also sleepy, overheated and cranky from the argument, suddenly erupted at Shai, "Try paying attention some time Shai! If you recall, most were NOT...killed during the attack!"

They both suddenly felt an assault of sorrow for Thia's loss. Really it was all of their loss as they loved her too. But Dae went on trying to keep pace of the conversation hoping the grief would flow away with it, "Even the ones that stayed behind trying to get as many out as possible were only captured, not destroyed."

There was a long pause before anyone replied. All relived and absorbed that day in their minds, eventually realizing how right Dae was.

Shai found a little of Thia's hope after getting over the initial shock of Dae's aggression and the memory of that time, "Alright so say there are a bunch locked up somewhere, any ideas Dae on how to locate them?"

Dae returned to calm the very second after he blew up as he's never been known to stay upset or hold a grudge. "Not sure, it's been too hard trying to keep our location unknown. But I am sure what we continue to learn from Thomas will come in handy."

They all agreed and let the matter rest for the time being. At that not another word was said, they just napped in the sun until they had enough rest.

That is when another well known attribute declares its turn, often enough to keep them in a little healthy trouble, the urge to get a little rowdy simply drives them insane. For this too, having a large secluded place to stretch out was a necessity. The middle state, the coalesce state, was called.

Some daylight hours are reserved and spent in disciplined practice on lessons past. To keep it up-to-date and interesting, new items caught while watching old and new movies are added. It didn't take long to master the new tricks since a strong base was already established. Depending on what they felt like doing, sometimes practice was done together while other things worked better alone.

Shai ran off some energy through the trees at top speed then climbed them jumping from one to the other to the very top of the tallest. There he sat watching the eagles. He admires the quiet power they have, unyielding and wise. He daydreamt of what it must be like to soar through the air, free and afraid of nothing.

Dae preferred to relax on the grass and sleep longer. When he was through sleeping, he packed a small book to read or brought along some trinket to examine. Either way, his attention was best kept by some variety of study. He loved to dissect how things work. The items were typically nothing more than a little piece of junk to the other two. But to Dae it was so much more, a doorway to discovery.

Any opportunity he got he tried to grab something from the Pallas before getting chased out for good. He researches these things recovered and reverse engineers them in hopes that he can find a way to counter it or at least learn more about who was after them and what they are capable of. No matter the type of item, he inspects everything from weapons, pieces of tracking devices and bugs to communication. It also helped that his friend Thomas works with the chemical aspects as Dae was more into the mechanics.

And then there is Thia, who chooses to dance in her alone time.

Nightfall came. Dae, Shai and Thia were standing around arguing.

"Fine, I'll go first." Thia caved.

It was time for more serious practice now that it was dark and more difficult for human eyes to see what they would be doing, just in case, "Okay, hit me!"

Thia held her chain weapon in the ready stance. They started slow. Shai sent some small rocks at her. She easily blocked them with the whip.

She gave Shai a bored, "Really?"

"Just warming up." he responded in a playful defense.

Then a couple bigger rocks sailed at her. She sent the point of the chain in the middle of them cracking them down into large pieces falling to the ground.

Then more came, bigger and faster. Spinning and turning her body getting just the right speed and force behind each hit, she had no problem keeping up.

"Dae, you too." She wanted to step it up. After all there were a lot more than one on the Pallas side.

Then a neat line of water from the stream headed straight for her. She changed the action of the chain to spin, faster and faster, so fast it was a blur, forcing the water into a spray when it hit and the rocks rebound off in every direction. Then something strange happened. First the whip started slowing down and the water took on a more controlled spiral shape. And the rocks that hit the water now danced off then turned red hot and exploded into a million pieces like small fireworks.

Her brothers couldn't believe their eyes.

"Shai, look at her face." Dae kept his voice very low and calm careful not to distract her.

Shai saw she was starring into everything that was circling with a curious look on her face. Her eyes changed too. But it wasn't her cat properties that shocked them, it was the new color they became. Only it wasn't just a change in her color, it's like they were glowing some sort of blue.

A deer sprang out of the trees into the clearing. The abrupt movement was enough to break Thia's concentration so all of the water and remaining stones washed over her like a small tidal wave.

"Thia! How'd you do that?" Shai asked excited.

"...I don't know. I was just watching it all sort of slow down and ...I don't know how to describe it. Everything just looked different. Like it was glowing?"

"Do it again!" Shai was enthralled by his sister's new trick.

Dae was very interested too but less vocal about it.

She looked back and forth between the two, "I don't know if we should. We don't want to attract any attention like Nomad said, right?"

"It'll be fine, right Dae? Thia just try." Shai pushed not known for his patience or any ounce of caution.

Thia was struggling with the decision. Though she heard Nomad's warnings again and again in her head counseling her not to, deep down she really wants to. It was finally a harmless glimpse into what she could do. A chance for her to practice what she was born with was right in front of her. All along her brothers could apply and occupy themselves with their special gifts without much concern. But she was always instructed not to even try until she could be properly and completely trained. Not to mention she was too afraid after hurting everyone, especially Dae. She couldn't help but look at his scar when she thought of this.

"Thia" Dae comforted instantly knowing and regretting that she continues to torture herself about that day.

Shai got frustrated with her, "Thia, just remember and do what you just did. That's all."

She looked to Dae for approval as he is always the most level headed one. However this time curiosity got the best of him too so he nodded in approval with a reassuring and trusting smile.

"Okay, here goes." excited she began spinning the chain again.

Dae and Shai sent their elements at her just like before. And again the water sprayed and the rocks bounced off. She glared into the spiral concentrating hard to get the glow to come back. Seconds went by, then minutes but nothing.

Tired and disappointed now she gave up, "Stop, I can't get it."

That moment the elements fell to the ground and she let the chain drop to the side.

"What's wrong? Why didn't it work this time?" Shai was just as dissatisfied.

"I don't know, it just won't do it. I can't get the glow back." Thia answered shortly as she didn't care to dwell on her failure. "Who's next?"

Dae felt bad for her, "You sure?"

"Yes" again short in her answer. Her brothers knew this meant it was her final decision.

"I'll go." Shai said ready to move on and see if he too could do something new and cool.

They traded positions and started up again. Thia walked around picking up the rocks that fell from her turn so she could send them at Shai while Dae kicked up a nasty wind. Thia forgot how strong it got and had to replant her footing to keep from getting knocked down by the wind and debris it carried. Then she decided to move slightly behind Dae where it was a bit more quiet and safe. And they began.

When Shai wanted more she would toss them in the air and kick them at him. After he raised a thin piece of ground in front of him to block the wind, Thia was able to knock a couple through his barrier. All they heard was "ouch!" Thia felt Dea's mood change. When she looked over he was smirking as a massive wave of water jumped over them and Shai's wall, dumping down on top of him.

"Hey! No fair guys!" Shai yelled thoroughly drenched all the way through.

Dae explained, "You are supposed to be prepared for the worst Shai, that's why we do this."

Thia just started laughing.

"Whatever. Dae, it is your turn." Shai didn't bother hiding that he wanted to get back at him.

So Dae calmly switched places with half angry, half pouting Shai. Both of them could tell Shai's intentions from a mile away but Dae was clearly not concerned. This only fueled the fire.

As expected, Shai tried to catch Dae off guard before he was ready, tossing a bowling ball sized rock at him. However Thia, also knowing her brother very well, expected it and kicked it back at him where it landed square in his stomach.

Holding his stomach, "Hey what happened to being prepared?!"

"I was, why weren't you?!" Thia shot back at lightning speed.

Mad at them both now, "Whatever you two, for real now."

Thia was fed up with his childishness, "Don't pout, you tried to cheat! We're also supposed to watch each other's backs if you remember."

Shai just ignored her. He wouldn't acknowledge she was right and he was reacting off of emotion, another of Nomad's lessons #4 – Do not permit emotion to cloud the Phelidae clarity.

Dae nodded he was ready and waited for his siblings attacks. This time a less emotional Shai conjured up a fireball, a hot one, and flung it at him. Dae pulled all the water he was standing in from Shai's attack and threw up an instant wall, swallowing the ball of fire whole then spat out the remaining slush of ash to the ground. Thia shot her chain at him and with the force of tornado sucked it right out of her hand.

All night they continued to challenge each other practicing through the night. They don't usually carry on so long but this time did since they felt guilty for not properly practicing in months. They all heard the Nomad that wasn't physically there in the back of their minds, strictly enforcing and urging constant practice during his lessons so they would be prepared just in case anything like the last invasion threatened them again.

The Encounter

One cool fall evening, the three where in their clearing deep in the woods. Shai was tired from hunting and decided maybe for once he'd take a look at what Dae brought this time, hoping it might be interesting. Dae pulled out what looked like a burnt up piece of a clock wheel. Happy Shai was finally showing some interest, Dae went on to explain to him how it worked but tried to keep it simple so as to not lose him.

"I did some research and it turns out it's an old timer used to trip the altered flash bomb setup in their back yard at the old house. The Pallas planned on surprising us at 9pm, then driving us to the back where the bomb would go off at 9:05pm stunning us with a bright flash of light and a loud ear ringing sound long enough to hit us with tranquilizers."

Shai grabbed the scrap out of Dae's hand to take a look, "You got all that out this piece of junk?"

Before Dae got too deep into explaining how he had done exactly that to Shai, Thia asked Dae to make it snow and the wind sing for her so she could go off and dance. All too happy to accommodate, his eyes changed their emerald green and he returned his attention to Shai.

In her own little corner, away from her brothers, a small but heavy grey cloud appeared and hung over her. She altered the material wrapped around her to hang to the ground just in time as huge fluffy snowflakes began to fall quickly covering the ground all around her. She stared up to the sky full of cleansing peace then closed her eyes enjoying the snow tickle her face and melt. Then the wind started to blow through the leaves on the trees and holes in stumps as a slow and tranquil flute-like song flowed through them.

Her hands floated away from her gown, up to the sky and began to slowly twirl in the cool snowfall. Her hair blew around her face soft and free. It looked like a quiet ballet mixed with the sensual moves of a belly dancer. Her hips twisted in figure eights, up and down, side to side moving in fluid motion. Her shoulders rolled as her arms met forming a circle around her head. She twirled around, her hands forming the lotus flower then broke and slowly descended down towards her face as her fingers and wrists continue to twist and turned in small rings, then slowly sway down to her hips. She danced her magical dance for what seemed like forever, until something that didn't belong caught her attention. She stopped and shot a look into the woods hearing something coming.

It was approaching fast. Thia flew over to her brothers staring alert in the same direction of the noise. Her brothers first felt Thia's reaction then heard the noise shortly after. All three of them were set to act. *Have they found us already? Probably, we were just getting to like this place,* was the shared prediction.

A girl about the age of fourteen came tearing into the clearing. She was running as fast as she possibly could. They could tell by her desperate breath and tears streaming down her dirty face, covered in long matted black hair, she was terrified and exhausted. She spotted them, hesitated, then changed course in their direction.

Barely able to talk she tried screaming, "Help! Help me PLEASE! They're going to get me!"

Without a moment needed to think, reacting in pure concentrated instinct, they were at her side. Shocked by the lack of time it took them to get to her, she slid on the moist ground. Most would be afraid but it seemed whatever was after her frightened her much more.

They waited patiently until four more came from where she did, faster than she moved, or any human for that matter. They were unnerving indeed. They looked like nothing Thia or her brothers had ever seen before, with skin so white, no, almost a bluish grey like when blood is absent from hands that are ice cold. Thia, having the strongest sense of smell instantly knew something about them was not right. The warm and strong human essence was completely absent.

She wasn't sure what they were but it didn't matter. The girl was definitely human and threatened by them. She was running from them and they pursued her. This much was certain. Still the assessment continued to be prepared for the worst. All three noticed they moved like cold animal hunters, staring at the girl like she was their prey, not a living breathing person. The girl whimpered and they sensed her body stiffen in fear then she crawled behind Dae grabbing onto his leg to hide.

Then another violent shift in the mood was felt.

A quick glint of amber flashed in Thia's eyes, first looking at the girl through the corner of them then switching to the oncoming danger. Her brothers felt it, and glanced at each other cautiously. As the red covered more of her iris Thia tightened her jaw as she closed her eyes tight trying to suppress the instinctual power she feared. The hair on the back of her neck stood up, and so did her brothers warning her efforts were not working.

She took a deep breath, slowly in then out mentally pushing out the piercing face of the hunters. Finally gaining control she opened her eyes and focused on the approaching group again studying each movement. Thia feeling more and more untrusting of them slid into the beginning of a defensive stance. Her brothers did the same as the bond with them proved stronger than ever with the inclusion of their little Blood Bond experiment, taking it to new and still unknown heights.

The four strangers saw where the girl was now and stopped, they could tell the three did not fear them but didn't understand why.

"Do they not know what stands in front of them?" the one asked another under his breath so human ears could not hear.

The moon is revealed from the clouds and all three sets of glowing eyes shifted over to him. This shocks the four but they are quick to recompose. The two groups stood silent, knowing something was very different with this encounter.

Then one of the grays, that's what Shai called them from then on, spoke as they slowly begin their approach again. "This is not your business strangers. We will take her and be on our way." The other three hissed in agreement.

Every muscle in Thia's body tightened from the arrogant order, still she was able to keep the red at bay, just barely. *Who do they think they are? And did I just hear hissing? Who does that?!*, she thought. Her brothers physically reacted in the same way.

Shai coolly replied, "Leave now, the girl stays."

"Byron!" the tall skinny one loudly whispered. "We don't have time for this! Find another pet dog." A breeze blew; he then sniffed the air, looked instantly irritated, and glanced to his side. "It is time to go!"

The one he was addressing turned and gave him a look of grave warning. *He must have spoken to him wrong,* Thia noticed. The tall skinny one retracted in fear of his misstep.

That one must be the leader., Thia further deduced.

With tensions already high it only got worse once a large dark brown wolf and then a slightly smaller sandy colored wolf came running at top speed into the clearing.

Why are they all coming from that same spot? It's not coincidence, but how could they all possibly be connected? Thia wondered.

The wolves appeared beat up and very angry. Thia and her brothers glanced over for a second then back at the strangers. The large new comers were not worth the distraction considering they were just typical knobby legged, rough fur and pointy nosed wolves.

But to the contrary, the grays seemed very troubled by their presents. The stocky grey's stance became impatient. Thia instantly picked up on his shift in weight and focused in on him. Thia could sense these sorts of things long before the other two and his body said he wanted to move. To her the sensation felt much like the pressure in the air changed. So she decided to take another quick look. *Perhaps there is something more to these wolves.*

That's when the stocky one got cocky. In a split second his muscles tightened as he prepared. Too fast for normal eyes to notice, Thia caught him lean forward, his eyes dilated on the girl and then...he made his move. In what seemed like slow motion, he lunged towards the girl intending on catching Dae off guard, knocking him out of the way. But as he moved through the air, something sharp and solid struck him in the face, across his lower left jaw and neck. He fell back in the wrong direction as if it just hit a wall. He smashed into the ground head first with his body to follow.

Thia instantly reset ready again for another attack, not noticing the strange blood on her hand. The moment the grey decided to move forward, Thia with a look of pure intentional rage, struck him down mid flight with her right hand before he knew what happened. To her brothers the force might have been considered a bit much, however they'd been with her in other threatening situations. They understood the things that set off her boiling fury. The past moments of protecting life, while risking exposure. The young potential victims especially, drew out her unrealized maternal instincts. At least this was Dae's theory.

In this frozen moment, all eyes, greys, wolves and the girl alike were fixed on the two of them. Thia's body remained ready and her stare unwavering. Thanks to Nomad's teachings, their kind made the most use of peripheral vision, able to focus in the general direction while watching all at once. This degree of focus came easy to them though. By nature they don't dignify the unworthy, with the act of respect through direct eye contact. Even worse the Phelidae's expressions were cold now, another tactic of Nomad's, "Clear any and all expression. Leave only a stone cold glare to send chills thought the enemy's soul thus weakening any trace of courage."

The girl, still safe behind Dae and Shai watched their devices in amazement. Now that some of the fear left her she began to feel ashamed for dragging them into this. She tried to justify her actions. She was desperate and afraid, but she knew better, she knew what was after her and that she should not have endangered their lives too. But these three turned out to be special. *Maybe it was meant to be.*

The other three greys were dumbfounded by the stocky one's face. Even the wolves stood dead in their tracks yards away in shock of what they witnessed.

The stocky one pulled himself up off of the ground attempting to shake off the blow. He straightened up attempting to face Thia's direction still stunned. The leader, Byron stares at the four thick deep gashes. For now the strike itself didn't have his attention, but the marks it left did. Rather than what one would expect to see from a hand or fist, it looked much more like something from a large clawed attack. His eyebrows crunched together confused by the sight. His eyes searched yet for evidence of some sort of weapon, was nowhere to be found.

The stocky grey reached up and touched the sensitive area receiving so much attention. Pulling his hand back covered in his own blood he studies it like it wasn't his own. Then he looked up at Thia and her brothers still in disbelief. The sting sets in as his expression changed to reflect pain, his eyes squinted and watering.

Half a second later the shock wore off and he became aware of his audience. Realizing the event made a fool of him, he quickly growled angry. The other two reacted with a shallow mirrored threat. Other than the one called Byron the rest of the grays didn't seem to have a mind of their own at all. They just followed what each other did.

All four then hissed but the Phelidae didn't budge beyond a slow forming cocky smirk.

The wolves stood still watching then Dae caught the big one glance at the girl.

Thia slightly in front and her brothers at her side, moving in perfect synchronization, as if they were somehow wired together with an invisible fishing line, clinched their jaws revealing their canines, which now seemed somehow more enhanced than before, tightened their shoulders pulling up their upper arms, forearms and clawed hands. During the physical transformation they let out what started off as a subtle, and then grew to be a deep and ground shaking growl. As intended, this sent a strong and serious animalistic warning.

The girl behind them was still a little frightened but not by her new guardians. Instead she seemed to behave with a bizarre sense of security among the odd group of three, understandable as they were currently protecting her from the ones that have come for her. For her own reason her attention shifted over to the wolves. The larger one noticed and nodded at the girl. Dae constantly in tune with her whereabouts and actions witnessed the connection. Oddly, the character of the wolf seemed caring. *They know each other*. he thought. *I wonder if they are friends. Or might she be their master?*

The grays, unnerved by the unfamiliar and unexpected sound, recoiled wide eyed and assessed their surroundings. Knowing Thia and her brothers were unlike any they had encountered before, they decided to give up the girl and retreat back in the direction from which they came. They walked away, one at all times keeping an eye on the three and the wolves. They did not like nor were they used to losing, however a single small girl was not worth fighting something unknown with apparently similar strengths and speed.

The wolves crouched down and still baring teeth, ready to go after the greys at the first sign of misstep.

Thia and her brothers watched both as they let them leave, and stood a little more upright but also ready until they were gone from sight and could no longer hear their light footsteps. They didn't bother going after them as it is not their way to hunt other than for food. The grays too were equally a dangerous unknown, but not yet enemy to them as long as they stayed away.

Thia's mind began, *I know what our topic will be when we get home. Dae's got a new project to consume his time. Should be interesting to see what he finds. Only a very faint and shallow heartbeat could be heard but they too seem strong...now to see what these odd wolves are about.*

Guarding the girl continued to be their sole intent as attention shifted to the two wolves. The animals felt the new interest in turn breaking their glare from where the grays disappeared. With an ear aimed towards the woods, they stopped growling and looked back at the three.

As the two groups studied each other the girl sprung out from behind the three running in the direction of the wolves. Thia and Shai wanted to go after her but stopped when Dae put out his hand. Unsure of what he meant by it, what he'd seen, they chose to stay put and watch. They knew how far she could go before it was too far for them to help. She was clearly not afraid of them. And rather than feasting their eyes on her as food, like the grays, these wolves, especially the bigger one, held a look of endearment as he lowered his head and slowly approached her. Normal wild animals would find someone rushing at them to be a threat and attack or run. These did neither.

Thia and her brothers still sure the girl was within range and in no immediate danger, unhurriedly headed in their direction. The girl leapt to the large wolf wrapping her arms around it and kissed its furry face. Dae was sure now that she must be its master.

As Thia and her brothers got close to the girl she turned to them, "Thank you! Thank you all!"

"You are very welcome." Dae answered back. "Do you know these wolves? Are they your pets?" he asked.

"Ha ha! No" she said in a laugh. "This is my brother and cousin."

The big wolf let out a low grumble.

Dae's expression dropped as he exchanged confused looks with Thia and Shai. Though not possible, all must have heard her wrong.

"I'm sorry, did you say you are related to them?" a perplexed Shai needed to confirm what he thought he just heard.

"Yes", she cheerfully answered.

"Show them." she insisted to the wolves.

The wolves looked at her for a moment in what seemed like disbelief then the big one shook it's head.

She attempted to reason with the animal, "Oh come on! You saw the same thing I did. They are not normal either"

Thia and her brothers straightened up anxious as they didn't like her flippant and revealing comment. Until now it always meant exposure, resulting in running again. However this time was very different. Curiosity getting the best of them they didn't move needing to know what they were on the verge of finding out.

Then the big one considered her point, bowed in a nod and walked off into the woods with the other wolf. A moment later two men came out wearing rags and covered in dirt, blood, bruises and scratches.

"See!" she said excited.

"BEN?!" they all recognized him from the club kitchen, an extremely reliable employee who didn't speak much.

Dae shook his head, "Wait I'm afraid we don't understand." Dae noticing a familiarity in the eyes, and understanding what was just implied, but never hearing of such a thing being true.

"They are werewolves." she answered as if it should be obvious.

All three let out a little laugh then Shai chimed in, "Like in the movies?"

"That's enough Alana", Ben said in a stern and cautious voice. He behaved much older than he looked to be. "We know nothing of them yet."

Alana scoffed, "What do you mean you know nothing? You've been working for them, haven't you?"

Dae spoke up agreeing it was only fair to begin by at least properly introducing his family, "I am Dae, this is my sister Thia and my brother Shai." He hesitated then went on. "As your sister mentioned, we too are…different."

Dae visually queues them and heads for the cover of some nearby trees with his siblings reluctantly following.

"This scares me." Thia admitted in a whisper.

"Me too, but they are much like us. We must earn their trust and learn more." Dae rationalized back.

Alana, and the men gasped at what emerged from the very spot the three entered. Thia and her brothers appear in the clearing in Phelidae form. The wolf family could not believe their eyes. All three cats built thick of nothing but powerful muscle, covered in perfectly clean and groomed fur, returned to the others with an overwhelming majestic grace commanding respect with their very presence.

Thia and Shai sat a little behind Dae and waited. It took some time for Alana and the other two to get over what they were witnessing, what sat waiting in front of them now. The cats sat patiently without a care as tall as the humans stood and at least three times as wide.

Alana was the first to speak, "Oh! You're beautiful!"

She went to pet Dae but Ben grabbed her by the arm pulling her back and scolded her, "Alana this is what I mean when I tell you that you are too trusting. Look at them again. They have enough size and strength to crush you before you have time to blink again and we would not be able to stop it."

Alana lost her temper and quickly snapped back at him, "But they wouldn't would they, considering they just *saved me from the Vampires*!"

Her brother backed off as the cats got up. They returned to the woods coming out again in human form.

"I am sorry, but what did you call those creatures again?" Thia asked once they got back. The question had been eating at her and she is not known for her patience.

The big one looked at Thia suspiciously then back at Dae, "I am Benjamin, but you can still call me Ben, this is Abe and my sister Alana. Thank you for what you did."

Dae looked at Thia out of the corner of his eye. He knew being ignored would get under her skin, "You are welcome. Our kind exist to protect life, it is our way."

"Your *kind*? What exactly is your kind?" Ben asked suspicious.

Thia was growing angrier and Dae could feel it, but went on to answer the question, "We are Phelidae. Much like you are part wolf, we are part cat."

Ben's eyes sharpened, "I see. So how can fellow animals of the wild not know a vampire when they see one?"

"It's time to go, now!" Thia erupted through clinched teeth. She could take no more of his rudeness nor did she trust him now considering they'd been working side by side and had no idea what he really was.

Dae sighed in defeat as he closed his eyes and dropped his head. He knew it was only a matter of time before she blew and that time had come all too soon. Thia was not going to let them stay and find out more. Both brothers knew better so they turned to go.

"Please don't go!" Alana jumped at Thia, apologetic about her brother. "My brother doesn't mean to be rude. He was sent away to be taught our old ways once he first changed. One extremely dated flaw of those ways, teaches respecting men above women. But now happily he is back home with us and realizing how backwards that behavior is. He *has* been getting better. Our mother doesn't care much for it either as our father was never like that. He's very easy going where as she can be quite headstrong."

Thia just huffed in response as Ben looked mortified at Alana both surprised and embarrassed. She also knew how much Dae wanted to stay.

"*Those* were vampires? We've seen those in movies too but never thought they were actually real. And as a matter of *fact, we* have *never* seen one before." Shai stabbed adding insult to injury for Ben but at the same time back an appreciative Thia.

"Oh they are real alright! They are our natural born enemies." Abe burst out slightly insulted by the lack of seriousness of the situation.

Ben broke off from his lingering and accusing glare at Alana and turned to Abe.

Abe reacted to the redirect, "What? She gets to tell all the good stuff and I don't?"

"What were you doing so far into the woods?" Thia asked Alana. "There's nothing around here for miles."

"May I show you?" Alana asked in a heartbeat.

"Alana!" Ben yelled astonished at how free she was with all of her family secrets.

"Ben back off! I am not missing out on making new friends like us! Besides you worry too much."

Ben was not backing down this time, "And I wonder why that is?! Maybe if you weren't getting yourself almost killed all of the time I wouldn't need to worry!"

Thia interrupted their argument, desperately wanting to know, "What do you mean by show me?"

"I can't shift but I can show things that I've seen. Some of our kind have powers of the mind; some can even control, not me though. It's said that loyalist of families are the ones worthy of such gifts." she smiled with great pride.

She approached Thia. Thia stepped back not quite ready to commit, unsure what to make of it all. She looked to Dae for approval. He nodded, she thought for a moment, and then nervously sat down on the cool, wet ground. Alana knelt down in front of her and gently touched Thia's forehead with her middle finger and instructed Thia to close her eyes. And as quick as she closed them Thia was rushed to another place in the woods, in the opposite direction of where they lived.

She saw Alana peacefully walking through the woods in search of something. Wild flowers she guessed as she was already holding a bunch of white and blue. Then the vampires appeared out of a blur. She wandered too close to the vampires passing through and they caught her scent. They told her they were following her, hunting her, until she was far enough in the woods that no one would hear her scream. She knew exactly what they were so she did just that and ran dropping the flowers creating a trail for someone to find her.

Then the wolves came up quickly behind the vampires. Abe later explained her friend told them where she was going. As it was getting late they decided to head in that direction. They weren't far off when they heard her scream so they changed and caught up.

Alana stopped so the boys could catch up. When they arrived the vampires had her surrounded. The wolves attacked knocking three of the four down. Being out numbered, the vampires beat the wolves down, but they fought hard keeping all four busy giving Alana long enough to get a head start. Unfortunately she was forced to head in the wrong direction as the battle was blocking her way back home.

She looked back as she ran. The vampires gave chase. The wolves in crippling pain struggled, but got up and pursued the vampires taking them down one by one as they could until they all stopped again to gang up on the wolves. When they were sure the wolves would stay down they resumed their pursuit of her and that is when they caught up in the clearing.

Everything went black. Thia opened her eyes blinking a couple times and realized she was back with the others in the present time, all of which were staring at her. "So they just went after you...like...food, like hunting you was a game." she stated, still shocked by it. "I should've hit him harder."

They all laughed and agreed.

Ben replied this time, also a little confused but a bit more relaxed now, "Yes, they do that. Seriously, you've really *never* met a vampire?"

"Nope. We…don't get out much." she said back. Then she and her brothers chuckled at the lunacy in her explanation. They were hardly ever home just usually didn't interact with anyone.

"I guess", Ben replied a little baffled.

Thia saw a scratch on Ben's arm then remembered what it looked like in the vision Alana showed her, "You guys must heal quickly like us? You were pretty beat up before you got here."

"Yes, we do heal very fast though it mostly depends on the severity of the injury."

"As with us too." Dae added.

Ben looked up at the now very dark sky, "It's getting late. I'd better get her home before our lives are threatened again from what awaits at home. I'm sure mother is nervous now that it is after dark."

Alana was clearly disappointed but could not argue his point.

Thia had to ask one more thing, "Why did the big one act funny after I hit him? He had thick old scars so I'm sure he's been hit before."

Ben didn't mind answering, "I was wondering that myself. They usually heal a little faster than us but your cuts stayed open."

Thia turned to Dae for an explanation so he gave it a shot, "Well, this is just a guess but we do have a type of oil in our claws that tends to stay behind. Maybe that is what kept the cuts open?"

Shai smiled in satisfaction, "I bet they stung too. He looked like it hurt."

"Yeah, pain isn't usually a problem for them." Abe offered.

Alana could tell they craved information, and she wasn't quite ready to go home, so she shared some more things that came to mind, "Some Vampires have different kinds of abilities too."

"Uh-oh, like what?" Thia had to know.

Alana was all too happy to go on, "Well most all of them can put you in a trance if you look them in the eyes too long. They are very fast and strong. However some have abilities beyond these. Some can gain memories from drinking their blood. Some can move things with their minds. And though we have a heightened sense of smell that picks up fear, theirs is even more sensitive. They can actually smell more emotions."

Dae spoke up, "We can smell that too, we just haven't had all the practice we need yet to recognize the more complicated ones."

"They also control each other, that is, if they made them or are an elder with the same bloodline."

"Made them, as in turned them, yes?" Thia was getting some of the same ideas she was mentioning from the movies.

"Yep." Then Alana turned somber, "And unfortunately, if one were to bite one of us, *if* it was old enough and powerful enough, they could control us too. These werewolves forced to act against their own will are called Lycanthrope as it is considered an irreversible curse among our people."

They all looked at each other a little troubled. No one said anything for a while.

Ben, deciding to break the silence, asked trying to keep his voice neutral, "You guys staying around here?"

"Yeah, back that way." Shai pointed in the opposite direction.

Abe had an idea where he meant, "Not the old military place? I thought I heard someone bought that. But usually you just assume the new owner is some creepy old hermit."

Shai laughed, "Yep, that'd be us, except for the creepy, old hermit part. T did good in fixing it up. You wouldn't even recognize the place now."

Thia added, "You should stop over sometime." She wanted to know everything about them and the vampires.

Ben forced a smile avoiding eye contact with Thia, "That'd be great. We really better get her back home now."

The two parties said their goodbyes and separated in their opposite directions.

It was silent for a few minutes until they heard a far off high pitched giggle from the Alana. When they knew they were far enough away not to be heard, even by animal ears, Shai was the first to break the silence, "What was that all about T?!"

Thia laughed, "There it is! I knew you couldn't hold your tongue for long! What was what?"

Shai was squirming with excitement waiting to pick on her, "You know, your little flirt session just now?"

"You're right Shai, he's totally hot and I want to go back and take him right now!" she went straight for shock value to pay him back.

"Gross!" It worked. Shai did not want to hear those kinds of things from his sister.

"That's what you get for assuming! I mean really? Do you not know what just happened? Is the last five minutes all that's sunk in from tonight? In all of our years of running, we just met someone as close to our kind as there is, that we didn't even know existed and you just want to send them off never to be heard from again?"

Dae agreed with Thia, "Thia is right, think of all we can learn from them."

"Whatever Dae, you just liked how the girl hid behind you. Made you feel all special." Shai teased.

Dae coolly responded as only he can, "Shai, I'm guessing she's about fourteen. I think I still have some time to find someone my own age. Have a little faith in me."

Shai shrugged him off, "Besides, it's not like they'll just up and disappear, Ben freaking works for us."

Dae showed some concern, "Yeah, assuming he still shows on Monday. I hope tonight didn't scare him off."

Shai thought for a moment, "Funny someone like that has been right under our noses and we had no idea. I mean I knew he smelled like dog, but I just thought he had a mutt at home. He doesn't talk much."

Thia more serious now, "Hey guys? I'm guessing from the long pause you were thinking this too, but what if we get bit by one of those vampires. You think that would happen to us too, that we could be controlled?"

Shai was the first to reply, "Yeah that's a little scary huh. What do you think Dae?"

Dae too was very concerned now, "Honestly I just don't know. I wish Nomad was here, he would probably know. Strange he never mentioned these types of threats before."

Dae's response was not what his siblings expected and made them worry. Dae always had a good answer but this time it was only empty and desperate. They walked on in silence the rest of the way back.

That night after the encounter, Thia started having severe dreams about the vampires. This wreaked havoc on their possessions. She kept seeing their cold grey skin and over dilated eyes. More than ever she wanted to talk with Ben. She wanted to know more about the wolves and vampires. In truth all three did. So the next day they hopped on the internet to see if they could find more since Ben was not at work.

Shai was driving the search, "Doesn't help we didn't get a last name when we hired him. Still this area is pretty small. How many Ben's could there be?"

After hours of searching they found nothing.

In desperation Thia suggested, "Maybe we should head out to that clearing again. Maybe they will come back soon?"

"We gonna setup camp while we wait for your boyfriend to show T?" Shai rolled his eyes.

"Oh I'm sorry Shai, what was your better idea again?" Thia searched for a large object nearby to hit him with but found none.

Dae, being the voice of reason, "Alright you two. We don't have much choice right now other than to hang out there. Or I suppose we could try asking around town?"

His idea immediately made Thia uncomfortable, "I don't know if I want the whole town knowing we are looking for someone. What if they don't want that kind of attention? What did Sally say his reason was for calling in sick again?"

"Just that something came up and he would be out for a week or two." Dae explained again.

Shai threw the rubber ball he was tossing up against the wall, "This sucks. Fine let's go."

So they decided to head out after all. As luck would have it Ben and his cousin were already there. It seemed both parties were apparently very curious about one another.

Ben spotted them the moment they came out of the woods and met them halfway, "Hey! Sorry about the call. Our family had to meet about what happened and figure out what to do with all of it. I couldn't risk talking about it at work and hoped you'd end up back here."

"We thought about stopping by, but figured we would try this first. Didn't want to come off rude too soon." Abe laughed.

Shai got stuck on a part of what Ben said, "Figure out what to *do*? Do with what?"

Ben explained, "We worry a lot about exposure."

Shai nodded, "Ah, us too."

So they all talked for a while exchanging information then Thia invited them over for dinner. They accepted and split up. Thia and her brothers returned home to prepare for their dinner guests. Later that night the door bell rang and Shai opened the door. Ben, Abe and Alana arrived.

Ben starts off apologizing, "Hi. I hope you don't mind that we brought Alana. We wouldn't hear the end of it otherwise."

Alana elbowed Ben in the ribs.

Shai laughed, "Ha! Must be a girl thing. Not a problem, Thia cooks for a small army anyway."

The two groups spent the whole evening eating, talking, laughing and learning. Like a sudden adrenaline rush, life became more interesting and exciting with the new friend they made. Thia, her bothers and even the wolves gained new hope knowing others exist like them. They were pleased to find they had so much in common and even more enthusiastic by all they had yet to learn from each other.

The Phelidae wanted to know about the wolves and the vampires and how they've managed to live in a single area for so long in secret. And the wolves wanted to learn all about the Phelidae people. The wolves were fascinated to find the Phelidae had been around for so long and yet no one had ever heard of them or the Pallas.

Too Soon

Continuing to have issues with the vampire nightmares, and destroying the house, Thia chose to visit their old home thinking it might be safe to retrieve some possessions they were forced to leave behind. One item she was particularly attached to came to mind considering recent events.

She wanted to find the dream catcher Shai made for her when they were growing up. The accident was the one other time her dreams wouldn't stop haunting her and brought embarrassing attention to her family. Ignoring her mother's pleas she refused to return home from the cave; that is until Shai brought his gift for her. To this day she believes it really works.

The run took her a few hours at top speed. She didn't mind the amount of time it took though. It was rare that she got to truly be free and run without worry of being monitored or discovered in some way. It also helped that it was an absolutely perfect day.

The forest was cool and only a little moist as the sun beams snuck through holes in the canopy of trees. A slight breeze in addition to the air flowing through her hair from moving so fast, kept the moisture from turning to muggy, sticky humidity. It was early morning when she started off, not yet giving the day time to warm up and dry most of the slippery dew.

Unaffected she flew through the trees with unheard of precision, appearing only as a blur as she passed by, horribly frightening a group of feeding deer attempting to rip up and enjoy some tender seedlings near a large tree. The scare came and went so fast they had no time to react. She imagined it took them a little while to calm down though being as skittish as they tend to be. Later she passed more deer, some foxes and wild turkeys. *Mmm, we haven't had Turkey in a while. I should pick one up on the way back,* she thought. *With an abundance of deer in the area it would be nice to switch it up for a change.*

Then her planning was interrupted as she felt something, like she was being followed. After stopping behind a tree and searching for what might have triggered this, she found nothing as far as she could see or hear so she picked up the pace intending to lose whatever it might or might not be.

In human form she could be a little clumsy, embarrassed and teased for tripping on furniture that hasn't been moved in months, cracking her head on cabinets left open and falling up stairs. However when in her coalesce state, she never misses a step.

Other supernatural's are either their true form all of the time or phased from one to another, but Thia's people could choose one of three states. Human, coalesce and Phelidae. The human form took no effort being the easiest. This was a natural state for them since they were born this way and their abilities develop later.

The Phelidae form took little focus to get into, but once there, again there was no extra effort needed as this too was instinctual during the infant stage of life. The coalesce state however takes some mastering. Bringing the two together in equal parts was trickier than it seemed but after getting the hang of it, it became second nature to sustain. In this state all senses are heightened and tuned in to the conscience bringing everything Phelidae power to human form.

Self control comes natural to them simply because they are a calm natured people, so there is no breaking of deep rooted habits required. When they get angry, they don't turn green, start smashing things or rip someone's head off. If they get hungry there's no need to worry about losing command of themselves and attacking a stranger, or even loved one, just because they could not help but see, hear and smell some tasty warm blood rushing through their veins. No, instead they have a different type of issue all together.

Staying hidden is their unfair challenge. Hiding itself is not the hard part but having to constantly remember and give in to, not being you. This is what they struggled with most and continues to be difficult even with the passage of time and much practice. It is most challenging when the occasional confrontation arises.

So many times when faced with a trouble making inferior being, these three especially have to fight the overwhelming urge to simply end the altercation quickly and be done with the annoyance. But knowing this simply is not an option, as they are hunted, getting some sort of gratification out of it seems justified to make the imposition a little more tolerable.

With a bit of modest yet careful fun in such situations proved to do just that. It was still of the utmost importance to make sure no one was around to witness any mysterious things that might happen. Things like random acts of nature and so on.

About 500 feet from the large cottage, she slowed down to a jog. She kept a keen ear and nose alert. Her intent, to detect anything that might require her to reverse course and head back home long before her presents is discovered. She patiently waited to see if anything moved. Dangerous things are usually too impatient to sit still for very long. But cats are very enduring. Finally deciding the coast was clear, she approached the remains of where they used to call home.

The site of what was left made her heart drop into the pit of her stomach and stole the live giving breath from her as she gasped in horror. Absolute destruction is all that was left of their once beautiful home. She recalls all the manual work she put into it, hand planting the flowers and shrubs, painting and maintaining inside and out...all gone. Thought she knew better, anyone else would've sworn a tornado devoured and spat it out.

This cottage, deep in the respected private property lot of forest, far from the road, is where they enjoyed the quiet and avoided passerby's accidently spotting anything unusual. It was made of logs but it was nowhere near what is traditionally considered a log cabin. The modern structure, sitting two stories high with a big picture frame window in the front and back secured its place out of that category.

All had something they favored about this home. Both Shai and Dae's centered around the privacy aspect but Thia was all about the view. She watched and listened to the fluffy squirrels, various types of birds, twitchy fuzzy bunnies and peaceful deer pass by on many lazy afternoons. Some of the animals became so comfortable in their daily routine of this route that they would stop for a couple hours to nap in the bed of sun warmed grass created by a small opening in the trees around the house.

She instantly fell in love with the clumsy little spotted fawns. They were so very tiny when they started off. As their mothers rested, they would hop around and run after each other as if playing a child's game of tag. When it was time to go, the mothers would nudge at them and head on to the next stop. If the babies weren't close enough Thia heard the mothers call for them and next saw the little baby's heads pop up and then spring off to the source of the call.

Watching nature made for a most tranquil setting. Thia and her brothers spent much of their afternoons laying around sprawled out on some piece of overly padded furniture in the living room. Every so often they enjoyed the most luxurious, muscle invigorating stretch followed by pure contentment and exquisite comfort melting away any possible trace of tension.

Pushing such sidetrack memories aside she very slowly approached, closer and closer watching and listening in all directions. When she decided it was safe, she moved to enter. Both front and back doors were caved in at the frame and buried but she found a huge hole in the side of the house she could easily fit through.

Sifting through the charred, blackened and broken remains, Thia found a statue of a long black and very sleek looking cat. She remembered buying this one at a random trinket shop as it reminded her so much of Dae with his easy going and serene demeanor.

Surrounding the statue lay spent rounds and she remembers how very different he is in battle. Unintentionally he is able to lure the enemy in as falsely they assume he is easiest and slowest target of the three. After ignorantly making such a dangerously sloppy judgment of him, thus first assaulting his siblings, they met an end none imagined possible. Even his siblings wouldn't watch when it came down to that. They know it is not who he really is, not what any of them are, only what they are forced to be for the sake of survival.

Packing up a few items in her bag, the feeling she wasn't alone again washed over her like a sixth sense alarm, a panic induced warning. She remembered on her way over, she thought for a moment she was being followed. However if someone or something was, it was too far back, and coming from the wrong direction to tell what.

If her brothers had been with her she would've sent Shai to investigate. He loves a good game of, "hunt the hunter" he called it. But sadly that was not an option this time. So she stood perfectly still for a few minutes breathing as shallow as possible. She waited for a while behind the nearest half wall but heard nothing beyond the background noises of the forest. She resumed her search, speeding it up a bit moving on to where her room used to be.

Her mind wandered into a paranoid rant as she dug for Shai's gift, *They couldn't have found us already? Whatever might have been back there couldn't have been them. I'm sure they still bring that stupid energy sensor equipment and I would've felt that. Plus it was moving too fast to be them. Must have just been an animal.*

Never the less, I better finish up here and head back home. Now where is that thing?

Thia's brothers had no need for expensive gadgets used by the Pallas. They have their own indicators of when Thia's mood skyrocketed or plummeted when she wasn't paying attention. The first stage and most common side effect is when the hair on their necks and arms stand up on end like in static electricity science experiments. They wasted no time teasing her when this happened which avoided the stronger later stages including static shocks, power drains and finally cracking foundations.

Finding the dream catcher, her reason for coming, she continued sifting through the remains of their destroyed home packing a few more small items in her shoulder bag until, something moved on the other side of the far wall. She could already tell it wasn't a stray cat, or any other animal for that matter. The new movements were careful but still heavy and clumsy through the debris. These were human footsteps. The pungent burnt smell drowned out any other possible scents and there was no breeze there to clear it.

Thia's heart sank, *whoever it is has been very patient. Crap, it has to be a member of the Pallas.*

Instantly she regretted not telling her brothers where she ran off to before she left. She was so sure nothing was going to happen, only thinking, *If worse came to worse, they can follow my scent after my call.* Not absolutely sure it was someone from the Pallas or just a trash picker, she didn't move, but scanned for the fastest way out.

But her suspicion was correct; she was spotted by the hunter watching not far from the site. Thia's guard was down considering until now the Pallas never returned after they'd lost the Phelidae, but instead went back to base to monitor for next signs of settlement. However this was not one of the regular personnel.

A wind picked up and gave away the identity her secret visitor. His attempt to camouflage his natural greedy stench with the latest in retched hunting cologne failed. Thia knew exactly which of the Pallas it was the moment his scent crept around the wall to her. It was Deacon, the young, overly ambitious but wealthy one. Deacon has an embarrassing habit of trying too hard to prove himself to his peers and most of all to his unnoticing father, the head of the Pallas. His father was too consumed by the job to realize or care that he had any offspring, but got an thwarting reminder every time Deacon screwed up.

Because of Deacon's ridiculously large bank account, setup of course to keep him out of his father's hair, he could afford the best. In the past he's tried many things. "Tries and fails at everything." was his father's comment to the entire team when Deacon ruined the latest expensive extraction mission. The one at the very house she was in now. Perhaps that is why he was still there, that day left a scar.

The three were relaxing as they often do in the living room that Saturday afternoon. Thia was on the couch at the window, head resting on her arms, watching her animal friends. Then a funny smell swept through the house carried in on a heavy breeze, the deer became startled and ran. To her watching animals was not only relaxing but, especially in this case, informative too. If they fled, there was something out there that didn't belong. She instantly tensed up and her brothers felt it.

"What's up T?" Shai asked over the top of his car magazine.

"Shhh..." in a volume too low for human ears to hear she motioned then she tipped her nose up signaling that something was in the air. Thia has the more sensitive nose of the bunch but the others soon caught it too.

The three of them very quietly, so as not to alert the uninvited visitors, began preparing just as they'd been taught. They moved through the house undetectable to any listening devices. They gathered their bags and carefully peeked out special spots in the house they installed for this very type of situation. Windows and door peep holes would be monitored but these spots were camouflaged to be unnoticeable from the outside.

Dae let out a low growl and the other two were at his side. Each of them took a look at what he called them to see. It was a large group of men in army looking gear down on the ground hiding behind trees and starting to work their way around the house. As suspected a listening device was aimed directly at them. At the click of a door latch the raid began but it was too late for they were already out of the house.

Arrows are Deacon's new favorite. Primitive as it may seem, these are unlike any available at a common hunting shop. Upon impact, burrowing deep inside the muscle from the hair splitting sharp edges, the metal tip opens into three thick blades with fishing hook-like ends, making quick removal impossible. Simply pulling them out like traditional arrows was no longer an option. These are much more painful and destructive. Yet there's more to these beyond the added entry and removal complications.

The real pain comes from an excreted toxin stored in the tip. The toxin is excruciating as well as demobilizing. It temporarily paralyzes muscles in direct contact and those nearby that blood carries it to. It causes a constant sharp pain pulsing through the system thus weakening senses. Severe headaches, blurred vision, numbed smell, ringing in the ears are all just a bonus side effect of the toxin.

The true intent and purpose is to prevent the Phelidae from changing into their full feline form because of the paralyzing affect. It was a pleasant surprise to Deacon when the rest was discovered, serving as a way to slow them down during the chase. Deacon is ever determined to demonstrate to his father that he would find the missing piece in capturing the last ones he most desired alive and well. These poison arrows were the latest invention Deacon secretly financed to prove his worth.

"Father relies too much on the old hunting methods." he'd say after every failed attempt, he didn't cause.

Deacon knew technology was the key to unlocking the impenetrable wall between him and his father. "I will show him the obvious answer that stubborn old coot refuses to recognize.

He'll see it will only make the hunt more efficient and finally successful if harnessed properly."

Unbeknownst to Father, this has been the latest small victory for them tested in less important hunts, mostly of those trying to escape, perfect for his trial run. Deacon knew it would only help that the Phelidae are too spread out and cut off from each other to spread the word on this one.

The Phelidae are also for the most part defenseless. Using their powers meant they would ultimately have to kill the hunter and or any other possibly innocent witnesses, something against their very nature *unless* the situation escalates to a half step short of self-preservation. So far it has not come to that. The Pallas need living specimens.

Deacon jumps out from behind the wall. Backpack secured Thia bounds off the wall behind her pulverizing it, and rolls out an opening. Deacon clumsily jumps through the dust and rubble to follow her. The chase is on.

Before she could get much distance between them Deacon stops and gets a few shots off through one of the broken windows, knowing he was going to lose her if he didn't play it smart. He hits her with one of his prized arrows. It penetrated deep in the back of her left leg. Though he could tell she definitely felt it judging by a slight miss step when it hit, much to his chagrin, it didn't seem to slow her down.

His jaw drops and he whispers to himself in disbelief, "She is still running without as much as a limp! Maybe there is not enough toxin in them?"

But he did not give up. "More arrows mean more toxin." It works, he knew, the results were undeniable.

He ran out after her until he felt she was getting too far way so he decided to stop, aim and shoot again. And only by pure luck, one ricocheted off of a tall thick root and planted deep in her back, underneath the backpack, into her right bottom two ribs. She let out a blood curdling scream, staggered a few feet and finally slammed against a tree a little late in catching herself with her hands, knocking some of the wind out of her.

She was still far from her new home and her beloved brothers. The whole time she ran in a staggered pattern, even though she desperately wanted to go straight home. Only half of her longed that they could feel that she needed them. *No, maybe it is better this way so they don't get caught up yet again in more destructive trouble I bring. Maybe this will end it all and they will finally be free of me. Then again, he is only human. Still...he got me good with that last one.*

Struggling to turn around and face her foe, her shoulder and head hit and rested against the rough bark. She began slowly sliding down as the one in her leg increased its torment. Catching her breath became increasingly difficult as her lower back and ribs blazed from the spreading poison. Her forehead also began to bleed a bit from the force of hitting the tree but that cut closed shortly after. Suddenly, like a red hot ice pick, another one slammed into her front left shoulder.

Deacon found a clear shot in the trees once he got closer and made the best of it. She cried out in agony. It was becoming too much. Taking over her thoughts *...hurts to breathe...can't see...* Everything was blurring up and her eyes overflowed with tears. She blinked hard and tried to stand up wanting to shake it off and regain control, but it only grew more intense as her limbs stopped responding. With her sight unfocused, a deafening ring in her ears and the rest of her senses dulled, she could do nothing as the violent icy burn became all she knew.

He finally caught up keeping his crossbow fixed on her but staying out of her reach while recalling a lesson he'd learned his first time out in the field against her kind. First and foremost, she is a quick, strong and fierce animal.

He was pathetically out of breath from all the running. She hadn't yet reached her normal speed before the arrows hit. Then they did in fact slow her down. Deacon remained oblivious thinking he wasn't doing half bad in keeping up.

He positioned himself up against a large tree across from her. Then when he finally found the air and courage to make his demands he managed to spit out, "Prove you're Athena! Do what they say you can do to try and free yourself!"

Wow, he is still new at this. she thought taking in slow deep calculated breaths, his face still a blur.

"Do it!" he urged impatiently.

Thia just turned her head and looked away. He wanted her to use powers against him, but she refused. She wasn't about to take orders from him. She wouldn't try to speak yet revealing the state she was in. Instead she let her body language make the "request denied" statement for her.

Though not surprised her refusal ate at him. He again, took deep breaths, attempting to slow down his over accelerated breathing and painfully beating heart. Then attempting to be more assertive, he again gave the order, this time failing to deliver the intended condescending "manly" voice. What managed to come out was deeper but still quivering.

Again she did nothing, her attention coming and going between his buffoonery and the searing burn. The toxin actually had a freezing sensation at first but it was so cold that it actually burned. But through the almost numbing pain, she was honestly a little embarrassed for him. *I hope he's got a backup plan. What does he think this foul breath shouting is going to accomplish?*

The lack of progress and reaction on her part angered him as he indeed had no plan B. He is closer than he's ever been before, than *anyone* one has been before, in winning his father's attention and respect from those that have made fun of him for so long now. He actually has her captured – this moment is real. Right here, right now. But he hasn't won yet. He knows he has to come up with something. He has to know without a doubt it is her. He can't afford any more embarrassments.

He pushed the last incident out of his mind and returned to what he had to do now to secure his catch. *It has to be her.* She looks very close to the old and fuzzy surveillance pictures on the training projector screen at the base. And, now that he was so close to her, he had to admit she was much better looking in person. The picture had a convenient store, mug shot quality to it. He interrupted his own wandering thought. *Now is your chance, you have her! The others won't believe it. Father won't believe it! I've done alone what all of them failed to do.*

Thia noticed the distraction from his internal struggle and decided it was time do make a bold move. They were trained not only in physical combat but a few psychological tactics as well. One lesson that came to mind taught, more times than not the enemy tends to make mistakes when you get them angry breaking their focus and clouding judgment with emotion. Nomad's Lesson #3, Cloud the Enemy with Emotion and Fear.

She cleared her dry throat so she wouldn't start off sounding raspy or weak, "Alone, are we? Too afraid to fail in front of your small army again?"

He looked at her confused, she kept going. "Say, have you been working out since last time I saw you? Wait, no. It hasn't been long enough I don't think. I mean to gain that level of mass in such a short period of time...uh oh, you haven't resorted to..." she sniffed the air slowly and accusingly in his direction. "Steroids, really?"

She made this part up as she could not recall ever actually seeing him during any of the attacks but heard he was there for a few of them. She also got an idea from some of the stories that got around, how he is viewed as nothing more than a spoiled skinny screw up and treated poorly for it.

She shook her head in a mockingly sympathetic way, "Daddy still not paying any precious attention to you? What a shame."

Her venomous jabs worked. He got mad, very mad in fact. It was the father comment that struck a nerve just as she was sure it would with him.

Unsure why but able to gain some of her focus back, she was not only looking at him but he was sure she was peering right through him. This made him nervous. Just moments ago he was excited he had her, then she was kind of attractive, then she angered him and now she frightened him.

He quickly broke away from her upsetting gaze and searched around trying to think of what to do. He was so turned around he didn't know what to do. Then it came to him. Now, he was going to get what he wanted for sure.

He rushed upon her, just as she secretly wanted him to, getting him within reach. He quickly reached up, careful not to look her in the eyes for fear of losing his nerve, wrapped his pale long fingers around the shiny cool arrow still lodged in her left shoulder, tightened his grip and ever so slowly twisted.

Thia wide eyed now witnessing what he was doing, at first shocked that he mustered up the courage, clinched down hard on her teeth to deal with the all new heights of pain. While doing her best to maintain control, she felt a trickle of something thick and warm fall from her nose. The stress and pressure caused it to bleed, fighting the overwhelming urge to change and annihilate him.

"It is the Phelidae way. We, only if *absolutely* necessary, match force, never over powering those inferior to us." She played over and over in her mind like a broken record.

Beneath her locked jaw scream and bloody nose, her crunched closed eyes began to change. This mere human boy, barely worth calling enemy if it weren't for his new toy, had no idea what was creeping up inside her preparing to strike. The stories and lessons he half paid attention to while daydreaming of his own all-star moment were just small fragments of the impending reality. As self preservation attempted to impose a new leader, the beast, she managed to open her eyes, barely a slit.

It was enough for him to get a perpetual rush of adrenaline from what he caught a glimpse of. Her eyes drastically morphed from the normal human grey to something else, something not human. Now, they took on a piercing crystal blue. But strangely enough that wasn't the heart stopping part. He never imagined it possible or heard it mentioned before that the pupil itself had gone from like his, to a sharp and courage swallowing abyss of a deep black and wide slit. He had heard literally hundreds of stories about these creatures but now it is all here, up close and horribly real.

"You *are* Athena." he whispered in pure fright. "I knew I recognized you. You were right there in the middle when we broke up that last tribe."

His words hit her like a ton of bricks. She too remembered something of this memory. Everything in her mind was gone now, only blackness existed. She was forcefully thrown back to that time; the time she lost her mother as she held her in her arms helplessly watching the life fade from her eyes. As she slowly looked up blinking the tears away, her vision clearing, she realized his face *was* there. *He* was the one that fired the fatal shot.

An invigorating shadow took over her. The beast arrived.

A confusing flash thought of her brothers popped in her mind but was gone again as fast as it came like a doused flame. They were trying to call her to find out what was going on, why they could feel something was very wrong, but her focus on her mother's killer was too strong.

"YOU!" came out in a trebling growl through her fierce teeth. She felt no pain now.

"You killed my mother!" her fingers curling up like large claws. "She was pure and good and you ended her! She did NOTHING to you!" her voice a bit higher, tortured and quivering but sadistic.

She looked him up and down, "You ignorant insignificant little rat. If only you knew her, even you would've loved her, not that a sniveling little brat like you would've deserved it."

His face was blank and afraid now, but she didn't notice. She wasn't talking to him she was talking *at it*. This was no longer a person in front of her, but a thieving monster.

She shoved him off of her sending him flying out into an open area next to them. He rolled over trying to catch his breath and watched as she transformed into her true self, a massive and beautiful snow white tiger. Angrily, she dug her claws in pulverizing the tree behind her. She could no longer feel the arrows that were still buried deep in her flesh. Then she leapt to attack him.

As she soared at him she imagined the many terrible things she was going to do to him; shattering his face beneath her massive paw, ripping his head clean off with her immense jaws, she envisioned plucking him apart like a hawk with a small rabbit.

Just as she was about to land on him a great force intercepted her. It was Ben in wolf form. He knocked her to the side then circled back and nudged her to let her know it was him. She growled and kicked him away with little to no effort, then turned back ready again to attack Deacon. The arrows were now all bent from the force of landing on them. She jumped again, but this time her brothers, also in animal form, stopped her forcing her to the ground. She growled and hissed, twisting and turning in frustration trying to escape.

Ben, shaking off the knock Thia dealt, was nervous around them for the first time from the pure force she demonstrated merely as a second thought. Still at the same time his trust remained intact. The shock lasted only a short time as he saw her brothers holding her down. The large cats let out short roars, attempting to comfort her.

The great panther changed into Dae and he pulled two cloths from a large bag that was around his neck covering himself and a changing Thia. Then once Dae had a good hold on her Shai changed and covered up too. Ben did the same.

The agonizing memory and physical pain left her weak. Her brothers could not believe their eyes as Thia's old healed gashes from that awful day reopened before them. Ben joining them gasped at the size of them, overwhelmed by the sight.

All of the new discoveries took Ben back to the time when his true nature was revealed to him. Ben was sure his life and anything he'd ever known was over the first time he became a werewolf. He eventually adjusted, but his new cat friends have brought joy back to his life and opened his eyes to possibilities he's never known before.

Thia pleaded, "He killed her. He took her from me, from us!"

"Thia…we can't. He is just a human." Dae trying to remind her of who she is. They've been away from their people for so long each of them felt like something was fading away soon to be forgotten.

Another image of her dying mother sparked in her mind. It ignited strength and she fought back lifting both of them until they countered.

She tried to convince them, "He is not, he's a monster. He stole life, *her* life!"

Rage exploded in her. She threw her brothers off and lunged at Deacon, covered in only rags, bloody wounds and arrows. Ben intercepted her, scooping her up and threw her over his shoulder. Her brothers again took over for him once she became unmanageable.

"Thanks Ben. Can you deal with him? The longer he is here the longer this will go on." Shai motioned over at Deacon.

Ben nodded and approached Deacon back in wolf form.

Deacon recoiled in fear, "NO! What are you?!"

With a single swing, Ben flung him into a tree knocking him unconscious. He then tossed Deacon up on his back and ran off.

The pain from the agonizing tools embedded deep in her shoulder, back and leg returned; draining her of all energy and most sanity.

"We need to get her home and get these out." Dae told Shai.

Exhausted, and with her new vision, she looked over to find a very large wolf returning without her tormentor. Struggling to calm down, she again closed her eyes. She had to take long struggled deep breaths to regain her control. Once she was able to settle down she opened her eyes again no longer seeing the wolf but a human Ben. She smiled.

"I can have my friend take a look at her. He can be trusted. He takes care of our kind and helps keep us a secret." Ben offered before noticing for the first time what a beautiful smile she has.

Thia was half out of it but spending her last bit of energy suddenly thinking about Ben. *Ben. What wonderfully unexpected benefit of moving to this remote place. He's not one of us but as close as they come these days. He is a good man. We all will become great friends I think, and stay that way even if we do have to move on.* Thia wanted to trust her new friend more than anything. By nature she would be a very trusting person had it not been for their situation. It's been very lonely on the run, perpetually separated from their own for so long. At this Thia faded out.

"How did you guys know to come, and get here so fast?" Ben asked.

Dae started explaining as he wrapped Thia up getting her ready to move, "We tried calling to Thia but the cat threw us out before we were able to get any details. We've never been thrown out like that before, or felt the way she did when we were in, so we knew we had to find her fast. It was enough for us to know she was in serious trouble, enraged and in lots of pain. So far we've learned, as calling is a little new to us, if fear, pain or anger is strong enough it can send out a call without us even trying, much like an alarm. We left home and ran as fast as we could following her scent."

Shai wondered the same thing about Ben, "How did you end up here?"

"Oh, I was out hunting when I caught a faint trace of her scent. She must have been going fast because it wasn't too spread out yet. I wasn't that hungry so I thought I'd see what she was up to or if she wanted to partner up. You guys hunt, I assume?"

"Yep", Shai said suspiciously. Ever since Caleb's attack on Thia he's been very protective of her.

Ben went on, "Then I smelled blood that didn't belong to an animal that I'd ever caught before and thought she might be in trouble. To be safe I assumed the worse and wound up here just before you guys."

"Okay she's ready, let's go." Dae had her in his arms after dressing her old wounds and doing what he could with the new ones so the movement from the journey didn't further aggravate them.

Ben led the way to his friend. After they dropped Thia off, Ben and Shai returned for Deacon. After many bad ideas they chose to leave him at the old house beaten up and unconscious. They were banking on the hope he wouldn't be able to remember which way he was heading when he was after Thia. Even in excruciating pain, she was still able to stagger the path. Successfully, Thia did very well in her redirections, denying any possibility of memorizing the route.

Dae examined but found he was at a loss on how to deal with the new weapon. Ben gave the doctor a call before they arrived. He cryptically explained why it was impossible for her to be brought to the hospital but that she still needed immediate attention, *his* attention. He said he thought she had a condition much like his but not exactly. This was enough to signal the doctor to come quickly. Her brothers kept an eye out for the doctor and quietly discussed the situation as Ben took turn watching over Thia.

To Ben, Thia seemed to have a silent confidence about her. Initially some first impressions are that she comes off almost unapproachable, that is, until she smiles at you. The genuineness of it can unhinge the poorest of moods, of which he's had many. He couldn't help but notice she was also one that favored direct eye contact when speaking, though she didn't waste it on just anyone.

She's been perfect when longing for someone to listen. Ben wasn't a big talker but when he chose to, there was no one better for the job than she. She glues herself to every word, then speaks back like she's been through it, even when some of those experiences would be impossible. One might become nervous wondering if she was in their head, though he already knew this was not one of her talents.

Thia had a likewise attraction, or maybe better described as a curiosity. Ben was not like others. She found she trusts Ben faster than she has anyone before but couldn't figure out why.

Something New

While everyone waited for the doctor to arrive, Ben stayed with Thia patiently trying his best to care for her. Alana got there shortly after he called her. Right away she noticed Ben's unusual attention to Thia, cautiously watched and gently coached. She gave him warm damp cloths to softly cleanse and rinse the deep wounds, a cool cloth to lay on her forehead to keep the fever down as well as dropping additional yet subtle hints guiding him along. She made sure she stayed just far enough away to keep him from realizing what she suspected, knowing this would only embarrass him and make him stop.

She'd never seen her only brother behave this way before. She could tell he felt something special for her. She wasn't sure if it was the likeness between their kinds or if it was something more but she loved her bother dearly and wanted nothing more than to see him find happiness. Until now his purpose was to be nothing more than a guardian of their people and family.

Thia lay on her side propped up with pillows coming in and out of consciousness, her bothers checking on her often. When she was awake she tried to talk without much success. They could only make out parts of what she was trying to say before she was out again. Occasionally, when she faded out, she experienced vivid dreams of her past. One strong one took her back to the decision in time when she tried to free her brothers of the burden she felt she imposed upon them for far too long.

After running and separating from one of their city homes before, she fell into deep a depression. Consistently a single thought returned, nagging at her; *they don't deserve this...constant running. It's because of me. They've sacrificed everything, and for what? Me? Why? I owe them so much. I owe them freedom...at least freedom from me. That is all I can give them for now. They need to find and be with their real families. Mine is broken but theirs doesn't have to be. I won't force them to protect me any longer. Nomad should've never made them promise. I'm going to do something about it this time.*

Once her mind was made up she didn't contact them like they'd done all the times before. They left worried messages, but she wouldn't respond, unsure of what to say.

She didn't want them to think something had happened to her so she finally replied only saying, "Do not worry, I am fine. But I will not be meeting up with you this time. You deserve to be free, at least of me. Don't bother responding as this is the last time I will be on. I love you both dearly which is why I have to do this. Thia."

Even though, she said she wouldn't, she still checked her messages, each time breaking her heart not to answer their begging requests for a response, to rejoin them, but she knew this is what she had to do. Solitude was her sacrifice for them.

She didn't feel like she could hide in a city, at least not for a while so she traveled until she came across a quaint little country town in southern Illinois called Wayne City. She had only a little money left and couldn't risk cashing out an account revealing her location, so she asked around about a place to rent and a job. A portly but very friendly clerk sent her to the farm of an older couple.

The friendly couple instantly liked her, having lost a daughter around her age, and took her in renting the small in-law suite behind their house. It was a little dusty but didn't take her long to tidy up. It was perfect. Thia loved the unusual décor. Little apple and cinnamon jar candles with checkered ribbons, ceramic chickens in the kitchen, dried grapevine wreaths and sprays above the doors, hand stitched quilts on the bed and walls, hand painted signs with cute sayings and hand sewn dolls, all done in a color theme of dark red, navy blue and beige. It was welcoming, quiet and comfortable.

She visited the local library to catch up on her email and national news. She would've offered to help at the farm but they had nephews doing the work so instead she found something at the little eatery down the road. She filled in where needed, sometimes waitress, hostess, dishwasher and cashier once they trusted her, which didn't take long.

Work wasn't too far from where she was staying so she enjoyed walking there. One day a friendly little mangy mutt found and followed her. She thought he looked hungry so during a break she shared some of her lunch and saved table scraps. He didn't leave her side after that. He wouldn't stay in the house with her but returned every day to walk with her to and from work.

One day, Thia happy to have her friend join her, fed him some scraps she got into the habit of saving and bringing along, "Hey there little guy! You know what? I think I'll call you Bengie. What do you think of that name?"

The perky eared dog just happily wagged his tail and trotted alongside her.

Sometime later Thia heard some clanging and noise out back so she followed where it was coming from. She found some mean young teenage boys teasing and abusing the dog, throwing broken glass bottles and rusty pieces of metal from the garbage at him. She ran out after them yelling for them to leave him alone. One of the bigger boys chose to be defiant and approached her.

He spoke in only a way a bully could, "And what if we don't."

Thia felt a slight jump of excitement inside from the challenge but wasn't sure where to go with it. All of her strength, and special abilities yet she was stumped on what to do with this oversized human farm boy. Then it came to her, she decided to have a little harmless fun.

Knowing his friends were too far back to see, she looked down at the ground and simply said, "Just get out of here if you know what's good for you." Then she slid her gaze up and stopped directly in his eyes and only for a split second, changed to her cat eyes and back.

At first the boy stood frozen. Then he swallowed hard, started shaking and wet himself. His friends saw his pants and called out to him. He didn't move. Thia not breaking eye contact tilted her head to the side. The boy jumped and ran off dragging his bike behind him. His friends followed looking back confused by what just happened.

Little did Thia know but the boy's aunt worked for the paper of the larger town over. His story ended up in it but luckily was met only with comparisons to UFO stories and laughter. They young man already had a reputation for causing trouble. Still Thia regretted her actions, and hoped it was too small of a town to be noticed by anyone that would come looking for her, specifically the Pallas.

Weeks went by and nothing happened so she was able to relax. She'd just begun her shift when a little boy and his family drove up in an older station wagon. Thia's mangy friend was out front and batted an old ball at the little boy, making him and his parents laugh and watch until they decided it was time to go in. Thia seated them and got their drinks. When she went back to take their food order she noticed the little boy was crying.

It broke her heart to see such a sweet little boy upset. Thia couldn't help but ask, "Oh, what's wrong?"

The little boy sniffled and explained, "My doggie went to heaven. He was my best friend. I miss him."

Thia searched out the window for her little friend to find he was right there looking back at them.

"Miss, do you know whose dog that is out front? We didn't see a collar on him." the father asked.

Thia looked at the boy then back at the father, "Um, some around here call him Bengie but honestly I don't think he has a home."

The little boy got all excited, "Daddy can we keep him?! Please, oh please!"

"We'll see son. Maybe after dinner we will see if he would like to come with us."

Though sad at the thought of losing her little companion, Thia felt a little better watching the boy dance in his seat at the thought of taking home a new friend.

After the family finished with their food they paid and returned to their car. The little boy pulled out a biscuit and little piece of hamburger he'd saved for the dog and gave it to him. All got in the car but the dad standing with his hand on the open back door by the boy. The boy called out with the biggest smile, "Come on boy!" and patted the seat next to him.

Strangely enough Bengie looked at Thia through the window of the diner, bowed his head as if he were saying goodbye, then jumped in the car and sat wagging his tail as they pulled away. Teary eyed Thia smiled and waved. She didn't want him to go but somehow she knew the little boy and his family would love him and treat him right. This made her feel much better.

"Bengie", she whispered with a sad smile starting to wake up.

"Yeah, thanks for the new nickname. Of course no one here has already started picking on me for it.", Ben said with a gorgeous smile.

Getting over the fact she'd never seen him smile, it took her a moment to get what he said, then let out a weak little laugh, "Oh, sorry. Why…where did you come from?" she asked out of breath and her eyes rolling around trying to stay awake.

But before he could answer a somber darkness cleared any trace left of a smile, "What did you guys end up doing with…Deacon?"

Ben's stomach dropped seeing how the sound of her enemy's name affected her, "I knocked him out, though I'm pretty sure Shai wanted to, and then we took him back to your old place and tied him to a tree."

"And to answer your first question, I was hunting and caught your scent." he said very plainly. Seeing how bad off she was his mind became occupied with the whereabouts of the doctor. She should be but was not getting better. If it were possible he was sure more color had left her face.

"So you were the one I felt following me." Thia closed her eyes and tried to take a deep breath.

Ben was getting antsy and yelled out to her brothers, "Are you guys sure I can't pull these out?" referring to the arrows. It seemed ridiculous to him that they should stay.

He shook his head frustrated, "They look like they are angering your wounds. I've removed things like this before. When I hunt sometimes I cross human hunter's paths and they've shot me with arrows, bullets, buck shot, you name it."

Thia tried to smile, "I don't doubt your abilities Ben. But no, you can't remove them. These are very different. They have been made special for our kind. Regular hunters don't have these and probably never will. You are correct, they are…angering… where they remain." Drained it took her a moment to regain her energy after being reminded about the pain they cause. "This is because they have a poison in them. But…" she was unable to finish as her head hit the table bed again.

And her dream resumed.

Staying hidden from her bothers was harder than she thought. She missed them so bad. *This too will pass as it did with mom*, she told herself trying to find comfort as she continued to ignore the emptiness.

But eventually the news story did get noticed. Both her brothers and the Pallas quickly found her. Luckily her brothers arrived first and they were able to get out just before the Pallas showed up. Thankfully none in the town were harmed.

Ben got increasingly anxious each time she stopped talking. He'd grab her face turning it towards him checking if she was still breathing. He found little relief when he saw that her breaths were becoming shallower as time passed.

Ben went back to his cleansing routine. Barely ringing out the wash cloth from the bowl of warm water he'd slowly squeezed it over each spot where the arrows protrude from, hoping he could somehow dilute the toxin that festered in her open wounds. He had no way of knowing if it was actually working or not. But he gained hope each time she came back.

"Hey" she whispered. He jumped, not expecting it. She let out another weak laugh.

"Ow", she winced from the added pain of the laugh.

She had only enough energy left for whispering now, "Why did you stop me?"

He answered nervous and quick, "I don't know, seemed like the right thing to do. You didn't seem yourself."

"Hey! Where is he?!" Ben yelled out the door at Alana.

Thia jumped and winced from the shock of his impatient shouting.

Alana yelled back, "I don't know. I'll call again."

"Maybe *I'm* the bad guy?" she half suggested to him.

He turned to her confused by the ridiculousness of the idea, "You are not. Even I can figure that one out. Besides who's the one with the most injuries?"

She weakly smiled back, "And I seem to remember three strong men needing to stop me from doing something very bad. Still, why risk your own life, even the lives of your family, for someone you barely know?"

"I…I don't know. I just did. I knew I wanted to…I should." Ben got flustered, "You shouldn't ask so many questions."

"right" Thia said as she closed her eyes.

Her silence made Ben feel guilty. His sister was right, he doesn't treat women the way he should, "Look, I'm not trying to be a jerk. I just don't know. We haven't met any like us. I guess I don't understand, it's been too easy trusting you guys. It makes me nervous."

She appreciated his honesty and chose to offer some back, "I'm not sure why either, but we trust you too. Maybe it's like you say, we don't want to be alone anymore." *Enough with the heavy talk,* she thought. "Regardless, now it seems I owe you." she ended with a smirk.

"You don't owe me anything." he said grabbing a cloth from the bowl again.

"Yes, I do, and we make good on our debts." she grabbed his hand headed for the bowl and bit the tip of his finger.

"Ouch! What was that for? You know if you are hungry just say so and I can get you something that tastes much better than my finger!"

She smiled, her lips so dry that the bottom one cracked open. She then took his finger and brought it to her mouth again. He recoiled, but she held tighter. He was shocked again by her strength, for a girl. She then kissed his finger with her broken lip.

"Wow, that's kind of gross. You haven't been holding something back from me have you?", he said with a raised brow.

Thia wasn't sure what he meant, "Like what?"

He just rolled his eyes, "Oh, I don't know, like you are actually part vampire? You know, my arch enemy? Cuz that might change things between us."

She smiled, "No, I'm not. Do I feel dead to you?"

Ben crumpled his eyebrows with concern, "No, but you aren't far from looking it."

She imagined she looked pretty bad but wanted to lighten up the mood, "Gee, thanks. You need to work on your compliments. Actually, I bit you to help repay my debt."

He wondered if she was slipping into deliriousness, "I'm not following."

"Now we have a bond." She told him. "If you are ever in trouble, I will know it and where to find you…without having to stalk *you*."

"Hey, I wasn't stalking you." he started but then broke off into a smile.

She started breathing hard and looking green again, "Sure, sure…" and again she faded out.

The next time she woke, her brothers were at her side as well as Ben, Alana and an older, grey haired man. Everyone feverously worked bringing in and setting up medical supplies and tools. The instruments didn't look brand new but were in good condition.

Ben noticed Thia's eyes were open and watching all that was going on around her. "Hey you're back. Thia this is Daniel. He is going to help you. He fixes us up all the time."

The professor looking man spoke fast and out of breath as he quickly tried to set up, "I apologize it took me so long, I don't live here in town. I've only gotten a quick explanation but I must admit I am already extremely fascinated by your kind. I have never met any like you, with your uh, composition I mean…but given the arrows are embedded mostly in muscle tissue I should still be able to remove them without much damage, but I have to tell you it won't be quick or easy."

When it was time to start both Dae and Shai stood over him, arms crossed and cautious watching every move. Thia thought this might have made him a bit nervous as he fumbled about moving too fast.

Once everything was in place Daniel took a deep breath to collect himself and asked everyone to leave the room. He explained that he needed to check her over to see exactly how bad the damage was and if there was anything else that may need his attention. However Thia's not so quick to trust body guards didn't budge. Ben and Alana understood and left them there with their sister.

Dae could tell the doctor was uneasy so he thought he would speak up and offer some information before he got started, which was good because Daniel jumped at the first sound of Dae's deep booming voice. "We used to be able to snap them off when they first made them of wood. But now they are making them out of a light metal, so they still fly but can't be quickly broken off." He went on to explain his theory about the tip of the arrow and the poison.

This did indeed calm the doctor as his interest seemed to distract his nerves.

"I see." Was all Daniel said, and then he went to work. He had Dae and Shai help since they were there. He told them what to do as he bottled samples of the poison and inspected the entry wounds. Then he pulled out his scalpel to finally attempt removing the first arrow.

"Oh" he stopped. "Shouldn't we sedate her?"

"No, it doesn't work on us." Dae explained.

His brows furrowed, "Mmmm…how unfortunate."

"You're telling us!" Shai added.

Shai was no match for the doctors lack of humor, "Very well, here we go."

Daniel moved to begin but was interrupted, by a low growl.

Dae acted quickly, "Uh, now that you mention it, it might be better if we hold her…hand." He signaled to Shai.

Both bothers grabbed a part of Thia and nodded for Daniel to go ahead. He began the first incision to further open the area and untangle its hold, but froze perplexed, it wasn't working.

Determined he tried again but again stopped in a huff, "Well this isn't going to work."

"Why not?" Dae questioned.

"You apparently heal way too fast, even faster than the wolves. Every time I make a shallow cut it closes right back up!"

"What if you make them bigger?" Dae suggested.

He looked up at Dae through his thick framed glasses, "I just tried that, still just as fast even though she is very weak. You truly are fascinating. May I study you?"

Shai was surprised and aggravated by his lack of sensitivity, "First we fix her. Now what do we do?"

"Thia?" Dae leaned in softly after thinking for other options.

"Yeah?" came out tired and raspy.

Dae gently explained, "We can't get the arrows out. You are going to have to push them out."

"Huh?" She said exhausted and confused.

"What do you mean she is going to have to push them out? You can do something like that?" the perplexed doctor inquired.

Dae spoke looking only at Thia, "She is going to have to try. We've done it with bullets before. Try to do it like we move wounds."

She whimpered, "I can't. I'm so tired. Just rip them out. I don't care how bad it will be, I just want them out already."

Dae and Shai looked at each other, like they were talking to one another without saying a word as the doctor helplessly observed taking mental notes. Finally Shai gave in and volunteered. She was conscience again so he started.

He took her hand, "Thia fight it out. We'll help you."

"Can't. I'm so tired" she whispered weakly.

"I said fight!", he yanked on her locking his hand with hers as Dae grabbed the other.

"I can't" she half cried and whined.

"Fine I'll make you!" at that he did just as Deacon did and grabbed the one in her shoulder and started pulling, only gently.

The pain woke her up a bit, "Ow! What's wrong with you?!"

"Now, are you going to push them out or what?" Shai said smartly.

"Get away from me! Leave me alone." she tried pulling her hand out of his.

He tugged at the same one in her shoulder again and she snapped around and growled at him this time.

"You sound tough, now let's see tough." and he flicked it.

"Ahh!" she screamed and this time sat up and kicked him through the wall. Ben, who had snuck in as Dae and Shai were deciding who would be the one to play bad cop, watched the whole time and was again impressed by her strength. Then Dae took over.

He grabbed Thia's face with both hands and looked her straight in her tear filled and streaming eyes, "Thia I think with your help we can work these out along with the poison. I need you to try, like Nomad showed us with the cuts."

Her attention turned to Shai coming back in, dusting himself off. Dae turned her head at him again forcing her attention. She nodded, very much aware now. She closed her eyes pushing the rest of the tears down her cheeks and onto Dae's hands and focused on the one that hurt most, the one in her back.

She took a deep painful breath and slowly, and a bit wobbly, straightened up as it was very sore. And just like in their lessons, they all imagined with her flesh and skin rejecting the arrow in her back and the poison oozing out with it.

Dae had a feeling this could work and if so would be a huge step for them. The doctor gasped in surprise as the arrow started to move. It hurt badly as it shifted but Thia slowly exhaled while squeezing her brother's hands, flinching every so often in reaction to the pain but refusing to stop realizing the progress. Slowly it twisted and turned, working its way out until it finally hit the table with a loud clang.

Dae smiled with pride, "Very good Thia! Keep going. You have to push out the poison before you can fully heal."

The hole slowly closed up once she was able to get rid of the rest of the thick yellow liquid. The doctor tried to help by rinsing the wound but the substance was like oil so the solution just ran off of it as rubbing only spread it.

Thia, with the help of her bothers, was able to remove the others the same way but the last one in her shoulder proved a bit more difficult as it slipped under a bone during the fight. When it was all over the doctor cleaned her up and had her rest for a while on the couch. Then the ecstatic man quickly gathered his instruments and ran down the hall to his lab to examine the liquid and determine its components. Dae also very curious joined him.

Starting to doze off Thia asked, "Shai, why does it smell like dog food in here? Where are we?"

But before he could answer she was out.

Shai decided to get some fresh air and stretch his legs for a bit from sitting with Thia. As she rested he sat outside across the way from a much calmer Ben. "So how did you find Dan?"

"That is an embarrassing story. I guess I didn't take the news very well when I found out I was far from normal. I took off and thought it'd be fun to play Chicken with an oncoming semi truck. I lost. Daniel said he was driving by and saw me in pretty bad shape, dog shape, on the side of the road. So he put me in his car and took me back here to his office and got me all fixed up. I failed to mention before, but as you've no doubt figured out, he isn't a people doctor so much but a vet. Anyway he was quite shocked when he checked on me one day and found a human in the cage instead of an animal. He never told, and ever since then we come to him."

Shai just laughed, "As messed up as this is, it kind of makes sense. Whatever works, right? Oh, and tell him sorry about the wall. We'll fix it soon."

Ben couldn't wait any longer, "I've been wanting to ask...where did her other wounds come from, the ones on her stomach?"

Shai hung his head and nodded, "Yeah, those. Most of the time when we are injured it's during a fight. So Dae says our bodies hide them quickly so we can focus on the fight and look less injured and weak. It's some survival thing. After the fight the cuts and stuff are still there healing even though we can't see them. Sometimes if we get physically or emotionally drained they will appear again since there is not enough energy to keep them away. Thia's however are different. We can't figure those out because she got them so long ago they should've been fully healed by now. We don't understand how or what would've reopened her scars."

Ben with Shai and Daniel with Dae are ever fascinated by their kind. They asked question after question, actually excited by the opportunity to finally speak with one of them. They found they were so much like their friends the wolves but also had very different qualities. The fast healing was the same as was the speed and heightened senses. But only Ben got to learn about their eyes and extra abilities and eagerly wanted to know more.

Inside, Daniel and Dae carefully studied the left over traces of the toxin.

Dae admitted it was thicker than he expected, "It must be to keep it there and not run out so it will last longer"

"Yes, yes that's good!" the doctor excitedly agreed.

Back and forth they exchanged ideas and deductions. Dae got so caught up in the investigation of it all that he completely forgot his prior prejudice of the unknown stranger.

"Your sister didn't seem to be in as much pain as I thought she would be in." He was amazed by this.

"The females have a higher tolerance for pain."

"Ah, yes I should've guessed."

Realizing how hungry they were once everything settled down, Shai and Ben went back in to check on the others and Thia, who was still sleeping.

"Dae and Daniel seem to be getting along." Ben noticed.

"Yeah, Dae can't really talk about that stuff with us. We can never keep up, or stay interested long enough. He has a friend he used to visit and bounce ideas off of but he doesn't get to see him very often." Shai admitted.

Once Thia woke up and was okay to travel, she and her brothers headed home after properly thanking Ben and Daniel for all they had done. The brothers also made sure they knew someone would be coming in the next day or so to fix the wall.

About a week after the whole ordeal there was a knock on the door. Shai answered to find it was Ben.

"Hey! Come on in. Guys it's Ben!" he shouted into the house.

They all met in the living room and Shai motioned for Ben to have a seat, "Hey, sorry to drop by unannounced but Alana wouldn't stop bugging me about checking on you guys. That and she wants to know if you would like to come over for dinner one night."

"What is it with you girls and food all the time?", Shai asked Thia as she placed a large bowl of chips on the coffee table.

Then she plopped down on the couch and kicked her feet up smiling, "The way to a man's heart is through his stomach."

Shai popped a hand full of chips in his mouth, "Is that some kind of code you are taught in girl school?"

Thia, behaving a little more refined grabbed only a couple, "Works doesn't it?"

Ben smiled at their endearing and playful bickering. It was reassuring knowing it wasn't only him and his sister that did it. It also helped him feel at home and almost part of the family since they weren't shy about being themselves around him now, unlike when they first met.

"Can I ask you guys something?" Ben seemed concerned. "Ever since that day at the vet, weird things have been happening."

Thia's face went blank and eyes wide. *Uh-oh*, she thought. She was connected to him and forgot to tell her brothers what she'd done.

Ben went on, "I don't know if it is that poison or what but doc says I might be experiencing some sort of side effects?"

Thia's mind franticly raced on how to change the subject but it was too late, Dae was already thoroughly intrigued, "What kind of side effects?"

"First I started to get really tired in the middle of the day. I thought maybe it was all that went on and I just needed some extra sleep. But then I woke up 3 hours later and it's been happening ever since."

Shai nodded in approval, "Now that's some quality napping."

Dae butted in wanting to hear more, "You said side *effects*? What else are you experiencing?"

"I was out playing ball with my friends, wolf friends that is since we can't really be around our old friends anymore, and I noticed…no matter how or from where I fell, I kept landing on my feet. And it is still like that. I actually really like that one, but it's a little weird that it just started out of nowhere. We've always played rough so I'm used to wiping out even when we end up fighting sometimes. The guys are getting a little jealous since they can't do it and end up all bruised and sore while I walk away without barely a scratch anymore."

Then Ben looked over at Thia, "You okay?"

Thia looked up at him still biting her lip, "Uh, yeah, why do you ask?"

"I don't know, you seem nervous or something." He could feel something was up.

"Thia!" Dae caught on to what happened.

She jumped, "What?!"

Dae was not happy, "Did you…you know?!"

She innocently shrugged, "…maybe?"

"What were you thinking?" he asked scolding her.

She responded remorseful and unsure, "I don't know that I really was, thinking clearly I mean."

Dae, worried about the possible fatality of the act, turned to Ben and began the inquisition, "Ben is there anything else? How do you feel?"

All three were interested in what he was experiencing. They've learned quite a bit on how it affected each other and were told what it did to humans but this was undiscovered territory.

Dae remained upset with Thia. It was irresponsible of her to do it without thinking it through and talking to them first. "Though he did help us we still don't know them very well. Not to mention we have no idea how it will affect him. So far we've been lucky but what if something goes wrong?" Dae reprimanded her.

She left the room upset and he followed. She admitted she didn't really think about any of it. She just did what she felt was the right thing to do at the time. This did not surprise Dae. Thia was mostly quiet and could be harsh at times but also has a very big heart, for those that deserved it. They spoke about how the bond was done.

Dae returned without Thia, "I am sorry Ben. It should've been discussed with you and us first before she did it."

"Did what? The only thing she did was bite my finger and say something weird I didn't really get. She said it would help her know if I was in trouble so she could help me and "repay her debt". I told her she owes nothing, but she wouldn't listen."

Dae hung his head ashamed, "Yes she meant well but the blood bond is not entirely known to us yet. We are still learning. One thing we do know though is that it has killed humans in the past."

Ben wasn't very concerned, he more felt bad for Thia now, "Oh, well I am not human…anymore so I should be okay, right?"

"Yes, I think. It killed the human quickly, but that was with a large…dose. So far you just seem to have taken on some of our…traits."

Ben left later feeling better having some sort of explanation for the strange experiences.

Thia recovered well from the toxin and felt fine within a few days. Dae checked in on Ben to find everything was fine then later spoke to Daniel to see if he found out more about the toxin.

Daniel was amazed but still didn't have much on it yet, "One thing I do know is if injected into anyone else, it would've killed them instantly. The poison is strong."

Dr. Daniel, or "Dan" as Ben continuously corrected the respectful Phelidae, had proven to be very trustworthy. They quickly developed into a small and very special tight knit group having the same types of tough experiences in the past, naturally caused by what they were.

The past few weeks solidified new hope in Thia. As they sat around the table at Ben and Alana's house, taking in the smells from the wonderful food they were enjoying and the sounds of the laughter and conversations, she looked around finally feeling a sense of peace, *these people are different, like us, and they are still here, undiscovered. It sounds like they've been here a very long time too.* Maybe it was their turn now. Maybe this would be the last time they had to move. *Could this be the place we finally get to call home?* She spent the rest of the evening daydreaming about the possibility as she happily watched her brothers enjoying the company.

Doctor Daniel, clearly a curious and apparently fairly fearless man, was determined to do all he could to learn everything about the toxin. Knowing Dae too was just as interested, he offered to have him come along and observe his next experiment if he wished. Daniel an awkward yet genuine man wanted more than anything for the new comers to trust him as Ben has come to. He considers himself very fortunate to have been exposed to what others have not. Dae saw this in him and gladly accepted his offer.

Numerous failed trials later they still had little to go off of. Knowing they'd finally tried everything they could, Daniel presented an idea. It was risky but he wanted more than anything to try it.

Seeking clarification, hoping his assumption was terribly wrong, Dae asked, "What exactly do you mean by *try it*?"

Doc half talking to himself and Dae, "I think it will be safe to do so if we are cautious enough and conduct it right. I feel it is well worth the risk if we can learn from it."

Dae stared in disbelief, "You do realize the *risk* is death."

Dae was finding out that the good doctor seemed to have taken on a new crusade to find answers to help his new friends. From a couple of the stories he'd shared, it seemed to stem from his intolerance of threats over the helpless. He too must have been under the same entrapping circumstances at one time, and still to small degree with some corrected by surgery. He was not open to explaining the cause yet of his limp, though they had a strong feeling it was no mere accident. This being the only thing he was not open about, no one ever pushed.

Dae also quickly learned that once Docs mind was made up there was no talking him out of it. He was as stubborn as they come. So when the day came for Doc to try the toxin on himself, they both brought some support. Doc had Ben and Alana and Dae of course had Thia and Shai. They were all going to meet at Doc's place at first, but once Dae decided he trusted them enough, he offered, after obtaining permission from his siblings, their converted yet secure old military facility home. They all came to an agreement that it would be less risky than at the office where someone with an animal in trouble might walk in on something this bunch would prefer to remain unknown.

All but Doc were uneasy about trying the toxin on a human, but they trusted Doc and Dae enough not to have to listen to the long and boring explanations on how they deduced it should be done. So as all were in hesitant agreement, the experiment commenced.

The response was beyond what any of them attempted to hypothesize. With only the smallest prick on his hand and just a hint of the toxin on the tip, the poison was slow at first to react. Then it rapidly melted and spread from the warmth of docs body, eating away at his skin and moving up the arm. They were able to uncover that it starts off as a butter consistency solid in cool enough temperatures, but then changes to oil once warmed.

"My arm feels like it's on fire!" Doc cried out in terrible pain and it was getting worse.

Dae made way to him to attempt stealing it like Nomad showed them from Daniel, but Thia intercepted and shoved him out of the way. She would spare her brothers any pain she could and she knew she could take it better than him.

She clamped her hand around the area, nails gently dug in, not breaking the skin but to keep solid contact. She figured that this would also be a good way to distract the subject long enough to remove it quickly with the least amount of resistance.

She was successful, all astonished but her brothers. Doc relaxed with a sigh of relief. The flame ignited under her hand she uncovered the new wound. Though still very painful, the wound was surface only so it was easy to clean and took no recovery compared to the embedded arrows.

They worked until the wee hours in the morning recording and discussing all they learned, had a midnight snack then were shown to their guest rooms, all but Ben who decided to stay up a while longer with Shai. Shai and Ben talked about their plans to take their bikes out on some old abandoned dirt roads the next day.

As much as Thia loved to dance, when in a foul mood she equally adored escaping with the sounds of thunderstorms. She tried the recorded ones but her ears are too good to fool with that. So as she recovered from the failed experiment, Dae put her to sleep with the most soothing thunder storm he could conger up. As she bundled herself up in the fluffiest comforter made, she drifted away at the sounds of Dae's thoughtful gratitude for her sacrifice and fell in a long needed deep slumber.

Much of Thia and her brother's communication was not vocal. Their new friends noticed this immediately when they spoke few words but were always of the same mind. They just knew, they could feel, what each other felt. Ben was getting a small taste of this, thanks to Thia, but still didn't fully understand what it was he was feeling. He couldn't tell what were his wants verses theirs. After speaking more on it with Dae, it seemed the bond translated differently across the species. Dae knew something else was changing too; Ben's feelings for them, especially Thia. Being respectful, those private things were pushed out and ignored. But not by Shai.

Ben longed to see Thia again, and when he finally worked up the nerve, and decided enough time had passed, he headed down the hall to her room. When he got there, he found Shai standing outside the door like a security guard.

"She's already in a much needed deep sleep. In this type of sleep we heal best. Morning would be a better time friend." he said in a very mild and kind manor, not like him at all. Ben had learned by now there should've been smirks and teasing.

"There is a room a couple of doors down you are welcome to." Ben, still taken back by this new man before him, a man now worthy of being Thia's brother, thought for a split second and nodded in acceptance. His eagerness gave way to contentment and respect.

The next morning Ben woke up. He had a nice long stretch and for once laid there to enjoy the sensation. He opened his eyes, sat up and looked out the window. He couldn't help but notice how beautifully the sun was shining, the birds were sweetly chirping and the air was so fresh. It was a gorgeous morning. *Wait, since when have I ever cared about any of this stuff?!* He suddenly thought. Then it came to him.

She's awake! He felt his heart jump a little. It was strange, then something else hit him, *Must be part of that bond they were telling me about, hmmm, kind of handy…unless it keeps making me think like a chick.,* he laughed and then looked a little worried. *I better ask her brothers how far this goes. They seem okay though.* Then a thick smell of sizzling bacon interrupted the racing train of thoughts and awoke his rumbling stomach. His mouth watered from the smells filling the room. He couldn't cleanup fast enough to get to the kitchen.

Thia was already up cooking to accommodate their guest. Her brothers knew their fate if they hadn't insisted they stay the night knowing how late it was. One by one they all found their way following the aroma and gathered in the kitchen. Thia prepared a feast of a breakfast. Daniel puzzled by her rapid recovery made a b-line straight to Dae where he explained the difference between surface skin reactions to deep penetrating muscle affects.

Hearing she was the topic of discussion, Thia sat back and watched them go back and forth engulfed in the topic and smiled. They were naturally glued to each other's every word. And how Dae loved and deserved the attention. How long had he waited for such company. Shai, Ben and Abe played race games on TV and Alana buzzed about, all too happy to help in the kitchen. Thia grew happier as time went by and their new relationships developed. Perhaps this time she chose right. Her brothers found kindred spirits, this place seemed to be a haven for the unnatural and she had a place to dance. Everything was in perfect harmony, for now.

What's coming?, she wondered. *It's like a dream, or the calm before a storm but something will be along to wake us soon enough. I just wonder what it will be this time.*

"Everything okay?" Alana noticed the concerned look on Thia's face. Thia heard the question but couldn't answer right away as she felt someone else's concern and turned her attention to the living room. They both found Ben looking back, then Dae and Shai. Ben asked Alana through their thoughts if everything was okay. Alana could hear but could not speak back without physical contact so she just mouthed the words, "Everything is fine."

Thia's brother's just smiled and went back to what they were doing.

Alana, a little embarrassed just said, "Wow that bond thing you guys have is pretty neat."

Thia went back to drying dishes, "Yes, it comes in handy sometimes. But it can also be a bit invasive too. We are getting better at tuning the start of *certain* feelings out."

"So what is all of that?" Alana was referring to Thia's dirty and half open bag on the side counter.

"Oh, that's some stuff I brought back from our old house. Most everything else was destroyed but I was able to find what I was looking for and a few other things." Thia put the towel down, grabbed an old rag from under the sink then walked over and pulled everything out of the bag and began cleaning it.

Ben joined them in the kitchen, "Sorry to intrude but my mood wasn't matching the game."

Thia laughed, "Sorry, you'll learn to ignore it after some practice. We have as you can tell."

"Why do they hunt you?" Alana seemed sad now too trying to understand.

"For the most part they want circus slaves to make them money." Thia said plainly.

Ben didn't like seeing either of the girls upset. Then he recognized the item Thia was fidgeting with, "Hey a dream catcher. It looks homemade?"

"Yes it is" she smiled looking at it, but then became very serious and hesitant explaining the rest of the memory. "Back home there was an accident…it affected everyone differently. I was having a hard time sleeping so Shai made it for me. After our more recent little encounter with you and those…grays, some bad dreams returned. So I went back home to get this."

"Old home." Alana corrected.

Thia was confused, "Huh?"

Ben just smiled. He knew where his sister was going with it.

"You went back to your *old* home, to bring it back to your new, better and permanent home." Alana said with a big beaming smile.

Thia smiled back in appreciation. She admires Alana's rare innocence and compassion. "I sincerely hope you are right. More than anything I want this to be the last time too. But I've held high hopes for this before and it's not worked out that way yet." She ended in disappointed.

"It's different now. You have us and we have you." Alana was very good at discouraging negativity.

Thia just looked at her and smiled, "You are sweet."

"Awe, I think I am going to cry." Shai mocked as he stood in the doorway breaking up the moment.

Thia threw the heavy and still dirty panther statue at him knowing he would catch it, in his stomach and nice clean clothes.

"Hey! You know you are going to have to wash this anyway!" He took his shirt off and threw it at Thia's head.

Alana turned a little red announcing her secret crush.

"It's still worth it", she said as she next threw a very wet dish rag and nailed him in the chest, spraying water everywhere.

"Awe, gross! It's your fault you know! You guys were getting so sappy in here I couldn't concentrate on the game! I'm used to tuning you out T, but since you got wolf boy over here joining in, you double teamed me. Cut it out would ya?" He said as he slid over attempting to put Thia in a wet head lock.

She retaliated by tickling him, knowing he *hates* it being so very ticklish.

He immediately backed off yelling, "UNCLE! I give."

Dae and Doc sat where they were watching and laughing. Abe however missed all of it completely glued to the TV.

Though they spent a lot of time at the Phelidae's house, most time was spent in the clearing where they needed to hide nothing.

Dae was lying in the sun with Thia and Alana.

Abe sat and watched Shai and Ben throw the football back and forth, "So what do you guys do here in your free time?"

Shai answered in between catches, "We come out here and hunt, practice or just relax."

"I get the hunt and relax part but what do you practice?"

"We had an old teacher that taught us some defense stuff in case we ever needed it. It's come in handy a time or two."

This got Ben's attention, "Nice, like what?"

Shai stopped throwing the ball and called his siblings over, "Hey, Ben wants to see some moves."

And so Ben got to see just what they meant as they demonstrated some of the lessons they practice in the field. He quickly found his two favorite moves. One was when Shai kick jumped off of Dae to gain momentum and tackled a couple trees. Yes he could definitely see they were part cat. Cats have more agility and balance than dogs and it shows in everything they do.

The other move was when Thia ran full speed at Dae and Shai. They attempted a last second clothes line on her but she was quick enough to slide under, caught their arms and swung on them like an uneven bar. When she came back around she kicked their sides and they flew to the ground rolling. With not much room left she still landed on her feet, of course…cats do that too.

There was also plenty of smack talk and teasing that went on and Ben loved all of it. Alana told Thia that when he went away he came back unhappy and cold. But his humanity and the loving brother she knew, was coming back the more time he spent with them.

Ben wanted to learn from them and they gladly taught him. The only price he paid was getting included in the teasing, but he didn't mind at all. Ben spent much of his time with them and they loved having him.

A few hours after the sun went down Thia was tired so she got up to head home, "See you guys, I'm heading home."

"Night Thia, we won't be much longer." Dae assured her.

Ben quickly jumped up, "Hey, I'll walk with you."

"Okay" Thia was pleasant but indifferent.

Shai and Dae exchange suspicious looks and smirks as they walked off. They knew Thia wasn't up to anything but they were all too sure about Ben's intentions.

"This should be interesting." Dae admitted with a raised brow.

Shai just winked, "I couldn't have said it better."

Ben, uneasy by the loud crickets and blanket of silence between them tried to strike up a conversation, "They can do some pretty cool stuff with all that element bending. Which ones can you do?"

She stiffened up, "I...can't do what they do." was all she said back as she stared at the ground. She didn't like lying but really didn't feel like explaining what would've been her real answer. "You can go back with them if you like. I'm fine. I'm just tired and plan on crashing when I get home."

"Need some crashing company?" he said playfully getting closer. She laughed, pushed at him and kept going.

"Alright, I get the hint. Just...*think*...if you change your mind." he laughed and headed back.

Over time Ben became a best friend to the trio, something they've never actually had. All were careful not to get too distracted at work, but after, the boys would come back to the house and play games till all hours of the night. Even Ben's family knew where to find him if they needed to call on him.

Ben also got really good at getting Thia to laugh. Her brothers especially liked this part as they hadn't seen much of it until these past few months. Yes, this time is different, just as Shai said before they split up from the last attack. Everywhere Thia and her brothers had been before, they were never able to really get close to anyone around them for fear slipping up, just once, but that was not an issue with Ben and his people.

The next morning all were up enjoying what Thia left out for breakfast. She already ate and was off doing laundry.

Ben thought it was a good time and asked quietly, "Hey, how come she can't do that element stuff you guys can do?"

Shai snickered almost choking on his food while staring at the television, plate in hand, "No use whispering, she can hear you." Then Ben's question sunk in, "Wait…is that what she told you?"

"Yeah." Ben was perplexed by Shai's reaction.

"What did she say *exactly*?" curiosity tearing Shai away from the TV for longer than normal.

"She said she can't do what you guys do." trying to remember and repeat verbatim what he was told.

"Hmmm, well that part is true I guess. I can't do what Dae does either. But she still has her own gift. She just refuses to use it." Then he took another bite, turning back to the TV.

"Why would she do that?" The idea seemed ridiculous to him.

"Shai don't." Dae warned from the other couch with his nose still in his book.

"Because of *The Great Accident!*" now flipping channels with the remote bored by with what was on.

"Shai, just stop." was again heard from behind the book.

Shai of coarse ignore Dae's counsel, "Hers is different than the rest of us and even the wisest of our kind can't figure it out. That and she, well none of us really, have finished proper training. But unlike ours, or anyone else's, her power keeps growing stronger as she gets older. With us, ours were done when we got them. It's actually getting harder to hide."

Shai's dodge and redirect of the accident explanation spared him from the preconceived flying heavy objects Dae was warning to, as he spotted her coming around the corner flashing Shai a look that would kill if it could.

The boys took off on another of their weekly rides so Thia took a nap since she got all of the chores out of the way early. She woke up much earlier than she wanted too from a bad dream, then had a hard time going back to sleep as her thoughts wandered thinking and worrying about Matteus.

When the guys got back they found the door was slightly open and the window broken. They cautiously walked into the living room to find it a huge mess. Everything that was on shelves was now scattered all over the floor. They all continued to sniff the air and listened for anything that shouldn't be there but could only hear her soft breathing and smell Thia's shampoo.

Ben whispered, "Is she in the shower? Is she hurt? Did someone break in?"

Dae answered, "No, I hear no running water and the sent is faded. Her breathing sounds like she is sleeping. She must have showered and is now down for a nap."

"That's what happened! Dae, how do we get her to stop dreaming about those vampires?! The house is going to be a pile of rubble if we can't get her to stop soon." He looked over at the TV.

"See! That's the third one we've been through!" Shai stormed off to his room to appraise the rest of the damage.

Ben wasn't sure what they were talking about. "Thia did this?"

Dae confirmed, "Yes, she can't really control how her nightmares project her powers, sometimes destroying parts of the house."

"OH COME ON!" they heard from Shai's room as he ran out. "I'm getting tired of cleaning up glass shot all over my stuff from my exploding TV! Why doesn't any of her things blow up?!"

Thia woke up from all the yelling and came out of her room groggy, "What's going on?" She got to the living room, looked around and then her eyes shot over to Shai's face. "Oh, no. I'm sorry. I didn't mean to. They slowed down but won't completely stop, even with your dream catcher this time."

Shai calmed down a little, remembering when he made it for her and felt bad for going off. Deep down he knows she can't help it and remembers Dae's talks about being patient with her. As much as he likes his expensive things, he would rather not lose her again like the last time she ran. If it wasn't for that little local paper last time they'd still be looking.

Shai walked over, head down and gave her a hug, "It's okay T. Sorry I went off."

"I'll clean it all up and order you a new one. I'll get started now."

But before she got to the broom closet Dae had an idea, "Ben would you mind telling us all you know about vampires? Maybe if Thia knows more about them they won't consume her thoughts and dreams so much."

"Sure." Ben agreed.

Shai's guilt faded away and his sarcasm returned, "We are willing to try anything at this point. I think shock therapy might be a good follow up option!"

Thia gave him a little zap for that one.

Something Old

Thia and her brothers felt something. For some reason there was a heavy mood shift. It was different than what they had grown used to but it was still very familiar, actually it was old and welcoming. A moment later the door bell rang. They weren't expecting any visitors today. They all went to answer it driven by curiosity, mainly by the possible origin of their altered state.

"Nomad! What are you doing here? How have you been? Where have you been?", Thia asked while pulling him in and dragging him through the house to the kitchen, brothers close by also awaiting the answers.

Nomad stopped her, "Good grief woman, you act as if it's been...well I guess it has been quite a while, hasn't it."

"What would you like to eat? I just went shopping so I can make you just about anything. Cinnamon toast first? Is that still your favorite?" she was beaming.

"My, someone is talking more!" he commented.

"Not really, it must be you. You always bring out the best in people don't you?" Shai corrected and teased.

Nomad loves all breakfast food. Even though she went through the formality of asking the questions, she didn't wait for the answers, she just made him everything. Her brothers certainly didn't complain as they are healthy eaters and love her cooking. All were in the kitchen catching up as she prepared and plated each course.

They covered everything, about how they ended up here and what this place was like. Then he explained where he had been all this time and what he was doing. He told of adventures in faraway lands with exotic people and animals, new discoveries as well as new friends.

Nomad always had adventures. All while they were growing up he would come and go. He would be gone for weeks, months and on occasion a year or two.

Once they got through the greetings, mountains of food and catching up, Nomad came to the reason for the visit. Though he had always kept tabs on them he explained visiting was too risky which is why he made a rule not to. It took him a little while to track them down this last time but had to as he had some bad news to share with them.

"And now for the unfortunate basis for breaking my own rule, in my travels I've come to learn of significant alliances that have formed over time… alliances formed with the Pallas."

"How significant?" Dae asked first for the three.

All three hung on Nomad's next words, "Caleb and his sister have been confirmed connected with them."

"I knew they were no good but to turn on our own kind? Why?" Thia asked upset.

"For selfish gain I'm sure." Nomad speculated. "The Pallas have deep pockets and are not stingy in rewarding those worth the exchange."

This was very bad, now at least two of their own are on the wrong side and looking for them. This eliminated the one advantage the siblings had against them. However Nomad saw something like this coming and had his own plan in motion. Though to some he may come off a little…unstable or *eccentric* as some politely call it, none the less, he is very wise.

"So now that the bad news is out of the way, I will further explain *why* I've been where I have. Once I learned of the treachery I knew we needed greater numbers, new allies, alliances of our own. Luckily for us the Phelidae are not the only creatures the Pallas have hunted and enslaved. A few of whom I speak of are on their way and will be here soon. There is much training to be done, together, to learn what each group can offer and how best to use it. It will only make us that much stronger once the inevitable happens, and it will…come down to a great battle."

Thia not one for formal entertaining of strangers, wasn't prepared for this. There were plenty of rooms but not all yet suitable for occupancy. So once they were done planning, Nomad took the one room she did have set for a single guest. He needed some rest from his trip and his full belly just added to the drowsiness. Thia offered coffee as she had many more questions but Nomad declined. He didn't drink such things. The closest to it he would drink was tea, but he usually carried his own.

Her brothers went down for a midday nap too. She would've but there was much work to be done now. She franticly ran out to the store to pick up some things for the rooms. She bought sheets, blankets, pillows and covers. She got some more food. Then she tried to remember how her mother would prepare and ran to get some social party appropriate items.

She stopped for a moment with a car full of items to think if there was anything else she might have been missing. Then it hit her that she hadn't even cleaned the rooms. So she went back to the grocery store to find out they were fresh out of cleaning supplies but would get more next week. This was too late. She would have to go to the next city to get some.

Waiting while the cashier rung up and bagged her purchase Thia noticed a sample of free vanilla scented hand sanitizer. *Curious stuff* she thought and decided to try some believing it safe, vanilla being one of the less offensive options. She pushed down on the plunger and a flood of it came pouring out much faster than anticipated. So in applying a generous amount to her hands the stinging alcohol cloud engulfed and burnt her nose causing her eyes to relentlessly water. Almost immediately she was crudely reminded the precise location of the deep paper cut she just received from one of the bags. "Ow!" The cut was feverishly red and throbbing. *How can a stupid little cut sting so bad?!* she thought. The random thoughts never ceased.

Finally she returned back home and began dinner. She threw something in the oven then moved on to fixing up the rooms. Within a few hours she was finished, just in time to clean up and complete dinner. Once everyone was again fed, dishes and kitchen cleaned up, Thia was finally able to join the rest in the living room and relax.

Dae and Nomad sat at the table discussing location and plans for training. Shai sat in his usual spot in front of the TV but Thia noticed he didn't seem to be paying much attention to it. In fact he wasn't even looking at the screen. He just stared off thinking. Judging by the expression on his face, whatever the subject, it wasn't pleasant. Still somewhat early in the evening Shai turned in for the night without a word.

The next morning Shai was already up and out aggressively working on Thia's old car. This is how he deals with things that bother him. Rather than talking when in a bad mood, he prefers to work it out physically. From the moment Nomad explained that the twins had turned against their own people, all of the old memories of them came back to trouble Shai, knowing he would have to see them again soon but as the enemy now.

Any time the troublesome pair visited with their aunt, a quiet woman who mostly kept to herself, it was never a good time for anyone else. The other villagers stayed indoors when they came around to avoid the rude comments that were sure to come. Their aunt was prideful, as the village they came from, but not mean like the twins. In short, the two were always pretentious busy bodies which would be harmless in and of itself. However this was not the case, for beyond all else they are most of all dangerously competitive.

Back then Dae, Thia and Shai didn't let the twins bother them though. They knew they could hold their own and just found them to be annoying. But things are much different now, especially for Shai.

Shai became consumed by Caleb and Kasha being the enemy now. As he physically worked on the car he mentally analyzed and planned. Shai remembered during the races impromptu or not, he won every time in speed, but in the other trials Caleb beat him in strength, *but not by much*, he told himself. The thought of being beaten by a try-to-hard like Caleb infuriated Shai. The more he thought about it, the more it ate at him until he could take it no more. Thia and Dae watched out the front window as Shai pealed down the driveway in his truck.

When he came back he unloaded a complete workout bench set from the truck into his room. He would take care of the physical part, but what angered him the most is how he mistreated Thia. Shai always thought him a coward for picking on someone that couldn't fight back. But maybe that was just it; she could fight back if she really wanted to. *Is that what he wanted, the challenge of power, even if it could mean the end of him?*

Nomad, Dae and Thia all knew to leave Shai to work things out on his own, in his way. Interfering in the process only failed in the past. When he is ready he will emerge. In the mean time Thia made sure he was well fed.

Shai seemed to break out of his full on mission, even if only temporarily when Ben stopped by to see if he wanted to ride. Ben was fighting with his parents about settling down and needed to get out of the house.

Ben paced Shai's room, "I swear they drive me insane sometimes."

Shai sat up on the bench panting and sweaty, "Yeah, mine used to bug me about that too. I kind of miss it now."

Ben hung his head suddenly feeling bad for complaining, "Sorry"

"Nah, it's okay." Shai wiped his face and neck with a towel.

"So who's that guy talking to Thia?"

"Oh, that's Nomad. You didn't get to meet him?" Shai finished wiping down then got up to put on a fresh shirt.

Ben sat down on the bench and started pressing, "No, Dae answered the door and brought me back here. What are you up to on this?"

"One hundred and fifty so far. But I just started."

Ben scoffed, "Show off."

They went for a ride then after Ben hung out and met Nomad. They got to know each other and before long Nomad approved of their new friend.

A few days later the first of the new visitors arrived. Nomad introduced everyone and began the training sessions right away. Of the ones he gathered, none were cat-like, as most were dead, captured or too hard to find, so they too were fascinated by the Phelidae attributes when their eyes changed to thick slits and various colors. Even Thia's striping trick found its way to her brothers, thanks to the bond. Shai's leopard print appeared out of his hair line and down his neck. Dae's was less noticeable as marking but more resembled thick tattooing, so much that one of the younger visitors nicknamed him Blade.

As the others went over the day's lesson, Nomad pulled Thia aside at the table, "Thia, I need you to pack some things as I will be taking you on a trip for specialized training."

Thia perked up, "Specialized training? Nice! But if we all go, what will we do with your friends?"

Nomad shook his head, "No Thia, not the boys, just you."

Thia became disappointed, "Just me? Why can't they come too? Or better yet, can't we just do it here?" She really didn't want to leave her bothers.

He solemnly shook his head again denying her request, "I'm afraid not. The level we need will be far too risky."

Shai came down the hall from his room, "What's going on? T, what's wrong?"

Dae showed up a second later, "What's wrong? Why's everyone so worried?"

Nomad, perplexed looked at Thia and the boys trying to figure out, "How did you know…no. The Blood Bond… you didn't!"

"We did?" Thia apologetically admitted.

"I knew it would work but no one ever wanted to try it!" he slapped his knee, "You three never cease to amaze me."

The three smiled. To them any bit of praise from him was a real accomplishment.

Ben joined them.

Nomad denying further satisfying his curiosity with a plethora of questions, jumped straight back to it, "Thia has to leave with me for a little while. We need to quickly define and learn to focus and control her abilities. I can't do this alone and you boys can't come because she only worries about a repeat of the accident when you are around." Nomad motioned at Dae. "There's no time to waste now."

Ben instantly felt Thia's deep pit of guilt, a hole darker than he'd ever known before. He looked up at Dae never considering once the huge scar might've been caused by her.

Nomad continued, "Where we have to go is a special place that very few can know about. And we can't take a chance on trying it here. The slightest mistake would attract much unwanted attention. I understand that you are all very happy here. You should not have to keep moving around and hiding. Whether we like it or not, it is time to resist. And the only way to stand a chance is by getting Thia's gift to be a part of the equation. Right now they are counting on her fear. We can use that to our advantage."

Despite the fact of being both self-conscious and nervous, Thia felt a spark of hope pulse through her. Nomad was back to finish what he started. It would be so nice to be able to do more than just the basics. She admitted to herself she gets a little jealous when her brothers play with their gifts. They could make awesome things happen while she could only sit back and watch. Not to mention finally putting an end to the embarrassing mood related accidents that come about every so often. The majority of them ended up laughable and her brothers enjoy teasing her. Their favorite to this day is the story about the hole in the attic.

She was digging around in the attic of one of their first few places, not a preferred room, but she found some cool old stuff before so she wanted to see what else might be up there. It was a typical dark and dusty mess so she brought a couple camping lamps with her so she could see and gloves so not to directly touch anything gross or creepy.

Her brothers weren't interested in joining no matter how bad she begged. Shai just told her to yell if she needed him to lift something heavy for her and laughed. At this insult, she launched one of the large ball shaped marble decorative stones from the hall table at him, which landed perfectly in his stomach causing him some discomfort and went on her way.

She pulled down the ladder and dragged up all her gear. In addition to the lamps she had a couple of boxes to bring stuff down in and some wet wipes to clean them off. The other box she brought to sit on. Within an hour she found old bullets, some army clothing, pictures of scantily clad women and an old pistol. Then she spotted something in a corner of the attic. As she reached for the strange red cylinder a rat came flying out at her.

The cleanup took a couple of weeks. Dae had to do some research and pickup supplies to then teach Shai how to patch a building. It was well worth it considering the laugh they got out of the whole thing. The object she reached for in the corner was an old stick of dynamite. Her brothers ran to her after the explosion to see if she was okay and found her covered in dust and blood. At first they were more confused than worried.

"Thia, why do you look so embarrassed?! Are you okay?" Dae asked franticly.

"You're covered in blood! Where are you hurt?!" Shai followed.

"I'm fine, it's not mine."

"Well who's is it then?" Dae insisted.

Just then Shai fell on the debris covered floor laughing. Thia, still sulking looked over at Dae who was still very confused.

"Shai?"

Shai couldn't stop. He only managed to point to the top of Thia's head.

Dae reached his hand to where Shai was pointing, grabbed something and pulled it back, "Oh" Dae replied this time with a bit of a poorly contained smirk.

"Ewww" Thia said glaring at what was left.

It was a rat tail...without a rat. Thia's scare exploded the rat and anything in the vicinity became collateral damage. The boys were both laughing so hard now she couldn't help not joining them. That home ended up with a new loft with a very nice skylight.

Shai dreamt that night of one of Nomad's lessons when they were growing up, "Remember all things come from the four elements, Earth, Wind, Fire and Water. Once you are totally in tune with your elements, you can manipulate almost anything. The earth gift can eventually alter metals, the water gift can control blood…"

Shai remembered cutting him off. "What can Thia's do?"

All fell silent. Nomad had an idea but refused to disclose it. "We are not yet sure." was all he would say.

Thia was instructed to pack minimally for the trip, no more than would fit in a backpack. She said her goodbyes during the small gathering the night before. It wasn't a huge event, just the few close friends from the area they'd made including Ben, Alana, Abe and Doc.

Doc and Dae were off talking about more of their ideas on countering the toxin and maybe using some sort of suit to repel the arrow head blades. They also wanted to discuss ways to reinforce their home since it was previously an old base anyway. This would be very useful for the oncoming threat. Abe joined in wanting to be helpful, mentioning he noticed a new shipment of scrap metal that came into the yard from a demolition job in the next town over.

Thia was in the kitchen listening to the many stories and various questions Alana rattled off at an alarming pace. A pace so fast they really couldn't be answered. They ranged from what was happening at school to what she was making and all while she danced around the room. Alana seemed to be a nonstop ball of energy tonight. Cats don't much care for jittery things so naturally Thia was a bit annoyed. Alana also interjected every so often with some of her own home recipes her mother taught her how to prepare. This part Thia didn't mind as it brought back memories of when she cooked with her mother too.

Abe and Shai ended up in the living room kicked back on the couches munching on snacks Thia placed out earlier, while watching and yelling at a game on the big screen. One thing Thia learned from her mother's social parties is that just about every available surface should have something edible on it and kept full at all times.

Ben who could usually be found with either Shai or Thia, was oddly planted in front of Nomad hanging on his every word as he told a few of the stories of his travels. When he first met Nomad he quickly wrote him of, as a strange old homeless looking person who didn't particularly smell all that great. He was at a complete loss on how this man came to know these three. *He is so plain and old and they are so young and fascinating.* But his wrong first impression was promptly righted.

He first noticed the almost reverence they paid him. Confused by this he couldn't help but to observe more of their behavior around him. It was clear to all who looked on, that they had a deep seeded and unwavering respect for Nomad. It's not obvious at first, but if they keep watching, the evidence becomes clear.

Nomad was having a good time too. He loved the attention as he didn't get many opportunities with a captive audience. And he was enjoying some of the *old food*, as he called it, that Thia started preparing, inspired by her chatty little sous chef in the kitchen who later left to join in on story time. It had been a long time since he tasted some these dishes. In fact the new food coming out changed the mood of all the rooms as everything calmed down.

Each of the dwellers of this home had an unintentional but powerful effect on their company. Nomad was quiet now, pretending to eat slowly so he could carefully study the situation. The others around him sat back and ate too but didn't wander far in case there were more stories to follow. Nomad saw that Thia stayed in the kitchen alone filling herself with the memories and preparation of the dishes. She was amazed at how much had come back to her after all this time.

Dae had since left Daniel and sat down at the dining room table, also eating slowly staring off lost in his own head. Shai's once glued eyes were no longer looking at the TV. He appeared to be gazing through his plate at his memories.

The rest of the guests focus too seemed to be on the food but instead they were intrigued by the unfamiliar tastes they were experiencing. The food was delicious but nothing like they'd ever had before.

Nomad wondered if what filled their heads was all memories of their past lives or the quickly approaching separation that was about to occur. Thia and her bothers didn't spend much time apart, they couldn't, not if they wanted to survive.

The next morning Nomad and Thia slipped out before anyone woke up. They traveled for days, stopping for rest and a hunted bite to eat on occasion. It was a perfect arrangement. She hunted and he prepared with special spices he carried from his journies. This helped them travel light. As they were walking a wonderfully sweet smell over came them.

"We're almost there." Nomad announced with a pleasant and peaceful smile.

Thia's heart jumped with excitement. She knew the smell but couldn't place it. She didn't spend much time on it though. They don't make shoes prepared for this amount of walking and was grateful it was about to end.

Even though she tried paying attention, she still had no idea where they were. They took so many twists and turns that her sense of direction was gone. She tried to at least watch the sun to see what way they followed but it didn't help much on the completely overcast days, which were most.

They stopped at the edge of the woods at a large clearing.

And with a sigh of delight and contentment he introduced her, "Welcome to Summers Meadow. This is a place of absolute warmth and peace, a place where the young call on the old."

The forest circled around the rolling hills and neatly kept grassy areas surrounding an old and beautiful castle like building in the middle. She thought of Matteus once she saw the beautiful white and pink blossom covered cherry trees scattered all around. *That was that smell back there.*

Then Thia oddly noticed, *There's no road...anywhere. Not so much as a path even.*

There were a few people walking around. She guessed they were Nomads people the way they were dressed and carried themselves much like him. *But how do they all get here? Does everyone just walk for days?*

They arrived at the steps of the ivy covered building and entered the double large wooden and black metal doors already wide open as if they were welcoming a long lost loved one home. The inside was even more breath taking than the outside. Any castles Thia had ever seen pictures of always looked cold, broken and bleak. However this one was different. This one was warm, inviting and full of life.

Rich colors accented every feature of the halls Nomad escorted Thia down. Large red velvet banners with heavy gold rope and tassels draped from the ceiling. She looked down to find a lush emerald green carpet keeping the floor from feeling like stone. And the walls were light, not grey like normal but white with thin grey streaks like marble.

"This is where you will be staying Thia." Nomad stopped and motioned to an arched door. "It's late so I will bid you good night. Meet me by the entrance in the morning and I will show you around then we will get started."

Thia nodded, "Good night", was all she could say. Thia felt their long journey catch up with her. Her eyes felt heavy as did her limbs. She entered the room and Nomad gently shut the door behind her. The room was warm even though the evening already cooled the air. She put her bag down on the upholstered chair and sat back on the bed.

Before she had a chance to get to know the room Thia sunk into the overly plush bed. For her the softer the better. She closed her eyes and slowly fell back into the thick feather comforter. Her whole body just melted. The bed was a luxurious change from the hard ground they'd been sleeping on for days. She kicked her shoes off and let the sensation fully take over. Her aching back and muscles were instantly soothed and relaxed as the pain simply floated away.

The next morning she found she was in the exact same position. She rubbed her eyes and heard the most beautiful song coming from a bird nearby. *Wow I must have been tired.* She freshened up and headed to where Nomad said to meet him.

"There's my sleepy head student!" he greeted her with a firm pat on the back. First things first, some breakfast."

Almost on queue her stomach growled loudly. She blushed a bit embarrassed and followed Nomad to the dining room. It was a large room filled with wonderful breakfast smells and already buzzing with people and their conversations.

Nomad pulled out a chair from one of the few empty tables left, "Thia you sit here and I will grab us something to eat."

She watched as he headed over to the over flowing buffet of food. Seeing all the food caused her stomach to protest even louder.

"Someone's hungry!", a squeaky voice giggled.

"Wha...oh, hi.", she searched and found the origin of the young voice.

A young boy stood behind her with bright eyes and the friendliest of smiles.

"You are new here! Hi, I'm Adam" and he held out his little hand.

"It's nice to meet you Adam. I am Thia." She met him back with a warm smile shaking his hand.

He pulled out the chair next to her and sat down and directly asked her, "So what do you do?"

Unsure of what precisely he meant by his question, "What do I do? What do you mean?"

His head tilted to the side, "Your special thing. What can you do? Everyone that comes here can do something special."

"Oh, well I guess that is why I am here. I'm not really sure what exactly I can do."

"Yeah we get those too." He said so grown and matter of fact.

Thia couldn't help but laugh a little, "So what do you do?"

He swung his legs that were too short to touch the floor, "I mostly clean and help out where ever I can."

Thia laughed again, "I meant your...special ability."

"Oh! No, I can't do anything. I can't even go outside in the day cuz I get sick. I was left here so they took me in. It's all I know really. I would *love* to see the outside. But I'm not allowed until I'm older Mr. Alfred says."

Thia hadn't heard that name before, "Who's Mr. Alfred?"

"He's the old guy here that everyone listens to."

The old guy? she looked around, curious who he was talking about.

"This place is great! You'll like it. Everyone is real nice. Especially Mr. Alfred. He comes off all mean like he doesn't want to talk to you but he's really nice once you get to know him. He just doesn't like to show it." He leans in and whispers, "But the big lady that passes out food behind the counter is not very nice. I don't talk to her.", he hid slightly behind Thia then looked over at the sour faced woman he was referring to wearing a hairnet.

"Well, thanks for the tips. I'll make sure I remember what you've told me." she whispered back to him with a wink and a smile.

"Hello Adam, and how are you this morning?" Nomad was back with heaping plates of piping hot food.

"Hi Mr. Brendon.", Adam greeted respectfully.

Mr. Brendon? Thia realized she never knew Nomad's real name.

Nomad patted Adam on the head, "I see you've met our Miss Thia"

"Yes, I was just telling her how nice it is here, except for lunch Lady Cowler…and how I can't do anything cool." his voice dropped in unsettled disappointment.

"Ah, but you are the hardest little worker of anyone I know, and you are getting very good at your lessons. As a matter of fact I've been meaning to ask you if you would be interested in helping me teach some of them next class." Nomad watched as the boy's face lit up as bright as the sun.

"Really?!" he asked with a renewed excitement.

"Of course."

"I can't wait to tell the others. Bye Thia!" And as quick as he came, he ran off and disappeared.

She couldn't help but smile watching him run as fast as he could, "Wow, you know how to cheer someone up!"

Nomad sat down across form Thia at the table, "He is a good boy."

She pulled her plate closer and began eating, "How did he end up here?"

"Alfred said his father dropped him off after his mother died. He couldn't deal with it all and left in the night. We think his parents are vampires."

"So that's why he gets sick when he goes out in the day?"

"Yes"

"That's good to know, I mean not for him, he seems very sweet. I was referring to the ones we ran into when we met Ben, the real Ben."

Nomad cautioned her, "Be careful, not all are exactly alike. There are different...eh...breeds I guess is how one might describe it. Not all of the folklore rules apply. The sun, for example, affects them in different ways. Some die instantly from exposure where others may not be bothered by it in the least."

They continued to eat.

"Figures. That advantage was short lived. What else can we not really count on?"

"Hmmm, let's see. From what I've been told, there are commonalities that do tend to be true. All are fast, some faster than others. Some have special talents, but not all, few in fact, and they all do require blood for survival."

Thia whispered, "Have any tried ours, like that human that died?"

"Not that I am aware. I'm not even sure they know you exist. It'd be best to keep it that way if possible. We need to keep our enemies down to a minimum. Speaking of which, finish up, we need to get started." He scraped his plate clean as she took a few more bites.

With her mouth half full, "What do you think would happen?"

"I honestly do not know, but will admit I am quite curious. Eat up, we have a long day ahead of us." He went up for seconds.

They finished their breakfast in silence, consumed by their thoughts, full of speculation. All while the others around them stay busy with their own business. But they too noticed the new girl like little Adam, including the *old guy* who watched all from the windows above. Unbeknownst to her, their intent to help her discover and hone her talents was not entirely selfless.

Nomad knows she is very powerful, he's seen it. Her parents were of the strongest, wisest and most respected in her tribe and paired because so by nature. He's seen their strong rooted qualities in her as well as some emerging of her own. But now her people were broken and scattered, protecting their young and few left. Balance has to be restored.

Facing Fears

Thia followed Nomad through the grounds as he described the origin of the place he calls home. She's never heard him call anywhere home. But she wasn't really paying attention to where they were headed but rather all the things that were going on around them, so much so that she almost ran right into him when he suddenly stopped deciding where he wanted to start.

These are definitely his people, she thought. Everyone so far appeared a little odd but very courteous. They slightly resemble monks with their solitary location and clothing but are not the silent kind. This place and its inhabitants are just the opposite, full of color and life, all kinds of life. The theme seems to be taking in misfit strays and providing them a fair and normal chance at life.

As they walked on Nomad reminded her how he too, like many here, never knew his parents. The monks, as Thia went on to call them, were all he knew of his past and what they told him, "She wasn't a careless woman and seemed to become very upset the night before she left without me they've said. I believe what they tell me to be the truth as the story remained consistent no matter the teller."

Nomad finally stopped at a particular group and sat down outside the circle, Thia did the same. Judging by their position, they were there to observe not participate. They did this for most of the day, moving from group to group watching and discussing the different kinds of students, what the groups were for and how they were being helped.

They moved on to the final group for the day.

"This one is a young and very powerful mind reader. He can also control some." Nomad whispered as they watched another student behaving oddly like a duck from the influence.

The boy noticed the new audience members, looked over to Nomad and read his mind. Surprisingly somehow Nomad knew and just smirked and winked back at him as if he made some clever comment. Then the boy moved on to Thia. At first he got nothing so he tried harder.

The boy's strange gaze made her very uncomfortable. She then became distracted by what looked like a stream of something dust like floating through the air towards her head then tickling her forehead. She even reached up to brush it off but found nothing there. Still her forehead itched a little, and then it stopped.

The boy, never experiencing resistance before, stubbornly tried again with more aggression. This time Thia's head started aching as a trickle of blood fell from her nose. She wiped away the blood then looked to Nomad, but her stomach dropped when her eyes met his expression.

He was seriously alarmed about something. Before she could ask him why he looked so upset, she felt something start to take over. A familiar hot wave washed over her. Before she could realize what was happening, her eyes changed, she growled and shot a threatening look as her body twisted in preparation to attack the boy.

The stuff that floated at her before was back but thicker and stung as it attempted to cover her head. Feeling somewhat suffocated by it, panic set in and she violently willed the substance away sending it rushing back at the boy.   The student's back arched and he grabbing his head in searing pain and bellowed falling to his knees.

"Thia!" was heard muddled as Nomad shouted.

Thia turned at him, still defensive. He knew not to grab her for he is not as strong as her brothers.

Sound still muffled she heard him say, "Stop what you are doing to him. I know you can. Everything is fine. He did not mean to hurt you. He too is learning."

She looked back at the boy still suffering. She released her anger and saw the substance dissipate into the air. She found it easy to back off and calm down this time. The boy's body fell to the ground still holding his head, eyes watering and breathing heavily. Nomad and the other instructor promptly ran to his aid. Nomad laid his hand on the boys head.

They spoke quietly, but not too low for Thia to hear, "He will have quite a headache but with some rest he should be good as new."

They nodded in agreement and the instructor had a couple of the other students assist the boy back to the castle as Nomad returned to Thia. Thia expected the group to turn on her with accusing eyes, like her piers back home did after the accident, but strangely none did.

"He will be fine." the tall and lanky man declared with a kind smile to the group, then Thia. "Let's continue."

"I'm sorry." she stuttered as Nomad wrapped his arm around her shoulders and escorted her from the group.

Nomad spoke in a fatherly tone trying to comfort her, "It's alright Thia. That is precisely why you are here. Why all of them are here. You'll find no judgment among the students because they were just as you are."

She hung her head defeated, "When will I stop hurting people? I can't do this."

"Remember child, he hurt you first, also unintentionally but it naturally triggered your survival instincts." He justified to her.

"Point taken, but who again has to be escorted away to recover and who just needed to wipe her nose? I saw the look on your face. You were afraid." Never before had she been so direct with him.

Surprisingly he agreed as they walked on, "That was my fault. I had no idea your defenses had become so strong since we last trained. We should've started off smaller. Nevertheless this is what we must to do to discover and study what you are capable of. Once we know what we are working with, then we can move on to helping you master it."

She wanted to understand, "Seems more dangerous than it should be, no? I mean, why don't my brother's heads explode then when we talk like that?"

"I suspect it has to do with your kind and maybe a part of the blood bond but I am not certain on that. Though that boy from the group has a gift, and a powerful one at that, he is still only human. I don't believe he has the capacity he would need with you and your brothers. This is not a surprise though, the Phelidae are very dominant in every way from your physical strength, the quantity of energy of your abilities and even your personal bonds are unyielding."

"Are you sure he is only human? Ben's sister has mind abilities too and her family is wolf." She couldn't remember sharing this information with him before.

"Interesting." Was all he said back.

She knew she lost him after that. When trying to figure something out, he could hear nothing else around him. So she let him go.

They were almost back to the castle where everyone was returning to now. Thia didn't remember walking so far, "Well it's getting dark and is time now for dinner. I think that is more than plenty for one day."

The day came to an end and they headed to the hall for supper. When they finished eating Thia was instructed to go back to her room for the night. Nomad wanted her to spend some time alone to take in all she's seen today.

She closed the door and locked it. She hopped in the shower and set it about as hot as it would go. The water beat down on her like a warm and relaxing massage releasing the days tension from the muscles in her shoulders. After towel drying and combing her hair she dressed for bed, this time in the softest pair of sweats with the bottoms of the legs pulled down over her heals keeping her ankles warm. She dove into the overly comfortable bed again, and was tired but did not fall asleep right away.

As she laid there staring out the window the sound of the rain grew louder over the crackling fire place. A big storm was coming tonight and this was just the beginning. A sigh of relief escaped her. Her and her brothers could always smell it coming, such a clean and fresh smell. No matter how loud the thunder clapped, the rhythm of the rain always lulled her to sleep and kept her there.

But tonight would be different. She was not falling asleep, not right away for she was home sick and missed her brothers terribly. Wondering what they were up to she stared off and thought about them. Her thoughts went deep. Then her cell phone rang. *Oops! Nomad told me to turn it off. I'll just get it this time and then turn it off.*

"Hello?" she answered without looking at it. She had a feeling she knew who it was.

"Thia?" she heard.

Her heart jumped with excitement, "Dae!"

He was happy to hear her voice too, "How are you?! Where are you?"

Then Shai's voice chimed in, "Hey, are you talking to Thia? Thia! When are you coming back? Dae can't cook!"

She just laughed. "I am good, homesick, but good. How are you guys? How is home?"

They caught up for a couple of hours but when they all grew tired, they said good night.

"I miss you guys. Sleep tight. And don't forget to take the garbage out. I don't want to come home to a smelly house." They agreed with tired laughs then said good bye. Thia drifted asleep while the storm passed through.

The next day with her breakfast tray in hand Thia saw the mind reader boy. She wanted to apologize but shied away and headed to the other side of the room. She sat down in the place that Nomad and she seemed to claim and waited for him. As she looked around she found Nomad heading towards their table with the boy.

As soon as they got to the table Nomad began his introductions, "Thia, this is Chase. Chase, Thia."

He held out his hand, not afraid of her at all, "It's very nice to meet you Thia. I wanted to apologize for yesterday. I shouldn't have been so invasive."

Thia was shocked by what he said, barely shaking his hand back, "*You're* sorry? I'm not the one that ended up in the clinic. If anyone should apologize, it's me."

He smiled, "Then we are both sorry."

She paused, then smiled back, "Yeah, okay."

"Well I will leave you two to get acquainted while I see to some breakfast." And Nomad was off after stealing Thia's tray.

"Have you been here long?" Thia asked as Chase sat down with his food.

He coyly answered with a question, "I guess that depends on what you consider a long time?"

"I guess what I am getting at is; how long does this training take? I'm on a bit of a deadline I'm afraid." Thia was thinking of her brothers and what was coming.

"It takes as long as it takes. You can't rush something like this. If you do, you may end up worse off than when you started." He argued back staring into his eggs.

Thia interpreted his awkward reaction, "You know something of this?"

Chase chuckled, "You know, you sound like...Nomad, as you call him."

She laughed knowing how true it was, "Yeah, I suppose we should. We've known him a long time."

"It shows. You are very reserved and controlled like he is, not reckless like the rest of us your age." he shoveled a fork full of eggs in his mouth.

Thia snickered, "Controlled. That's funny. Is that what you call what happened yesterday?"

He swallowed harder than planned to answer, "That's not quite what I meant but now that you bring it up, you did stop when he asked you to. I saw what happened from others while I was down. I'm the one that went overboard. I've never met someone I couldn't read before. I didn't know how far to go and chose poorly. Thanks to you I now know what I need to work on next", he ended in a wink and continued to eat.

"You do well at turning bad into good. You've also studied with Nomad?", she took a bite.

"A little bit, but not as much as I would like. He doesn't stay long. He was here for a while years ago but then he caught wind of something big and was gone again just like that. And now, here both of you are. I get the feeling he's been searching for something, maybe you for a while. Or just waiting for the right moment, I could never tell for sure. He is very difficult to figure out sometimes. I can always read his mind but he is very good at only letting me hear what he wants."

"He does the same with us, my brothers and me. We find it pretty frustrating."

"You know it just hit me. I don't mean to be presumptuous but would you mind if we try again? I do like a challenge." He smiled playfully at her.

She smiled back. He was nice and she knew he was good, especially if Nomad was willing to teach him, but her brother's scar would haunt her always, serving as a constant reminder of what could happen if left unchecked.

Not to mention the fresh new images of Chase holding his head and collapsing on the ground, "Thanks, but I don't think that is a good idea. Much worse has happened without me even being aware of it."

But Chase was determined, "Oh, I think I can take it."

She shook her head, "No, no. I wouldn't want to chance it. Maybe once I've been properly trained."

She didn't want to disappoint but she really didn't want to possibly kill him just to spare it.

"So I trust you've come to know each other by now?" Nomad startled away the stale mood that had suspended their conversation. "Sorry I took so long but I had to wait for fresh hash browns. You know how I love hash browns."

"Yes" they answered in tandem. Then Thia felt an ugly bit of jealousy of Chase getting to know Nomad so well. But it soon faded.

They sat in on many other lessons that day. During one with children floating sticks back and forth, something she's seen a million times at home, Nomad noticed Thia starring off smiling.

"Thia you are going to have to stop that." Nomad ordered quietly.

She snapped out of it, "Sorry. I just wanted to check in. They seem happy and to be getting along well with the visitors."

"I know you miss them but the risk of exposing this place it too great. They have mind readers on their side too. This is my home and these people trust me as well as any anyone I represent." He stopped and thought for a moment.

"That will be our lesson for today then. We will teach you how to control your thoughts so no one can get in. We've found already that you have your own self defense mechanism, however when we first arrived one of the mind reading instructors searched both of us, first me, then you. When she read you, she wasn't able to pick up much as she quickly came down with a severe migraine. She later explained that she's never experienced that reaction before. You truly are special Thia. Our keeper is very curious how you will turn out. However your mother did tell me she was able to read you without you noticing. This can be dangerous if they are able to get in."

"okay" Then she remembered something, "You know, now that you mention it, I did see some of that stuff around me when we first got here too. I just thought it was pollen or something."

Nomad was very excited about this new information, "You actually see something when they try to read your thoughts?"

"Yeah, it's like... dust or something?" she was unsure how to describe it.

"Very interesting! We can use this. It's about lunch time now, why don't you head in and I will meet you there. I have to share this. It may be the very key we looking for to help you find your control." At this, he rushed off.

Thia didn't feel much like eating by herself in a room full of people so she grabbed a sandwich, salad and an apple to take back to her room. She sat and ate slowly feeling a little sad and alone, desperately wanting to know how her brothers were doing. But Nomad would be upset with her if she called so she decided against it. A little bored after she ate she went to the window for some fresh air and to see if anything fun was going on.

She knelt down on the bench under the window, laid her arms on the window sill and rested her chin on them. She saw some of the younger kids running around playing with each other. They were playing tag but one was an air bender and kept knocking down the one after him. A few older ones were too busy flirting to notice the nearby sudden gusts of wind. One girl even took advantage of it and fell into the boy.

Thia again noticed the floating substance outside but didn't pay much attention to it this time seeing it wasn't meant for her. The younger ones flirting made her think of Matteus and their time together at his house. She liked him a lot and found she was disappointed that he hadn't even tried to contact her since the last time she saw him. *I hope he's okay. Maybe he got better and his family talked some sense into him convincing him I am a pet after all? It was too good to be true anyway, right?*

Thia kept remembering the few times they had together; she could still feel his exquisite embrace when he held her close under the tree. He made her feel special, especially in front of his disdainful friends.

Tired of watching the others she wanted to try to take a quick nap. She closed her eyes and promptly fell asleep. Her vivid dreams came quickly, Matteus being the subject of them.

She dreamt of the places they'd been, laughing and being held by him. She felt safe with him, trusted him despite most things still unknown. Then everything went dark and the floor disappeared beneath her. She couldn't tell if she was floating or falling. When it stopped she was in a new place without moving at all. It's a little like when she talks with her brothers but she didn't remember calling for either of them.

The place was familiar, then it hit her, it was the club she and Matteus went to on their first date for his birthday. Then she felt confusion, but not hers, then a need to go to the mirror. She saw Matteus's reflection. He looked terrible. His hair was a mess and his clothes torn and dirty. His face was feverish and covered in cuts and bruises. He brought his hands up over his face upset and embarrassed.

What happened? she gasped in awe.

He dropped his hands revealing a look of shock then spoke, "Thia?"

He heard me? How can that be? He never...it's not possible... she gasped. *The grocery store I cut my finger on the bottle.*

Before she could say anything she was ripped from the reflection and the place.

When she woke up Nomad was looking down on her. "Were you with your bothers again?! Thia I told you not to..."

Still a little groggy she tried to answer, "No, I...it wasn't them. I accidently connected with Matteus."

Nomad tried to recall, "Matteus? Ah, the boyfriend. Does he know about you and your brothers?"

"no" she simply confirmed.

"That could prove troublesome. Do you trust him?", she felt like he was looking through her with this question.

She carefully hesitated before answering, "I do, I think. But honestly I don't know him that well. I was just thinking about him and ended up in his head while I was dreaming. I wasn't trying to. I didn't even remember that he'd kissed my finger when I cut it. He didn't look good. He's all beat up and…he heard me."

"Heard you? Mmmm…well I guess we have no choice but to deal with this at another time. For now we must stay on task. It is time to get started." he said with a large grin.

Her eyes lit up, "Oh! You guys came up with something?"

"Yes, now let's go join the group." He headed for the door.

She followed reluctantly, "We have to try your experiment in front of others?"

He stood by the door and addressed every concern he knew she had, "Yes and you will be fine…and so will everyone else so do not worry, it only inhibits your concentration."

"Whatever you say." she said warily.

When Nomad and Thia arrived the group had already started. A little girl was making some flowers floating and dancing around all the members' heads like butterflies.

Next was Thia's turn so she steps in the middle. *Unlike training growing up, everyone here is very nice,* she thought. *It's funny how misfits are more forgiving.*

Nomad broke away from the discussion with his fellow instructor and handed Thia a clear light bulb.

Thia smiled and looked around not understanding, "Uh, what's this for?"

Nomad told her with complete seriousness, "I want you to light it."

It took her a second, first thinking that the nearest lamp was probably in the castle. Then it sunk in what he intended and her curious smile faded into fret.

She swallowed hard, "Don't you think everyone is a little too close?" she stressed as her voice strained.

"No we don't. Please proceed when ready." his tone was not mean but very dry.

Her stomach knotted up and she spoke stern but softly, "I didn't ask what *we* thought, I asked what *you* think. *They* know nothing."

He got closer to her and quietly directed, "I need you to take a deep breath, and relax."

Her eyes never leaving him as he backed away, she attempted to do so trusting him.

Seeing that she was having a tough time he chose a different method. "Thia, I need you to look at the filament in the bulb and describe it to me."

With frustrated hesitation she did, "A frail metal coil?"

"Yes. Focus on just how frail is it, how thin and fragile it is."

It was so quiet it was like no one else was around. Nomad's trick worked. He'd drawn her attention from the circle of potential victims, to the intricate details of the object in her hand.

She stared deep inside the bulb. "Okay."

He spoke in a softer tone as if she were in hypnosis, "Good. Now with something so thin, how much energy do you think it might take to light it?"

Her eyes were fixed on the thin wire, "I wouldn't imagine much at all."

"Correct -- so light it. It's just like we learned to move wounds." She only heard his voice now looking into the glass.

Her eyebrows furrowed, "I don't see how this is like that at all."

"Sure it is. Instead of peeling off the gash and watching it travel to its new destination, imagine a spot on one end of the coil start to glow, watch the energy fill and travel through the coil."

She took a moment to absorb what he said.

When he thought she had enough time, "Are you ready to try?"

She nodded trancelike, "Yes, I think so."

When she looked up to answer him this time she realized again they were not alone and she got nervous and relapsed, "But don't you think, just in case, everyone should watch from further away, including you?"

He cut her off in a scold for not beginning already, for allowing herself to get distracted, "The coil Thia. That is the only thing that should be in your mind now."

"Right." and she quickly did as she was told. Nomad is not one for wasting time and it was very rare that he got upset.

She held the metal part of the bulb in her right hand pulling it closer to her face. She closed her eyes trying to remove everything but the bulb as she was instructed. She opened them again looking deep into coil.

Now that she was paying more attention she started to notice more details about the coil. She saw where it was soldered to the wires on the ends. How the coil was imperfect with a rough surface and multiple shades of dull grey and pits. The coil shivered at the slightest movement.

The solder spot is where she chose to imagine the glow. She wanted it to turn red and then white hot like metal heated by a blacksmith's fire. Then she started to notice it was in fact turning red, yellow then white. She jumped with excitement and the bulb exploded showering everyone in glass.

"Ha ha!!! Very good Thia!" Nomad was ecstatic with the progress she made.

Both puzzled and disappointed she couldn't help but ask, "What are you talking about? Everyone is covered in shards and the bulb is dust now."

He grabbed her by the arms, "Ha! You wonderful and silly girl! Don't you see? It only exploded when you got excited. But before that, you did it! And on the first try, *again*. My dear girl you truly are a natural. Oh the things you'll be able to do."

Everyone clapped.

Thia laughed, not expecting their acceptance and support.

"Never, never dismiss improvement! Now we just need to work on taming the effects those powerful emotions of yours have on your abilities. Come, that is enough for one day.", as he turned and began walking quickly back to the castle.

She had to jog to catch up, "Enough? We just did one thing and it's the middle of the day. Let's try more!"

"You're hooked? Good. Oh you'll be trying more. I've got a whole box of bulbs for you to take back to your room for practice."

"…Nomad?" she asked trying to keep up with the new speed she'd never know he was capable of.

He grinned but didn't slow, "Ah, this is going to be a seasoned question. I can tell by your tone and the use of my name. Go on, I can't wait to hear it."

"Um, okay." His comment threw her off for a second. "What do you think happened when I hurt everyone? Why did just the light bulb explode instead of …you know, what happened back then?"

"And once again, you have not let me down. I do have a theory. Actually our little experiment just now brought me much closer in the direction I was already headed."

He went on to be blunt in his honesty explaining exactly what he thought happened. As it turns out, Nomad was clearly not a fan of the instructor's predictable and ill prepared teaching attempt, "First off, your stubborn and feeble minded teacher failed you. Rather than trying to save face for his ignorance, he should've consulted with someone on how to approach your training. When you tried your power, it was not focused. The radius was too wide, and the target too far away, thus applying your power to everything instead of only on the lone object."

She took a deep breath, "Why did Dae get hurt the worst? Why didn't some sort of bond instinct kick in to save him instead of hurt him?"

Nomad slowed down dropping his head, "Within every being, the survival instinct is very strong. Self first is natures rule." He regained speed.

She emanated with reborn determination, "Please, teach me to override it."

Nomad did as he promised and delivered a box to her room after lunch. The rest of the day she practiced. Again, she watched the melted metal heat up. The first few were the same until she was able to keep the thrill at bay.

Finally she took a break to stand up and stretch. She walked over to the window and scanned the grounds. She didn't realize how long she'd been at it. It was getting dark now, the air cool and invigorating. She leaned against the pane as her eyes wandered up searching to find her favorite stars peeking out. Though she was tired, she knew if her brothers were here she could find the energy to dance. It was a perfect night for it.

Becoming very home sick and missing her brothers again, she went away from the window. She wasn't sure if her new spike in motivation came from honorable determination or, more likely, pure impatience, but regardless she went back to diligently practicing. *I have to get this right…tonight.* She wasn't very good at setting actual goals so this one sounded as good as any when it came to quenching her impatient need to complete something.

She sat back on the floor, grabbed a fresh bulb and started again. But in that moment, she realized something about Nomad, *he totally knows how impatient I am! He so just worked me, getting me to sit here like this until I get it.* Rather than getting mad at the fact, as she fully trusts him, *Hmmm…good for him. Maybe he will teach me how to work people some time.*

The summit of connection heated up in the bulb. The smell of hot metal escaped the glass and filled her overly sensitive nose. A molten red snake slowly and smoothly wound its way through the coil to the other side. She stared at it with deep curiosity as she half willed the flow of the lava to change from red to orange, intensify to yellow and finally reach the hottest white.

Once she came to the realization that she'd accomplished lighting the still intact test item in her hand, the room was now completely filled with warm light from the brightly glowing bulb. She mindfully caught herself, careful not to get too excited. She decided she would settle for pleased – there was enough glass on the floor for one night.

The next morning came faster than expected as she continued practicing through the night, able to consistently reproduce results in singles, then trying multiple bulbs, dimming them at the same time and different times until there was a knock at the door.

Already knowing who it was by his scent, Thia flung the door open in excitement to find a very tired looking Nomad.

Before he could get a word out she shouted, "Nomad I got it!"

"I know." he calmly answered rubbing his eyes.

Confused by his comment she asked, "How could you know?"

He walked over to her window, looked down at all of the glass on the floor that crunched under his sandals, then back at her.

Facetiously she explained, "Failed attempts from earlier."

"My room is the next level down over there." he pointed out her window to one adjacent to hers." The excessive light kept me and a few neighbors up half the night. I finally piled enough against the window to get my room dark enough to sleep. Thia, the bulbs aren't built to even go that bright. For the first time in my long life you've afforded me an abundance of mysteries to solve."

She looked at him blankly, "Is that good?" Then she couldn't wait to show him, "Never mind, watch!"

She proudly demonstrated her new newly acquired control over the handful of surviving light bulbs, lighting, dimming, one then three at a time. She even got them to change to brilliant colors of red, blue and purple.

"Thia I am very impressed by your progress in such a short amount of time. So what have you learned? What are you doing differently?" Nomad asked now in a very teacher like manner.

"I knew you were going to ask that so I've been trying to figure it out. The only thing I can come up with is, well it's like I was trying so hard to pull the light through the element. But it wouldn't work and I got frustrated and tired. But I didn't want to stop until I got it to work at least once. So I tried to calm down and relax. When I tried it again instead just kind of watching it instead of forcing it, it seemed to move along by itself? Does that make any sense?"

"It does indeed. You always seem to do much better when you don't try. When you try to force your power, your results if any, end up erratic. However when you allow proper focus, letting your power to freely flow gently guided by suggestion, the results are clean and consistent."

Since they had opened up a way for Thia to recognize the use of her gift, Nomad wanted to get started on ways for her to better direct her power. They walked through the castle grounds passing many of the groups as Nomad explained their next lesson, "You've learned all you can now from the bulbs. Sitting alone staring at a lifeless item is not going to help you when it comes to guiding your powers especially when there are distractions around. We need an open area for out next trial. Have you and your bothers been practicing your Martial arts forms?"

She was a little ashamed for all three of them, "Not as much as we should've but we've gotten a lot better at making time to practice, why?"

"You will need some of the core items for this next lesson."

They headed around and behind the castle finally stopping at a large garden containing a small pumpkin patch.

Thia's eyes widened from the awe inspiring vibrant colors of the well organized plot of land, "Oh, this is beautiful. I really need to get a garden going at home. Then again we normally wouldn't be there long enough to reap what we would've sown."

Nomad did what he did best and carried on like he heard nothing. Then again he really might not have heard her, full of his own plans for the vegetation. "You are going to use your hands and body for meditation and directing. The theory being that you should be able to channel it through your body and movements."

Mentally set on his decided approach he turned to her and began his instructions, "Now, plant your feet in a solid stance, just like in our early lessons. This will help you maximize control and increase the force of a hit." They walked through some together encouraging grace in the flow and adding emphasis and pop on the stopping points.

When he felt she had refreshed enough on the form, he picked up a large and not quite ripe yellow and green pumpkin from the patch and placed it in front of her.

"Thia I want you to move this gourd with the movements we just reviewed. Slowly push your arms forward to move it forward. Then side to side, up and down and so on."

The day passes with no progress. Both are exhausted.

Nomad at last stands up, "Thia that is enough for today, it is time for dinner."

Frustrated she is short with him, "No, I have to get this!"

"Do not worry, we can try again tomorrow." as he turns to go.

She crosses her arms and stares angrily at the target, "You go, I'm staying."

"No one can focus on an empty stomach. I've heard yours growling for over an hour now. It is time to stop and eat. Then we can come back if you wish."

"No."

He almost stomped when he spoke, "Now is not the time for stubbornness Thia. You know very well, the outcome will not improve with the mood you are in."

She didn't move.

It never having to come to this before, he straighten up, "Thia, I am no longer asking."

Her shoulders drop and she turns to him utterly defeated. "Why won't it work?"

He offered his arm and slowly walked her back to the castle, "Though it may not seem so, this is much more advanced. It will take time and patience, both of which you are not known for."

She didn't bother arguing a point she knew was absolutely spot on.

They arrived at the dinner hall and ran into Chase, "Hey! You guys are out late."

"Hi", Thia still looked upset.

Before Chase could ask what was wrong, Nomad jumped in, "Chase, can I ask a favor of you when you are finished with dinner?"

"Sure, I'm actually done already. One of the other kids in my group wouldn't stop thinking about food since he woke up late and missed breakfast, it made me really hungry. Turns out I learned today I can subconsciously send that type of suggestion to those fairly close by. We all ended up so absorbed by the thought of eating we agreed to finish early." He laughed.

Nomad sent Thia off, "Thia, go get started. I will be with you shortly."

"See ya Chase." And Thia did as she was told. She grabbed a plate and looked over to them. Chase was reading Nomad's mind for his instructions. Thia found it frustrating not being able to hear what Nomad was planning, but judging by some of the body language she guessed it involved something outside, her failure perhaps.

"What can I get you?!" Thia jumped from the loud, rude lady behind the counter barking at her.

Not all that hungry despite the claims her stomach made, Thia grabbed a few small items to eat, sat down and reluctantly took a bite. Nomad joined her. There were many conversations going on around them but not much between them was said as they finished.

Returning their dishes to the counter Nomad offered, "Do you still want to go back and try some more?"

Thia hesitated, a little surprised. She was sure he was done with her for the night but decided to be honest, "yes"

Weary but willing to help her try again he accepted, "Alright then, let's go."

When they exited the giant doors she saw what Nomad had asked Chase to do. A path of torches lit the way to the pumpkin patch.

An hour passes, and Thia plops down on the ground yawning then lays back looking up at the black sky sprinkled with little sparkling stars. She then looks over to Nomad who is slumped over fast asleep. *How does he do it? He can sleep anywhere.* She lets out a little laugh at him as he snores. Not wanting to disturb him just yet her attention returns to the stars.

The longer she looked at them the more seemed to pop up, twinkling like little spinning crystals suspended in front of lint free black velvet cloth. She rubbed her eyes as it was getting pretty late. Almost ready to call it quits she decides to try one last time for the heck of it.

She sits up and looks at the giant pumpkin still attached to the vine. She gives it its own personality. *Why are you so stubborn? Just move when I tell you.* And as she talks to it in her mind she notices something new. It's fuzzy at first. Then it looks like it's crawling, like little fireflies, on the vine to the stem and over the surface of the pumpkin.

Nomad chokes and snorts a bit waking up sensing a change in the air. Thia's gaze at the pumpkin wasn't disrupted at all by all the noise; she'd been hearing it long enough tonight to tune it out. He was careful not to move noticing the same expression she had with her bulb success.

Still unaware that Nomad is awake; Thia tips her head to the side then lifts her hand attempting to push it a little. The pumpkin moves. She lets out a slight gasp but quickly tamed it while still in the trance. The fireflies are getting brighter and moving a little faster now.

Nomad sees her eyebrows furrow then looks at the pumpkin. It's slowly growing and the colors are changing. The yellow color moves from the bottom half to the top chasing the green away. Then the yellow gives way to a deep rich orange.

Thia sees these changes too. Then she imagines mentally influencing the fireflies. She points and lifts her finger telling them to lift the vine, and they do so. Then bringing the rest her fingers up she tells them to make the pumpkin bigger by spreading her fingers out around the pumpkin, and they do. Then she couldn't help herself. She imagined the pumpkin was a big balloon and makes it grow even faster. This was getting fun.

Nomad still observing her succeed notices the new smile on her face. Knowing it will lead to her getting over excited, he attempts to remind her, "Thia remem…"

The pumpkin explodes. Thia blinks out of her trance to find them both completely covered in pumpkin guts and seeds.

"…ber to control your excitement." Nomad trails off.

Both exhausted but happy now, they agree to clean up and call it a night.

The next few days first thing after breakfast they head back to the patch.

"Nomad, why don't we practice with the others? They are all in groups." Then she spots the old man staring out the window. "And who is that guy that watches us?"

Without looking he knew who she meant, "I had to get permission to bring you here. He is the Keeper. He was intrigued when I told him about you. He observes and helps us, the instructors, come up with how to best train the students. You and I don't train with the others yet because they would still distract you setting you back. We have not the time to lose. Once you are truly ready, we will join the others to further teach you how to avoid additional diversions."

They reviewed what happened each night and increased the level of difficulty. Thia was on a roll now as she gained confidence from becoming more comfortable, finally able to understand how to do what she could do. Both grew with each lesson. Nomad gained new and valuable ideas on how to approach the others student's challenges that he thought he'd tried everything with.

Nomad explained the fireflies she saw to the Keeper and they came to the conclusion it must be the energy that surrounds everything, and that when she slows down enough, that is when she is able to see it. With a few days of rapid progress under her belt she was drained from the mentally strenuous practice. Her nights were thankfully blessed with deep sleep that is until one night she was woken up from an unprovoked but none the less disturbing nightmare.

She was all alone in a field by the castle. She heard a noise and turned to look but found nothing. But when she turned back a strange old man suddenly appeared in front of her, "The Dark is coming. This world will fade." And then he was gone.

Almost immediately after that she thought of her brothers and the phone rang.

"Thia you okay? What's wrong." Dae spoke for both.

Thia still a little weirded out by the dream, "I'm fine, just had a weird nightmare. Some crazy old guy…"

He finished her portrayal, "said the Dark is coming?"

She found some relief knowing she wasn't the only one for once, "Yeah. What's that all about?"

He offered no further comfort, "I'm not sure, but Nomad might know since we all saw it."

Her stomach sunk, she didn't want to think that it could actually have meaning, "You're probably right. I'll ask him in the morning."

"Did he say when you might be coming home?"

"No, not yet but we've been getting a lot done. I doubt it will be much longer. How are things going there?"

"Pretty good, everyone is catching on quick now."

"Glad to hear it. I'll let him know that too. Although he's going to be pissed I'm talking to you on the phone."

Shai chimed in, "Oh, he'll get over it. This seems kind of important."

Dae agreed, "Shai's right. He may be upset at first but this might need some attention. We'll let you go now so you aren't on too long."

"Alright, take care." And they hung up.

I miss home. She thought curling up tight in the bed to go back to sleep.

The next morning Thia and Nomad were at breakfast when Chase came to join them.

"Good morning guys!" he said enthusiastic.

"Good morning Chase." Nomad spat out with a full mouth.

In the middle of a bite Chase remembered something, "Hey…Nomad, I wanted to ask you about something. Last night I had a strange vision about an old man in the field on the side of the castle. He said *the Dark* was coming. What do you make of that?"

Thia sat up in her seat, "Hey, I had the same nightmare, and my brothers saw it too!"

Nomad looked uncomfortable at the news, "This is the first I've heard of it. When you two are finished go back to your rooms and wait there. I'll stop by after I speak with the Keeper." His plate half full he left walking much quicker than normal.

Chase stopped eating, "Okay that makes me nervous. I've never seen him react like that before. Nothing scares Nomad."

Thia nodded, "Agreed. I think we should go now and take our food with us."

"Good idea, see you later." And they both quickly headed off to their rooms.

Thia nervously sat in hers, not sure if she wanted to see Nomad soon or not depending on what news he brought. When that got old she started pacing and watching out the window but there was still no sign of Nomad. After a while she decided she did want to see him just to get the suspense over with. The sky was growing dark like another storm was coming. *It's just rain, don't get all paranoid* she tried to rationalize. Then her brothers called again.

It was Shai and he was out of breath, "Thia, they're here, in town, you gotta come home now."

An explosion goes off in the field shaking the castle.

"What was that?" he asked.

She ran to the window, "I don't know. I have a very bad feeling that dream was right. I may need to help here first."

Static filled the connection, "Alright, be careful. I'll let Dae know. Nothing's happened yet but they are definitely in town and they brought a lot of big stuff with them so it's only a matter of time now."

She hears a knock on the door, "Okay, I'll do what I can. Gotta go, someone's at the door."

There was another loud knock at her door then it wildly opened and Chase came rushing in.

He flew in and grabbed her arm, "Hey, we gotta stick together and find Nomad. He'll know what to do."

She grabbed her bag, "Good idea. Do you know where the keeper stays? We should try there first."

Chase did know the way as they ran through the castle of panicked and screaming children. All were told to head to the dining room at the center of the castle. Teachers lined the halls and checked the rooms for anyone left behind.

Almost to the room Nomad and the Keeper headed them off.

"Where are you two going?" the Keeper asked.

"We came looking for Nomad to see what we should do." Chase answered out of breath.

"Very well. We'll need you to join the others in the dining room. We'll be there shortly." Nomad said calmly.

"Yes sir." And Chase grabbed Thia's arm again to escort her there.

Thia resisted and spoke up, "Nomad, they've arrived back home."

Nomad no longer looked calm.

Thia continued, "Shai said nothings started yet but they brought a lot with them. What should I do?"

"This is orchestrated." The Keeper declared.

She spoke again talking to Nomad, "I will stay and help here first then head back, yes?"

He nodded once, "Yes. For now please join the others."

She looked back at him as she left with Chase. She wasn't scared like all the others. Instead she was worried for her brothers more than anything. But the hidden Phelidae down deep was creeping up inside of her, the preservation instinct filling her. It felt good. She'd denied her cat form for too long, weeks, not once changing to her other self and running free. She had a small urge to ignore his order and go fight, and it was only getting stronger the closer she got to the room with all the young and old human targets gathered in it.

Chase whispered to her, "Thia, why are you pacing so much? Others are starting to watch." She could barely hear him over the murmurs in the room and more explosions outside.

Thia's stripes came out, "I can't help it. I need out."

"Wow, that's cool." Chase was in awe of her new face.

Another large boom shook the room as dust fell from the ceiling. The lights flickered not darker but brighter. Nomad and the Keeper stood towards the front of the room discussing plans with the other teachers. Both took turns keeping an eye on Thia. She paced like a cat trapped in a cage.

After the next flicker Nomad came to see her, "I can tell you are anxious. We think your energy might prove more useful outside."

Chase laughed, "You mean before she blows out the lights?"

It was as if he'd given her a present she'd always wanted, "Oh thank you! I will see what is out there and come back to let you know once I find out."

"Can I go?" Chase jumped up eager to go with her, to help.

All of her nervous energy made him antsy. In fact the older ones of the group noticed this to be the theme of the room. Any other time they would've been afraid, but this time she was there, influencing, like her kind do.

Nomad admired his courage, "I'm afraid not, not yet at least. First we should know what we are up against. We'll all get a chance to do our part."

"Me too?", asked little Adam appearing from behind Nomad.

"Yes, you too." Nomad smiled.

Thia could wait no longer and dropped her bag, "Be right back." And out without a sound she leapt up and out the open second story window at the back of the room.

About fifteen minutes later she returned through the same window.

"She didn't change?", one of the teachers asked Nomad.

Nomad simply responded, "She is a white tiger, they would've seen her."

"Ah, smart" the teacher admitted in a surreal daze.

"It's the Pallas." She said as she approached Nomad. "They don't have much gear with them. I'm guessing because it's such a haul here. But I am surprised they didn't bring the chopper."

The Keeper spoke up but not directly to Thia, "It would do them no good. You see we have unseen, and to most unknown, ways of remaining undetectable." This was the first time she heard him really speak since she'd gotten there. He had a deep resonating voice, a voice of authority.

"That explains a couple things. They are getting close but still seem to be blindly shooting in the dark."

Then the enemy got lucky. A rocket hit the castle tearing a hole in the roof. Some with gifts were able to act fast enough that no one got hurt from the large pieces of falling stone.

Thia still itching to do something, "I need to go back and fight. We need to end this before it really starts."

Nomad already had a plan, "Agreed. We will only send a few."

And they did so. Nomad led Thia and a few of the more experienced including Chase. They were successful in putting up enough of a resistance to send them away but not without some injuries. Most were minor but Chase had been hit with a bullet during one of the panic induced sprays. Against many protests she steals the wound for her own. It went deeper than she anticipated but didn't let on.

Once the attack was over they returned to the castle. All the others went inside but Nomad pulling Thia aside.

"We can handle things from here. I have a feeling this was just a side project for them with minimal effort, which means the brunt of it is waiting for you back home. Pack your things and go now. They will need you as soon as possible and I will be there once I know everything here is alright." Before he let her go Nomad stressed to her, "No matter what happens, you are very, very important Thia. You must be very careful and keep fresh in your mind all that you've learned here."

Headed Off

"Go to them Thia. Your training is far from done but you have come a long way. Remember all you've learned, now is the time to use it, be careful." were Nomads last words to her before she left him with a backdrop of the broken castle and smoke.

Running from Nomad's home leaving them all behind, many thoughts flood her mind as guilt settled in. *This is somehow my fault. How could I have exposed such a peaceful and noble place? What did it? How did they find us? Could it have been from talking to my brothers, or maybe seeing Matteus? Nomad should've never brought me. Bad things happen around me all the time. How could he have forgotten that?*

Her thoughts ran fast and furious with her. Though her wound was hidden it still hurt. It was a deep one that would take some time to heal. The bullet passed through but it nicked something on the way out. It would heal faster if she could rest but that was not an option for the time being. She tried to think harder on what she learned to distract from the pain. She tried to remember everyone she encountered during the time she spent there, *I don't remember anyone that looked suspicious.* No reason for the attack would come to her.

Nomad told her to head south east until she recognized the area and she did so. On her way back she was not stopping as they did on the trip there, she was running straight through. It was drizzling, depressing and grey but this didn't slow her down, she didn't slip once. She only wanted to stop to call her brothers but she decided it was best to keep going.

Getting closer to home, still at top speed the wind blows a faint familiar scent in her direction. *Matteus? Can't be, what would he be doing out here?* So instinctively she slowed down knowing the source of the scent was not far off judging by its concentration. If there is ever a chance a Phelidae could be seen behaving like a non human by an outsider, they were to avoid it at almost all cost, survival the exception. She slowed to a walk when a strong call took over.

Dae was out of breath surrounded by a lot of noise, "Thia, where are you? It's begun and is getting bad here. Nomad was right, they have a lot and of all kinds. It seems to be half vampires and half gifted humans with Caleb and Kasha in the lead. We underestimated them and the connections they've gained. We've never prepared and fought an attack like this."

She spoke back to him in her head much like she did with her mother, "I'm already on my way. We had some trouble at Nomad's but I should be there soon. Hang in there. Run if you have to."

"Thia we can't run. Ben's people are here and fighting with us. They keep trying to get at Shai and me but the wolves have us fully covered. We can't leave them with this, especially now."

"Alright. I am moving as fast as I can. I'll see you soon." It was getting late and darker by the minute. *Hopefully this will give us an advantage over the humans at least*, she hoped starting to plan how to handle the new information.

When she came out of the call, Matteus appeared directly in front of her. She jumped back in shock.

His face and tone full of remorse, "Thia."

Despite the fact that she missed him, now wasn't the best time, "um, hi. I'm sorry but I'm in a bit of a hurry. Can we talk later?"

"No." He was different, his voice cold and dry not like him at all.

Regardless, his answer was what caught her attention. "Okay, well either way I have to go, it's an emergency." Very confused she had to first ask, "What are you doing all the way out here?"

Still somber and barely able to look her in the eyes, "Thia I'm here to stop you."

She was completely lost, "Stop me, from what? That doesn't make any sense. How did you know I would be here?"

Matteus did not respond at first, just looked down.

Thia's frustration grew, "As always, so full of answers. You know what, it doesn't even matter. Feel free to keep your distance like you have been. Good bye."

She turned to leave but he said something horrifying, "I felt you coming. I don't understand how it is possible but I felt when you were near. Thia, I've never been one at a loss for words…but…I need you. I…I am so very sorry. The last thing I wanted was to stay away. I so desperately wanted to see you. I cannot tell you how regretful I am about this. I will explain once we get there but right now I can't let you go. You must come with me Thia, please." And he extended his hand.

Thia's frustration boiled looking at his hand. He was keeping her from her brothers, "I'm sorry, did you just say can't *let*….oh, don't worry about it. You don't *get* that choice!"

Thia takes off, not at top speed but faster than she should have in front of a human. She ran faster than he should be able to handle yet somehow he keeps up. *What the…how is he doing it?*, Thia wondered. So she cuts off in another direction but again he stays with her. So she goes a bit faster but he's still at her side. She stops.

She's very angry at him, "How are you doing that?! You shouldn't be able to keep up with me. What's going on? And this time I demand answers!"

Matteus obviously very upset, "Honestly? I am not sure anymore. Thia you've changed me, even before you -- changed me. At first when we met I found you interesting and attractive. I don't know if you realize but you emanate *life* despite your closed off facade. When I first saw you at the diner, I couldn't take my eyes off of you. I had to meet you. Then after we met I found it impossible to stop thinking about you. I deeply regretted not being able to find you sooner. Then when I saw you at the store...I was...dead I suppose it's called. But from that day that I kissed your finger I've been...changing. My skin feels so warm, almost feverish compared to before. I crave food and rest when I haven't done those things in...a very long time..."

"...Matteus, I have no idea what you are going on about but if you insist, we'll have to discuss it later. I have to get back home, *now*." She turns to run but this time he simply appears in front of her.

Thia gasps not expecting such speed from him.

Matteus gently takes Thia by the arms, "You are right, I owe you an explanation. You remember the ones you fought in the clearing that night with the little girl and the wolves?"

Thia is cautious now leaning back, "How could you know about that?"

Matteus was ashamed, "They are the family that I told you were coming to town the night of the party."

"I'm so confused. What does that have to do with...?" she stopped and her expression dropped. During the last vision from Dae she saw one of the four there from that night. Then it all made sense to her.

A look of ultimate betrayal washed over her. "You're a...vampire?"

After some more thought she stiffened up. "If you are here to kill me then let's not waste anymore time." She broke free from his grip. Her eyes changed to piercing slits, her deep dark stripes came out creeping up the back of her neck finally resting around her face as she made her defense stance.

Matteus's stood in awe over the instant transformation. It took his breath away, "Fascinating. You are even more beautiful in this form."

"You've seen nothing, yet." as her teeth grew slightly.

"I told you Matteus!" a new voice boomed from the woods which startled them both. They were too involved in the conversation to notice his approach.

"Darius, why are you here?" Matteus looked half concerned but half ready in his own guard.

"I'm here to properly meet, your little *pet*." He seemed to hiss while slinking towards them from between the trees.

"I'm not his anything", Thia corrected Darius. Then she turned to Matteus and with a slight growl, "You were wise to bring backup."

Matteus however, with affection and extreme anxiety, "Thia please, that is not what this is."

Darius thoroughly appalled, "Matteus, do not disgrace yourself pleading to this animal!"

Thia smiled at his pompous mumblings. "Your kind are nothing more than walking infectious death. My *kind* protect life. I gladly take being an animal over a parasite maggot."

Darius's hand fell to his chest, "Oh my, she does have some fire in her Matteus, I give you that. In fact I'm embarrassed to admit I'm possibly starting to understand your bizarre interest in her."

Matteus growled at Darius. Thia looked at him surprised by his unexpected reaction. She couldn't help but still care about him, though she hadn't shared it with him yet she found him special too. But, she remained unmoving in her decision to let him go as he was so quick to release her, or so she initially thought.

Darius, persistently snide, "Ah that's right. Matteus is, how did you say, *infectious death* too dear, remember?" Then he turned psychotically angry, "That is until you poisoned him! We don't take too kindly to such interference. Because of you, he actually had a brief moment where he thought he was suddenly too good his own family, wanting to go off and have nothing to do with us, without any bit of rational. But fear not, he may be a few degrees warmer now but we were able to remind him who and what he really is. We will not lose one of our best to the likes of *you*."

Instantly insulted by the accusation, "Poison? I did no such thing!"

He didn't acknowledge her statement attempting to add injury to insult but squinted, "But please if you will, tell us how you did it? He had the hardest time figuring out why he fell ill. It took some time for your poison to set in but when it did our Matteus was almost gone from us. He was weak, burning up and covered in bruises when he was brought to the club. According to Giles, the blood in his veins has flowed slowly for so long now that the rapid increase in speed and volume nearly caused him to bleed to death internally as the stress caused multiple bursts. Well done dear. However, you did *not* succeed. You see our kind heal very fast. That and our beloved Simone, after escorting him from your dirty little club, found him at his home just in time and tended to him *personally*. She was sure to meet his *every* need."

Darius was accurate in his intentional mind game attack. Thia indeed felt a jolt of jealousy pulse through her.

But Matteus was the one that could take no more, "ENOUGH Darius!" For the first time Darius looked afraid of Matteus but only for a moment.

Matteus again gently took Thia by the arm, "Thia it was nothing like that. It's true I was sick, and Simone did insist on being there to watch over me, but nothing happened beyond that. You *must* believe me. Your trust is very important to me."

Thia realized they'd wasted too much time, she had to end this now, "My trust?! You disappear with no word leaving me to believe I'd done something wrong. And now this attempt at holding me against my will to listen to you two banter on about your dysfunctional family matters. I do not have time for this! I'm leaving…NOW!"

Darius tittered a fake little laugh, "Oh, I'm afraid not…" He was cut off by the gust of wind announcing her rude and unexcused departure. She was up to top speed but it didn't take long for them to catch up to her.

"My, she's fast too!" Darius said running on her left commenting to Matteus shadowing on her right.

Then she catapulted up, flying above the trees as they watched in amazement. Still when she came down they were again close by. Annoyed she dug in and came to a complete stop, they blew past her but quickly returned.

"This useless game needs to end!" she said in a blinding fury now.

Darius's evil smile grew, "Matteus she is right."

Matteus shouted at him, "Darius you promised, if I stopped her she would not be harmed."

Darius folded his arms, "Ah yes Matteus but I have yet to see her stopped."

"*Me* not harmed? You struck some back alley deal with this…and what of my brothers and our friends?"

"Collateral damage I'm afraid dear. Those Pallas can be very persuasive when they want to be." Darius voice rang out in a sickening sing song tone.

Thia turned to Matteus in disbelief, "You were going to allow my brothers, the only loved ones I have left, that mean the world to me, be taken just like that?"

Matteus distressed with tears in his eyes, "Thia I did not know what else to do. I cannot lose you. And you are terribly outnumbered."

Darius sat quiet for long enough, "Oh, how sickeningly sweet."

She let out a ground rumbling roar, "I will lose no more family to anyone or thing!"

Darius was momentarily unsettled by her power, remembering reports of the strike she dealt in the field, but quickly regained his composure, "Impressive, but we shall see." And in a split second Darius attacked.

Thia and Darius fight blow after blow but get nowhere.

Darius was enraged, "Matteus, help me end her!"

Quick and unattached, "I will not."

"Traitor!" he hissed at him.

At the most inopportune time Thia gets another call, a strong one. She is instantly incapacitated. Matteus sees this and in a poorly controlled panic tries to divert Darius's attention. "Traitor?! You are the one that has gone back on our agreement?! You will pay. You will see when Giles hears of your broken word! He will know you cannot be trusted…"

But it was too late. Darius already noticed the quick look of concern on his face and turned to find Thia nonresponsive, "Clever, but not quick enough Matteus."

He saunters over to her, "What have we here?"

Matteus's hands ball up into fists, "Darius I implore you, stop this madness!"

An evil smile crawled across his cold face, "Oh, this is too delicious to leave be."

Matteus is unable to stop him for he is bound by his coven's union which prohibits him from acting against his own kind. But, fighting against the crushing urge of Darius's orders, he refuses to hurt Thia. Helpless he winced in pain as Darius struck leaving a deep gape in Thia's side. Still, she failed to react as her body fell to the ground.

"No!" Matteus cried out rushing to her side.

Something strange happens as they watch over her confused by her state. Though her eyes were wide, blinking and moving her body was motionless and limp. Matteus stared furious at Darius for hurting her at all much less by taking such a cheap shot while she stood there helpless. But his attention returned to Thia seeing Darius blink and squint watching the bullet wound appeared on the other side of her stomach.

Thia was still out. Her vision this time was a long one showing her the fight had sadly escalated not in their favor. Some of the people Nomad brought were seriously injured and a few captured. Dae turned just in time for Thia to witness Shai get taken down, then the vision cut off instead of fading out like usual. She panicked as fright set in *I have to get there now!* The affects were wearing off and she saw the two figures that stood over her. Pure anger took over Thia as her company came in focus.

Matteus and Darius were still lingering, curious. Her eyes went narrow again and she slowly blinked as she came too. Once her focus was fully back her face turned angry, scaring them as she sprung off the ground twisted around kicking the two of them away from her. Matteus hit the ground and slid as Darius slammed hard in to a thick tree that didn't give.

Before Darius has a chance to recover she attacks him and doesn't let up. He is overwhelmed and cannot fight back. Matteus crawls to and grabs on tight to the nearest tree fighting the overwhelming urge to come to Darius's aid. His fingers bled as he dug in fighting it. Thia didn't notice. A new fierce rage drove her every move. Darius was keeping her from the only family she had left when they needed her most and now they were hurt, or worse.

She backed off of Darius after all but killing him, she was done wasting time and would be heading home. However he finds the strength enough to get one solid hit off into her stomach sending her to the ground. She's down now and squirming from the distress in the large open wounds.

Matteus quickly approaches her and inspects, "You're hurt bad."

"Don't!" she orders through gritted teeth and pain filled eyes.

Matteus shakes his head, "Thia please, I must confess to you, it is all so complicated but...I love you. Please, let me help you."

While Matteus attempts to plead with her, Darius manages to slowly get up. Matteus doesn't see him coming up from behind as he is too concerned about Thia's condition. She catches sight of him, forgetting the pain she twists around and kicks off springing high up in the air over Matteus. She comes down on top of Darius pinning him to the ground.

Thia places both hands on his stomach and digs her fingers and nails in drawing his cold blood. Her eyes go wide and angry peering dead in his eyes. She was deciding but her choice didn't take long. She closed her eyes and transfers both large wounds and major bruises to Darius. None had shown them how to do this and she guessed none had ever tried but as she guessed, it worked much like stealing did. It took a second but when she was through, he writhed in pain he'd never known. The wounds were too large and deep for his kind to heal fast enough.

Matteus pulls Thia off by her waist watching Darius embrace his own affliction.

"Matteus… heal me…now!" as he holds his stomach from the pain, panicking, as he knew he was quickly running out of time.

Matteus fights as he spins Thia around and jerks her close, forehead to forehead. With his left arm holding her tight against him as he struggles still fighting the urge, he takes her face with his right hand and takes her lips into his, not letting go again as the urge to assist Darius attempts to interrupt with each of Darius's screams.

Finally he gently pulls away exhausted from the conflict, "Thia go, I cannot resist much longer. I'm not sure how I've been able to this far but I suspect it has something to do with you. I *have* to help him, so you must go…now."

Torn, both confused and still very upset at him she pulls away. He fights as long as he can to send her off. Finally she turns and runs as fast as she can disappearing from sight in seconds.

"Matteus! You will pay dearly for this!" Darius struggled to yell, furious with him.

Quietly Matteus acknowledges his fate, "I know." was the last she heard as she ran on.

She couldn't help but want to go back for him. *What terrible things are they going to do to him? What have they done to him already? Oh God, what are they doing to my brothers?! If they…I swear for the sake of their kind my brothers better be okay...* And she ran faster, faster than ever before.

After some time Thia didn't slow a bit even knowing the road that cut between the woods was coming up from the smell of the evening cooling pavement. It was not as windy here so there was less air noise going past her ears for her to pick up on something horrific.

Darius was healed enough to come after her again. She could hear, he alone, closing in as she tried to decide what to do. *He is too fast and strong for me to lead straight home. Things there are bad enough; I don't need to make it worse.*

With the road visible now she thought about maybe just jumping it hoping no one would see or that the highway wasn't wider than it looked but she wasn't positive she would get high enough to clear tall trucks. Then, in the distance she could heard a motorcycle coming. She could tell by the sound it was one of the fastest record breaking bikes that just came out, Shai's favorite. Thia could never get the different names down. As it got closer she guessed from the dealer looking plates that this may be a test drive. At that point she knew exactly what she was going to try.

The rider was having some fun first scanning for cops then climbing to the bikes top speed. This was fortunate for two reasons; one it would get her faster than Darius could go, so she hoped. And two, there was no other traffic around it which meant no attention to what she had planned to do.

"Where do you think you can go, *cat*?!" Thia could start to make out some of what he was yelling as he got closer.

"You destroyed him! Do not think I will not make you pay for forcing me to do what I must for his betrayal!" for the first time she heard he was slightly winded from the injuries and the run.

Ignoring Darius's continued threats of all the atrocious things he had planned for her once he caught her, she zero's in on the bike. Thia backs up a bit into the woods just far enough for a running start but still keeping her way out of site. This got her a little closer to Darius which cut out some of her lead time, but this was not going to distract her, it had to be done.

When the bike was almost to her, she checked both ways to again confirm there would be no witnesses from either direction. Then she tore off running leaving behind divots in the ground and a cloud of leaves. She blew out of the woods with a blur of twigs and dust, and with the bike and its rider directly in front, vaulted from the edge of the road. She reached the rider and flipped in the air, kicking him off as she spun around landing on the seat and grabbing the handles.

As soon as she was secure on the bike she checked back to confirm the rider had safely landed in the bushes she pre-calculated for him. In her left mirror showing the opposite side of the road, the side she came from, she found in the shadows, stood a livid Darius staring intently at her definite escape. Even he knew the bike was too fast for him to keep up with so he reentered the woods and disappeared.

Taking the road route was going to be a little more distance but she would easily make up the time using the speed the bike offered and the fact the gas tank was full. *The boys are going to love this thing, especially Shai. Not sure what to do about it being stolen and all though.* She refused to even consider the chance of an alternate ending.

The Stand

Back home, before the initial alert to Thia was necessary, her brothers become restless taking a break from practice and decide to go hang out with their new friends. Dae visited Doc Daniel to see what fun experiments he might be up to and bringing some of his own project ideas. Shai gave Ben a call to come over so they could race on one of their favorite abandoned roads. The sheriffs here didn't care as long as they weren't destroying anything. Of course the lack of challenge and thrill of the chase disappointed Shai a little.

Over all they were very happy and settled in. Thia did very well in her choice of location. The boys didn't think they would like it at first since it was so small, dull and remote, naturally mind-numbing in comparison to their previous homes, but they never told her this. She probably wouldn't have taken it very well.

Giving the place a chance, they found the food was good, for the most part people minded their own business, meaning they didn't go as far as snooping around, and they found much more freedom without so many eyes watching all the time.

All things considered, everything worked out surprisingly well. The town was quiet, content and predictable but they knew it wouldn't last forever. With Nomad's news of the twins, they recognized the fact that many would be seeking them out since joined with the Pallas. And that is just what happened.

A couple days later Dae was researching on the computer and received an emergency message from his friend Thomas. Since the last time they met he and Sarah had moved away, also to stay on the move and hidden, but sadly the Pallas found him anyway. Though not dead, he was in bad shape when they were finished with him leaving him for dead.

T-Mas: I am very sorry friend but they know where you are now and will be coming soon! Leave the moment you get this.

D-Day: I don't understand. How can this have happened?

T-Mas: They showed up here at the house. I held out as long as I could but then they turned to Sarah and I couldn't let them hurt her. The pair you mentioned before, Caleb and Kasha seemed to be willingly helping them.

D-Day: Do not worry dear friend, I understand. Thank you for risking sending this news. We will not be leaving this time. If all goes well I will be in touch and explain later.

There was a new twist this time. The Pallas had something vital they never possessed before, Caleb and Kasha, up for hire undoubtedly seeking to fulfill their own goals. All along none recognize the signs.

The twins felt even their own kind were unworthy of them, they were special, they have dual powers. Never mind the other three. Caleb wanted to lead, it was the only conclusion as far as he was concerned. With the more powerful ones out of the way they would be free to change things as they saw fit.

After they finished with Thomas, the twins met up with the army. Caleb instructed the Pallas not to come with them to Thomas's home. He'd already heard of and witnessed plenty of their failures and didn't want a strong lead like Thomas to flee before they had a word. Caleb knew instead that sensing his own kind approaching guaranteed Thomas would at least hesitate to see who it might be before leaving.

In addition to the army, the twins gained other exceptional acquaintances along the way. During their own travels and research of the area they were now heading to, Caleb and his sister came across some fascinating tales about oddities occurring in the surrounding area. The stories of these phenomenons seem to coincide with some news stories on suspected peculiar bear attacks during their hibernation season.

After some research and reaching out, they stumbled upon a group of vampires that had some issues with Ben's group. In particular he found a teenagers blog about a clan war. Already dismissed as typical teenage angst by any who noticed it until now, Caleb was not so quick to do so. Something about it drew Caleb, he was sure it was real and was right, using it as his way in.

While messaging back and forth with the boy, who loved the sudden attention, he came to understand it started as a dispute over the territory. The vampire clan had to leave their previous home due to too much attention and rising suspicion. So they settled on this one, attempted to take over, but lost…badly.

He met up with the boy gaining his trust and then with his clan. He promised if they joined the new alliance he would help them get what they wanted. No more needed to be said. A well known trait across all vampires would be their immense sense of pride and as an extension of this they don't like to lose. It was a chance to ultimately win and they jumped at it without any thought spent on potential consequences.

Back home Dae spread the urgent news and gathered everyone together to meet and discuss how to deal with what was confirmed coming and fast. He didn't bother calling for Thia as he felt her lessons were more important for now, to her and them, in the long run. Shai did not agree with his decision. He felt if they waited she would not arrive on time and they were certainly going to be outmatched, but in the end he didn't bother arguing with Dae. He usually ended up being right anyways.

Just a couple of short weeks later a rush of rumors spread fast through town about a large group of strange people with big black trucks and SUVs staying at the motel just outside the town limits. Described as 'very rude' and 'secretive', Dae and Shai knew it was the Pallas that had arrived and began conducting their business. The rumor that did it was one that came from the loud old man who runs the motel.

He was sitting next to Dae, Shai and Ben and rambled on to the waitress behind the diner counter, "They paid upfront in cash for a month! No one's ever done that before! I've never seen such big bills. I thought they were fake at first. They didn't want the cleaning service though. I thought that was strange cuz everyone wants that. Hmmm…very peculiar. But I'm not one to gossip. What they do is their own business, just as long as they don't destroy the place."

All three instantly knew who this must be and quickly departed to set Nomad's preconceived plan in motion. During the prior two weeks Ben already spread the word to gather his family and out of town friends asking for their assistance when the time was needed and many said they would come. Now that the army was here he alerted them. That's when Dae called Thia. Dae still didn't want to bother Thia but after considering Shai's point, he decided to anyway.

This time Thia and her brothers could not just pull anchor and move on to the next place. This time others are involved. There was no choice but to take a stand and fight. Back at the busy house buzzing with the visitors and many wolves preparing, Dae and Shai freeze and straighten up the moment they felt Caleb get close. They rushed to the window to find him waving a yellow flag.

Shai went for the door but Dae grabbed him, "You sure you want to go out there? If you do you have to keep your cool, he is only here to talk right now."

Shai was already worked up but nodded that he would.

Everyone got quiet, gathered at the windows and watched. Some scanned the surrounding area in case Caleb was not alone.

Though not fully complete with preparation, mentally they were ready to begin if necessary.

Before they opened the door Shai spoke low through clinched teeth, "I don't want him in this house."

Dae's eyebrows furrowed as he looked down to where he had a hold of Shai's arm, "Wow, all that working out seems to have come to fruition."

Shai yanked his arm free, "I don't know what the hell you just said. Let's go."

Dae's attempt at knocking him down an aggressive notch or two with a compliment failed.

He looked back at Ben, "We'll be right back. Try to keep it down. We don't want to let on any more than we can help."

Ben understood, "got it"

They slowly headed out the door.

"Fellas, long time no see!" Caleb behaved as if they'd been best friends all along.

"Not long enough." Shai snapped at him.

"Well that no way to greet someone." Caleb jeered with fake disappointment.

Dae cut to it, to end the nonsense, "We know why you are here and who you've come with. Let's get to why you've come to our home now, alone."

Caleb's smugness disappeared, "Very well. The Pallas wanted to give you a chance to surrender unharmed. They said if all three of you came quietly you would be well treated. By the way, where's our dear Thia?"

Shai stiffened up but Dae took care of it, "She's not home. And we are not interested. Now please leave." Caleb went to speak but Dae stopped him, "I will only ask once."

Caleb stood there for a bit looking thoroughly irritated but carefully considered Dae's last words then named the place, "We shall meet in the clearing then a few miles north of here. I trust you know where I mean. You will be sorry." And he ran down the drive way.

"I'm proud.   I didn't think you would be able to stop yourself." Dae admitted.

"I'll get mine soon enough." Shai said with satisfaction still staring down the driveway.

Finally the time came and place was set.   Human casualties were not necessary, and all involved could do without the added attention.   The vampires the twins brought included the four Thia and her brothers met earlier, who cowered behind the others of course, yet somehow still managed to act beyond arrogant.   They grew so used to everyone fearing them that they've come to expected it.   Even the twins were a bit nervous around them, but Dae and Shai already saw what they were made of and were completely indifferent.

The lead vampire noticed the difference in reactions and already wondered if Caleb and Kasha were even the same as Dae and Shai as they carried themselves complete different.   Dae and Shai instead had a quiet yet majestic fierceness about them, almost like royalty but with a tribal edge.

The lead could not ignore his observations.   Experiencing the actions of the twins during their time together and the immediate and unwavering impression the brothers left, they'd already earned unspoken respect from him.   The twins however lost some value to him.   But then he remembered why he was there and who *he* was. The effortless manipulation for selfish greed angered him, casting doubt on his true purpose for being there.

Ben's family and some friends showed up in wolf form but forced Doc to stay away.   Not as many showed as he received positive responses for, but he was grateful to those that did as were the Phelidae.   As ready as they could be, all stood by their lifelong friends.   Once you prove yourself to the Phelidae, the strongest of pacts is guaranteed.   However just as severe are the consequences if ever betrayed.

The fight began after a new Pallas recruit, with an itchy trigger finger, fired a round.   Thia was nowhere to be found.

"Something must be wrong. Where is she?" Ben said worried, after killing a vampire.

"We can't think about that now." Dae urgently dismissed, also killing one.

All three, especially Shai, kept a close eye on Caleb located on the other side supervising. So they didn't miss when he abruptly turned his attention to the woods as if he heard something then disappeared in them away from the battle.

"Where's he think he's going?" Ben asked.

"Thia's here" Shai answered, both brothers sharing the same satisfied expression. They sensed her.

"Now the real fun's going to begin." Shai added. "Dae, can you feel it? She's different."

The Pallas-vampire mix were there trying to capture the brothers but were unable to as Ben's people and the visitors very mission was to prevent it. The Pallas wanted them for very different reasons given to Caleb and his sister.

Everything and everyone stopped hearing a faint strange sound. All heads looked around for a second and then spotted something coming from the end of the clearing Caleb just entered. It was small at first then grew closer and bigger, it was a person, yelling. Finally Thia crashed to the ground on her back, digging a large grove in the ground and slid until it gave no more, ending in a couple rolls. The wind was knocked out of her from the landing. Every onlooker stood frozen. Was she dead?

Ben ran to her. The others stiffened up reacting to his movement but ultimately did nothing. Certainly anyone would be dead after a fall like that. Her brothers arrived at her side in one leap from the same direction. The others still did nothing.

Shai checked her over, "T, you okay?"

As they were looking her over checking for anything serious, Caleb came out of the woods. Still all watched and didn't move.

"What are you waiting for, huh?!" shouted Caleb. "You three are *the best*. At least that's what I've been told for so long I hear it in my sleep! HA! I have to say I'm very disappointed!"

"What *are* we waiting for?" Shai growled to Dae and Thia with Ben still kneeling with them.

Dae explained how it had to be, "It's got to be all three of us. He doesn't play fair, we all know that."

"Come on Thia", Shai pleaded.

"Now my brother is going to join in on the heckling?" Thia said attempting to get up now. "No, I'll fight but not with that. My training is far from over. Nomad said it himself before I left."

"Come on! You've been gone for weeks! You can't tell me you learned nothing, you told us you were making progress." Shai was frustrated.

"NO! We will do fine without it and he will stop and go away once he figures out nothing is going to happen." She justified.

Shai snapped at her, "Thia, that's ridiculous! You know as well as we do that is not what's going to happen." He took a breath, "Just try?"

"No...I can't!!! I 'm not good enough yet! I can't control it" she fought off a glance at Dae's scar.

"Face it. He's not going to stop until we stop him. It's as plain as that." Shai knew he was right, not even Dae was contradicting him.

A dirty bloody mess, she looks over to the side at Nomad who just showed up with desperation in her eyes. Caleb catches this as he continued his approach. It hits him. He now sees their link, the real reason for her hesitation, the Nomad. With an evil grin, he signals Kasha and changes direction.

Thia looked back in time to see the exchange and new heading. "What's he doing? No!"

Kasha stood in her place, stiff as a board and focused in on them.

All three get up to run and beat him to Nomad. Caleb speeds up. Out of nowhere all three hit an invisible wall. They bounce off and fly back but land on their feet. Approaching the wall they look over at Kasha. Now she has her hand up controlling the water wall made of strong mist. They try everything to get out from behind it but it was an impenetrable dome. Even Dae could not get it to come down.

"Dae do something!" Thia yelled.

"I'm trying but Kasha's had more training than I. I…can't", he admitted ashamed.

"Aaaaaaaahhhhhh!!!!!" an enraged scream came from Thia.

All bystanders covered their non cat ears, pulsing in pain.

Nomad looks Thia deep in her eyes. Knowing how it was likely to turn out, he said goodbye and let her know she is ready, all in one glace, only like Nomad can. They watch helplessly as Caleb reaches Nomad.

Ben arrives at the wall to try to help but is pulled in. Next his friends try to come to the rescue but Kasha is able to stop them too. After all of the attempts they watch in horror as Caleb picks up Nomad without even touching him.

"This isn't happening", Thia won't believe what her eyes are showing her.

"Thia…" Dae said sad and soft.

"NOOOOO!" she screams in the deepest earth tearing, teeth bearing growl, much like the time she held her mother in her last moment. The others looked at her and saw something they'd never seen before, ever. Her skin was getting more pale than usual and some of her cat markings were appearing up the back of her neck like before but now also crawling down her arms and legs.

Ben and Shai pushing against the wall suddenly fell forward. The wall was gone. Ben looked over at Kasha to find her holding her head between her hands clinching in terrible pain. The wolves found they were free now too and tore off running again to assist Nomad. Dae and Shai were already in pursuit.

Caleb, too focused on sucking the breath and life out of Nomad's almost lifeless looking body didn't see them coming. Shai got to them first, as he is the fastest and tackled Caleb to the ground, leaving Nomad to fall into Dae's massive arms and setting him down.

Shai was then thrown from Caleb back to where Nomad lay.

"Watch over him", Dae ordered.

Shai coughed a bit from the hit then nodded and began to search for signs of life.

Dae caught Caleb in mid attack, pulled him around and punched him dead in his chest before he could do anything. With Dae being much stronger than Caleb physically, Caleb went flying to the center of the field and landed on his back then flipped over to his stomach. He curled up coughing and clutching his chest where Dae's hit landed.

"Fix him!" Thia ordered to her brothers from a distance, noticing Dae's sad eyes.

Nomad had a small army around him now but Thia still saw no sign of life.

Moments later Dae and Shai's mood changes from worry to confusion as they hover over Nomad.

Ben gets nervous from their change in reaction, "What? Why do you guys look like that? I feel weird too, what's going on?"

Then they look back in the field. The two realize what's going on. Thia is now walking away from them to the middle of the field in Caleb's direction. With his hand still on his chest he looks over at Kasha.

It wasn't a caring look, but one you would use when staring at someone who had failed you. She was on her knees now trying to look at him, still holding her head but now with a nose bleed and tears streaming down from his disappointment. Then her attention is diverted to the oncoming Thia, or who she at first thought was Thia.

Caleb turns to see what thing greater than he, could possibly pull his sister's attention from his scolding. Then he saw Thia, really saw Thia. Aside from the streams left on her dirty cheeks and torn rags being the only resemblance of her former self, she looks like a completely different person now.

She no longer appeared meek and sad. In fact, she has no expression whatsoever. Her face is dead; dead accept for her fiery eyes. Her posture changed as well. She was no longer confined but instead truly free and confident. All restraint and heavy measures of safety she's had built up for all of her life dissolved away.

Caleb took a closer look at her eyes again, they were not her human grey anymore. The pupils were huge and pointed at the top and bottom. The color replaced by an electric blue, but it is not a fixed color. Bursts of glowing blue and silver moved like the tail of a comet. In addition there is a hazy blue glow all around her and in the glow are small sparks jumping around.

She stopped and turned her head only slightly in her family's direction.

"We should be clear right?" Shai asked Dae a little nervous.

Dae shot him a look, "Isn't this what you asked for?"

Then a big smile crosses Shai's face and he quietly admits, "It's about time."

Dae too shares a proud smile seeing what his sister has become.

All others forgotten a while ago, proved insignificant to the event, like ants on a side walk.

"Is that what it feels like when you steal breath?" Thia asked staring at his chest with an nearly wicked smirk.

He could barely talk but would not let her have the last word, "Care to find out?"

Caleb works on getting up. He sees the crowd to the right, the ones he came with, now flush with the trees, fewer and hidden from those that remained. Thia's group on the left stood strong and ready, but in shock to what they were witnessing. The Pallas and vampires had seen some of what Caleb and Kasha could do, but nothing like Thia's display.

Caleb looked on at the leader of the Pallas, wondering what he was waiting for. But the leader was not going to waste any of his men if it was going to be a futile attempt.

Caleb ridiculed them under his breath, "Cowards. I should've known better".

He finally stood up facing Thia, doing his best to hide the way the new her made him feel – afraid. He made the first move striking at her with his fist but missing. They fought hand to hand again, as this was the honorable way to fight, but unlike before, she held her own.

He was the one struggling now. She didn't break a sweat as he becomes winded. Her moves were fast and exact while he stumbled about. He was very nervous now, getting a taste of what 'they' meant all along. Why these were labeled *the best*, though they would never acknowledge it. At the most inopportune time he remembered something. It was mentioned during a lesson he sat in on at the Pallas compound shortly after joining them.

"Stay away from their trainer. They are very close to him. We can't afford to anger them. This will make them unpredictable and be counterproductive to their capture." instructed the faceless lecturer in a lab coat.

It all made sense to him now. He'd just done the very thing that triggered her change. The very thing he didn't want to do if he had any chance of getting them back in one, well enough of a piece to get his promised reward. He saw in her eyes she was not going to stop. He broke their cardinal rule when he was interrupted trying to take an innocent life. *She will avenge her Nomad* he thought to himself.

Just then his stubbornness reared its ugly head, *No, if I can just get her down long enough to catch a wisp of her breath...* he planned, finding a final burst of energy. It was cheating and dishonorable but he knew his energy was about spent.

After another missed blow he instructed his sister with a simple look and she understood. Pushing aside the fright of Thia's new image, once again more afraid of her brother, Kasha trapped Thia. In this moment Caleb attacked with everything he had. Kasha removing the barrier just in time for Caleb, he rushed upon Thia knocking her to the ground pushing just enough breath out of her, pinned her down and begin his thievery.

Thia never experienced the affects of his gift. She laid there paralyzed, unable to move. A bolder was sent speeding through the air at Caleb, only to bounce off of the new barrier Kasha wrapped and reinforced around Caleb and Thia. Vicious wind, fire, rocks and debris were sent in Kasha's direction, again to be blocked by her own protective wall. Thia remained motionless.

She thought to herself feeling everything around her fade, *How easy it would be to just lay down, relax and accept what is coming. Would it be so bad to leave this world and move on,* to see her mother? *I miss her so much, her flowing strawberry blond hair, her fair skin and her perfectly soft and warm smile.* The temptation called to her.

However this train of thought didn't last long. She could hear or feel something trying to interrupt, something faint in the background. Then it got louder. Her brothers were calling to her. Her deep love for them took over as sudden rush of energy swept through her as her brothers became her focus.

Starting to come back, she lay there and become aware of a faint glowing line around everything, just like with the pumpkin experiment. But the lines seemed to vibrate. They were thicker and moved more on the lives around her. The outline on the other living things such as trees and grass were thinner and moved much slower. The colors were different too. The things of nature had a soft green. The people she would describe as 'good' were light blue. And the others she considered 'bad' burned red.

Though it felt like an eternity the whole awakening only took a few seconds.

Then like a slap in the face she felt her brother's calls. She began to struggle, feeling her life preserving instincts prevail. But this time she was calm and focused. Ben and her brothers would not need to hold her back a second time. She imagined holding her breath, what was left, much like how she stopped Nomad from taking her extra wound. As she held it Caleb reacted like pulling a chain that suddenly had no give. He tried to begin again but could no longer pull anything from her. It just stopped. He tried again and again but nothing. This has never happened to him before.

While he struggled she saw the orange glow of the invisible shield around them. And then she saw a thick orange line connecting it back to Kasha. She wasn't sure what to do so she tried the first thing that came to mind. She thought about popping the bubble. The orange blew apart and Kasha screams, thrown back flat on the ground and rendered her unconscious.

Another massive rock flew into Caleb ripping him from Thia, knocking him back about fifty feet. Dae knew the shield was gone once he heard Kasha's shriek. Too worried about himself, Caleb didn't bother looking in his sister's direction this time. In a final desperate attempt he changed to his Phelidae form and lunged at Thia, still down on the ground but sitting up now.

She saw the glow of his evil red energy coming at her in slow motion. She then saught out her brothers and found their color was white. *They must emit their intention or guilt or something. They know when they are doing wrong, they feel it.* She found it very curious that the lead vampire on the other side stood out as white as the others around him remained crimson red. He did not fit in with those proud to be bad.

She studied his slow approach looking even deeper inside him and seeing the energy deep down, around his heart. Again unsure of what to do so she tried what seemed to come natural.

She kept her eyes on the jagged energy band around his heart. Then she reached out envisioning wrapping her fingers around it. And she squeezed. Caleb, saw her motions then felt an immobilizing intense pain in his chest. He, who had been all but unstoppable, did in fact stop, immediately. He fell to the ground holding his chest. He managed to seek the truth, eyes reaching up to her in disbelief.

Evident that Caleb and his sister failed, the army slowly moved in. Thia's attention was diverted to them. The vampires stood back and watched no longer confident in the competence of their new partners. Caleb ran the moment he felt the break in pain and Thia went after him. Every time he turned she met his move like a shadow.

Caleb stopped panicked. Thia quickly checked to make sure her brothers were still okay or if they needed help. He took advantage of this fleeting distraction and pulled out the two guns he had tucked away behind him. Thia heard them load, *never played fair, even after all these years* she deliberated. She formed an imaginary shield of energy catching and crushing the bullet and before her head made it around to confirm what she heard, a half sphere of distorted vision rushed at him. The bullets, already half way to her, exploded in mid air and he was again knocked to the ground as his guns too turned to dust.

Dae and Shai joined Thia's side while Ben guarded Nomad. An explosion beside them caught them off guard, throwing them into the lake. The army fired a shot to stun them and was pleased to find them floating face down in the water.

Dae was the first to regain consciousness and used the water to lift all of them up on a gentle magic carpet of water away from the edge of the lake where the others waited. He wanted to give his siblings time to recover without interruption. Thia and Shai woke up and were quickly right again so Dae brought everyone back down to calf high water on the other side. Thia could not only see but feel their powers for the first time and used their Blood bond to borrow, draining them only for an instant.

Then she spread the sensation of all powers combined across all three of them including some of her own in turn strengthening theirs. Dae and Shai felt an adrenalin like surge, but much stronger.

"Damn T. I think I'm getting what happened now." Shai admitted in a daze referring to the day Dae earned his scar.

Caleb still looking to redeem himself, thinking they had to have been injured from the blast, enters the water to go after them. All three instantly know when he gets close and without looking, zaps him clear out of the water back to the middle of the clearing.

Another bomb sores at Thia and her brothers but all three float on a cloud of mist back to the clearing and send it back to its origin instantly destroying most of the expensive machinery the Pallas brought with them and a large group nearby with it. The rest retreat rendering the all mighty Pallas's fight short lived.

"Retreat!" the leader yelled dragging himself out from under a large piece of damaged metal.

Lying on the ground, smoke rolling off of his singed clothes, he snaps out of the stun at the sound of the order.

In a final attempt he launches into the air and turns into a Jaguar. The other three do the same. Caleb turns to Thia for a face off, challenging her. Aware the vampires have not yet left, the Phelidae keep a cocked ear ever in that direction. Caleb, impatiently jumps but Shai matches him. It's the moment Shai's waited and prepared for, for so long. It evolves into a fierce cat fight with clawing, wrestling, massive blows, hissing and growling.

Shai went at him with a full on attack, reigning blow after powerful blow down upon him until Caleb could fight no more.

"Aaaahh!!!!" Caleb screams in defeat rolling back turning again to exhausted human form.

Shai changed back to human too, "Time to end this."

"No!" Thia yelled, also human again, as well as Dae.

"He's had more than enough chances to do anything right." Shai justified.

She didn't want to take a Phelidae life by choice but even she couldn't argue Shai's point. Despite the consequences she didn't want to, she couldn't.

"Thia he can't be given another possibility to murder more of our kind." Dae pleaded.

"Ha ha ha! Yeah all mighty Thia, do it!" Caleb mocked sounding a little out of his mind. Then it turned to vicious fury, "You freaking misfit. No wonder your own kind sold you out!"

Shai couldn't take him abusing her anymore and bound at him. Caleb got up and ran at Shai, then when they met, Caleb clotheslined Shai to the ground knowing it would work since he was reacting on mostly emotion, them bent over him to seize his life. Dae started in their direction until he heard something from Thia.

"fine, I'll take care of it" she regretfully whispered.

Up until now they tried everything they could to spare his life but he refused to stop. He'd broken all teachings of their ways for greed. He could've been forgiven, banished, but forgiven if he'd only stopped. It was clear this was not an option for him so he had to be destroyed.

It was not an easy decision. If something like this happened back home the elders took care of it far away from the village. She wished she could simply hand off the judgment to them now but that was impossible. She wished Nomad could tell her what to do, but that too was not possible.

Greif stricken, she stared at the ground, it started to rumble. The wind blew towards her whipping her hair up and out of her face. Her eyes began glowing brighter and the blue sparks floating around her grew bigger. Her brothers backed away.

She planted her feet and raised her eyes to Caleb. Two massive bolts of lightning hit the ground at each side of her. Anyone within proximity felt the hair on their arms and necks stand on end. At least she would be able to make it quick for him. In an instant she leaned forward and clapped her hands. A thunderous boom sounded and anything left over from the Pallas exploded in to dust. Caleb was knocked out cold by the blast and blown over next to Kasha also still out.

Tears rolled down her face. She couldn't do it. Her brothers said nothing for they too shared what overwhelmed her.

When Caleb and the Pallas failed the vampires still hiding in the shadows, the rest stepped in. All glowed red announcing their intentions. The one that was white was gone. Since it was clear they would not be getting the coveted trio, the vampires decided to move on to plan B; settling for the twins. After all, they had powers and the Phelidae blood too. But before they scooped up their consolation prize they had one more trick up their cold sleeves.

Matteus, beaten and unconscious was dragged in and thrown to the ground by Darius.

"Darius" Thia grumbled under her breath.

"T, you know him?" Shai asked quietly.

She nodded, "Unfortunately. That is why I was late."

Darius addressed Thia and her brothers, "Before we depart *cats*, we wish for you to watch as one of our own is punished properly for the act of betrayal."

Darius crouched down over Matteus, "So much for you being chosen for next in line by Gilles over me. Fool." at this a couple scrawnier vampires, at a speed faster than normal human eyes can see, plant a stake in the ground and tie Matteus to it. Then they bring out torches.

Thia gasped.

Attempting to burn Matteus actually backfired as Shai turned the flames on them then Dae sprayed them out. During all of the excitement the vampire with the white glow came out of nowhere, removed Matteus from the post and dashed out of site with him before being noticed.

His missing victim angered Darius, "Alistair! I should've known an old friend of Matteus could not be trusted to obey the coven! You will no doubt go into hiding but we will find you!"

Plans badly foiled the vampires also chose to leave but when they go to collect the twins, the found Caleb and Kasha were gone. This would have sent them in to a fury had it not been stopped by the unsettling sight of glowing eyes staring at them in the dark, so they chose to depart quickly.

Shai slapped her on the back, "We knew you could do it sis."

"Wow!" Ben said approaching.

Seeing Ben reminded her, "Nomad!" and ran past them to him.

All three looked at each other remorsefully.

When she got there her heart sank. He was pale and still. She knelt down next to him and started to cry.

"Why are you crying? I told you that you could do it." Nomad whispered in a weak and raspy voice.

She laughed wiping away her tears and gave Nomad a big hug, too big actually.

Nomad coughed, "Ouch, easy."

All four laughed relieved and glad their old friend was going to be okay. Thia and her brothers spoke with each member of the group, graciously thanking Ben's friends and Nomad's visitors for standing with them and inviting them back to the house for food before they departed back to their homes.

Most headed back but a few discussions carried on. Thia finished up her last one abruptly after she saw something moving on the edge of the clearing. It didn't look like an animal and stood upright. Nervous the fight might not be over she slipped away to investigate. She didn't want to alarm anyone just yet until she had a chance to check it out first. When she got to the spot the person was gone but she found an odd trail of what looked like dark blue or purple glowing fireflies crawling away on the ground deeper in the woods. Thia instinctively fixated had to follow them.

Back in the clearing Shai sensed Thia's mood and spotted her, "T? Hey where are you going?", Shai called to her and tried get up to go after her, but Nomad stopped him.

Dae helped Nomad sit up, "Let her go, it is time she knew."

The flowing vein like path started fading so she sped up not wanting to lose where it was leading. The closer she got to the trail Thia noticed how everything felt cold and dry as the lights left. She watched and noted they appear to have a draining affect on everything they touch. The leaves on the trees in contact display the first sign as they shrivel.

Concerned she wondered what evil could possibly cause life to slowly drain from living things. *What could do this, and why?*

She touched the fragile bark of a small affected tree and felt sad for it wishing she could fix it, to put the life back in to all that suffered. Just then a neat stream of champagne white light poured from under her hand to the tree and quickly spread to the rest of the area. She smiled as their health restored.

Oh, wow. Then she remembered what caused it, *But where'd that purple stuff go? I have to find and stop whatever is doing this.*

Still not yet feeling threatened she jogged catching up, running over and past the little lights as the terrain changed. The area transformed from flat to hills rather quickly the deeper she entered. As she got closer, the lights were brighter and the stream grew thicker finally coagulating to a solid line laying over the next tall hill.

She slows down sensing the source is very close, *Oh, what now? I'm getting confused with all of these new sensations.* Whatever it was was not completely foreign to her.

She crept up the large hill trying now to tip off what it was she sought out. Once at the top, she saw a young man facing the opposite direction on the next hill. The lights led directly to him. He turned slowly in her direction. She froze not sure if she should run or stay put. Then the moment he saw her, the lights vanished.

They stood silent staring at each other. The slim young man was about her age and height with a friendly face. *He doesn't look like a bad guy, assuming he would if he was,* she half joked to herself.

I'm not bad, a male voice answered in her head.

You are a mind reader, a Phelidae mind reader. She tried to stay cool but couldn't help feeling a little excited finding another of their kind and so close to home.

He simply responded, *Yes.*

What is your mark? Somehow she instinctively knew he had a gift and wanted to know which to further confirm her suspicion on what it was.

He hesitated, *I really shouldn't...but I can't help but trust you. This is crazy but I feel like I already know you* and he showed her his arm.

A darker version of the one she possesses sat in the exact same position on his arm. Fighting her natural urge, she did very well in keeping her thoughts simple. Her mother taught her a couple quick tricks to stop them from wandering off potentially revealing too much.

His gaze at her converted to more curious than cautious, *You've had training. Your mind is quiet. It's nice.*

Thia just nodded, then looked down at her arm and showed it to him. She hadn't noticed before but her mark was white now.

He smiled seeing the same and jumped down his hill and climbed up towards her. With a little more forced caution than he, she headed down to meet him as she struggled to remember to be careful no matter how comfortable she felt. Everything in this moment was off.

None of what was happening seemed real. It had to be a dream. It was hard for her to recall anything she'd learned and had became second nature throughout the years. All the worrying, needing to be on guard and hiding, for the first time none of it came to her easily. It all felt like a dark and distant nightmare.

The two stopped in front of each other and examined, like eyes, like faces.

Then he spoke out loud, "I think you are my twin sister."

Thia's jaw dropped. "Your what?"

He too was very happy about his new company and could hold it in no longer. A childlike excitement caused him to ignore her shock and pour out all that came to mind, "You know our parents? You were not told of me? I was only just told of you, then tonight I felt you, from the energy in your fight. I had to come. I knew it was you!"

The sound of a horn made Thia jump and broke his rambling, "Uh-oh, that's for me. I have to go." And he turned to run off.

Her hand automatically reached out, "Wait! No! Where are you going?"

"My time is up, I have to go back." he was anxious now.

She shook her head and started to follow, "Back where? L...let me come with you. I want to know more. I have to know more."

He stopped, "Ha! No you can't come. I would get in *so* much trouble!" the horn blew again. "Oh, now I *really* have to go. Three times would be very bad." And he took off.

Her voice broke with sorrow as her mind spun trying to keep up, "Will I ever see you again?"

"Of course you will. I know how and where to find you now!" he shouted back with an assuring smile.

Thia desperately wanted to know so much more but watched helplessly as her euphoria vanished with him and the cold and empty reality crept back, but not entirely this time.

A small smile returned to her face with her warm thought, "I have a twin brother."

Home

Back at the house, some of the wolves, a few of Nomad's friends, Thia and her brothers enjoyed a late night feast of pizza, the only place open at that hour. The delivery guy dropped off the order, completely oblivious to the horrors not that far from there that could've changed everything. He did however seem surprised by how much of dirty mess Thia and Shai were when she paid and he took the steaming hot boxes.

Most left for their own homes shortly after eating considering it had been weeks since they'd been back. Only a few stayed to get a full nights rest and leave early the next morning.

Finally in the quiet living room with the fireplace burning, Ben, Dae, Shai and Thia were all that were left still awake and sat listening as Nomad explained, "Yes Thia he is your twin brother. Your mother and father secretly sent him away to a safe place once they found he was a telepath. And yes it is very possible, even likely, that he too has the gift of energy. If I had to guess from what you described, it would seem his is negative energy, where yours is positive. Did he say when he would come to visit? I would very much like to finally meet him."

"No, he just said he knew how to find me now and took off." Thia shrugged.

"Oh boy, we are in trouble now. I don't know if I can handle two of you T." Shai teased.

"Hey!" she laughed hurling a nearby magazine at him.

Her mood turned somber, "I hope he comes before we have to leave. I don't know that we can stay here very long. I'm sure that will not be the last we see of either group. The last thing we needed was to double our enemies. Now that they know where we live, we should probably assume there will be many more to come. It will happen again. We can't drag you and your family down with us Ben."

Offended Ben thoroughly reprimands her, "I know I speak for all when I say we'd prefer you stay. The time for running and living in fear is over. We proved that tonight. Besides, if you leave and they come back, we are outnumbered. And what if more of your family hears you are here? They may come, others may come. Your brother..." he stopped as it didn't sound right, looked at Shai and Dae, then corrected himself "...other brother may come. It's just not worth it. Dae did mention your desire to find the rest of your kind and you will. So, just as they prepare, so will we."

A very surprised and put in her place Thia didn't argue, as she's been known to do. Instead she just smiled, admiring his honesty and hoping more than anything he is right.

Then another thought occurred to her, "Nomad, how did they find the castle?"

Nomad found out the answer shortly after she left for home, "They had a mind reader hiding by your house here. They remembered during an interrogation of another captive, one mentioned a castle. They tortured him until he took them there. That was the old man the bunch of you saw. He was close enough to warn the boys and you Thia through them."

Ben had an idea, "Tomorrow we should search around the house to make sure no one's still around, then lock up and head back to the Blast Zone and see what we can find from that army. That is assuming Thia didn't dust it all."

"The Blast Zone?", Dae asked.

"Yeah, Abe named it that in honor of you guys blasting them out of here! I think it's great." Ben explained and laughed.

"I like it!" approved Shai.

Dae was happy someone else was thinking at least a little like him, "That is a good idea, I'll join you. Also, I will have to call Daniel first thing tomorrow. He will be upset with me if I fail to provide details soon."

Thia had another question, "Nomad, how did Caleb learn to take people's breath? I can't believe our kind would teach such a cruel thing."

Nomad agreed, "You are correct Thia, they wouldn't. If I had to guess I would think the Pallas came up with that barbarism."

Shai very seriously followed up, "Speaking of Caleb and Kasha, what do you suppose happened to them?"

Nomad did his best to speculate, "I imagine they've hidden themselves. I know word has spread of their treachery to all connected Phelidae as I've heard from a few not directly in contact. Even with the lack of a formal society, they are considered banished. I imagine the Pallas no longer trust them. And there'll be no help from our kind for them."

Thia stared off, "What now? What does it all mean?"

Nomad answered, "I believe it is safe to assume the tables have turned."

Proud, Shai agreed, "Yeah, I mean if you think about it the Pallas had two advantages on us. Then when those weren't working they tried to be sneaky and hit us when we weren't looking. They brought all that fancy equipment and it was reduced to nothing in an instant. And that had to have been the good stuff. There's no way they came to an opportunity like that with anything less. Face it, last night changed the future, our future."

Thia thought the idea sounded too good to be true, "Oh come on."

However Nomad pursued Shai's point, "I agree with Shai which is why I too will be leaving early in the morning. In light of what has happened, there is much to be done and I must get started right away. I promise I will return as soon as I can. We must continue with training. In the mean time you are to keep practicing and work with your trustworthy friends here on ways to better your surveillance. If they choose to try again, which I find highly unlikely, you'll need all the notice you can get."

Shai wanted to squeeze one more answer out of him, "Nomad, one more thing? I've been stronger since Thia...I don't know, super charged us? Will it stay?"

Nomad always tried to be honest with them, "I am sorry boys, but I can offer no wisdom on this. Nothing comparable to this has happened before. Either the effects will fade or what she did changed you both permanently. Only time will tell."

Thia yawned and stretched, "Alright, I'm done for tonight. See you all in the morning."

She walked over to Nomad and gave him a big hug, "And you be careful. Thank you for all you've done."

He assured her, "Do not worry Thia, your training is still incomplete. I will need to steal you away again before long."

Everyone followed her example as the events of the long day caught up with them.

Thia hung back hoping to catch Nomad alone as he moved slower, "Nomad, since you have to go, would you want to try the bond? I know the boys wouldn't mind, especially not with you."

"That is very generous and tempting, but I must decline. Remember I am only half Phelidae so it may not be safe for me.

But thank you just the same for the offer." Nomad patted her on the arm and retreated to his room.

The next afternoon before the time the rest agreed upon, Thia returns to the place deemed the "Blast Zone" but didn't stop there. She continued on to where she met her twin brother. Remembering the way, she saw no signs that either of them were actually there. Even though she knew better, for a split second she entertained the notion that it might have all been just a dream. It felt like one.

She climbed the last hill and stood where she first saw him. The memory was vivid but something changed on the hill he stood on. She jumped over to check it out. At the top of the hill on the tree to her right, a purple ribbon had been tied with a little box hanging from it. She opened the attached tag and it read,

I knew you would be back. Here's a little something to remember me by. It was not a dream.

See you around,
Thaddeus

Thia's eyes widened, "Oh my gosh! I never asked him his name. How stupid of me." She smiled, "Thaddeus. That's a nice name."

Inside the box lay a breaded leather necklace with a large purple and white swirled stone pendent. She put it on right away.

Then she wondered *what I should leave him. Oh, I have a beautiful Tiger eye on a chain at home! That'll be perfect.*

She ran home, put the Tiger eye in the same box, grabbed a white ribbon and headed back. Excited she tied the box in the same place. She placed her hands on the tree and beautiful white and purple blossoms bloomed on the branch her gift hung.

"That ought to let him know I've been here." She said very pleased.

On her way back she was head down admiring her gift. Next to Shai's handmade dream catcher, it meant the most to her.

"Hey! Did you find anything?" Ben's unexpected voice made her jump.

She was glowing, "Hey. I did, but not from the Pallas. My brother left this for me."

She looked around and noticed they were alone, "So, no one wanted to join you out here?"

He shook his head and walked over to where the Pallas were located the night before. He searched the ground picking up and inspecting anything he found, "Everyone's still asleep and it's almost noon. I couldn't wait any longer. There's got to be something good out here."

Thia felt him get very nervous but didn't let on.

Shortly after, the cause revealed itself, "I meant to tell you, it was really great, all the stuff you did here. And..." he took a deep breath. "Though I meant what I said on why you should stay, that wasn't all of it. Some of my reasoning is also somewhat selfish."

Afraid to ask but not wanting to be rude she did anyway, "What do you mean?"

"I uh...oh! Hey, look at this. I better go show this to Dae", turns out he wasn't quite ready and ran off.

Thia waited till he was gone and let out the laugh and sigh of relief she caught and held in for what seemed like an eternity. It was flattering, and he is a good guy and also nice looking, but Thia keeps thinking of Matteus wondering if she will see him again. And if she did, what would happen? Would they still feel the same? Would he be able to return if Darius was right and he and his friend had to go into hiding?

She hung out a bit longer half sifting through the left over mess. She found nothing interesting and returned home to find Dae awake and on the computer.

Dae sent a message to his friend Thomas not sure when and if he would get it. But just in case he was on, he had to let Thomas know they were okay. As chance would have it Dae was delighted to find Thomas respond.

D-Day: Hello friend. Everyone is okay. They are gone now.

T-Mas: I'm so glad you are all well. How'd you do it?

D-Day: It was a combined effort but T really came through.

T-Mas: And what of the twins?

D-Day: They disappeared after being defeated and their deal with the Pallas void. They are considered banished among us.

T-Mas: Understood. The others will agree with me when I say you three truly are amazing. Please be sure to keep in contact once you settle in your new home friend.

D-Day: There'll be no need for that. I am pleased to say there's been a change in plans for all Phelidae. We are staying. We will be hunted no more. We took a stand and won. Now it's time to find the others and join together again.

Three young Phelidae, heroes of the past who were on the run, just changed the game. If they are twice top of the food chain then why are they the ones fleeing? This question haunted them everywhere they went. If only they could regroup they would be able to become strong again and go back to the way it was, once again restoring order.

$\mathcal{S}$helía $\mathcal{W}$eíss, wife and mother of two began writing when she, "could hold it in no longer...the story gradually filled me up until it finally spilled out onto paper." in 2010. Not known to pick up a book often she was quite surprised when the writing bug sunk in its teeth. Drawn by the entertainment world in search of her place since she can remember, she's been a professional Belly dancer, Model, Actor and now Author.

She lives in Cleveland, Ohio with her family.

CPSIA information can be obtained at www.ICGtesting.com
Printed in the USA
BVOW070708051211

277588BV00001B/7/P